WORTHY OF THE CALLING

The Seventh Book in the Rebecca Series

WORTHY OF THE CALLING

WALKER BUCKALEW

Fideli Publishing Inc.
WWW.FIDELIPUBLISHING.COM

Library of Congress Control Number:

    ISBN: 978-1-962402-13-2 (hardcover)
    ISBN: 978-1-962402-12-5 (paperback)

This is a work of fiction. Names, characters, places and incidents are products of the
author's imagination or are used fictitiously.

Copyediting by FRANCES ARCHER
Cover art, design and photo by REEL VIDEO & STILLS

Published by Fideli Publishing, Inc., Martinsville, IN 46151

Author's Note

This book may be read separately from the previous books in the Rebecca Series, but new readers may wish to know that it is a sequel to these titles:

The Face of the Enemy
By Many or By Few
Such Thy Mercies
Choose You This Day
A Fearful Thing
A Whip of Cords

The first four novels are set in the 1970s and early 1980s. The fifth and sixth take place in the summer of 1985. The new story is set in 1986. Readers will want to be conscious of the fact that the Cold War between the U.S. and the Soviet Union is in full swing throughout those years.

In the 1970s and 1980s, technology was changing rapidly. However, even in the new story, nearly all computers are desktops, not laptops, and handheld devices are just beginning to emerge. Telephones still have cords and are just… telephones.

Regular readers of these stories are aware that, except where a setting must be fictional — for example, "The Lodge," near Birmingham, England — real sites, presented fictionally, are used whenever feasible: for example, St. David's Cathedral in Wales in the first novel; Navy-Marine Corps Stadium in Annapolis, Maryland, in the second; the Italian coastal village of Amalfi in the third; Israel's Yad Vashem and Tel Megiddo in the fourth; the Washington, D.C., area in the fifth; Duxford Royal Air Force Base, near Cambridge, England, in the sixth; and New York City, in all seven.

The central character, Rebecca Manguson Clark, is 26 years old in *The Face of the Enemy*; she is 34 in this story. In this fictional world, she was an internationally ranked tennis player on the women's professional circuit until, at age 24, she retired from tennis, having realized that her life needed to shift its direction.

The antagonists in each novel are conspicuously evil. That word is capitalized when the reference is to supernatural forces. Not every "evil" character is "Evil."

In each story at least one new "good" character is introduced, and some of them have become part of the permanent cast. Each novel features at least one love story, as well. The love story in a given novel is never what the book is mainly about, but the love story is never unimportant, either. Love stories matter in all of life.

Walker Buckalew
Greer, SC

"I therefore… beg you to lead a life
worthy of the calling
to which you have been called…"

— Ephesians 4:1

CHAPTER ONE

Monday, June 1986, New York City

DR. ELEANOR CHAPEL, DISTINGUISHED OLD TESTAMENT lecturer, scholar, and teacher, walked briskly in the June sunshine toward the New York City Public Library. She had left her and her husband's Morningside Heights apartment, near Union Theological Seminary, at 9 a.m. sharp, and had been scurrying south on Broadway for nearly 40 minutes. She was well over halfway to the library, a 4-mile walk from home.

Her pace remained fast and steady although the street-level temperature was already rising through the high 80s. Dressed as usual in a gray, mid-calf summer skirt and off-white sleeveless blouse, she carried over one arm a gray, summer-weight sweater against the expected chill of the library's air conditioning. The studied grayness was offset by one of her trademark iridescent red silk scarves. Other than her wedding band, she wore a single piece of jewelry: a delicate gold cross pendant.

And she wore proudly her new, formerly white Adidas running shoes — her first-ever pair of purpose-built running shoes — that had already collected sufficient dirt and grime from the city streets to look well-worn.

That was the footwear look she preferred: well-worn.

She found that she was not tiring in the heat, even though her leg muscles, especially her calves, were still working to adjust to the unusual weight of the new shoes. Their weight was approximately doubled — and somewhat unbalanced — thanks to the insistence of her detective husband, who had, with her grudging permission, paid the New York Police Department's cobbler to custom-alter the new Adidas.

The innocent-looking running shoes now boasted steel toes — thereby having been effectively "weaponized" — as her ever-protective husband had proudly announced when he brought them home to her. She thought the whole idea silly, but had learned to defer to her husband on the subject of security. On that topic, Sidney Belton always knew exactly what he was talking about.

As she crossed 52nd Street, still on Broadway, she smiled to herself, thinking of her husband's continual concern for her safety. Who but Sidney would think to weaponize the feet of his 85-pound, 4-foot-10-inch, 72-year-old wife?

"Eleanor," he had said repeatedly, "yer a walkin' target. Yer a tiny woman, older than dirt, an' yer cute as a button, too. One a' these dirtbags is gonna grab ya an' throw ya in his trunk an' I'll never see ya again.

"Know what I mean?

"Hm?"

She had laughed her tinkling laugh, but she knew there was truth in his law-enforcement-bred analysis of her vulnerability. And, she admitted, now laughing again to herself, that he was not wrong to call her "cute as a button." She couldn't really help that. She had a "pixie face," as he had often noted, "pocket-size" stature, "baby doll" blue-green eyes, and a childlike innocence of appearance.

Although she was 14 years older than her husband — he, having just turned 58 — any stranger, upon being told of the 14-year age difference, would have guessed that it was he who was the older. For Eleanor Chapel appeared, especially when in motion, to be perhaps early 50s. Belton, in contrast, wizened and wounded from countless injuries incurred in the U.S. military, New York City police and detective work, and now private detective employment, looked to be the 70-something that, in fact, his wife was. His aged-warrior appearance was reinforced by his hesitant, cane-assisted gait.

The only qualities in Belton that bespoke youthfulness were his sense of humor and his razor-sharp intellect. His legendary analytical wizardry had over the years caused his name to be spoken with highest respect in police, detective, and national intelligence agencies ranging across half the globe: from San Francisco to Washington to New York to London to Tel Aviv to Moscow.

Belton had not, however, won the couple's recent argument about her hairstyle. The decision to abandon her longtime preference for pulling her gray hair into a tight bun, and now, instead, for allowing her hair to fall unbound to her shoulders, produced a torrent of objections from her husband.

"Now yer gonna look all soft and feminine," he had said. "Yer just gonna make yerself a tastier target fer th' bad guys, Eleanor. Get yer hair off yer shoulders and pull it back like ya always have."

"Sidney Belton," she had said to him just the day before, "I'm tired of looking like an aging schoolmarm. My hair is still manageable when it's unbound, touching my shoulders … and besides … I've noticed you seem quite accepting of this … 'all soft and feminine' appearance in the morning when I'm wearing this ratty bathrobe.

"Or is shoulder-length hair okay only in combination with ratty bathrobes?"

She smiled again at the recollection of his familiar cackling laughter in response to her teasing question.

The few individuals who were allowed to know Eleanor Chapel and Sidney Belton as a couple, rather than singly as professionals, knew well that the two were not only in love with each other, they also loved being *with* each other.

Wedded late in life, they had, nevertheless, not imagined that they would relish their mature years to this extent. They were supremely happy together despite the apparent incongruity in their backgrounds: he, a lifelong Roman Catholic from Brooklyn, and she, a Southern Baptist from the Deep South; he, a former NYPD and now private detective, and she, a lifelong scholar and teacher; he, a committed bachelor, and she, a settled widow for almost her entire adult lifetime, her first husband having been a World War II casualty, flying a P-47 Thunderbolt more than four decades earlier.

But they were both devoted Christians who prayed and worshipped daily in ways that suited their individual backgrounds. This fact transcended all others.

They had immense respect for each other's faith commitments, and acknowledged both privately to each other, and publicly to anyone who asked, that they had never been so happy as they now were. But they also acknowledged the larger picture. That is, they acknowledged the persistent danger that was woven into the fabric of their lives. And the fact of that danger, she now reminded herself as she approached 50th Street, was why she tolerated Sidney's having arranged for the alterations in her new running shoes. And there was more.

He had also insisted that her soft-cover briefcase be modified by the same NYPD footwear-and-clothing artisan who had altered her shoes, so that the briefcase now included an unobtrusive pocket on one side. The briefcase's long shoulder strap allowed her hands to be free so that, if suddenly necessary, her right hand could reach down to the external pocket and extract a small can of chemical mace.

Belton had badgered her to practice daily in their apartment, and she had done so until he was satisfied that her automatic response to sudden threat was "reach-and-spray," "turn-and-kick," and, finally, "run-and-scream."

Now, having passed the Winter Garden Theatre on her left, she turned left — that is, east — away from the Hudson and toward the East River. The turn would take her shortly to Fifth Avenue, whereupon, at the corner of 50th and Fifth, she would turn south. In eight short blocks from that turn, she would arrive at the library.

She loved walking in the city as she, in fact, loved most things about New York. She and Sidney did own a dilapidated, much-dented car, and she used it some days to drive to Lower Manhattan for lunch with her husband and his detective-agency partner, Jaakov Adelman, but she much preferred to walk everywhere.

This was the first Monday of the sabbatical semester granted her by Union Theological Seminary where she had held the post of full professor and department chair of Old Testament for more than a decade. She looked forward to a full working Monday using the resources of the famed library, as she began her half-year of research into the Minor Prophets of the Old Testament and their collective role in what she, with the late C. S. Lewis, viewed as "God's long preparation of a people for the central event in history." She was eager to dive into the research. She had quickly decided to ignore her husband's repeated urgings that she take a three-month break before launching the research project.

"Sidney," she had said to him the previous evening at dinner, "if you tell me one more time I should take a break before beginning my sabbatical I'm going to take that walking cane out of your hands and crack you on the noggin. You'll stagger around wondering what hit you and while you do, I'll go spend half your NYPD pension check on the research materials I'll need to get started.

"You won't even have enough money to get into the Yankees game tomorrow. In fact, you might not have enough to buy a hot dog in the parking lot. You'll be so destitute you'll be asking me for bus fare to a Greenwich Village movie."

Belton had then laughed his unique laugh, delighted as always at his wife's playful put-downs, delivered invariably at his expense. He loved it.

"You try 'n take my cane from me, Eleanor," he'd said in his rumbling Brooklynese, "an' I'll toss yer puny 85-pound self right down th' laundry chute an' y' won't be found 'til Christmas."

Now she smiled, yet again, at the recollection. What fun!

But she acknowledged to herself that her husband's polished walking cane was also thoroughly weaponized, and much more formidably so than her steel-toed running shoes. His numerous irreversible injuries, suffered over the course of a professional lifetime, made the walking cane necessary, and the fact that his right arm was frozen at the elbow meant that the cane was always handled with his left hand. Belton leaned to that side whether walking or standing.

The handle of the cane contained a recessed trigger that enabled the detective to release, in a split second, a spring-loaded knife blade from the base of the cane. Belton's strong left arm and hand could drive the blade into an enemy's lower leg with considerable force, quickly incapacitating an assailant.

She smiled again, noting to herself that both she and her husband appeared utterly harmless to those who did not know them. But they were not.

Now moving east on 50th Street, she passed Rockefeller Center and then turned right onto Fifth Avenue. In fewer than 10 minutes she would be able to see the New York City Library's Beaux-Arts structure just on the other side of 42nd Street.

Indeed, as 10 a.m. arrived, the library came into view as she stopped for the signal at 42nd. The light changed and she started across the intersection in company with a clutch of other pedestrians, but her attention was immediately drawn to the sight of two very large men, both masked, emerging from an illegally parked van not 20 feet from her. Their purpose, as they moved straight toward her, was unmistakable.

Calling instantly on her freshly learned and thoroughly practiced defensive repertoire, she crouched, drew the mace from its pocket on the side of her briefcase, and directed a long stream of the irritant into the eyes of the first assailant who, outpacing his partner, was already reaching for her shoulder. As the spray hit the attacker squarely in the eyes, she pivoted toward the other and, as he raised his hands to protect his eyes, she drove one steel-toed Adidas into his shin with astonishing force for a diminutive septuagenarian.

Both men yowled in pain as Professor Eleanor Chapel, distinguished Biblical lecturer, screamed like a banshee and ran back to the curb.

Her fellow pedestrians reacted in myriad ways. Some ran away; others ran to her side; and two others, both women in 3-inch heels, conservative business suits, and carrying hard-shell briefcases, raced toward the attackers.

Converging on the two momentarily disabled assailants, the two women screamed obscenities and swung their heavy briefcases wildly at the men's unprotected skulls. The men dived back toward the van.

One of the men, dragging his throbbing leg behind him, steered his momentarily blinded partner toward the van's open side door. As the two fell into the van, the long, nondescript vehicle, its motor already running and its driver impatient, lurched from the curb. Fighting its way through a red light, the van dodged, horn blasting, across the wide intersection, finally disappearing on the other side of Fifth Avenue and into the Monday morning traffic on 42ⁿᵈ Street.

That same evening, in their simply furnished, fourth-floor Morningside Heights apartment, Eleanor and Belton sat at their small kitchen table to begin their just-delivered dinner: a medium half-and-half mushroom and pepperoni pizza. They bowed their heads while she offered one of her typically exquisite blessings, one which, on this evening, concluded with a phrase that she recited verbatim from the Church of England Book of Common Prayer.

She had immersed herself in the book's evocative prayers since, the previous summer, her husband had purchased the small volume during one of his emergency trips to England. His purpose there had been to assist Rebecca Manguson Clark and her family as they confronted yet another potentially cataclysmic threat to the faith, to the people of the U.K., and to themselves.

Now, Belton stiffened as he heard his wife conclude her blessing by quoting the words formulated in the prayer book's language, words, and phrases originating from the year 1662: "And we yield thee praise and thanksgiving for our deliverance from those great and apparent dangers wherewith we were compassed … Amen."

He opened his eyes and looked up at her.

She met his eyes, smiled sweetly, and picked up a slice of the pizza, taking a dainty bite from the mushroom and cheese portion.

"Great an' apparent dangers?" he said in his deep Brooklynese. "What *great an' apparent dangers* are ya talkin' about, Eleanor?"

She chewed, swallowed, and smiled again.

"Oh," she said, "you'll be so pleased to know that I used my chemical mace *and* my steel-toed Adidas this morning, Sidney. I wish I had it all on film. I was textbook perfect … really … I did just what you taught me."

By the time she was halfway through her casual summary he was on his feet and beginning to hobble around the table.

"Whad'ya mean? Th' chemical mace … th' steel toes … whad'ya *talkin'* about, Eleanor? Don't be cute with me about this sorta stuff.

"Whad'ya *talkin'* about?"

She put her pizza slice down.

"It was just a little blip in my day, dear," she said. "It was over in an eyeblink. And you should have *seen* two of my fellow pedestrians go after those two brutes.

"Two women dressed to the nines, screaming at my attackers and swinging their briefcases. Those animals couldn't get out of there quick enough.

"It was spectacular, Sidney!"

By then she saw that Sidney was ready to explode, so she stood, stepped to him, threw both arms around his waist, and, with the side of her face pressed against his chest, recounted the incident with as much precision as she could muster.

He was not mollified.

He placed his left hand on her small shoulder and moved her gently to arm's length. He fixed her with his most intense stare, one that had led dozens of police suspects over the years to avert their eyes and begin to confess everything they had been trying to avoid confessing. Such techniques had no impact on his wife.

She smiled her pixie smile and said, "Sidney, you're going to blow a gasket." Then she paused, musing aloud, "You know, dear … I've always wondered what that actually means, haven't you?

"I mean," she continued, "what, exactly, is a gasket?"

He dropped his hand from her shoulder, sighed, limped back to his chair, sat down, and picked up a slice of pepperoni, shaking his head. Seeing his response, she moved behind his chair and leaned down over him, placing her arms around his neck.

"I'm sorry, dearest," she said softly, "but I don't know anything else to tell you about what happened. I really didn't see anything that would possibly be useful to you or to the NYPD people.

"I just saw the attackers coming and I automatically went through the maneuvers you'd taught me. I saw two women swinging their briefcases at the men, and then I ran back to the curb, still screaming, while several people came to comfort me. I never really saw the vehicle enough to tell you even what color it was. And I just *think* it was some kind of van.

"I don't know anything else, Sidney. Really … I just don't."

It was the feel of her arms around his neck, more so than her words, which calmed and relaxed the hard-bitten detective. He slowly put his pizza slice down on his plate, slid his chair back from the little table, and pulled his wife around and into his lap. He smiled his crooked smile at her and nodded.

"Okay, Miss New York City street fighter of th' month," he said, "ya can keep me from blowin' a gasket — maybe — by tellin' me why ya waited … let's see

… about *eight hours* t' mention anything about this t' me … or t' th' NYPD … or t' anybody at all. Ya gotta know by now, after livin' with me fer all this time, that every minute that passes after a street assault lessens th' chances a' findin' th' dirtbags who did it.

"What in th' world were ya *thinkin'*, Miss Smarter-than-anybody-else-in-th'-city, Old Testament expert?

"Hm?

"What were ya *thinkin'*?"

"Well," she said, snuggling into his chest as she balanced herself lightly on his bony lap, "I was just thinking about diving into my research, Sidney.

"I just wanted to get to the library and start to work. I didn't want to spend time making reports and giving descriptions — especially since I didn't really have any — and my mind went straight from the fracas to the Old Testament book of Amos.

"Did you know that Amos," she continued, warming to her subject, "whose Biblical words are so powerful and so often erudite, was not among the highly educated of his era? Sidney, he was a *shepherd!*

"Did you know that, dear?"

He sighed, shook his head slowly, and pulled her tighter.

"No, Eleanor," he said quietly. "I did not know that Amos was a shepherd." He kissed her temple.

"Tell me more about Amos," he said, nuzzling her ear.

A half-hour later, dishes and glasses washed and put away, the couple sat down on their well-worn sofa to begin their evening reading time. As she picked up her Thomas Merton from the coffee table, he placed a hand gently on hers to indicate he needed her attention before she resumed *The Seven Storey Mountain*.

She smiled and attended to him. She had known that their conversation about the morning's events was not finished. Not for Sidney Belton.

"Okay, dear," he said to her, "here's what I'm thinkin'."

She waited.

He organized his thoughts, then began.

"First, I'm thinkin' that this morning's attack — th' one you an' yer lady friends blew up in 10 seconds — took a lot a' planning. *A lot* a' planning.

"Fer them t' be waitin' fer ya right there … right then … they had t' know ya were gonna be leavin' home on foot at 9 a.m., headed fer th' library on Fifth Avenue an' 42nd Street. They had t' know how fast ya usually walk, an' they had t' know th' route ya were gonna take. If you'd walked down Central Park West instead a' Broadway, or taken a different street from Broadway over t' Fifth, yer timin' woulda been different …

"Eleanor … they *knew* ya were gonna go t' th' library this morning, an' they knew *exactly* when ya were gonna get there.

"How'd they know that?

"Hm?"

She knew he was not really asking a question, and she knew he was not finished. She continued to listen.

"How'd they know anything at all about yer plans fer Monday, and how'd they know t' wait fer ya about *4 miles* from our apartment, and at exactly 10 a.m.?

"Hm?"

She continued to wait.

"An' then I gotta ask this, Eleanor. *Why* were they waitin' fer ya?

"Those dirtbags were gonna throw ya in a van an' take ya somewhere. That usually means that ignorant hammerheads like these people want a hostage. An' that usually means they got big-deal plans, an' havin' Dr. Eleanor Chapel as a hostage would hafta be th' first step in their big-deal plans.

"What would their big-deal plans look like, Eleanor?

"An' whose big-deal plans would they be?

"Hm?"

He looked at her. She shook her head.

"I don't know, Sidney," she said. "I don't know about any of that, but my mind is stuck on your first question … how did they know to wait for me at the corner of Fifth Avenue and 42nd Street at 10 a.m. on this particular Monday?

"That frightens me more than the bigger-picture questions … you know … what bigger plans could this be part of, and whose plans could they be? For those bullies to know these little things about my life on this Monday morning … they must somehow have access to details about my everyday life at the seminary, Sidney. Someone at our seminary must have given those people information about me and my plans … my routine, day-to-day plans.

"It's terribly disconcerting to think someone I know at the seminary could have been part of what almost happened to me this morning, even if the part they played was … possibly … accidental … which it could have been."

"Whad'ya mean … *accidental,* Eleanor?"

"We publish a little weekly blurb that says what our faculty members are doing … you know … vacation plans … study projects … writing projects … that sort of thing. *Anyone* at our seminary could have known where I'd be spending the day today. And if one of our seminary people passed the little weekly publication along to outsiders, then those outsiders could just have waited to see me leave our building this morning. Then they could have simply followed along behind me on foot … or in a vehicle … just long enough to see my route … then they could have anticipated my arrival at that intersection at 10 a.m., and driven there to intercept me.

"Not really very difficult … but who shared our little weekly publication with the people that tried to do this to me? Who passed that along to people who would want to kidnap me and … you know …"

They sat back, side-by-side on the little sofa, holding hands, and thought in silence for long minutes. Finally, she turned to him and said, "I know what you're thinking now, dear."

He smiled his crooked smile and said, "No chance, Eleanor."

"Well … then go ahead and say, Mister Big-Shot New York City detective," she said, her blue-green eyes twinkling.

He cackled, took several seconds, turned serious, and began.

"Maybe this is as simple as th' New York City Russian Mafia wantin' revenge fer what happened t' 'em last summer … th' FBI raid that cost 'em millions a' dollars an' wrecked their organization.

"They knew that we — you an' me an' Rebecca an' Luke an' th' others — laid th' groundwork fer that FBI raid. Maybe they're just mad, Eleanor."

She nodded.

"That's what I *knew* you were thinking, Sidney."

He shook his head.

"Nope," he said. "Yer wrong, Miss Old Testament genius person … I was just leadin' ya down th' garden path …

"Think about it. Why would th' Russian Mafia dirtbags want a hostage, if they just want revenge? Hostages are a lot a' trouble … an' takin' a hostage is a ridiculous, roundabout way of gettin' back at somebody. If they're just mad, Eleanor, they'd just get their guns an' shoot us … an' be done with us. End of story.

"Know what I mean?

"Hm?"

She was thoughtful.

He waited.

Then she nodded.

"Yes, dear," she said, "I see. The hostage idea doesn't make very good sense, if this was simply about revenge for last summer."

"Right," he said. "Th' attack this mornin' was about somethin' else."

He continued.

"I'm thinkin' this has got nothin' t' do with those Mafia guys. They don't want a hostage … an' besides … th' Russian Mafia in New York is gonna need t' stay under their rock fer quite a while, Eleanor.

"Nah … this is not th' Russians. At least, it's not *those* Russians.

"This has gotta be a different bunch a' scumbags … with a completely different *kind* of agenda.

"This is somebody that doesn't want Dr. Eleanor Chapel t' appear on that week- long string a' panel discussions in Washington, D.C., next week. They don't want ya as a hostage, Eleanor. They want t' take ya outta circulation.

"They don't want ya t' be part a' next week's Washington, D.C., circus.

"Know what I mean, Eleanor?

"Hm?"

She was surprised.

She was quiet, thinking, still holding hands with her husband.

Finally, she turned to him.

"Well, dear," she said, "that's not at all what I was thinking. I *was* thinking about the Mafia people. I was thinking the Mafia people picked me because I'm easier to snatch than you, or any of the others …

"I'm more available to people who are, as you say, mad at us. And I'm also, as you'd say, a high profile person … you know … public lectures, books, articles … all the things I've managed to become … um … well-known for …

"I'd make an excellent hostage, you know … but, as you've said … to what end? How does that accomplish anything for the Mafia people? That couldn't have been what the assault was about, could it? I'm just wrong.

"Right?"

"Right … yer wrong."

"Oh," she said, "but I do hope you're *not* right that I'm wrong. The last thing we need is some new group of … *dirtbags…* who want to … who want to …"

Her voice trailed off.

He squeezed her hand. She looked into his eyes and continued.

"I just never thought about my appearances next week in Washington until this moment … as being a reason for someone to assault me at a Manhattan intersection … that never crossed my mind."

They were quiet … quiet together … for several more minutes, thinking. Finally, she turned to him again.

"So, Sidney," she said, incredulity in her voice.

"You're telling me that this morning's commotion was all about … this thing in Washington? This assault was about … *liberation theology?*"

He shook his head.

"I don't even know what that is, Eleanor. What is it?"

"Umm," she murmured, "the short answer is that it's a perspective on Christianity that emphasizes liberation of the oppressed … concern for the poor … political liberation of oppressed peoples.

"It was spawned within Catholicism in the 1960s after the Second Vatican Council, and, later, highlighted by the World Synod of Catholic Bishops in 1971. That synod's theme was … let me think … yes … 'Justice in the World.'

"More recently, for example, several priests in Northern Ireland have embraced the right of communities to create alternative education, welfare, and political structures. And they have *not* condemned paramilitary groups when those groups presented themselves as alternative police or alternative armies.

"Alternative *armies*, Sidney.

"Some of them may be coming to Washington next week."

"Yikes."

"Yikes, indeed," she agreed.

Once again, they fell silent.

After several moments, he rose from the sofa, turned off the floor lamp behind him, picked up his cane, then crossed to her side of the sofa and turned off the table lamp next to her. Darkness enveloped the small living room, the only light in the apartment now coming faintly from the kitchen.

Belton then clumped across the room to a spot near the window and stood to one side, looking down at the street, four stories below. He studied the scene, then, still in near-complete darkness, returned to the sofa and sat again, once more taking his wife's hand in his. She did not need to ask why he had done what she had just observed.

"What did you see down there, dear?" she asked.

"Surveillance," he replied simply.

"Whoever this is, Eleanor, they know ya walk everywhere ya go. They're just waitin' t' see ya walk outta th' building in th' mornin'. They're not gonna wait this time, until yer at th' library. They're gonna snatch ya up right away.

"They're not givin' up, Eleanor. They're not kiddin' around."

She waited.

At length, he resumed their discussion.

"So … keep goin', Eleanor. Liberation theology …"

"Well," she said after a moment, "I spoke about its Catholic origins, but possibly more important from an academic point of view is the fact that liberation theology has become a big thing in non-Catholic circles, too, such as non-Catholic Christian seminaries, and non-Catholic Christian undergraduate colleges.

"It has swept up the academic world across the board."

They sat silent in the dark, still thoughtful, still holding hands.

"Okay, Eleanor," said Belton finally, "I'm still workin' t' figure out why you — Miss Southern-Baptist Big-Shot Professor of Old Testament at Union Theological Seminary in New York City — would be singled out as a target fer what sounds like somethin' that started as a mostly Catholic thing.

"I mean … it's *me* who's th' Catholic in our two-person family. *I'm* th' one who goes t' St. Patrick's Cathedral fer early Mass almost every mornin' of th' year.

"I'm almost as easy a target as you are. Why not snatch *me?*"

"For the reasons you've already explained to me, dear. You're not on that panel in Washington next week. I am."

"Oh, yeah."

"But you're right," she resumed, "in asking 'why me?' I'm not publicly known for being either for, or against, liberation theology. Why would someone want to keep me away from those panel discussions and presentations next week?"

More silence.

"Well … *are* ya fer it, Eleanor? Or against it?"

"I've never been one for jumping on board these 'movements,' dear," she said. "I've never thought our faith should be coupled with something else, no matter what the 'something else' might be.

"Christianity is about belief. I try to stay focused on passages like … for example … the magnificent passage in the eighth chapter of Paul's letter to the Romans. You know the passage, Sidney."

"Yeah, but lemme hear it again. I don't know th' Bible like you do."

She closed her eyes and, in her high, lyrical voice, recited the passage verbatim from the King James Version, smiling as she did.

"'In all these things we are more than conquerors through Him that loved us. For I am persuaded that neither death, nor life, nor angels, nor principalities, nor powers, nor things present, nor things to come, nor height, nor depth, nor any created being, shall be able to separate us from the love of God, which is in Christ Jesus our Lord.'"

She opened her eyes and, still smiling, looked at him.

"I focus on that passage, dear," she said, "and on a handful of others ... like, for example, Jesus' astonishing parable of the sheep and the goats ... in Matthew's Gospel account ... you know ... when Jesus reminds his listeners ... *'Inasmuch as ye have done it unto one of the least of these my brethren, ye have done it unto Me ...'"*

Belton squeezed her hand to indicate he wanted to interrupt.

She paused. He could see her dimly in the darkened room, the distant light from the kitchen illuminating her face

"Y'know," he said, "that sheep-and-goats thing sounds a lot like what you were sayin' about liberation theology ... concern fer th' poor an' th' oppressed.

"That doesn't sound all that bad, Eleanor."

She nodded.

"No, it doesn't," she replied, "which is exactly how most of these movements get launched. Someone takes one of Christ's teachings and turns it into *the* teaching ... *the* main thing ... *the* focus of Christianity. And that means distortion, Sidney.

"Movements are about distortion. You can't take John 3:16 and 3:17 and turn that simple, heart-of-the-matter core pronouncement — that 'God so loved the world that He gave His Son ... so that the world, through Him, might be saved' — into something else and call the 'something else' the core pronouncement.

"And I know this, Sidney: The most effective Evil *is very nearly Good.*

"So, when the various movements have come along, I have always pushed back, trying to remind advocates of the movement-of-the-day that movements come and movements go. The central, core Gospel message remains."

He considered this for several moments, then said, "Well, Eleanor ... maybe that one thing — yer *pushin' back* — has been enough t' get somebody t' want t' keep ya away from next week's hoopla in Washington. Maybe that somebody is sittin' outside our apartment right now, down on th' street ...

"*Somebody* is sure sittin' outside our apartment, down on th' street, right now."

She nodded.

"Yes," she acknowledged, "and that reminds me to say that these various movements … even if a particular one might create just *a little* bit of distortion of one of Christ's ideas … can gather to themselves some very dangerous people.

"Movements can attract people who have an extremist bent … people who decide that the movement they're determined to embrace — in this case, perhaps, liberation theology — is worth fighting for … literally … fighting for. Perhaps even *killing* for. And such people are often capable of adopting approaches that are not just extreme, Sidney … they are violent … sometimes *terrorist-style* violent.

"You may think that liberation theology 'doesn't sound all that bad,' as you said a moment ago, but some of the people who are attracted to that perspective may be exactly those who will take their new insight, as they would see it, to any extreme whatsoever. Violence can become just one more hammer in their toolbox."

Belton cackled.

"Oh, man," he said delightedly. "You said 'one more hammer in their toolbox,' Eleanor … like you're one a' those construction guys that always talks in terms of two-by-fours an' plumb lines."

He laughed, but seeing her unsmiling face, he turned instantly serious again.

"I do get yer point … liberation theology might not be terrible as an idea … an idea that's not too far away from what Jesus was actually talkin' about … but it's *not* what He was actually talkin' about … an', if it pulls in enough dirtbags …

"I get what ya mean, Eleanor."

They were thoughtful again.

Finally, he turned to her once more in the darkness of their small living room, a secure haven from the evil poised in the darkness outside.

"Okay … then tell me more about th' thing next week, Eleanor. Who's there? What's it gonna look like? How much publicity is it gonna get? Who's gonna pay attention? How much money is ridin' on th' outcomes of th' discussions?

"Hm?"

He rose again, waiting for her response, picked up his cane, and hobbled to the window, again standing near in the darkened room, but to one side.

She was thoughtful.

"Georgetown University," she began, "a Jesuit institution, you know … will be hosting. The featured panel, as we are called, will be spotlighted each evening for three nights, as I understand it, Monday through Wednesday. Scholars from Notre Dame, Oxford, Cambridge, Virginia Theological Seminary, my seminary here in New York, other seminaries around the U.S., and, of course, Georgetown, will comprise the … um … 'disputants,' as we have been labeled in the announcements.

"Note, dear, that only Notre Dame and Georgetown are Catholic. Liberation theology has become Christianity-wide, insofar as academic interests are concerned … and not just academics now. Some public figures like … maybe … one or two of the Northern Ireland people I just mentioned … are expected to speak at various small seminars during the daytime portions of the program. Don't forget that I said *political* action is considered one of the cornerstones of liberation theology.

"But, as for me, Sidney, I appear to be … sort of … the Baptist 'representative' among these panelists. I imagine I was picked for the usual reasons I'm picked for such things: I'm an anomaly … you know … a Baptist at a not-even-remotely-Baptist seminary here in New York City … an Old Testament professor in a field that is almost entirely male … a theological traditionalist in a sea of theological liberals and radicals …

"An old person … a woman …

"The usual things, Sidney."

Still staring out the window, he replied after a moment's thought.

"Sounds like ya might be a thorn in th' side a' these guys, Eleanor … they're all guys, right? … an' yer gonna make 'em look foolish like ya usually do, right?

"I can see one or two of 'em wantin' t' get ya … uh … taken off th' program, if ya see what I mean … hm?"

She snorted.

"Oh please, Sidney! These brainy academic panelists wouldn't lift a finger to sweep me off the stage. They'll feel sure they can talk down their noses at me. They'll think of me as a minor annoyance … certainly not worth taking any physical action to eliminate me from these evening discussions."

"Eleanor," he replied immediately, "we just now talked about these movements sometimes pullin' in violent dirtbags … what makes ya think these 'brainy academic panelists' haven't pulled in th' kind a' meatheads who'd scoop a 72-year-old, 85-pound professor off th' street an' throw 'er in a van?

"Hm?"

He leaned toward her.

"Ya can't keep thinkin' yer lookin' at harmless little academic people, Eleanor, when you've already said movements like this can pull in violent toughs. Big, violent toughs like th' two thugs that were gonna throw ya in their van this mornin'.

"Hm?"

"Yes … yes … I suppose," she replied reluctantly.

"*Somebody* came after ya, Eleanor," he said.

"An' *somebody* is sittin' down there on th' street waitin' fer ya.

"Hm?

"Who are they?"

She shook her head.

More silence.

Then she brightened.

"Oh!" she exclaimed. "Maybe we're looking in the wrong place, Sidney. Maybe it's more to do with something you said 10 minutes ago."

"What's that?"

"You said … 'it's not the Russians,' but then you said, 'at least, it's not *those* Russians,' meaning not the New York City Russian Mafia."

He nodded.

"Yeah, I did say that."

"How about last summer's *other* Russians, Sidney? How about the Soviets? And … now that I think of it … why could it not be *both* things?"

"Hm? Whad'ya mean?"

"Why could it not be some of *those* Soviets … some of those *Marxists* … getting interested in liberation theology as a way to twist Christianity — Catholic, Protestant, Eastern Orthodox, all of it — away from the core idea of God's love for us and of our individual responses to His love … and into something this group of Soviets could exploit for their own purposes?"

Silence in the room grew long. Sounds from the street below were muffled.

Belton shuffled back to the sofa and sat again, once more taking her hand.

"That's good, Eleanor," he said. "An' I just thought a' somethin' else …

"Remember," said Belton, "last summer, when Jaakov did his summary a' those documents we'd photographed at th' headquarters a' th' Chaos organization? Remember what he said?"

She thought of Jaakov Adelman, her husband's partner in their Lower Manhattan detective agency. She tried to recall the former Mossad agent's overview, in summer of 1985, of the self-described terrorist organization that had called itself 'Chaos,' its very name accurately embodying its organizational Mission.

Finally, she said, "I remember Jaakov's doing a summary, dear, but I don't think I'm getting to what you have in mind."

Belton leaned toward his wife and took her hand in both his.

"Jaakov reported that the Chaos people who were terrorizin' England last summer appeared t' be the U.K. branch of … let's see … I think his words were, 'a multifaceted, full-service, criminal organization' whose origins were Middle Eastern. He said we were lookin' at one branch — th' United Kingdom branch — of somethin' that was becomin' 'global in scope.'

"Remember?"

She nodded in the semi-darkness.

"Yes … I do remember, Sidney.

"But how on earth can you recall so much of Jaakov's summary … apparently word for word?"

"I don't know, Eleanor … those phrases just stuck with me …

"Anyway … seems t' me … we might be dealin' with *those* people … maybe *those* Russian terrorists … or maybe not *Russian* terrorists at all … maybe *Middle Eastern* terrorists … there's plenty a' terrorists in that part a' th' world.

"Could be anybody, Eleanor."

Belton shook his head in the semi-darkness, irritated at the lack of clarity.

"Eleanor, I don't know what it is we're lookin' at here, but I know one thing."

"Yes, dear?"

"We gotta bail."

"We do?"

"Yeah. We can't keep doin' business as usual right here where we live … right here where we go t' church … right here where we each go t' work every day. We gotta get outta here.

"We gotta leave New York, Eleanor. We gotta get out … right now.

"Tonight."

CHAPTER TWO

Earlier that same Monday morning, June 1986, Washington, D.C.

AS MARIE CAMPBELL NEARED THE END OF HER DAILY 20-minute walk to her downtown Washington office, she found herself daydreaming happily about her upcoming one-year anniversaries. "Anniversaries" — plural — because the date would mark 12 months of marriage to Jack McGriff and, as well, of the extraordinary wedding gift to the couple from Sidney Belton and Jaakov Adelman.

That gift was their own branch office, along with an experienced administrative assistant, costs for both fully covered by the parent agency. She was still thrilled every morning to read the professionally lettered sign in the office window.

Belton and Adelman Detective Agency
New York City

Campbell and McGriff, D.C. Agents

Marie was dressed for work on this Monday in one of her numerous summer skirt-and-blouse combinations, this one a dark blue, knee-length skirt, coupled with a light pink, sleeveless, cotton blouse. She wore low-heeled navy walking shoes, their color a good match for the skirt. Her brown, shoulder-length hair was caught up in a ponytail, the ponytail held in place by a small gold barrette. The exquisite barrette was fashioned in the shape of a heart and had been given to her by her husband on the occasion of their first Christmas together as husband and wife.

As usual on her walks to and from work, she carried a leather ready-satchel by its long shoulder strap. The ready-satchel concept was one she had learned the previous summer through her experiences with Rebecca Manguson Clark and her family members in London. They often carried the capacious, multi-purpose totes in acknowledgement of the close-quarter dangers they and their associates had faced for years. Marie and Jack, as a result of their willing involvement with the Clarks in their desperate summer 1985 fight against a Soviet-backed terror campaign in the U.K., had known from the start that they would become heirs to those dangers.

Marie's ready-satchel contained some of the same ingredients found in Rebecca's own satchel — passport, cash, emergency contact information, a few toiletries — but some ingredients were specific to Marie. The latter included a can of chemical mace, whereas Rebecca's ready-satchel contained three of her prized 12-inch Barringtons Swords throwing knives. Of the members of Rebecca Clark's core group of family and associates, only Marie and her New York City friend and employer Eleanor Chapel carried the defensive aerosol spray instead of actual weaponry.

Ironically, those two women would be the only ones whose ready-satchels would come into play on this Monday morning.

Still musing about the upcoming anniversaries, Marie made the final turn onto the block on which the Campbell and McGriff office spaces were located. Thus preoccupied, she did not sense the running footsteps approaching from behind.

Suddenly, she was struck between the shoulder blades with enough force to send her crashing headlong into the pavement. Her hands came up in time to keep her face from smashing into the sidewalk, but that same reflexive movement dislodged the ready-satchel from her shoulder. Her assailant, hardly slowing, snatched the satchel from the pavement and accelerated, sprinting to the next corner and disappearing.

Pedestrians rushed to her aid and she, struggling to rise and screened by her rescuers, did not so much as glimpse the attacker as he fled. Helped to her feet, she conducted a quick self-inspection and found only matching sets of abrasions on her knees, elbows, and hands. She adjusted her skirt, gratefully accepted the return of one shoe, and assured her helpers that she would be alright to continue.

Two of her helpers, a man and a woman, refused to leave her until they had escorted her the remaining half-block to the office. As the three of them entered, Jack McGriff, who had been at work since 6 a.m., sprang from behind the reception desk, alarmed by his wife's bleeding knees and by the mere fact of her being helped along by two strangers. Joined quickly by the administrative assistant, McGriff thanked the two Good Samaritans, asked if they could describe his wife's attacker and, although they admitted they could not, jotted down their names and contact information.

Minutes before, as the assailant, running hard, approached the unsuspecting Marie Campbell from behind, a tall, athletic young man walking on the opposite side of the street saw the impending assault a full two seconds before impact. Even as Marie crashed onto the sidewalk, he was sprinting in pursuit.

Now, 10 minutes after the assault, Marie, seated at her desk in her own office, was astonished to see her ready-satchel being handed to her by a stranger. He had just been escorted to her door by the office assistant. The young man, having thanked the assistant, proceeded to introduce himself.

"My name is Jim Durham, Mrs. Campbell," he said courteously.

"I was pretty sure you'd like to have this back," he said, smiling. "Once I'd overtaken that kid and had read him the riot act, I looked inside your purse — that's quite a purse — to find your contact information and discovered your business cards. Too bad you didn't get a chance to use that can of chemical mace on the guy."

Jack McGriff had entered his wife's office in time to overhear Durham's self-introduction and comment.

The men shook hands.

"We can't thank you enough," said McGriff, "for getting Marie's ready-satchel back to her. How hard was it to overtake the thief and subdue him?"

"Oh," replied Durham, "I didn't really have to catch him or subdue him, Father McGriff. I just had to get close enough to shout at him. See … I know that kid. I'm a detective working with the precinct's juvenile division.

"He knew to stop when he realized it was me chasing him. He's in enough trouble without getting into a fight with a D.C. city detective."

Marie, just finishing applying antiseptic and bandages to her knees and elbows, now stood to shake Durham's hand.

"Let me add to my husband's thanks, Mr. Durham. I did not expect to ever see my things again. I've already asked our assistant — the young woman who escorted you to my office — to call the police … and our bank …

"Which reminds me … let me tell her what you've just said. You'll want to make the police report yourself, yes?"

"Yes, ma'am."

She left the room.

"I've been meaning to stop by to introduce myself, Father," said Durham. "I was aware of your opening last summer. Just never got around to it.

"All of us saw Sid Belton's name in the office window, and were impressed that he'd started a branch agency here in Washington. He must think a lot of you and Mrs. Campbell, as investigators."

"We've been working hard this first year, Jim," said McGriff, "not to disappoint him and Jaakov Adelman, his partner. Oh, by the way … how did you know I'm an Episcopal priest? I don't wear my collar to work here."

"Well," replied Durham, "I think everybody in our precinct knows that, sir. We've always been aware of your work in the community as a priest. We didn't know you had this other talent, though. We're just pleased you've stayed here in the city."

Marie re-entered the office, saying as she did, "Mr. Durham, can we get you a coffee or tea? We have both."

He shook his head.

"No thanks, ma'am, I need to get moving, but I appreciate the offer. And I'm not 'Mr. Durham,' please. I'm 'Jim,' and I'm just glad I happened to see the kid when I did. If I'd seen him a few seconds *before* I did, I could have shouted a warning."

"Please use our first names, too, Jim," she said. "I'm Marie and my husband is Jack, and we'd love to have a conversation with you about your work and ours, whenever you can spare the time to drop back in."

As Durham turned to go, he paused, smiled sheepishly, and said, "What did you say your assistant's name is, Mrs. Campbell … I mean … Marie?"

"I didn't," she replied, smiling. "Her name is Sarah Wilson."

Durham shifted his feet uncomfortably.

"Um … is she … ah … attached … um … you know … going with somebody… or … ah … you know …"

"Oh, no," said Marie. "Sarah has somehow been overlooked by the male population of Washington in the year she has been here. That's possibly because she worked in New York until our branch opened. Sid Belton knew of her work as an administrative assistant with the precinct in New York and gifted her to us, just as he gifted us this wonderful office space, Jim. I don't think Sarah has gotten out much since she moved here.

"She does go to our church, but I don't think …"

Marie paused, seeing her husband looking at her and shaking his head.

"What, Jack?" she said.

"We ought to let Sarah decide how much she wants Jim to know about her, Marie. She might be hoping to get to know somebody not engaged in law enforcement, you know, rather than just …"

"Oh, please, Jack," Marie said. "She'd *love* to get to know …"

But Jim Durham had left the room.

Marie waited a full minute, then walked to the door of her office and looked down the hallway toward the reception area. There she saw Jim Durham and Sarah Wilson chatting comfortably with each other.

She turned to her husband triumphantly.

"There!" she said. "It's obviously love at first sight."

McGriff rolled his eyes.

She returned to her desk and sat down, starting to paw through her ready-satchel, and was pleased to find the contents undisturbed.

"Looks like Jim was careful when he looked through my things," she said. "Everything is exactly where it's supposed to be."

McGriff took a seat across from her and asked if she was really alright after the assault. "Do you need to take a day, sweetheart? You've got to be shaken up. The guy had to whack you pretty hard to knock you flat like that."

"I'm fine, dear," she said, "but …"

She gave him a look.

"What?"

"I'm going to change the subject, dear."

"Okay," he said, sensing a *tone*.

"I read in the *Post* this morning about this series of panel discussions and presentations that are scheduled next week at Georgetown. The article said that Dr. Eleanor Chapel would be one of the featured panelists each evening. Have you heard from her or Sidney about this?"

McGriff froze. Then his shoulders slumped.

She glared.

"Are you *serious*, Jack McGriff?" she said.

He slapped his forehead comically, shaking his head in embarrassment.

"I forgot," he said.

She was stunned.

"Are you actually going to tell me that Sidney and Eleanor have been in touch, and you've *forgotten* to say a word to me about it?

"Jack McGriff!"

"I'm so sorry, Marie," he said contritely, "my mind …"

"Your *mind* …" she interrupted, rolling her eyes, "your *mind* has been so vacant that you neglected to *mention* that the couple who served as de facto parents at our wedding and who set us up in business at a prime downtown location and who hired our administrative assistant and paid her wages for a full year … *that* couple … is coming *here* … and you didn't think to *mention* that to me?

"What on *earth?*"

"Well, Marie," he said, searching desperately for an adequate excuse, "Sidney left a voicemail for me Friday evening, here at the office number, and every day I've meant to say something to you, but every day I've gotten sidetracked … and … oh, rats, Marie … I've got no excuse.

"Let me step into my office and get the notes I jotted down when I listened to his voice mail Saturday morning."

She rose from her chair.

He was already standing to go to his office, but he paused as she came around her desk. She walked directly to him and leaned into his chest. She looked up at him from her 5-foot-5-inch height, reached up, and gave him an affectionate punch to the chin. His long arms enveloped her as he smiled down from his six-foot-plus height, relieved to see a trace of playfulness in her response to his negligence.

"So, Jack," she asked, still leaning into his ample torso, "are they staying at our house next week, but you forgot? Are they coming early … maybe tomorrow … but you forgot? And are *you* perhaps on the program at next week's conference, but you also forgot to mention that?"

He lifted her lightweight body completely off the floor and planted a firm kiss on her small nose. "No," he said, "nothing like that, sweetheart.

"Sid's voicemail just said that Eleanor was going to be speaking at Georgetown University next week and that he and she would be staying at a hotel near the university … my notes say which hotel … and he said that he hoped they'd have a chance to drop by our office at some point, but he wasn't clear enough yet on Eleanor's speaking schedule … said he let us know.

"That's all … really."

"Well … okay," she said grudgingly.

"And Jack?"

"Yes?"

"Put me down."

Tuesday, 2 a.m., 4,000 feet above New Jersey and climbing

As Belton and Eleanor settled back in two of the cushy passenger seats of the Learjet 55C, the Central Intelligence Agency's two-man flight crew turned the sleek aircraft away from the Teterboro Airport and headed toward the Washington area's Andrews Air Force Base. The CIA's newest 55C had been configured to seat as many as six, but the Belton-Chapel couple were the only passengers on this unscheduled, emergency night flight.

After Belton's pronouncement to his wife, earlier that night, that they'd need to evacuate their New York City apartment, he had placed a call to the emergency hotline at CIA headquarters in Langley, Virginia. Over the years, Belton had developed many useful contacts among the intelligence agencies in the U.S., the U.K., Israel, and a handful of other countries. His reputation allowed him access to those agencies' resources at almost any time of the day or night.

The CIA duty officer had had the agency's standby pilots heading for Andrews, where their 55C was fueled and ready, within half-hour of Belton's call that night. At the Learjet's cruising speed of well over 400 mph, the flight from Washington to New Jersey to retrieve the couple had been brief.

Belton had requested an NYPD patrol car to drive himself and Eleanor across the Hudson to the Teterboro Airport. He knew that the enemy's surveillance team would witness their departure, but he knew also that this enemy, whoever that might turn out to be, would be helpless to intervene.

"They might as well know we've bailed, Eleanor," he had said to her. "No reason t' try t' hide that from 'em. They'd figure it out pretty quick anyway."

The flight was over so fast that it seemed to them both that they had left their Morningside Heights apartment just minutes before. As the couple stepped down from the Learjet, two CIA officers greeted them, took their two small pieces of luggage, and escorted them to their waiting unmarked car. By 3:45 a.m., they were unpacking in their government-furnished room at the CIA safe house at Langley.

"Mr. Belton," one of the officers had said on the drive to Langley from Andrews, "the chair of our five-person *Rebekka Yahalomin* unit requests a session with him — just him — late morning today, or whenever the two of you feel sufficiently rested. He's just anxious to know whether his unit needs to be on alert ... for something."

The Hebrew term, Rebekka Yahalomin, translated as "the Rebecca Communications Unit," had been coined by Mossad, the Israeli intelligence agency, when it had become apparent to them and to the CIA and MI6, their closest allies in the international intelligence community, that Rebecca Clark, her family, and several of their associates, were at times provided with information beyond any that they could develop on their own. The CIA and Mossad, following the lead of MI6, had eventually created small units to deal with what MI6 termed "unexplained and unexplainable data and their sources."

These three secular government agencies had remained officially noncommittal on the question of whether such "unexplainable" sources were, in fact, as Rebekka Yahalomin members steadfastly and unashamedly maintained, supernatural. The occasional newcomer to these small units was simply told that the Yahalomin themselves routinely made reference to "the Source," a word that was capitalized when written, and capitalized by oral emphasis when spoken.

Some veterans of these select, three-to-five member units had come to believe that much of the data in the Yahalomin's information array could only have supernatural origins. Other members were skeptical of that specific idea, but had come to trust the information anyway, being forced to acknowledge that the Yahalomin's track record had been unblemished for nearly a decade, and, supernatural or not, it would be absurd not to utilize whatever data happened to be given them by the Yahalomin.

And all members of these intelligence units understood that, at least in recent years, it was not actually the *group* called Rebekka Yahalomin that received the "unexplained and unexplainable" data. It was just one person, a woman named Rebecca Manguson Clark.

Tuesday 9 a.m., Campbell and McGriff detective agency, Washington, D.C.

McGriff walked down the short hallway to his wife's office, rapped lightly on the frame of her open door, and entered. She looked up at her husband and saw a quizzical smile on his face.

"Good morning ... again ... dear," she said brightly. "What's behind that smile?"

"Just got off the phone with Sid Belton, Marie," he replied. "He and Eleanor are *here*. They've flown overnight on a CIA Learjet to Andrews, and they've been placed in one of the rooms at the Langley safe house."

She gave him a suspicious look.

He raised his hands defensively.

"No, no … I'm completely innocent … this time. I had no idea they were coming *this* week. Sid says they had to evacuate their Manhattan place overnight. He said that Eleanor was attacked on the street yesterday morning on her way to the library. She's okay … she fended them off … but he and she realized they're under surveillance by … well … they're not sure who, but they think it *might* have something to do with the presentations that she'll be a part of … next week at Georgetown."

They were silent, turning this over in their minds.

"Jack," replied Marie, "you're saying that Eleanor was attacked yesterday morning in New York, and at roughly the same time I was attacked here in Washington … these were coordinated assaults, then?"

He shrugged.

"That's what Sidney and I were just asking each other on the phone. He didn't know, of course, about the attack here until I told him. And I didn't know about the attack on Eleanor until he told me.

"It put us in mind of those coordinated attacks in England, last summer … the coordinated attacks that kicked off the attempted terror bombings at Wimbledon … and then, had we not intervened … would have been expanded to attempted bombings at the Parliament building — the Palace of Westminster — and elsewhere …"

She shook her head.

"But, Jack … Jim Durham said the young man who hit me was just a kid … a teen … a teen-ager who's in the juvenile system here. He seems a really unlikely member of some kind of coordinated assault."

McGriff nodded.

"Exactly," he said. "That's what Sid and I said to each other … but then I said, 'Sid, how likely is it that two members of Rebekka Yahalomin would be attacked at almost exactly the same time in two different American cities?'

"Seriously, Marie, are we really supposed to conclude that these two highly similar events happened on the same morning, more than 200 miles apart, entirely through *coincidence*?"

She stood, circled her desk, and started for the door to the hallway. As she brushed past her husband, she touched him on the cheek and said, "I'm going to ask Sarah to get in touch with Jim Durham, dear … I want to hear more about this 'kid' that he overtook yesterday in the process of retrieving my ready-satchel.

"We need to know things about that young man, Jack."

Sarah Wilson smiled as Jim Durham entered the Campbell and McGriff reception area. He had arrived fewer than five minutes after she had phoned his pager.

"That was quick, Mr. Durham," she said brightly.

"That's 'Jim' to you, you know … well … I was just a couple of blocks away when your office number came up on my pager, Sarah. There didn't seem any point in finding a phone, when I could just trot over here in a few minutes.

"What's up?"

"Marie wants to talk to you," she said, "about the teen who knocked her down yesterday morning … you can go on back to her office."

He nodded.

"Sure … um … okay … um … do you have lunch plans, Sarah?"

She opened a drawer in her desk and wordlessly held up a lunch sack.

"Well," he said, "would that keep until tomorrow?

"I know a great lunch place …"

Sarah was already shaking her head.

"No … I like to eat and work at the same time. I just can't wrap my head around the idea of taking … what would you say … about an hour-and-a-half away from the office just to get something to eat?"

Durham looked embarrassed. She hastened to correct the impression her statement had given.

"I didn't mean all that time away from my desk would be absolutely *wasted*, Jim … I mean … I didn't mean to imply that talking to you would be a complete waste of time … I just don't want to do that during the workday.

"Do you understand?"

"Yes, I do," he said. "But it sounds like dinner would not ruin your day, right? I could come by whenever you expect to be finished this afternoon or evening. My workday doesn't really have a start and stop time. We could just walk from here to the place I would have taken you to lunch."

Sarah nodded.

"That sounds good … but am I dressed alright for that place?" she asked.

"Perfect," he said. "Will 6 o'clock work?"

She smiled and nodded again.

"Perfect," she said.

He walked down the hallway to Marie Campbell's office, and realized that, to his amusement, he was whistling.

As soon as he entered Marie's office, she buzzed her husband to join them, and she and McGriff quickly walked the young detective through the paired assaults in Washington and New York City the previous morning.

They knew that they could not, however, simply tell him about the two attacks and leave it there. For Durham to appreciate how extraordinary the situation appeared, they had to go further. The three of them sat down together in the small conversation area Marie had set up in one corner of her office. She and her husband sat on a small sofa; Durham, on the matching chair that faced them across a coffee table.

"Jim," said Marie after McGriff had described the attempt on Eleanor Chapel in Manhattan, as it had been explained to him by Sid Belton, "for you to understand how uncomfortable we are, we need to explain something … strange … to you. And for me to know how I can best say this, I must ask something quite intrusive."

"Ask away, Marie," Durham replied cheerily. "I'm pretty hard to intrude upon … I mean … I can't imagine what you'd ask that I'd regard as … um … intrusive."

"Okay," she said. "I'll start by asking whether or not you are a Christian.

"Are you a believer, Jim?"

He grinned broadly.

"I am *now,* Marie. I got turned around a few years ago, while I was still in college. I've been a regular on Sundays for years, over at Foundry Methodist, on 16th Street."

Marie nodded and smiled.

"I need to push a little more, Jim … so tell me … do you pray?"

"Wow, Marie!" he said good-naturedly. "Where are we going with this? … But … yes … my prayer life is very disciplined. I do early morning devotions and early morning prayers, before I get started on the day.

"I did ROTC in college, and so I served as an officer in the U.S. Army for three years after that. I found that doing my prayers at 0400 was the only way to ensure the thing happened at all.

"Of course … in the Army … and here, too … there are some days when that doesn't work, because of … you know … assignments that might keep me out all night or get me moving at, say 0300 … but, as a civilian, I do morning devotions and prayers in my study at home. I'm almost never interrupted by the phone or by my pager."

Durham reflected for a moment, then continued.

"Of course, in addition, I offer short, impromptu prayers any time of the day or night, but those are *responses* … responses to things that come up, or things that are coming up next … just catch-as-catch-can. Some days, there might be dozens of those little eyes-open prayers. Other days, there might not be a single one of those."

Marie smilingly nodded her understanding.

"Thank you," she said. "Jim, the reason for all these questions will become clear as I start explaining what we need you to understand. There is an Old Testament verse that applies here … I Samuel 3:1: 'The word of the Lord was rare in those days; visions were not widespread.'"

Durham nodded uncertainly. This was not remotely what he had expected when he had jogged to the Campbell and McGriff offices in response to being paged.

Marie continued.

"There is an Englishwoman," she said, "named Rebecca Manguson Clark … about my age … mid-30s … who, from time to time, over a period of nearly 10 years now, has been the recipient of dreams … visions … messages … from God. She thinks of herself as an ordinary Christian person, yet I find her just … different … from anyone I've ever known, and not just as the recipient of the occasional vision."

She paused, seeing Durham's face change as he seemed to search his mind for something. After a moment of reflection, he asked, "Is this the Rebecca Manguson who was an internationally ranked tennis player about 10 years back? I seem to remember that name in a tennis context."

McGriff responded.

"Yes," he said quickly. "That's exactly who this is. She retired from the circuit about then … about 10 years ago … and she's now the married mother of twin 5-year-olds. Her husband is an American, Matt Clark, a former U.S. Navy officer."

Durham nodded vigorously, pleased at his memory.

"Okay," said Durham. "I can actually picture her. I saw her play a couple of times in the U.S. Open ... tall, rangy ... big serve ... long, black hair caught up in a ponytail.

"I wondered what became of her. She disappeared from the circuit back then, and I had not heard her name again ... until this minute."

McGriff nodded. "Yes ... she decided that wasn't the life for her, and she just stopped, though she is still involved with youth tennis programs in England."

Durham nodded, then turned again to Marie.

"I've sidetracked you, Marie," said Durham. "Sorry ... please go on."

Marie resumed.

"Rebecca Manguson Clark," she said, "is sent, from time to time, what we call 'divine messages,' always at moments of crisis ... usually a crisis specific to certain Christians or maybe to Christianity itself, broadly speaking ... but always related to the faith in one way or another.

"Last summer," she continued, "Jack and I were swept up into Rebecca's world by a series of events that were focused, first, on a plot financed by the Russian Mafia in New York, and second, on a terror campaign driven by the Soviet KGB in England. Suddenly we were part of a small group of family members and ... associates ... a group that has actually been given a label ... a name.

"They ... that is, *we* ... are called 'the Rebecca Communications Unit' ... except that, since that label was coined by a member of Mossad, the Israeli intelligence agency, the actual label is 'Rebekka Yahalomin'... a Hebrew phrase."

She turned to her husband, who picked up the narrative.

"As Marie said," continued McGriff, "we have been part of Rebekka Yahalomin since last summer, and so is Dr. Eleanor Chapel. She is an Old Testament professor at Union Theological Seminary in New York, and she is the woman who was attacked in New York City yesterday morning, within a couple of hours of Marie's being smashed to the pavement just a half-block from here ... by the kid you chased down.

"We are having a hard time, Jim, believing that two members of Rebekka Yahalomin would be assaulted on the same day and at roughly the same time, 200 miles apart, without those two events being carefully coordinated and precisely orchestrated by someone.

"Do you see what we mean?"

Durham nodded thoughtfully, then asked a question.

"Has this organization — Rebekka Yahalomin — been placed on some kind of alert status ... I mean ... has Mrs. Clark communicated with the members about anything that seems to be coming up on her radar, so to speak?"

Marie laughed delightedly.

"Oh, Jim," she said, "what a great metaphor … 'coming up on her radar' … we'll have to relay that one to her.

"But, to answer your question," she continued, "the thing doesn't work like that. Each of us just goes about her or his life … in this country or in England …"

McGriff nodded, and added, "Last summer there were two separate events … as Marie just mentioned … but we understand that in most years there has been either just one crisis … or, just as often … no crisis at all."

Marie leaned forward from the little sofa, reached across the coffee table, and touched Durham on his knee. "Jim … you need to understand this, even if you understand nothing else … the initiative does not lie with Rebecca or with any of the rest of us who are part of Rebekka Yahalomin.

"We may find ourselves confronting something that *seems* to imply engagement by the Yahalomin, but God Himself initiates … and, thus, in a real sense … *activates* Rebekka Yahalomin."

She looked to her husband, who nodded his agreement.

"Right," said McGriff. "What Marie just said, Jim … that's really the only way to say it … and say it accurately."

Marie turned again to Durham.

"We have," she said, "received no recent communication from Rebecca … or from her brother, Luke … and so we have no idea whether these two attacks constitute the prelude to a Yahalomin-style crisis. But you can help us *prepare* to go into action, if we are called, by finding out whether or not the young man who struck me and took my ready-satchel yesterday was operating under direction from someone.

"Did he," she continued, "just see a woman walking down the sidewalk … and suddenly decide he would knock her down and steal what he assumed was a purse with, he hoped, lots of money? Or was he paid to do that by someone whose agenda is bigger than just knocking me down and taking my shoulder bag?"

CHAPTER THREE

Tuesday, 11 a.m., CIA headquarters, Langley, Virginia

LATER THAT MORNING, ACROSS THE POTOMAC FROM THE CITY, Belton and Eleanor took their seats in a conversation corner similar to the one Marie had set up in her own office downtown. This office, however, belonged to the CIA agent who called himself the "convener" of the five-person unit whose task was "to study, assist, and control" Rebekka Yahalomin. The members of this small CIA unit acknowledged among themselves that the third-listed item in its task list — to "control" the Yahalomin — constituted nothing more than a faint hope.

It was a hope never yet achieved … or even approached.

The convener welcomed the couple.

"It's great to see you two again. Thanks for giving me a few minutes this morning. You've got to be exhausted after the overnight you just pulled."

"We're grateful t' you an' yer boys," replied Belton, "fer gettin' us outta there last night. Not sure how we wouldda managed t' get away from there without yer help."

Eleanor quickly added, "And the Learjet pilots and the officers who met us at Andrews were so thoughtful. We've been treated like royalty, and the room you've given us in the safe house is just right. We hope not to intrude for long."

"No trouble at all," responded the CIA officer. "We'll be at your service whenever you need us … but tell me what's happened. We don't have any information."

The couple provided a summary of the New York portion of the story, but did not mention the Washington incident. Members of the Yahalomin had learned from experience that the allied intelligence agencies, while at times indispensable, were also in competition with each other and, in a sense, with Rebekka

Yahalomin. Each one — CIA, MI6, Mossad — felt that intelligence data about threats to national or international communities belonged to *them*, regardless of the "unexplainable" nature, or not, of the data source. The Yahalomin had learned to dispense information judiciously.

Once the intelligence agencies were given "the full bank" of information, their decisions regarding next steps inclined toward violence, sometimes lethal. Rebekka Yahalomin's actions inclined in the opposite direction, consistent with their understanding of their Christian mission. Violence, for them, was to be undertaken as a last resort, and only in desperate circumstances.

"So," said the convener after listening to their account, "your best guess is that those thugs in New York planned to kidnap you, Dr. Chapel, to keep you away from these sessions at Georgetown University next week?"

The couple nodded in unison.

"And," he continued, "you think that this could have something to do with the topic of next week's sessions … liberation theology?"

"Possibly," said Eleanor.

"Why, Dr. Chapel? I don't follow."

"Liberation theology," she replied, "leans heavily on political action to try to improve the lives of the poor and the oppressed around the globe. Liberation theology has become a 'movement' in which its advocates are aggressively engaged in pressing their agendas on governments, corporations, and institutions of all types, including seminaries and churches. The movement has taken on a militant flavor."

"And you, Dr. Chapel, oppose that?"

"Yes, I do, in the sense that militant movements engender widespread violence, and that kind of violence tends toward indiscriminate destruction, including loss of life as a kind of collateral damage.

"My opposition, however, has not been open … I've not written or commented publicly on liberation theology at all. After all, it's not my field."

"Then?"

"I've become 'high profile' in some Christian circles," she answered immediately, "and that means that the advocates for liberation theology, as with anyone else, have no trouble researching my writings, or gaining copies of my public presentations. And what they find is a perspective on the faith that eschews the whole idea of something that I, and others before me, like to call … 'Christianity *and*'.

"You can't legitimately attach an *'and'* to Christianity without distortion of Christ's life and of His message … that is, without turning Christianity into something different than what it, authentically, has always been. Anyone who does research on me can anticipate that I will be speaking in opposition to liberation theology."

"And," the convener asked skeptically, "someone might care enough about that to *kidnap* you, Dr. Chapel?"

"That's what we're guessin'," said Belton, "but we don't really know. We just knew we had ta' get outta there last night. They tried t' nab Eleanor yesterday mornin' an' they'd set up surveillance yesterday afternoon an' evenin' at our apartment complex. They *wanted* 'er."

"And you don't have a guess as to who ... or what ... might be behind this?"

Belton shook his head.

The convener again looked skeptical.

"You're not going to give me anything to work with, are you, Sid?" he said.

Belton smiled his crooked smile.

Tuesday, 6 p.m., Campbell and McGriff offices, Washington, D.C.

Sarah set the office alarm system, stepped onto the sidewalk behind Durham, and locked the door behind her. Her workday completed, she and her dinner companion started the short walk to the lunch café that, thanks to her unwillingness to leave the office for lunch, had turned into their dinner café.

They were a striking couple.

Sarah, 23, was 5 feet, 10 inches and slender, with curly hair that fell below her shoulders. In some lights, her hair appeared auburn, but in others, red. Her eyes were hazel. Her mouth was wide and expressive. Her cheekbones were high and prominent. She was beautiful without cosmetic assistance other than simple hoop earrings.

She chose skirts that were not quite knee-length and blouses whose sleeves were three-quarter length. Her work shoes of choice were flats. Today, her skirt was cream-colored, her blouse was light blue, and her flats were a cream color that was a near-match for the skirt.

Her posture was erect; her stride was athletic and confident.

Jim Durham was 6 feet, 3 inches, with the build of a distance runner, something he had, in fact, been in college, and was still, at age 27, participating often in 5K and 10K road races, along with the occasional half-marathon. The previous day's teen thief had had absolutely no chance to escape Durham on foot.

The youngster would have needed to be able to run hard and fast for at least a dozen miles to lose his determined and superbly conditioned pursuer. This particular teen could not, in fact, have run even a mile.

Now, Durham was dressed, as usual, in khakis, a short-sleeved off-white dress shirt, and a tie with subtle red-and-silver diagonal striping. He wore light brown deck shoes, his footwear of choice for most occasions. His sandy hair was close-cropped. His eyes were dark brown. His face was thin and angular.

Some would say he had the face of an ascetic, though he could be described as ascetic only in regard to his morning prayer discipline and his daily workout regimen. Aside from those lifestyle markers, Durham was relaxed in demeanor and at ease with himself and with others, unless he happened to see a teen-age boy knock a woman down, steal her ready-satchel, and run from the scene.

Now, he held open the café door while Sarah entered. They seated themselves and ordered soft drinks from their server while they studied the menu.

They sat in awkward silence until their server returned with the soft drinks and filled their water glasses. They both asked for BLTs, and the server left them to place the sandwich order with the kitchen.

They took a sip of their soft drinks, then Durham asked, "Tell me how you got to Campbell and McGriff, Sarah."

She thought for a moment, considering where to start her story. She decided to begin at the beginning.

"I went to work for the NYPD right out of high school," she replied. "I'd always wanted to work in law enforcement … I mean … the administrative side of law enforcement … not the policing side. My grandmother has been a lifelong friend of Dr. Eleanor Chapel … Sid Belton's wife. And Mr. Belton, you know, co-owns our agency here in Washington, with his New York partner, Mr. Adelman.

"Grandma wrote Dr. Chapel to ask if Mr. Belton could help me get a clerical position with the NYPD. He pulled some strings, and then kept tabs on me. I got a promotion pretty quickly, and he got to know my administrative work, because his own investigations often put him in contact with our precinct's investigations.

"I was nearly always the one," she continued, "asked to get stuff for Mr. Belton. So, when Mr. Belton and Mr. Adelman decided to open their branch office here …"

"You were the obvious choice to be the office administrator," said Durham, finishing the story for her.

Sarah smiled, shrugged, and nodded her assent.

Durham considered her account for a moment, then asked, "That accent of yours sounds pretty Southern, Sarah.

"Were you worried about coming north to the big city?"

She laughed.

"You're right about the 'pretty Southern' thing … I'm from small-town Alabama, like Dr. Chapel. My main problem, though, was not going to New York. My main problem was Mom's reaction to the idea of my not going to college right away.

"But Grandma and Dr. Chapel," she continued, "got Mom finally to relax about that. They told Mom I could start college in New York part-time, build up my job resume … and eventually graduate from college … probably without any debt. I think that's what convinced Mom … the 'no-debt' thing … and Dad, too."

"I get it, Sarah," he said. "Makes sense to me."

She continued.

"I became the precinct administrator by the time I was 20. I handled scheduling, transfers, job rotations, and paper trails on most investigations. That last thing is what got me in regular contact with Mr. Belton."

Their BLTs arrived.

Neither moved to pick up the food.

"And you've been here for about a year?" Durham asked.

She nodded.

"And how has it been?"

"It has been everything I hoped," she said, smiling at the thought. "Marie and Father Jack are great people to work for, and, since our firm is private, there's *so* much less paperwork than there was with the NYPD. I love it."

"College?"

She nodded.

"I've was taking one course per semester in New York, plus one each summer. I started two years ago at Fordham. I've transferred all my credits to American University here, and just finished spring semester."

Her story was finished. They smiled at each other and, without signal, bowed their heads. Durham murmured a blessing for their food, and, after hesitating, asked God to bless "the start of this friendship."

She looked up.

"Thank you for including our friendship in your blessing. That was nice."

"You're welcome," he replied. "Might as well ask for God's blessing right from the start of something like this."

She smiled.

"Something like what, Jim?"

He hesitated, returned the smile, and then said simply, "Well ... I don't know exactly ... just ... you know ... something."

She reached across the small table and touched his hand. "I'm sorry," she said. "That was sort of rude. No definitions needed."

Mutually embarrassed at this turn, they picked up their sandwiches and began to eat. After several moments, Durham picked up his questions again.

"You've accomplished a lot since leaving Alabama, Sarah," he said, impressed. "How old are you now? 45?"

She laughed again, a joyful sound in Durham's ears.

"I turned 23 in the spring, which means I've had six years to soften my Southern accent. At first, New Yorkers would laugh at my dialect. Now, they mostly don't seem to notice ... at least, they mostly don't comment.

"But ... what about you?" she said. "How old are you, Jim? You need to start talking, so I can start to eat my BLT. You'll have to wait to eat yours until you've given me as much about you as I've just given you about me."

Agreeably, Durham told her that he turned 27 the previous winter, that he earned his bachelor's degree from the University of Maryland, that he was in the university's ROTC program, and so his first real job was as an officer in the U.S. Army. His first tour was in Germany and his second was at the Pentagon. His responsibilities there included serving as liaison with the D.C. police force, which in turn led to his first civilian job, as a patrolman, walking a beat in downtown Washington.

"How was that ... being a patrolman?" she asked between bites.

"Usually boring ... occasionally dangerous," he replied, "but what the detectives were doing was always intriguing to me ... in fact, that's what intrigued me about studying criminology in college ... so, eventually I took the tests ..."

"And you're happy being a detective in this precinct?"

"I am," he replied, "but I can see bureaucracy creeping more and more into the picture. Eventually, maybe I can move into the private realm, like Mr. Belton did … and like Marie and Jack."

She nodded.

"Do you know Father Jack's background?" she asked, still working on her BLT.

"Well," answered Durham, "I know he is an ordained priest with the Episcopal church, and that he still does part-time counseling at the church where he met Marie. I understand he was her counselor for a couple of years before they … um …"

"Fell in love," she said.

"Or, better," she said, correcting herself, " … before they acknowledged to each other that they already *were* in love, and had been for a while."

"And they're good together at work … not just at home?"

She nodded vigorously.

"They seem to have figured out when he should lead, professionally … versus when she should lead … and it all seems to work perfectly. It's wonderful just to be around them, Jim. I hope someday to have a marriage like that."

Another uncomfortable moment ensued, which led them simultaneously to pick up their soft-drink glasses and drink, as if they had suddenly become thirsty.

"About Father Jack," she said after several moments, "did you know he was part-time with the CIA until last fall?"

"What? No."

"He was a recruiter for the CIA," she explained, "until he finally realized that he would never be happy working for an organization that had to practice deceit, even though he wasn't directly involved in that kind of thing. He says he is much happier now. He says detective work is 'straightforward' … one of his favorite words."

"But he and Marie acknowledge the necessity of intelligence agencies in today's world … they just don't want to work for them?"

"Right," she said. "They feel some people are cut out for that kind of work, and some people aren't. Father Jack decided eventually that he was not."

Durham nodded as he finished his BLT, while Sarah still nibbled at the remains of hers. He decided to introduce another topic.

"Sarah," he said, "Marie and Jack talked to me this morning about an Englishwoman named Rebecca Manguson Clark. I suppose you're familiar with everything connected with her … and with … um …"

"Rebekka Yahalomin," she said helpfully. "Yes … they talked to me about her and the Yahalomin as soon as I started, last summer.

"Nothing has been going on with that, though, since then," she continued, "and I gather that that is usually how things are with the Yahalomin. A year, or several years, may go by without any hint of the kind of crisis that brings them to active status.

"But why," she asked, "did they talk to you today about Rebecca?"

"Because," replied Durham, "your friend Dr. Eleanor Chapel was nearly a victim of a kidnapping on the streets of Manhattan yesterday morning, at about the same time Marie was knocked on her face near your office. And because of the assault on Dr. Chapel, she and Mr. Belton were flown to Langley by CIA jet overnight. They're in the CIA safe house over at Langley now. Mr. Belton phoned Jack today to report all that to him, which is when Jack told him about the assault on Marie.

"Since Dr. Chapel and Marie are both part of Rebekka Yahalomin," Durham continued, "they have all begun to wonder if this is not the … um … the prelude … to a new Yahalomin-style crisis.

"In fact," he concluded, "they want me to find the kid that hit Marie, and question him … to try to find out if he was paid to steal her ready-satchel … and, if so, why, and by whom. I'm meeting Jack tonight, so that we can go together to find the kid. I know where he usually hangs out on weeknights.

"I think we'll be able to find him."

"You're going to do that tonight?" she said, surprised. "Father Jack and Marie didn't say anything about that to me. They always keep me informed about everything."

Durham shrugged.

"Maybe I've just spilled the beans?"

She shook her head.

"No," she said, "They occasionally do business at night, without necessarily letting me know in advance. Father Jack will let me know, in the morning, on how your … investigation turns out … so I can keep the office log current.

"Our office log is a record of *everything* we do. They're insistent on that."

He nodded. "Good idea … good procedure."

Her face clouded.

"You'll be careful, Jim … really … you'll be *careful?*"

He looked into the hazel eyes of Sarah Wilson and suddenly felt as if he might somehow fall into them. His voice seemed to fail him.

He simply nodded, helpless to do more.

Tuesday, 10:30 p.m., near Union Station, Washington, D.C.

Durham slipped into the passenger seat of McGriff's fire-engine red, 1985 Jeep Cherokee, and buckled his seat belt.

"Thanks for the ride, Jack," he said. "This would have been a long walk."

McGriff shook his head. "You could have handled the distance easy, but this particular walk, at 10 o'clock at night, felt a little iffy to me."

"Yeah, I suppose," agreed Durham, "but I could have just turned it into a 3-mile run … maybe with a sprint at the end if people started chasing me."

McGriff chuckled and put the Jeep in gear, but then looked closely at his passenger, whose face was illuminated briefly by a nearby streetlamp.

"You have a goofy smile on your face, Jim. Why is that?" asked McGriff, a mischievous smile on his own face.

Durham shook his head and rolled his eyes.

"Can't help it, Jack. Can't get your administrative assistant off my mind."

"Why would you want to? Surely, you're going to see her again."

"Yep. We have a date to go to church Sunday. We'll go to hers … that is, to yours … first, then we'll go to mine the following week."

McGriff nodded.

"That sounds like *two* dates, Jim. Moving fast, huh?"

"Well … no … two BLTs and two worship services can't be considered 'fast,' unless you're comparing us to you and Marie. Two *years*, Jack?"

McGriff laughed his big laugh.

"Good point. You and Sarah are a couple of greyhounds compared to us."

Durham did not reply to this. He instead reached inside his jacket and checked the seating of the Beretta 9mm in the shoulder holster he had donned when he stopped at home after walking his date to her apartment building.

He, like McGriff, wore a loose-fitting windbreaker to protect against the night chill, but also to cover the shoulder holster and the Beretta. Otherwise, Durham was dressed as he had been for dinner at the café, sans necktie, but with a change of footwear from deck shoes into Nike running shoes.

McGriff parked the Cherokee next to a fire hydrant, under a streetlamp, and placed his detective's parking authorization placard on the dashboard. They were parked one block from Dunbar High School, just north of the Capitol building.

They walked together to a nearby park, a favorite hangout for a particular group of teens, several of whom were in Durham's juvenile system.

As they came around a corner and were suddenly visible to the young men, Durham shouted, "We need to talk to James … everybody else go away."

And a dozen teens melted into the copse behind the benches on which they sat, leaving only James, who stood uncertainly, obviously considering running.

Durham called to him.

"James, I caught you yesterday. I'll catch you tonight. Don't bother."

James slowly sank onto the bench.

The men sat down on each side of him.

"James," said Durham, "this is the Reverend Jack McGriff. He's one of the ministers at the Episcopal church not far from where you and I tangled yesterday morning. You know that church?"

James nodded.

McGriff offered his hand.

"You a reverend?" asked the young man.

McGriff nodded. "Yes."

James looked at the proffered hand … then took it, although without enthusiasm. He turned back to Durham.

"I just wanted the lady's purse," he said. "Didn't mean to hit her so hard.

"Is she okay?"

Durham nodded. "She is, but you can't hit somebody like that and expect them not to be hurt badly. This particular woman happens to be pretty tough."

Durham paused.

"You know … assault will get you in a lot more trouble than theft. I want you to remember that, James."

James nodded.

Durham switched gears.

"The woman you hit is the wife of Reverend McGriff. What would you like to say to Reverend McGriff right now?"

James turned back to McGriff.

"I'm sorry, Reverend."

"I'll let her know, James. Just remember what Mr. Durham just said."

"I will."

"James," resumed Durham, "what were you doing over there where Mrs. Campbell — that's the reverend's wife's name — was walking yesterday? That's a long way from your neighborhood."

"I don't know… just happened to be over there."

"No, you weren't," said Durham. "Tell me why, or we're going to continue this conversation over at the precinct office. And that's going to mean I enter your name into the precinct records … and that's going to mean you're going to court … again.

"So, tell us why you were there, James. Tell us now … one chance."

James studied the ground in front of his feet.

Durham stood.

"Okay, James, walk with us to our car and we'll take you to the precinct."

"No … no …" he said. "Monroe paid me 20 dollars … said he'd give me 20 more if I brought him the lady's purse … told me where she'd be … and what time …"

"Joseph Monroe?"

The teen nodded. "Monroe," he repeated, accenting the first syllable.

"Where is he right now?"

"He hangs with RJ and them … over at the pool hall."

"Near the train station?"

"Yeah."

"Okay," said Durham. "James, if you've lied to me, I'll be back, and I won't be giving you any choices. Clear on that?"

James nodded.

"Let me hear you say it."

"If I lied to you … you'll be back … and I won't have any choices."

Ten minutes later, McGriff parked the Jeep one block from the pool hall identified by young James as the favorite hangout of Joseph Monroe.

"Jack," said Durham, "we leave our jackets here in the car. We want everybody to see we're armed, as soon as we go through the door. Okay?"

"Okay."

Three minutes later, shoulder holsters clearly visible, they pushed through the door to the pool hall. They immediately split, Durham taking five quick steps to the right of the door, McGriff taking five to the left. They turned to face the assembled players and drinkers, numbering perhaps 15 altogether, almost all men.

The room fell silent.

Durham held his badge up, shoulder level.

"We need to talk with Joseph Monroe. Just Monroe. Everybody else can go back to what you were doing."

Both detectives saw several eyes cut toward a tall 20-something man, standing back from one of the pool tables, pool cue at the vertical. McGriff, former small-college offensive lineman, still well over 200 impressive pounds in his mid-30s, walked directly toward the man who had been identified unwittingly by his cohorts.

McGriff stopped 3 feet from the man presumed to be Monroe and gestured with one hand toward the door. "Let's talk outside," he said. "No need to go downtown for this … maybe a five-minute conversation."

The man hesitated, nodded, handed his pool cue to a woman seated just behind him, and walked around the table. McGriff stood aside and followed him to the door. Durham held the door and the three men stepped outside.

"We can talk here, Joseph," Durham said quietly, "or we can walk to our car to talk in private. Which is better for you?"

Monroe considered the question.

"Can I smoke in the car?"

"No," said McGriff.

"Here then," he said, and pulled out a cigarette.

"You gave your man, James," said Durham, "20 dollars to steal a purse from Mrs. Marie Campbell yesterday, over near the detective agency where she works."

No response.

"He knocked her down," continued Durham, "took the purse, and happened to do it when I was about 50 feet away, on the other side of the street. I ran him down and recovered Mrs. Campbell's satchel from him. Reverend McGriff and I …" here Durham gestured to McGriff with his eyes, "just spoke with James over near Dunbar High, and he gave us your name.

"You can't blame James for any of this, Joseph. He couldn't know I was right across the street from him when he hit Mrs. Campbell, and he couldn't know I can run 10 miles faster than he can run two.

"And he didn't give you up just now until I told him that, if he didn't, we would be on our way to precinct and he'd be in court … again …"

Durham waited for Monroe to process this, then said, "I'll say to you what I just said to James … you can tell me who paid you to have Mrs. Campbell assaulted … right here and now … or we can go to precinct and you can go through the interrogation process there … which means that your other run-ins with the law will be brought up … which means that you'll end up doing time … again… for ordering an assault and a theft, and for being a repeat offender.

"Joseph," Durham concluded, "that's not going to go well for you."

Monroe crushed out his unfinished cigarette on the sidewalk.

"I got no need," said Monroe, "t' keep her name from you. I don't like her. I don't need t' do business with her no more. She paid me $300, but I can get that much in two nights here at the pool hall."

"She?" asked Durham.

"Yeah."

"'She' who?"

"Millicent Thomas."

"*Congresswoman* Millicent Thomas?"

"Yeah."

"Why?" asked Durham, incredulous, "would a U.S. congresswoman want Marie Campbell to be assaulted on her way to work?"

"I don't know. I don't ask."

McGriff cleared his throat.

"Jim," he said to the detective, "I have some thoughts about that. I think we can probably let Mr. Monroe get back to his pool table now.

"Let's call it a night."

Durham was bewildered, but deferred to McGriff, who clearly knew things about this congresswoman that would clear up the confusion he was feeling.

Durham turned back to Monroe.

"Thanks for your help, Joseph. Stay out of trouble."

Wednesday, 9 a.m., offices of Campbell and McGriff

Eleanor, Belton, Marie, McGriff, and Durham took their seats around the conference table in the Campbell and McGriff office. Belton and Eleanor had been dropped off at the agency by one of the CIA's Langley employees.

McGriff opened the session with a prayer.

"Father … be present … be present…

"Be present as we seek to understand the Evil we face … lead us in the direction that we ought to go …

"Be present … be present …

"We pray in the name of Your Son, Jesus Christ ... Amen."

The "Amen" was echoed around the table.

McGriff and Durham began the session by summarizing for the others the events of Tuesday night, starting with the teenager at Dunbar High School and ending with Joseph Monroe at the pool hall. McGriff explained that, once Monroe had given them the name of Millicent Thomas, they let him go back to the pool hall.

"So," said Belton, "what's th' deal with this congresswoman?"

"Her name," said McGriff, "has come up quite a bit in our first year of operation, Sid. Usually just out of the blue, in situations that implied nothing political."

"Jack and I have been puzzled," Marie added, "by the number of times our inquiries have led back to her, though nothing concrete has ever resulted ... her name just floats around the periphery."

"We think," said McGriff, "that she engages in continual trading for favors ... you know ... 'I'll push this legislation forward if you'll pressure such-and-such corporation or such-and-such military supplier in the direction of doing business with one of the industries in my city or state or region ...' that kind of thing."

"Yeah?" said Belton. "So what? Sounds like pretty normal Washington stuff t' me ... where's she from? I never heard of 'er."

"Louisiana," said his wife.

"You've heard of 'er, Eleanor?" asked Belton, surprised.

"Everybody has heard of her, Sidney," she replied.

She rolled her eyes for effect.

"She's in the news nearly every week," Eleanor continued, "but you would have to read the financial sections or the business sections or the political commentaries to know that. See, dear ... if you just attend to the Yankees and the Knicks and the Jets and let the rest of the world go by ..."

Belton cackled, then asked the obvious.

"Okay, Ms. Know-Everything New York City Old-Testament Wizard," he said, "tell us exactly what this dirtbag politician woman from Louisiana wants with Ms. Campbell's ready-satchel. What's she want with that?

"Huh?

"Let's hear ya tell us about that, Ms. Super-Professor Person ..."

Eleanor smiled her patient smile at her husband and replied, "I've no idea, Sidney ... perhaps Marie or Jack can tell us?"

Their hosts shook their heads.

"We don't have an answer to that, Eleanor," said McGriff. "Marie and I talked about that when I got home, late last night. It doesn't make sense to us."

There was a knock on the conference-room door.

"Yes?" called McGriff.

The door opened and Sarah stepped into the room.

Durham's heart skipped a beat.

His eyes met hers and they both blushed, quickly looking somewhere else. Everyone in the room watched the display with amusement.

"Mr. Belton," she said, "Sergeant Morris — my old boss at NYPD — is on the line, and says he has something you need to know right away. Shall I put the call through to the conference room, or do you want privacy?"

"Well," said Belton, "let's put 'im through t' this phone, Sarah, if Marie an' Jack say that's okay with them."

Both nodded, and the assistant disappeared, closing the door behind her.

Belton, always alert for signs of romance among his co-workers, looked at Durham, smiled his crooked smile, and said, "You an' Miss Wilson turned red as beets, tryin' not t' pay attention t' each other … You courtin' th' young lady, Jim?"

Durham blushed again, leaned forward, and covered his face with his hands.

"Hmmm," he muttered, an unintelligible noise.

"I'll take that fer a 'yes'," said Belton, pleased with himself.

The conference-room telephone buzzed, and Belton rose and clumped in his cane-assisted walk to a small table in one corner of the room.

"How're ya doin', Sergeant Morris?" he rumbled into the phone.

Belton fell silent, listening, occasionally murmuring, "Uh huh."

Finally, he said, "appreciate th' call, Sergeant. Tell yer boys that Eleanor and I appreciate their pickin' up th' ball an' runnin' with it. Ya did great."

He rose and hobbled back to the conference table.

"Eleanor," he said, "as soon as th' squad car picked us up fr'm our apartment on Monday night … actually, I guess it was early Tuesday mornin' … another NYPD unit pulled in behind th' surveillance dirtbags, found some excuse t' take 'em in t' precinct, an' ran an interrogation on th' two dimwits who were watchin' us.

"Guess what they found out?"

Knowing the question was not a question, no one responded.

"Th' two meatheads finally admitted, after they'd been sweated fer most a' th' day yesterday an' then fer most a' last night, that th' person that was payin' 'em t' try t' kidnap you, Ms. High-Profile Old-Testament Person, was … anybody?"

"Congresswoman Millicent Thomas," said the chorus.

Two hours later, the group reassembled in the conference room, this time with Sarah also in attendance. Two hours of research, with all six of them working the phones, had resulted in a much more complete picture of the Louisiana congresswoman whose name was now attached both to the New York City attempt on Eleanor and to the Washington assault on Marie.

McGriff again opened the session with his familiar "Father … be present … be present …" prayer. Again the Amens echoed around the room.

McGriff looked up at the administrative assistant.

"Sarah," he said, "will you lead off for us?"

She did, and she was followed systematically around the conference table until, 20 minutes later, all six had reported the results of their phone calls and had answered each other's questions. Then they sat silent for minutes, thinking about the overall picture that had been sketched over the 20 minutes of reporting.

At that point, McGriff asked Belton, the most experienced investigator in the room, if he'd like to summarize what they had pieced together thus far.

"I'd rather you or Marie do that, Jack," replied Belton. "I'd never heard a' this woman until this mornin'. You got more background than I do."

McGriff nodded and looked to his wife.

"Go ahead, dear," she said.

McGriff organized his thoughts and began.

"Congresswoman Millicent Thomas," he said, "is almost certainly positioning herself to run for the U.S. Senate, and, plausibly, to use that as springboard to securing the nomination for vice-president of the United States. The current VP is obviously going to be his party's nominee for president when the time comes. He might decide that Ms. Thomas would balance the ticket nicely."

McGriff consulted his notes, then continued.

"A different, but related point, is that she is independently wealthy, having inherited her family's oil money, and, in addition, having negotiated a cushy divorce settlement about 10 years ago.

"Her Louisiana district has re-elected her five times to the U.S. House, and she maintains high-level visibility with her heavily Catholic district by financing numerous outreach projects with her local church."

Sarah moved her hand to indicate she had a question.

McGriff smiled. "Yes, Sarah?"

"Do you have the impression that Ms. Thomas is an actual believer ... or that she just uses her Catholic projects for political gain?

"In other words," Sarah continued, "is her Christian-ness genuine ... or do we not have any way of knowing that?"

The group was thoughtful.

Eleanor finally spoke.

"We can't," she replied, "know the answer to that question with any certainty, Sarah, but if she is, in fact, the force behind the attempt on me in New York City, or the assault here in Washington on Marie ... she may, at some point in her life, have wholeheartedly invited Evil — with a capital "E" — into the core of her being. And that is the kind of chaos-generating and chaos-proliferating act that has, in the past, led God to respond by calling forth Rebekka Yahalomin."

A lengthy, uncomfortable silence ensued.

Finally, McGriff offered a conclusion to his overview.

"We should all take note," he said, "of the fact that Ms. Thomas is on the program next week at Georgetown, although, unlike Eleanor, not as a featured presenter.

"Ms. Thomas is a participant in one of several concurrent panel discussions next week ... Monday, Tuesday, and Wednesday mornings ... those that are scheduled to be held in regular classrooms, not in an auditorium. The program for those days states that those sessions will focus on the specifically political implications, in the United States, of liberation theology.

"The program," continued McGriff, "lists Millicent Thomas as one of three politicians slated for those sessions, and it notes, in particular, her track record of 'concern for the poor and oppressed' in her home district in Louisiana. This could, as we've surmised, be part of a plan to attract more independent voters — those not aligned with either party — in an upcoming run for the U.S. Senate."

"And then for consideration for the vice presidency," added Durham.

"Indeed ... that, too," agreed McGriff.

McGriff then quickly summarized the remaining points, none of them as high impact as those already offered, and asked what other thoughts the group might have regarding the congresswoman's strategic objectives.

Eleanor was ready with her answer.

"The revolutionary nature of liberation theology," she noted, "gives her a platform to appear to care about the masses ... not just in her Louisiana district, but everywhere in the U.S. and beyond. And it's possible that she genuinely cares about 'the poor and oppressed,' as the liberation theology literature emphasizes.

"But a more sinister rationale," she continued, "can undergird this kind of strategic objective very well.

"That rationale is, in fact, one that fits with my observation that this woman may have, at some point in her lifetime, welcomed Evil into the very center of her being. And *that* is a rationale identical to the one that animated the Soviets last summer, especially the Soviets we faced in England. Their goal was the disruption and corruption of democratic society itself … a terroristic approach designed to produce the disintegration of norm-based, hopeful living.

"Their strategic objective," she added, "was to foster a national depression, by means of which whole democratic societies could be led into despair."

"And," inserted Marie, "as we said last summer … ultimately into a person-by-person despair within *individual people* … individual human beings throughout, first, the U.K., and then, systematically, other democracies around the globe."

"Exactly," agreed Eleanor.

More silence.

Finally, Belton spoke up again. "So," he said, "help this poor, dumb detective make th' connection, people. What does any a' that have t' do with Eleanor bein' kidnapped, as she almost was, or with Marie bein' whacked an' burglarized right here on th' street? What's all that got t' do with liberation theology an' this dirtbag woman's strategy?

"We're supposed t' think that, if ya knock a couple a' women around, society falls apart an' everybody throws in th' towel?

"Hm?

"That's what we're supposed t' think?"

Eleanor responded immediately. "Sidney," she said, "I find myself thinking again about last summer … in the first of the two crises … the one that brought Rebecca and the other London people over here to the U.S. We realized eventually that *Ataka* — that rogue Soviet group — wanted to create conditions that would lure Rebecca and the others to the U.S.

"They wanted to draw her out … thinking that their ultimate objectives were unlikely to be accomplished unless they could … um … 'eliminate' Rebecca herself. And they were very nearly successful.

"Perhaps Congresswoman Thomas has a similar idea."

Durham jumped in.

"That would make sense, Dr. Chapel," he said. "Kidnapping you would certainly get Mrs. Clark's attention … and the others in London, too. And grabbing

Marie's ready-satchel would provide Ms. Thomas — she would assume — with contact information and other data about Rebekka Yahalomin.

"I can see both these attacks," Durham continued excitedly, "fitting that kind of strategy. And Ms. Thomas has got the money and connections and influence to make things like that happen anytime she feels like it."

Eleanor again responded.

"If she does," she said, "in fact, embody the maximum Evil that humankind can absorb into itself, then small actions such as attacking women in the street, and colossal actions such as those available to a U.S. senator, are all of one piece.

"Evil at such levels," continued Eleanor, "does not discriminate. Evil at such levels is as delighted with the corruption of a single person as with the corruption of millions. In fact, Evil at such levels ultimately wants the moral and spiritual destruction of every *individual* human being, as Marie just said, and Evil's corruption of whole societies is nothing more than a vehicle to corrupt every single individual."

"Corresponding precisely," added McGriff, "to Christ's ultimate objective: saving every *individual* human being on the planet."

This exchange produced still more thoughtful silence.

Finally, Marie asked, "But how does the congresswoman know anything at all about Rebecca? How does she know that Eleanor and I have anything to do with the Yahalomin? It's not as if there's a membership list published somewhere. How could she know about us?"

"Marie," said her husband, "Millicent Thomas has contacts *everywhere*. Her people wouldn't need to search very hard to discover this thing — the Yahalomin — this ... um ... this *force* ... that has become increasingly conspicuous over the years. In the circles she apparently has chosen to move in, Rebecca Clark is *known*."

"An' *feared*," added Belton.

More thoughtful silence, until Marie asked a new question.

"So, Dr. Chapel," she said, "does all of this mean that we should get in touch with Rebecca in London?"

Eleanor shook her head.

"No, Marie," she said, "the initiative always lies with her ... with Rebecca ... because it is only via the 'divine messages' that she ... and then we ... are called into action as the Yahalomin. And, in this instance, that's especially pertinent, because Rebecca wrote Sidney and me some weeks ago to say that she and Matt were planning to take a driving vacation in Ireland.

"She and Matt planned to leave the twins with her parents in Birmingham for 10 days while she and Matt travel. She was excited about the chance to get away, with just her husband, and to see Ireland again. She was there previously only as a child.

"They left Monday. There is no way to reach them."

Marie thought about this for a moment, then said, "But, if Rebecca has one of her … one of her Yahalomin dreams … while she and Matt are traveling in Ireland, she would get in touch with us from there, wouldn't she?"

Eleanor nodded.

"Oh, yes," she said.

"If Rebecca dreams one of her Yahalomin dreams, Marie, she will take action of some kind. If the dream implies that she should contact us, there is no doubt that she would devise a way to do that … and to do that immediately.

"She," concluded Eleanor, "and we … have learned over and over the critical importance of immediate action in response to anything that calls Rebekka Yahalomin into action. Rebecca knows that better than any of us."

CHAPTER FOUR

Thursday, 4 a.m.

THE WOMAN WAS JARRED AWAKE BY AN INNER SIGNAL FROM Somewhere Beyond herself. She resisted an impulse to open her eyes, in obedience to a stronger impulse to keep them closed. And immediately a scene began to develop on the inside of her eyes ... a scene with bright contrasts and clear borders.

As seconds passed, the scene matured and evolved into two images ... two faces ... their countenances somehow divorced from their bodies.

The two images were stationary, allowing the dreamer to examine carefully each of the faces, knowing she would need to reconstruct her dream at some point. One of the images was that of a woman. She appeared to the dreamer to be in her middle years, perhaps mid-40s.

The woman's face was lean and heart-shaped, and was framed by close-cut, layered brown hair that contributed a certain harshness to the image. This severity was heightened by unsmiling, compressed lips, which seemed to want to turn downward. The eyes were also brown and, although unremarkable, contributed to the harshness by seeming to squint ... a sort of built-in narrowing of the eyes ... and to squint purposefully in the direction of the dreamer.

But the chief distinguishing feature of this woman's face was a vertical scar that ran from the left edge of the mouth, downward toward the chin line. The scar was readily visible, but the dreamer would later recall thinking, even during the dream, that the laceration had been sewn together by a skilled surgeon, one who could pull skin together so masterfully, and who could work the sutures so dexterously, that what might have been distracting and unsightly had been reduced to a barely noticeable mark, one made almost invisible by the woman's use of cosmetics.

A scar *almost* invisible.

The other face, portrayed to the dreamer just to one side of the woman's, was that of a man, a man considerably older than the woman, perhaps mid-70s. Unlike the woman's, this face was soft ... almost pudgy. The crown of the man's head was nearly bald, although a few strands of wispy hair had been combed over in an unsuccessful attempt to hide the baldness. The skin color was brown.

The lips were irregular, seemingly cast in a permanent snarl; the nose, broad; the eyes, deep brown, nearly black. There was an intensity in the gaze ... the suggestion of a powerful, and perhaps malevolent, intelligence residing there.

Powerful, *perhaps* malevolent, intelligence.

The dream remained in place for what the dreamer later decided might have been more than two minutes, which was more than enough time for her to absorb every detail portrayed. And as the dream began slowly to fade, the dreamer found herself experiencing sensations that communicated a daunting sense of threat ... presumably, she thought as she began to awaken, threat to be initiated by one or both faces ... but threat directed toward whom?

Later, she was unsure how this sense of threat had been transmitted to her, since nothing was altered in the appearance of the two faces, which were immobile throughout. But the threat was unmistakable. She *felt* threatened, and not just threatened personally, but on behalf of those about whom she cared.

Suddenly she found herself fully awake. And despite the brevity of the dream, she found she was soaked with perspiration.

And somehow exhausted.

She turned her head to look at the lighted digital clock on the nightstand. It read 4:10 a.m. ... still fully dark outside. She sat up with difficulty and turned on the reading lamp. Fighting through her exhaustion, she reached for her address book. She found the number she wanted and forced herself to dial immediately.

Eleanor Chapel, deep in sleep, slowly awoke to the sound of the ringing phone somewhere in the CIA safe house assigned to her and her husband. She sat up groggily, heard Sidney Belton's muffled snore beside her, and felt for her bedroom slippers. She pushed her small feet into the slippers and stood.

Now awake fully and concerned about a call at such an hour, she walked quickly to the kitchen, where the only phone in the safe house was mounted on the wall. She lifted the receiver and spoke.

"This is Eleanor Chapel," she said, her voice husky with sleep.

Later, she realized that she had fully expected, somehow, to hear Rebecca Clark's voice on the line. But the voice she heard was not Rebecca's familiar contralto. This voice was somewhat higher in pitch, and, rather than Rebecca's exquisite Oxford dialect, it traced the same soft, Southern accent that had once been characteristic of Eleanor's own diction.

"Dr. Chapel, this is Sarah Wilson. I'm so sorry, but I must tell you what has just happened. I have *dreamed.*

"This was a 'message dream,' Dr. Chapel. I've been told by Marie and Father Jack exactly what Mrs. Clark says her dreams are like.

"This was a Yahalomin dream."

Sarah's report to Eleanor took some time, the latter taking notes as the dreamer spoke. The older woman read the report back twice, going slowly, so as to make sure her account was complete and accurate.

"Sarah," she said finally, "are you going to be able to sleep now?"

"I don't know," she replied. "I'm exhausted, but somehow not sleepy."

"Why don't you sleep as late as you can, Sarah," said Eleanor, "and then phone me here at the safe house, so we can schedule a session at Marie and Jack's office for later this morning."

Having acknowledged, though not necessarily having agreed to, Dr. Chapel's suggestion, Sarah took her bedside Bible into her small living room, sat down, and tried to concentrate on her morning devotions and prayers. She found she could not.

Suddenly, on impulse, she rose, walked back to her bedroom, and consulted her address book once more. Fighting off the cautionary voice in her head that said, "Don't behave like an adolescent girl," she shook her head and dialed.

Jim Durham, interrupted in the midst of his own morning prayers, answered on the second ring. "Durham here."

The line was silent.

"Hello," he said. "Anyone there?"

"Yes," came a faint voice.

"Sarah?"

More silence.

"*Sarah?*" he repeated, "what's wrong?"

After another stretch of silence, she answered.

"Jim," she said hesitantly, "could you come over … now?"

He did not ask for an explanation.

"Yes," he said simply. "I'll be there in 10."

She went to her bathroom, washed her face, and put on shorts and a presentable tee-shirt. By this time, she was scolding herself for such a childish response to this unexpected and unsought intrusion into her well-ordered life. *Did Rebecca Clark respond this way when the first 'message dream' came?* she asked herself.

Of course not, was her answer.

The doorbell rang.

She opened the door to find Jim standing in front of her, wearing his warm-weather running attire — running shoes and shorts, tee-shirt, lightweight sweat-shirt with cut-off sleeves — and breathing hard from his high-speed, six-minute, 1-mile run from his apartment to hers. His face showed deep concern.

"Sarah," he said, "what is it?"

She tried to answer, could not, and suddenly felt his arms around her. She recoiled automatically, felt his arms tighten, and relaxed, allowing herself to be held. They stood motionless for what seemed a very long time to them both.

Finally, he said gently, "Should we sit down?"

She nodded. He closed the door.

Once seated next to him on her sofa, she pushed herself away from him, but only minimally. She moved just far enough away from him to be able to look into his eyes and begin her explanation.

She described the vision with the same exacting detail she had managed with Eleanor, then said, "I'm so embarrassed that I phoned you ... I don't know why I did that ... I'm not a child, and I shouldn't be frightened by this."

She paused.

"And I'm not even sure," she continued, "that 'frightened' is the right word. It's just that, having fulfilled my responsibility by reporting the dream to a knowledgeable listener, I wanted more ... I wanted to be face-to-face with someone ... and that someone was you. Yet I barely know you, Jim."

He shook his head. "Well, that's not exactly true. We've spent enough time together to know that we are both believers, that we both start our days with devotions and prayers, that we want to attend each other's churches so we can experience worship services together, and that we *really* like being together.

"I don't know about you," he continued, "but I can't say those things about anyone else ... just you. How many people can you say those things about?"

She smiled. "One."

A comfortable quiet ensued and they relaxed in the silence, suddenly conscious of the fact that they had taken each other's hand at some point, and that neither wanted to let go. Finally, he asked, "Did you finish your morning prayers?"

She shook her head. "I never started."

"Shall we do that next?" he asked, "and then talk about next steps?"

She consulted her watch. "I like to get to the office by 7:30, even though we don't officially open until 8:00. I think I need to send you home so I can get busy."

"Are you sure you'll be okay?" he asked seriously.

"No … but I think I'm going to be fine," she said. "You've given me exactly what I needed this morning. I can do a short version of my morning prayers, grab some cereal, get dressed, and be at the office by 7:30. Thank you so much for coming … and for not even asking why I needed you. I won't forget that … ever."

He smiled, rose, pulled her up and held her close again. Then he kissed her on the cheek, turned, and was gone.

Sarah did, indeed, arrive at the office by 7:30. McGriff was already there, as usual, working at his desk. She walked back to his doorway, said "Good morning, Father Jack," heard his cheery response, and returned to her desk in the reception area. She pulled out several file folders from the bottom drawer, opened the top one, and began to read, intending to make notes in the margins as she went.

She found she was unable to maintain concentration.

Sarah soon closed the file and sat back in her chair, thinking. She tried to assess her mental and physical state. She did not like what she found. She found herself beginning to tremble, tears welling. *This doesn't make sense*, she thought. *I'm not injured or wounded or ill. I should be fine.*

She closed her eyes and attempted to pray, but could not even concentrate on prayer. She found herself again wanting the presence of Jim Durham. *Well, Sarah,* she said audibly, *that is the most ridiculous thought you've had in … forever. You don't need Jim's presence, or his arms around you, to get yourself under control.*

She shook her head, sighed, opened the filing drawer again, and returned the folders she had removed just minutes earlier. She rose, walked back to McGriff's open office door, and rapped lightly on the doorframe. He looked up, smiling, and said, "How are you this morning, Sarah? You don't look quite yourself."

"Father Jack," she began, "I was awakened … forcibly… this morning at 4:00." To her annoyance, her voice was shaky.

She continued, determined. "I was given a 'message dream,' Father Jack, and I awakened Dr. Chapel at the safe house when it ended, so I could report. I knew that's what Rebecca Clark has always done, and that it's 'procedure.' But I was so … needy … after I reported to her, that I phoned Jim and asked him to come over. He did.

"We talked … I felt better … I sent him home … and now I'm here."

She took a deep breath and continued.

"Dr. Chapel suggested I try to sleep, so that all of us could meet later this morning to talk about the dream. But Father, I think I need to go home now … I'm just not functional. I haven't slept since the dream, and I think I should do what Dr. Chapel said … actually get some sleep … if I can."

By the time she was halfway through her statement, McGriff had risen, circled his desk, and now stood just in front of her. He reached for her hand and took it in both of his, looking intently into her eyes.

"This is extraordinary, Sarah," he said. *"Extraordinary!"*

He was beaming.

"I know that Rebecca and Luke's parents … and Matt Clark's mother … experienced 'message dreams' some years ago … but they are a generation older … and you are the first person of your generation, so far as I know, other than Rebecca herself, to have been given this high honor.

"This is such an incredible *tribute*," McGriff continued, "but, you're right, you need to recover, physically and mentally. These messaging events are tremendously draining for the recipient. Nearly every one of them that Rebecca has ever experienced left her exhausted, as I understand it.

"Eleanor is right … go back home. Let us know when you'd like us to get together to hear about the vision … to discuss its implications. For now, just rest."

She stopped at her desk, picked up her little purse, a clutch barely large enough to hold her house keys and wallet, and left the office. She looked down at herself as she started along the sidewalk and rolled her eyes at the color combination.

Her skirt was light blue, her blouse was dark green, and her flats were maroon. She sighed. *Really, Sarah,* she said to herself.

Her apartment was less than a 20-minute walk, but halfway there, she became conscious of an uncanny feeling of … she could only identify the feeling as … threat. She felt a sense of threat, exactly as she had in her dream … but threatened by what?

Surely, she thought, this is just a transitory collapse of the easy assurance she normally felt … the easy assurance that she knew exactly who she was … that she knew exactly what she was doing.

But the dream had shaken her. *Why should this kind of experience turn you into some kind of fear-filled creature, afraid of your own shadow?* she asked herself. *Think about Father Jack's reaction just moments ago,* she continued. *Father Jack said that your being sent this kind of dream is a great honor … a tribute … something to gladden your heart and lead you to rejoice. Then what is this enervating sense of threat? How much longer will you let this interior nonsense haunt you?*

She turned the corner onto her street and shook her head again. She forced herself to continue her purposeful walk. Yet the interior monologue resumed. *Transitory or not,* she acknowledged to herself, *this feeling of threat is not going away … this absurd feeling that someone is following …* She struggled against a gathering sense of fear … real fear … and tried to focus on simply getting to her apartment building as quickly as possible, but without breaking into a run.

Starting to run, she knew, would exacerbate the fear. She clenched her fists and fought to suppress the feeling, but without a trace of success.

Then suddenly she stopped, moved several steps to her left, and leaned against the wall of the office building she happened to be walking past. With her back against the rough brick wall, she looked behind her. Two people, a man and a woman, quickly looked away, and she knew.

She *was* being followed.

Suddenly she realized that another couple was approaching her, as well, from the other side of the street. They looked directly at her. She glanced back at the trailing couple and saw them turn and raise their arms, apparently signaling someone behind them. Meanwhile, the couple that was crossing the street had continued to advance and was now just a few feet from her, both people smiling in her direction.

"Miss Wilson," said the woman, "let me show you something, please."

The woman took a small container from her tote and held it up, apparently inviting Sarah to read the lettering on its side. The woman, still smiling reassuringly, opened the container near Sarah's face, took out a small canister, and in one quick motion sprayed her victim's eyes with a mixture of chemical mace similar to that used by Eleanor earlier that week on the streets of Manhattan.

Sarah tried desperately to turn her head, but the woman's male partner had already grasped her jaw with one powerful hand, holding her steady. The highly toxic spray saturated her eyes, and she recoiled as the irritant did its grisly work. Her hands went reflexively to her face.

The man released her jaw.

She doubled over, her mind numbed by the excruciating pain.

Helpless and blinded, she felt the man now scooping her bodily off the sidewalk, one arm under her back and the other under her knees. Simultaneously, she heard a vehicle braking harshly, apparently at the curb just in front of her.

She felt herself being carried in the direction of the vehicle that, she suddenly knew, waited to take her away to some destination she could not imagine. Her eyes still shut tight, she took her hands from her face and flailed at the man's face. He was unaffected by her feeble blows. He simply held her tighter to himself and tucked his face down and into her sternum, making it impossible for her to strike with effect. He carried her easily toward the vehicle she had heard as it had roared to a position just 15 feet from the wall against which she had pressed herself.

She sensed that other people in the immediate vicinity might be active. She did not know how many, beyond the two couples, might be engaged in the attack — perhaps none — but she shouted for help on the chance that uninvolved pedestrians, if any were near, would come to her rescue.

Had she been able to see the attack on herself from, say, a second-floor window, she would have seen that the waving signal, seconds before, given by the trailing couple, had summoned an unmarked ambulance that had driven slowly behind her from the moment she turned onto her street. From such an imaginary vantage point, she would also have seen the ambulance, having been signaled, racing to a stop just feet from her. And she would have seen, as well, the same trailing-and-signaling couple running to the double doors at the rear of the now-stationary ambulance.

Finally, she would have seen that same couple pulling open the ambulance doors, then standing to each side while the man carrying his blinded victim stepped off the curb, and, with the struggling young woman held tight to his chest, carried her into the ambulance's interior.

Now inside the ambulance, Sarah was slammed roughly down onto a mobile stretcher. As she felt her captor's hands release her, she also felt a mysterious calmness … an eerie serenity. Her muscles, without conscious direction from her mind, relaxed fully. She also felt herself, again without conscious direction, beginning to smile, even as she felt the man's female partner trying to force her hands into bindings for her wrists. Somehow, she now knew that the danger had passed completely. Somehow, she knew she was saved.

But how?

Later, she wondered by what means this sense of being rescued had come over her, though she felt certain, from the moment it happened, that the Source of the calmness could only be the Source that had transmitted the vision to her hours earlier … at 4:00 a.m. … while she lay in her own bed. *That* Source had forcibly intruded upon her sleep; now that same Source appeared determined to intervene in her attempted abduction in order to spare her life for missions of importance … missions that were not to be pushed aside by emissaries of ruin that had just assaulted her and appeared determined to take her captive.

While she never knew with certainty how she knew she was saved before the saving had happened, she understood that she did not need to know. She had only to know that the dream and the foreshadowing of rescue originated from One Source.

Days later, she realized further that, of all the events that had transpired since 4:00 a.m. that day, the most astonishing events, in a sense, were the ones that occurred next. Although blinded and able to see none of the events at the time they happened, she was able quite easily to piece them together afterwards.

The series of events took but seconds.

The trailing couple — the couple that had signaled the ambulance to come forward — was at that moment standing at the open double doors at the rear of the ambulance, preparing to finalize the kidnapping by slamming the doors shut. Both the man and the woman faced the interior of the ambulance, both reaching for the doors that, once closed, would seal Sarah Wilson's fate.

Thus engaged, they did not see what had materialized behind them.

They had no warning that two 12-inch Barringtons Swords throwing knives were to be hurled at them from a distance of 35 feet. Their first inkling of the disaster that had overtaken them was, for the man, the devastating shock and pain of a knife slamming into his right shoulder from behind. The knife, launched by means of a technically difficult, underhand, no-spin delivery, had been thrown by a world-class expert in the arcane practice of competition knife throwing.

The razor-sharp blade sliced through the man's flesh like an artillery shell through plaster. He screamed, falling forward into the ambulance cavity. Face down, he writhed on the grimy, hard rubber floor of the vehicle.

The woman, incredulous, spun around in time to glimpse the second knife a microsecond before it tore into the muscle of her left shoulder, driving her back into the ambulance, where she fell heavily onto her back. She lay prone, stunned, just 3 feet from her wounded colleague.

The woman's ear-piercing, higher-pitched scream joined with the man's in a cacophonous duet that filled the ambulance with a uniquely disjointed serenade. Had Sarah been able to see, she would have witnessed the knife thrower now closing the distance to the open rear doors of the ambulance and focusing intently on the second couple, the pair now seated on either side of her stretcher. Had she been able, she would have seen that *this* couple was now staring wide-eyed, first at the screaming human wreckage lying at their feet, and next, at the knife thrower.

Sarah also would have seen that her two assailants *knew* what they were facing, that they *knew* what would happen if they hesitated. They did not hesitate.

They immediately began to slide the stretcher, the patient now quiescent, out of the ambulance bay and onto the street surface. They roughly shoved aside their wounded, moaning colleagues in their single-minded haste to save themselves from becoming the next targets of the knife thrower.

As one, they looked up again at the knife thrower, who had closed the distance to just 15 feet and now stood poised to release another of her fearsome weapons, if necessary. The couple quickly stepped away from the stretcher and held their palms open toward the knife thrower in a wordless plea for mercy.

The fifth member of the kidnap unit, the ambulance driver, had observed the developing scene by means of the vehicle's side-view and interior mirrors. Seeing the staccato burst of violence ending, he slammed the ambulance in gear and roared away, causing his two wounded associates to slide, knives still embedded in their shoulders, out the back of the vehicle. They slammed onto the asphalt, the woman hitting the back of her head and being knocked unconscious, the man hitting face down and skidding, skin ripping from his face, along the road surface.

Departing, the driver left behind his four colleagues — two uninjured, two others wounded and concussed, and one of those two unconscious — plus their would-be victim, Sarah Wilson, and the startling apparition that had forestalled and dismantled the kidnapping. For "apparition" the knife thrower seemed to be, to those who had been tasked with the abduction. All five of them knew exactly who this knife thrower was. They had thought they knew *where* she was. They had thought the knife thrower was on the other side of the Atlantic Ocean.

They had been wrong.

The knife thrower strode briskly to the stretcher and looked closely into the victim's face. Despite her watering, inflamed, tightly shut eyes, the victim appeared astonishingly serene. The knife thrower placed a hand gently on the victim's forearm and spoke to her quietly.

"My name is Rebecca Clark," said the knife thrower, the Oxford accent getting the immediate attention of the American. "You appear uninjured except for the eye irritant, and … you seem … quite tranquil. Are you?"

The victim sat up energetically and swung her legs off the stretcher and onto the street surface. She stood and faced in the direction of the voice. At 5 feet, 10 inches, she was still 2 inches shorter than Rebecca Clark.

"Yes," she replied to the voice. "I do feel tranquil … because I somehow knew that I was going to be rescued … before the rescue even began. I became tranquil *before* you intervened, Mrs. Clark."

She hesitated, then added, "My name is Sarah Wilson. I am Marie Campbell and Jack McGriff's assistant … I was just walking home …"

Rebecca, although listening carefully to the young woman, was still looking steadily toward the two undamaged assailants. They were beginning to edge away from the knife thrower, obviously considering running, but conscious of the apparently considerable range of the woman's knife throws. Rebecca stepped around Sarah Wilson and fingered one of the remaining knives.

"Do not run," she said, her voice commanding. "Attend to your wounded colleagues, but do not try to remove the knives from their shoulders. You must wait for the arrival of medical personnel. Let them remove the weapons."

They nodded, still nervously eyeing the woman whose name they knew and feared. Each now knelt beside one of their wounded associates.

"Mrs. Clark," said Sarah from behind Rebecca, "if you'll please guide me to my purse, which I dropped when the man lifted me to carry me to the ambulance … and then if you'll lead me to one of the offices that I can picture on this block, I'll make sure someone has called 9-1-1 for us. I think I can picture an insurance office …"

Before Rebecca could respond, they both heard the sirens.

"They're coming, Sarah," said Rebecca, "but I do need you to get in touch with the precinct captain, Horace Johnstone. Do you know how to contact him?"

"Yes … he's given us his direct number. His information is in my little purse. If you can help me find the purse and then a telephone, I'll call him.

"What should I say, Mrs. Clark?"

"He knows me," said Rebecca, "from last summer's events. Tell him I've had to use my knives to disable two people who attempted to kidnap you. Tell him his officers are on their way, and I'll need him to radio them via his police network. Tell him I'd prefer not to be taken to jail for what his officers will deem vigilante activity. Citizens … and especially foreign nationals … are not supposed to throw knives at people. He'll need to explain to his officers … um … do you know the term 'Rebekka Yahalomin', Sarah?"

"Yes, ma'am."

"Use the term. Captain Johnstone will understand immediately."

Several pedestrians had begun to edge closer to the scene. Some were just curious, but others, viewing the two bleeding, suffering individuals now lying prone on the pavement, clearly wanted to assist if they could.

Addressing one of the latter, Rebecca said, "Sir, my friend has been temporarily blinded by chemical spray. Would you be kind enough to escort her, first, to her purse … which is lying on the sidewalk …" — here she pointed to Sarah's small clutch lying some 30 feet away — "and then … I think … lead her to that insurance agency … just there … so she can use its phone?"

The man nodded, took the young woman's hand, and led the way. Meanwhile, Rebecca approached the two uninjured assailants.

Rebecca was dressed for action in dark-blue tennis warm-ups, black tennis shoes, and a dark-blue, billed cap. The cap was slit in back to accept her straight, jet-black tresses which, bound in her trademark tight ponytail, fell more than halfway to her waist. Six feet tall, rangy and athletic, with regal features accentuated by a scar which ran from the right side of her mouth across her cheek and to her ear, in a shallow V-shape, she still held a foot-long throwing knife in each hand.

Despite her beauty, she was an intimidating presence. She stopped 5 feet from the couple, both of whom were kneeling on the already hot pavement, their hands on their fallen associates.

She affixed each of them in turn with her penetrating stare, the arresting gray eyes boring into each upturned face. Rebecca, seeing their fear, had no intention of placing them at ease.

Unsmiling, she said, "Tell me who paid you to attempt this crime."

They glanced at each other and hesitated.

Rebecca moved her right hand, turning the blade so that its lethal profile was more conspicuous. The man's eyes widened.

He swallowed, struggling to speak.

But finally, speak he did.

"Ms. Millicent Thomas."

"And who is Millicent Thomas?" replied the Englishwoman.

He swallowed again.

"Millicent Thomas," he repeated. "The congresswoman."

He glanced toward Sarah, as she was being led toward the insurance office, purse now in hand. He turned his face back to the knife-thrower.

"We weren't going to hurt her, ma'am. Really.

"We were being paid just to take her … somewhere."

"Where?"

"I don't know, ma'am," said the man nervously. "Our driver had the destination, but we didn't. We weren't told where Miss Wilson was to be taken. We were just paid to take her … without hurting her.

"And we did not hurt her, ma'am.

"We were really, really careful not to hurt her … and you saw her, ma'am … you saw she's got no injuries … and her eyes will be okay in a few minutes.

"Really, ma'am … we were very careful.

"Honest, ma'am … honest … we were so *careful* with her."

Thursday, 8:30 a.m.

After speaking with police, who had indeed been contacted by Captain Johnstone as a result of Sarah's phone call, the two women walked together back to Sarah's office. Rebecca wanted to talk with Marie and Jack to gain a clearer understanding of the situation.

And Sarah, having now shrugged off the confusion that she experienced in the hours following her 4:00 a.m. vision, now — despite the assault — felt renewed, clear-headed, strong … and angry. And she needed also to talk with Marie and Father McGriff about her dream, the ensuing drama, and its implications.

She had found that, by squinting through her painfully inflamed eyelids, she could see well enough to navigate the familiar route without assistance. Nevertheless, Rebecca protectively held her hand as they walked.

"Your demeanor," said Rebecca as they turned the corner toward the office, "when I first looked closely at you, Sarah, very much surprised me. You said you had become tranquil *before* my intervention. How?"

Sarah stopped and faced the Englishwoman. Their hands being joined, Rebecca automatically stopped and turned, as well.

"Mrs. Clark, at 4 a.m. today… I *dreamed*."

Rebecca was unsurprised.

"Yes," she said mildly, nodding her head.

Sarah's eyes widened. "You *expected* me to dream?"

"Not exactly," she replied, "but I am here because of a vision I was sent 36 hours ago, in Ireland. And once the dreams begin, I have learned that God is almost certainly going to be further engaged, and that subsequent events are likely to demonstrate His engagement in any number of ways.

"I did not *expect* there to be another visioner, Sarah, because there has not been another one, other than me, for some years now … but I did expect … *something*. And the 'something' was, I knew, as likely to be a second visioner as anything else available to Almighty God, which is to say … anything at all."

Sarah nodded her understanding and acceptance of the point.

The women then turned back toward the office and resumed their walk, no longer holding hands, but with Rebecca's hand now touching the younger woman's elbow.

"And so," said Sarah, confirming her understanding, "that's why you were not surprised that I reported becoming calm *before* you arrived on the scene?"

"Exactly."

Thursday, 8:45 a.m.

Marie arrived at her and her husband's office minutes before Sarah and her rescuer appeared at the agency's door. When they first entered, Marie saw only the unexpected figure … the woman whom she knew as *the* visioner.

Her jaw sagged.

"*Rebecca?*" she exclaimed so loudly that her husband jumped from his chair and trotted up the hallway toward the reception area.

"*Rebecca?*" he echoed incredulously.

But his and his wife's excited smiles faded as they took in their assistant's red, swollen, and watering eyes. They both went directly to her, rather than to Rebecca.

"What's happened, Sarah?" asked Marie.

After hearing a cursory explanation, McGriff suggested that the four of them go to the conference room, so they could examine all aspects of what was becoming not only a complex threat, but an expanding and highly personal one.

Rebecca quietly demurred.

"Father Jack," she said, "it's been 36 hours since my first vision in almost a year. Because of its content, I have been working furiously to get here in time."

She looked at Sarah.

"And I made it — from Ireland — with perhaps five *seconds* to spare.

"Furthermore, I've just wounded two people whom I don't know, people who may be good human beings who were promised money to do something they did not understand … something they did not want to do.

"In fact, other than the irritant, they were careful not to hurt Sarah."

She glanced again at Sarah, who was pressing tissues into her eyes.

Sarah nodded her agreement.

"In any case, Father," Rebecca continued, "I need time — alone — to pray. I need to pray about the fact that I wounded those two people and then purposefully intimidated their two associates. I need to pray to God about those things I was required to do to rescue Sarah. I've left my husband and children behind, in England, because my dream … my vision … compelled me to travel to Sarah as fast as possible, as I will explain. I've done what I had to do, according to the dream … but I have *wounded* people, Father … and I have *intimidated* people…

"As a Christian woman, I need time alone now … please."

Marie was stricken at the sight of *this* Rebecca … a Rebecca exhausted and distraught … a Rebecca that Marie had never seen until this moment.

She stepped to the Englishwoman and embraced her. More than a half-foot shorter than Rebecca, the side of her face was pressed against Rebecca's upper chest. Rebecca, reaching down, returned the embrace.

Marie looked up, into the deep … and suddenly sad … gray eyes.

"Rebecca," she said, "the guest office is unoccupied. Let's go."

McGriff placed his hand on Rebecca's shoulder.

"I'm sorry, Rebecca," he said. "I didn't realize …"

Rebecca held up her hand and shook her head.

"No need, Father," she said.

Marie took Rebecca's hand and led her down the hallway.

Thursday, 10:00 a.m.

More than an hour later, now mid-morning, Rebecca had completed her solitary prayers. She had also washed her face and brushed her hair, having extricated her well-used hairbrush from the small array of toiletries she carried in her ready-satchel.

That ready-satchel, the only "luggage" Rebecca had brought with her, now contained, in addition to a few grooming items and fresh underwear, her passport, U.K. and U.S. cash, and the two knives she had not needed in the rescue. Rebecca had also folded her cap, placed it inside the ready-satchel, and taken down her action-ready ponytail, allowing a cascade of glistening black hair to fall freely down her back.

The foursome now took seats around the agency's conference table. McGriff nodded to Rebecca, which she understood was his request for prayer.

"Yes, of course," she said.

They bowed their heads while Rebecca prayed on their behalf.

Father … be present … be present … she began, as she nearly always did.

We give thanks to You that You have spared our sister, Sarah, this morning, from the manifold dangers wherewith she was compassed.

And we give thanks to You, as well, Father, that You have chosen her to serve as a vessel for the transmission of your messages to us … to the Rebekka Yahalomin.

Now we ask Your guidance as we attempt to understand Your will for us, and as we begin to formulate our plans on Your behalf.

Once again, please … Father … be present … be present …

For we ask in the Name of Your Son, Jesus Christ.

Amen.

The others echoed her "Amen."

They then looked up expectantly, and Rebecca offered her story.

As was her long-standing habit, developed as a teacher of junior-school girls in one of London's inner-city Anglican schools, she stood and paced as she spoke, her hands moving expressively in front of her chest as she slowly circled the room.

"This is Thursday morning," she said, mentally putting together the timeline since the vision that had interrupted her driving tour of Ireland with her husband.

"Just yesterday," she continued, "Wednesday morning in Ireland, at 3:00 a.m., their time — which is to say, 10 p.m. Tuesday, your time, 36 hours ago — I was sent another of the 'message dreams' that the Holy Spirit has chosen to place before me repeatedly, over the years. The vision began, as it often has in the past, with a surge of inner warmth that awakened me ... that surge of divine energy that has always consumed me mentally and physically, causing perspiration to pour from me, head to toe, even though I remained prone and unmoving ... while a visual image formed in front of my tight-closed eyes.

"I have learned," Rebecca continued, "to keep my eyes shut during the visions, though I also have learned that the vision would proceed, and continue to be visible to my inner eye, whether my eyes were open or closed. This image took several seconds to form itself, and when it did, I saw something familiar to me ... the sidewalk in front of your detective agency, here in Washington.

"This very sidewalk that Sarah and I just used.

"I recognized the setting easily," continued Rebecca, "having been introduced to your office spaces during the tour you gave us last summer after your wedding ceremony. I knew instantly where this dream was set."

She paused, remembering.

"By then I was on highest alert, knowing that I would need to reconstruct every element of the vision as soon as it ended. And then I saw you, Sarah, as you walked out the office door ... and, to me ... you appeared to be troubled.

"Of course," Rebecca continued, "I did not know it was you. I'd never met you, nor seen a photograph of you. I just knew that a troubled young woman had exited this office and was walking with purpose toward ... I didn't know toward what."

Sarah stirred, indicating a question.

Rebecca smiled and nodded.

"Rebecca," asked Sarah hesitantly, "was I ... was the young woman ... dressed the way I'm dressed now?"

Rebecca smiled again, the smile that always caused the long scar on the right side of her face to contract briefly until her face relaxed again.

"That's a wonderful question, Sarah, but the answer is ... I don't know.

"In my visions, often the critical elements are crystal clear, while less critical components remain obscure. It's as though the Holy Spirit does not wish to overload my brain with data not central to the dreamed message.

"But the dreamed woman was certainly you … your face, your curly, reddish hair that falls below your shoulders, your nearly 6 feet of height, your carriage, your stride … I was shown *you* … and no one else in the world."

Sarah nodded her understanding.

"The perspective in the vision," continued Rebecca, "then shifted, so as to allow me, through my dreaming eyes, to observe your progress down the sidewalk.

"And as your image gradually receded in the dreamed distance, I watched you cross a side street and move on to the next block. There was no foot traffic; my dreaming view of you was not obstructed.

"Finally, as the dream closed, I observed you as you turned the corner, two blocks away from my viewpoint … and you disappeared from my view. Had there been nothing else in the vision, I don't know what I would have concluded.

"But there was something else. There is nearly always something else. And, in this case, it was a feeling … an oppressive feeling … that a vehicle — apparently an unmarked ambulance — that I saw crossing the intersection where you turned, was following you, and for purposes that were unmistakably evil.

"Evil was behind you … trailing you … and you were not aware that you were moving into the greatest danger of your life."

Rebecca drew a deep breath, paused, and offered her conclusion.

"The dream ended there. I awakened Matt and reported everything to him. We have learned never to hesitate. When a vision comes, we know that our response must be immediate. We phoned our airline, and learned the first flight from Dublin to Birmingham would depart at 5:30 a.m., giving us just enough time to pack, drive to Dublin, return the rental car, and board that flight.

"From the Birmingham airport, after we landed, we retrieved our own car and I dropped Matt at the Lodge, where the children are staying with my parents. I left him at the security gate. I knew that if I drove all the way up the hill to the Lodge itself, and saw the children, I would not be able to leave … at least, not quickly.

"So, I left Matt at the gate and I drove, fast, to the Royal Air Force Base at Brize Norton … the transport center for the RAF in England. I went directly to the commanding officer, explained that I needed to fly to the East Coast of the U.S. as soon as possible. I found, to my surprise, that my brother had done exactly the same thing two days earlier, and is right now consulting at Naval Air Base Oceana, near Norfolk, Virginia. Poor Luke knew that Matt and I desperately wanted an uninterrupted driving vacation in Ireland, and so he didn't even let me know."

Rebecca paused and shook her head at her brother's thoughtfulness and consideration. Then she smiled, remembering, before she continued.

"The commanding officer," she said, "knows Luke well ... knows that Luke is a naval reserve officer ... knows that Luke was a *legendary* Royal Navy boarding party leader ... and knows that Luke has had, for years, a standing request for himself and our family to fly RAF transport whenever there is an open seat.

"And, of course, open seat on a military transport aircraft simply means a space against a bulkhead large enough for a person to curl up out of the way of whatever is being transported ... military vehicles, weapons, supplies, anything at all. I was in the air before noon U.K. time ... before 7:00 a.m. yesterday here in the eastern U.S.

"I arrived at McGuire Air Force Base, near New York City, late yesterday afternoon, rode a bus into the city, and managed to catch a late-night AMTRAK to Union Station here in D.C. I was able to snatch a few hours' sleep on a bench in the main waiting area, having convinced security personnel that I was not homeless ... just needing to rest until 6:00 a.m. today.

"They were," Rebecca concluded, "very sweet to me. I actually did sleep a little, but I was awake and in a taxi, headed for this address, by 6:30 this morning. I waited, just down the block, Sarah, for you to appear, still not knowing who you were. Before very long, there you were, walking away from the office ... just as in the vision.

"I followed close, especially when you approached the corner where I knew you would turn. Then, when you turned, I was only 25 yards behind you, and the unmarked ambulance was already crossing the intersection in your wake."

Rebecca paused and looked to her listeners.

"This," she said, "is where Sarah's and my experience of the attempted kidnapping merge into a single experience from two perspectives. Do you want to hear Sarah's account of her vision, from 4:00 this morning, or do you want me to go ahead and describe the attempted kidnapping from my perspective?"

Marie and McGriff looked at each other.

"Marie?" asked McGriff of his wife.

"Oh," she replied, "... I think I'll do better if I hear your account of why you, Sarah, came to work, stayed just minutes, and then left. That's *never* happened, and, if you can help me understand why that happened, I'll be clearer on how these things fit together. I'll be readier to hear either of you talk about the rescue itself."

Sarah shook her head.

"But wait, Marie," she said.

"I can't get past the *timing* of all this. So … before I try to explain what happened to me early this morning … and in the hours after that … could I ask you — any of you — to explain the timing of all this to me. Rebecca, you've said that, 36 hours ago, in Ireland, you were given a vision about a woman, who turned out to be me. You've said that you traveled from Ireland to England to Washington as fast as possible.

"You've said you crossed the Irish Sea, arranged RAF transport across the Atlantic Ocean, caught AMTRAK to Washington, got a taxi to this street, and reached me with *five seconds* to spare. How can I grasp that, Rebecca?

"Did God wait until there was absolutely zero time to spare and *then* prompt Rebecca to scramble from Ireland to England to America … then to Washington … then to this street … and finally to me, to rescue me with *five seconds* to spare?

"Why?

"If God knows in advance that I'm going to be assaulted and kidnapped, and if He wants you to intervene in the kidnapping, why would He not send a vision to you, Rebecca, long before that?

"I can't grasp the timing of this, and I need to understand it."

Rebecca looked to Jack. "Father McGriff?" she said.

"I'll give my answer, Rebecca, and then you can clarify for Sarah.

"Is that okay?" he asked.

Marie groaned in protest.

"I can assure you, dear husband, that Sarah is not the only one who needs to be given clarification on this. You're speaking to Sarah *and* to me."

"Okay, you two," he replied good-naturedly. "Here goes."

He looked to his right, where Marie and Sarah sat near each other at the conference room table.

"God stands *outside* time," he began. "That's the first thing to understand. God does not experience time sequentially, like we do. All of time ... all of eternity ... stands before God in His 'unbounded now' ... a phrase from C. S. Lewis.

"So, when God sends a vision to Rebecca, He sees the entire development of her ensuing experiences as one, single ... *now* event ... not as 'ensuing experiences' at all. And this is how the classical disputes about 'predestination' versus 'free will' are resolved. Both concepts are true.

"Both are true because God sees everything *now*. He sees your birth, Sarah, as a *now* event. He sees your death, also, as a *now* event. However, the time and circumstances of your death are not 'predetermined' in any meaningful sense, simply because God sees it *now* ... nor is your 'free will' diminished in any meaningful sense, and for the same reason.

"God sent Rebecca," he continued, "a vision of a woman, Sarah, and observed the 'resulting' series of events as one thing ... not as a series of things ... and so, while, to Rebecca, she arrived at your crisis point with *five seconds* to spare, to God she arrived with an infinite amount of time to spare. His 'now' is unbounded.

"To God," concluded McGriff, "five seconds is eternity, and eternity is five seconds. Or, as St. Peter wrote in his Second Letter, ' ... one day is with the Lord as a thousand years, and a thousand years as one day'."

McGriff stopped and looked to Rebecca.

"Rebecca," he asked, "what should I have said?"

"You said exactly what I would have tried to say, Father," she replied, "but you said it better than I could have. Sarah? Marie?

"Does Father Jack's explanation work for you?"

Sarah and Marie looked at each other. Then they laughed.

"Well," said Marie, "we *heard* him, but ... well ..."

Then Rebecca also laughed.

"I know," she said. "Understanding that explanation ... and *comprehending* that explanation ... not quite the same thing, is it?"

"I think," said McGriff, "that the idea of God 'standing outside of time' is something we can accept, and, as you say, even understand, in our limited fashion, without necessarily being able to *comprehend* it. It's possible, I think, that *comprehending* the Divine Mind is always something that's a step or two beyond us.

"But remember ... 'In the beginning was the Word' ... that is ... the *Logos* ... the Divine Mind ... and, as is written in verse 14 of John's first chapter, ' ... the Word became flesh, and lived among us'."

"Yes," said Rebecca. "God sent His Son, as John's Gospel tells us, as a living witness to the eternal *fact* of the 'Divine Mind' …

"And we, as Christian people, know and even 'understand' that fact, while not being fully able to 'comprehend' the same fact. It's the same kind of thing.

"Wouldn't you agree, Sarah?"

"Yes," Sarah said. "Jesus Christ is with us, and in us, and I know that's true, through my own everyday experience. But *comprehending* Christ's being with me, and in me, is a step beyond … and a step that is not necessary."

"Marie?" inquired Rebecca.

"Oh, yes," she said. "As soon as Jack reminded me that God 'stands outside time,' the thing came together for me. And it makes me weak with the wonder of it all … that God placed His vision in Rebecca's sleeping mind, and that He *saw* the outcome at the same time that He placed the vision … but that does not mean that the outcome was 'predetermined' … it just makes His experience 'a thousand years' while for Rebecca and Sarah, there were just 'five seconds' to spare.

"So, yes," Marie concluded. "I'm quite happy with this, Jack. Thank you for the impromptu sermon … and you, too, Rebecca."

A comfortable silence then fell on the foursome, each processing the "wonder of it all," as Marie had said, and each conscious of the fact that Rebecca's prayer had been fulfilled in the little conference room.

For she had prayed, "Father … be present … be present …"

Thursday, 11:00 a.m.

Sarah, at length, interrupted the quietness by saying, "Well, Marie, it seems like it was quite some time ago that you asked that I give you *my* story, and I deflected your request into something that took us on a very long detour. I'm sorry."

Marie laughed her easy laugh. "Oh, please, Sarah," she said. "That was a wonderful detour, but now I'm hungrier than ever to hear your story. Tell us!"

"This feels funny to me," Sarah began, "because I feel as if I've already told my story … but that's because I *have* told it … twice, this morning … but only to Dr. Chapel, on the phone, and then to Jim … not to any of you. I did mention to Father Jack and to Rebecca that I experienced one of Rebecca's 'message dreams' at 4:00 a.m., but I haven't had a chance to describe the dream to them, or to you, Marie."

Sarah then talked her listeners through the vision, carefully describing the two faces and, as well, the powerful sense of threat that accompanied the paired faces. She then told of her immediate phone call to Eleanor at the CIA safe house, followed by her "pathetic" phone call — "pathetic" being her own term — to Jim to ask him to come to her apartment. She finished the account of her near-abduction quickly but precisely, including a careful description of her sense of being rescued, while still lying on the stretcher inside the ambulance, and well before the rescue became a fact.

That done, Rebecca took up the narrative again, recounting her story of seeing the actual abduction attempt as it developed, and of hurling her throwing knives into the shoulders of two of the kidnappers.

And she explained, mostly for Sarah's benefit, her years of training with the Barringtons Swords competition throwing knives, and the clarity she experienced when she turned the corner and saw the trailing couple signaling the ambulance. She explained how she ran quietly toward the ambulance as it braked to a stop near Sarah, and how she focused on the signaling couple as they prepared to close the ambulance doors to complete the act of kidnapping.

"I knew," Rebecca concluded, "that I had waited as long as I could, and that there were no more options available to me. I knew that, at that moment, I was called to use my weapons against flesh and blood.

"It's a terrible awareness when that happens, Sarah, but we — all the members of Rebekka Yahalomin — understand that we are permitted to use force against those who would hurt innocent people, when no other choices are available to us."

At that moment, they heard the soft bell chime that indicated the agency's front door had opened. Rebecca looked inquiringly at Marie.

"No need," said Marie, "for us to do anything about the door, Rebecca; our part-time receptionist arrives mid-morning, and will take care of any visitors who come in. She'll interrupt us, if we are needed."

Suddenly the conference room door opened and Durham burst into the room. He went directly to Sarah, his face twisted in an agony of fear, and, leaning down over her, he embraced her. She touched his face tenderly and said quietly, "I'm alright, Jim. I was rescued before anything terrible happened. My eyes still burn, but I'm not injured in any way."

Only then did Durham seem to realize that there were other people present, including one whom he did not know ... but whose identity he had no trouble guessing. He stood and moved around the corner of the table, his right hand extended.

"Don't get up, ma'am," he said to Rebecca. "Just let me shake your hand and thank you for what you've done this morning. I don't know how you did it, but I'll be forever grateful to you."

Rebecca, remaining seated, took his hand and smiled.

"You're welcome, sir," she said. "I'm going to *guess* that you are Jim Durham, one of the precinct detectives."

Rebecca then laughed and continued teasingly, adding, "If you're not, then I very much need an explanation for the affectionate entrance you just made. Sarah did *mention* you when she recounted her early morning experiences for us."

Durham blushed, glanced at Sarah, then pulled one of the extra chairs up to the table next to her. He sat down and took a deep breath.

Then, realizing the others would want to know how he knew to come to the agency at all, he said, "I was talking with two of my uniformed colleagues this morning, standing next to their patrol car. I heard Captain Johnstone's radio message on the police frequency, telling other officers — those who were on their way to the abduction scene — that the 'knife thrower,' as he described Mrs. Clark, was an important ally to D.C. and New York City law enforcement, and that she was not to be detained for her use of the weapons. But I was on the other side of the city.

"I was on foot, and I started running the minute I heard him say that a woman had thwarted a kidnapping attempt by hurling 12-inch knives into the perpetrators. I didn't stop running until I reached the scene of the assault. Uniformed police were still there, interviewing witnesses. That's when I first realized that you really were okay, Sarah, and that's when I stopped running. I walked the rest of the way here."

Durham's hands were resting on the table as he said this, and Sarah placed a hand on his. "Thank you, Jim," she said. "I knew you would have done the rescuing, if you'd been close by and had seen what was happening."

He smiled and said, "I certainly would have tried, but I think your rescuer was the perfect person to stop that action without … you know … taking a life in the process.

"I do carry a gun …" — here he touched the 9mm nestled in his shoulder holster — "but I know it's hard to *wound* somebody when you have to shoot them. Happily, I have never had to use my Beretta for anything but target practice."

He suddenly exclaimed, "Oh, say, have you described your vision to every-one, Sarah, and have you identified the woman in your dream?"

"Yes and no," she said. "I've given them the word-portraits of the two faces I was given in my vision, but we don't know …"

CHAPTER FIVE

Thursday, 11:15 a.m.

AT THAT MOMENT, SARAH WAS INTERRUPTED IN HER RESPONSE to Durham's question by the part-time receptionist, who rapped twice, then pushed the conference room door open just enough to admit her face.

"Mrs. Campbell," she said, addressing Marie, who was sitting close to the door, "we have a call from Dr. Chapel, at the CIA safe house. Do you want the call forwarded here, or should I just take a message?"

"I'll take it here, please," replied Marie.

As Marie rose to walk to the extension, it buzzed.

"Good morning, Eleanor," said Marie cheerily. "How are you today?"

The room was silent while Marie listened, then said, "Thank you so much for calling, Eleanor, and no, your timing was just right. We were just starting to talk about that very thing.

"Give my best to Sidney."

Marie returned to the conference table and said, "Eleanor apologized for interrupting, but even more for not realizing something early this morning when Sarah phoned her at the safe house and described her dream.

"She said she got out all of her materials today ... the ones she'd been sent by Georgetown regarding the liberation theology sessions next week ... and realized that, in the back of the conference program, there are head-and-shoulder photos of all the presenters. And guess who's right there ... Congresswoman Millicent Thomas, exactly as Sarah described her this morning, from her 4:00 a.m. vision.

"Eleanor said that, if you look at Ms. Thomas' photo closely, you can even see that faint, vertical scar that runs from one corner of her mouth down to her chin."

Sarah gasped and clutched Durham's shoulder.

Rebecca smiled. "Oh, Sarah," she said, her facial scar crinkling in response to the wide smile, "your reaction brings back so many memories for me. It's just so incredible, isn't it … to realize that you've been given something by the Holy Spirit that corresponds exactly to something in the real world that you'd never seen before in your life."

Durham contentedly reached for Sarah's hand, the one that had grasped his shoulder in surprise and amazement, and pressed it to his lips. The two looked deeply into each other's eyes, oblivious, for once, of their audience.

Suddenly, Rebecca straightened in her chair.

Her gray eyes widened.

"How did this congresswoman," she asked the room, "and her hired assailants know *anything* about Sarah? How did they know to target *her* for anything? For any reason whatsoever? Why would she — this congresswoman — instruct her people to attempt a kidnapping of *Sarah Wilson?*"

There was a lengthy silence.

Suddenly, Durham slammed his hands onto the table. "The CIA safe house phone is tapped!"

The others looked at him in wonderment, all thinking the same thing … *the CIA safe house is not safe?*

Durham continued. "Someone at the CIA had to be listening to Sarah's 4:00 a.m. call to Dr. Chapel. Someone heard Sarah's word-portrait and recognized the woman in her dream as Millicent Thomas. That's the only possible explanation. Just a few hours later, they tried to snatch Sarah off the street as she walked home.

"The safe house phone is tapped," he said, "and there has to be a mole within the CIA unit there … possibly, but not necessarily, in their five-person Rebecca Unit.

"He … or she … heard Sarah's phone message and relayed that information to the congresswoman, who is doubtless paying that person to do exactly that. Ms. Thomas ordered the abduction because she realized Sarah would eventually be able to identify her as a threat to … well … to whatever Ms. Thomas is planning."

Durham thought for a moment, then expanded his idea.

"Not only is the phone bugged," he continued, "but the apartment itself — the one they've placed Dr. Chapel and Mr. Belton in — is surely filled with microphones."

Silence.

"Oh, Jack, we should have guessed," said Marie to her husband after a moment. "Last year … last summer … there was a mole who contaminated the CIA's Rebecca Unit. The CIA leadership rooted him out so quickly, that I allowed myself to assume the thing was forever cleaned up there.

"We should have guessed, dear," she said again.

He nodded. "A rookie mistake on our part, Marie."

In minutes, McGriff was maneuvering his Jeep Cherokee through downtown Washington and across the Potomac to Langley. His passenger was Rebecca Clark. Their immediate mission was to communicate with Sid Belton and Eleanor Chapel without using the safe house telephone, and without offering an explanation while they were in their safe house apartment. They would chat casually with the couple while Rebecca showed them the written explanation she had typed.

The couple would read the statement, collect their things, and, feigning a trip to the grocery store, abandon the safe house for good.

A half-hour before Rebecca and McGriff had run from the office out to the Cherokee, when the group had first realized the extent of the problem, Rebecca had asked, "But where can we take Dr. Chapel and Mr. Belton that will allow us all to function as the Yahalomin?"

After a moment, McGriff had answered.

"Andrews Air Force Base," he had said. "Sid has *connections*, Rebecca. We need to transfer our operation to Andrews, rather than here or at Langley.

"Marie," he had then said to his wife and agency partner, "I suggest we ask our part-time receptionist if she will work full-time for a week or so. And I think, too, that we should bring in a security team to be with her every day, starting now.

"We'll set up a dedicated phone line from Andrews," he had concluded.

"That will give us a protected communications environment from which to work. Sid is great friends with the lieutenant colonel who handles all of the base logistics. They worked together beautifully just last summer.

"We should get started … now."

McGriff and Rebecca had gone immediately to the Jeep, while Durham sprinted to the nearby garage where he kept his silver, 2-year-old Dodge Ram. In 15 minutes, he was back at the agency in his truck. He picked up Sarah and Marie, who fit easily on the bench seat of the Dodge, and drove them, first, to Sarah's apartment to pack her things, then to Marie's house for the same purpose.

The stop at Marie's took longer than at Sarah's, because that stop included Marie's taking several minutes to collect everything her little calico, Penelope, would need for an indefinite stay elsewhere. With Penelope tucked into her pet carrier and the carrier resting on the floorboard of the truck under Marie's legs, and with all the necessary feline accoutrement riding behind them in the truck bed, the women were ready to be displaced for however long would be necessary.

They headed for the air base.

They arrived there shortly before 1:00 p.m., about 20 minutes after McGriff's Cherokee had passed through the main gate with Rebecca, Belton, and Eleanor as his passengers. Belton had phoned the lieutenant colonel from the guardhouse, and the colonel had come immediately to retrieve them.

From the lieutenant colonel's viewpoint, this was "Detective Sid Belton plus three others," none of the "others" being consequential in his mind. Once Durham, Sarah, and Marie arrived in the truck, they were quickly processed as part of the same group.

Thursday, 1:00 p.m., Andrews Air Force Base, Maryland

The lieutenant colonel led McGriff's Cherokee and Durham's truck in his own Jeep Wrangler to the base visitors' quarters a half-mile from the main gate. He, knowing Belton would not ask anything of him lightly, asked no questions.

It was clearly another emergency, perhaps similar in some way to the previous summer's situation in which he had been able to assist. That's all he needed to know in order to help with the arrangements. Once inside the quarters that he had assigned to Belton and his wife, the colonel interviewed the group in the small living room.

"Tell me what you'll need, detective," asked the officer. "I'd like to get everyone situated right now, so that you'll have everything you'll need for the time you're with us on the base. I don't want you to have to run around looking for me."

"I'm gonna ask Father McGriff an' Ms. Clark t' fill ya in, Colonel," replied Belton. "They're miles ahead of Eleanor an' me on what's been goin' on here."

The colonel turned to McGriff and Rebecca. He raised his eyebrows in question. The two exchanged glances, and McGriff began.

"Dr. Chapel here," he began, "was attacked on the streets of Manhattan on Monday, Colonel, which is why she and Sid were evacuated, at their request, by

CIA Learjet overnight Monday-Tuesday. As I think you know, sir, the detective firm operated by my wife and me is a branch of Sid's operation in New York; he can work from here as readily as from his home office. Sid and Eleanor stayed Tuesday and Wednesday nights at the CIA safe house in Langley, but we have excellent reason to believe that the CIA has tapped their phone … and probably bugged their room, too."

"No surprise there," observed the colonel dryly.

McGriff smiled and continued.

"We need to know, Colonel, if we might be allowed to operate our detective agency from your guest quarters here for … maybe … a week … which would mean not only housing us here, but allowing us to set up a dedicated and secure phone line."

The colonel looked at Rebecca and smiled.

"Sounds like none of you may know, ma'am, that your brother has contacted me this very morning, and will be on his way here, probably Saturday," he said. "Lieutenant Manguson will fly up from Naval Air Station Oceana, at Norfolk.

"Because of his phone call this morning, I've already set up quarters for him right here, in his usual unit, in case he comes in early. There's no time limit at all on his stay with us. He's pretty much a fixture on our base, you know. I'll just expand the arrangements to accommodate however many others you need."

Rebecca's look of surprise and delight comprised her wordless response.

The colonel smiled and continued.

"Let's see," he said, "I'll need to add Sid and Eleanor, here in this apartment … and you, Father, and your wife, in the adjacent one … and then a single unit for you, Mrs. Clark. Your brother is booked for a single, next to the one you'll use.

"Is that all you'll need, Father?"

McGriff shook his head.

"Colonel, this young woman is Sarah Wilson … she is our administrative assistant at the agency. We need to have her here, with us.

"Our enemies, and we clearly have some, although we do not yet understand everything about them, know where she works and where she lives.

"May we impose on you for a single unit for her, as well?"

Rebecca quickly intervened.

"No, Father," she said to McGriff. "Sarah should stay in my quarters with me."

She looked to the colonel.

"Would it be too much to arrange a double for Miss Wilson and me, sir? Or maybe a cot brought in to one of your singles? I don't think Sarah should be staying alone for a while. She's not accustomed to the sort of personal violence she has already encountered. I'd like to be with her."

The colonel nodded and jotted a note to himself.

He looked at Durham.

"How about you, sir?" he asked.

"Thank you, Colonel," Durham replied, "but I'll need to stay on the streets in D.C. I'm not private … I'm a detective in Captain Horace Johnstone's precinct. If you'll just arrange for me to have unlimited passage through the main gate for the next week, preferably just by showing my badge, I'll be in good shape."

"Done," said the colonel with satisfaction.

Thursday afternoon-evening, Andrews Air Force Base, guest quarters

Sarah and Rebecca had taken turns showering in their quarters, as the agreed-upon time for the evening meal approached. Sarah was getting dressed, while Rebecca was still drying her hair with a towel.

"Sarah," said Rebecca, "I feel I've been awake almost continually for two days now. I know it's only 6:00 in the evening here, but in England …

"I'm wondering … would you like to talk before I go to sleep? I think I'll pass on having dinner this evening."

"Oh, yes, Rebecca," she replied. "Just for a few minutes. Then I'll go back to Dr. Chapel and Mr. Belton's room, where the others are, and have dinner with them."

Rebecca, still drying her hair, nodded and turned down her bed sheets.

She was wearing the nightgown Sarah had been thoughtful enough to pack for her, once she realized Rebecca had been able to bring nothing with her, other than her ready-satchel. Although Rebecca was two inches taller, and broader at the shoulder than her roommate, they were otherwise the same size.

The nightgown fit well enough.

Sarah, now dressed for dinner, sat on the edge of her bed, facing Rebecca's, and said, "When you had your first experience with the 'message dreams,' what did you think? How did you feel? What did you do to cope?"

Rebecca fluffed her pillow, pulled the sheet up, and turned on her side to face Sarah. "I think my first response was to deny — as I talked to myself about it — that it was really anything special. I wanted to think it was just an unusual dream that contained … well … puzzling and … elaborate imagery.

"My brother and I were both second-year teachers, and lived together in an inexpensive flat in southwest London. I said nothing to him about the dream."

"Really? You just kept it to yourself?"

Rebecca nodded. "Yes … until the dream happened again … and then again. Finally, I couldn't tell myself that there was anything 'normal' about the dreams. That's when I told him about them."

"What did he say?"

"He said what I'd already been thinking, Sarah. He said that it sounded like the kind of dreams our parents had experienced when they were younger.

"He said we should drive to Birmingham, to the Lodge … that's with a capital 'L' … that's what our parents' inn is named. They have owned the inn, just outside Birmingham, for decades. He said we needed to tell them about the dreams.

"When we finally did that, we developed an understanding that, as soon as a vision happened, I needed to tell someone immediately, because the details mattered, and another person needed to hear those details so that two of us would be able to relate the story accurately to others."

"And your brother was the person you'd always talk to?"

"Yes … until Matt and I married, of course."

"And did you always feel better after you'd told someone?"

Rebecca thought for a moment before answering.

"I think I always felt I had done what I *should* do, but we all realized that these dreams were *sent* to me by God, just as with our parents, decades earlier.

"And we knew that the dreams implied action on our part … often action that would put us in dangerous situations. So, I'm not sure I felt *better* after telling Luke … and eventually, Matt … and eventually other members of Rebekka Yahalomin.

"I just knew that reporting the dreams was necessary … it was required … and it was a part of responding as a Christian person to something extraordinary … something that involved God Himself giving me, and us, a directive, one to which we were expected to respond, and to respond immediately."

Sarah nodded.

The two women were silent, each thinking about the fact that they were together, two of a tiny handful of living individuals who had experienced God's

Hand in this rather "Old Testament" fashion, as Marie Campbell had once said about Rebecca's visions. Finally, Sarah looked again at Rebecca, whose eyelids were becoming heavy, and said, "I know you need to sleep, Rebecca.

"But I do want to say that I, too, did not feel better, really, after I had phoned Dr. Chapel and reported the dream. I just knew that, as you've said, it's the thing you must always do, and it's the … required … thing to do.

"However, I was so unsettled … that I phoned Jim and asked him to come to my apartment. I'm still amazed that I did that. I just barely knew him, really, Rebecca … in fact, I *still* just barely know him.

"But he *ran* to my place and when he came in, I just melted into him. *That's* when I began to feel better. He held me for a long time, but when it came time for me to get ready for work, I sent him home, and I actually arrived at work on time.

"But, as you know so well … I didn't stay."

Rebecca nodded. "You needed to be comforted, Sarah. And that was *so* much better than what I did with my first vision … denial … and denial … and denial … until I reached the breaking point and talked to my brother."

Sarah smiled gratefully.

"Thank you, Rebecca," she replied. "That's something I really needed to hear … from you … now. Thank you."

They were silent again for several moments, then Rebecca shook her head to fight off the fatigue, and said, "And how do you feel about Jim, Sarah? What do you think of the relationship … so far, I mean?"

Sarah blushed.

"I think I'm … falling in love with him, Rebecca, which is ridiculous, I know. We don't know much more about each other than you might read in a short bio. I mean … our first date was *Tuesday,* Rebecca. This is *Thursday.* Can you imagine?"

She paused, reviewing her time with Jim in her mind.

"I think," she said after a moment, "something changed in me this morning, which seems forever long ago now … when I phoned him, distressed, and asked if he would come over … and he *ran* to me, Rebecca.

"He didn't even ask *why* I wanted him to come … he just said, 'I'll be there in ten …' and then he actually was. And when I opened the door, I couldn't say anything, and when he saw that, he just stepped forward and enfolded me in his arms.

"Then we sat on my sofa for a while, and when I sent him home so I could get dressed for work, he kissed me on the cheek, Rebecca … *on the cheek.*"

Rebecca smiled her wide smile, her mind going back to Matt Clark's similar, and oh-so-*careful* touching of her when they first met.

Sarah continued. "And you saw how Jim was when he burst into our meeting this morning … he just leaned over my chair and enveloped me … again … in his arms."

"Yes," said Rebecca, "and I saw how you responded, Sarah. I saw how you touched his face with your fingertips. You are *tender* with each other."

As these words left her mouth, Rebecca's eyes closed.

She was gone.

Sarah stood and tiptoed to the door. Then she turned and whispered, "Thank you, Rebecca. You've saved me again.

"Thank you."

Friday, 5:30 a.m., Washington, D.C.

Durham, having completed his early morning devotional readings and prayers, moved his Bible to one side and picked up the morning newspaper. He read the sports section first, and then turned to the editorial pages, leaving the news itself for last, as was his long-standing habit.

As he worked through the editorial section — commentaries on national and international news — his eyes stopped at the headline for a longish piece on the situation in Nicaragua, where civil war had broken out and the U.S. administration seemed to be acting in support of the side that called itself the "Contras." These fighters, the journalist explained, had risen up in opposition to the "Sandinistas," formally called the Sandinista National Liberation Front. The Contras, said the writer, had been formed five years earlier, in 1981, and were being trained and funded by the CIA.

Continuing, Durham raised his eyebrows at the next paragraph's opening: "The Sandinistas' official ideology is embodied in liberation theology, a perspective on Christianity advocating political action on behalf of the oppressed."

Durham lifted his eyes from the piece and considered the implications of the article for the upcoming liberation theology conference at Georgetown, which would feature Dr. Eleanor Chapel and, in a lesser role, Millicent Thomas. A connection between liberation theology and the Nicaraguan fighting had not occurred to him until this moment, and he found the thought disconcerting.

Was Dr. Chapel moving into an area fraught with Central American violence, despite her own lack of support for liberation theology? Were the assaults on her and on Sarah related, via liberation theology, to the Nicaraguan war?

He read on.

"The Sandinista government," wrote the columnist, "has instituted literacy programs, land reform, and quasi-universal health care, but it has come under international criticism for human rights abuses.

"These have included mass executions and the oppression of indigenous peoples. The Nicaraguan government has been criticized, as well, for mismanaging the national economy and overseeing runaway inflation."

The writer noted that the mass executions and "the oppression of indigenous peoples" animated both the Contras and the CIA-driven support for them. There was no more mention of liberation theology's role in the civil war, but Durham continued to focus on that theology as constituting the Sandinistas' official ideology.

How, he wondered, did Millicent Thomas' professional and political interests relate to this Central American imbroglio?

He finished the article, showered and dressed, then sat down at his work desk and picked up the top file. It contained a report written by a young Sudanese man named Kazim Deng. Durham had spoken often with Deng at the precinct offices where Deng worked part-time as a data analyst, and had been consistently impressed by Deng's work ethic and studiousness.

Durham also knew something of Deng's deeper history, that he had escaped with his family, as a boy, from Sudanese conflicts, first to England and then eventually, on scholarship, to a New Jersey boarding school. Durham knew, further, that Deng was a recent graduate of Georgetown University in mathematics, and that he was completing a doctorate in computer science at American University.

Deng also, Durham was aware, drove a taxi part-time to help with his school expenses. A young man of many talents and immense determination.

Deng's research report, Durham quickly saw, had taken him to documents that would have been impossible to access without assistance from someone of considerable political influence. Apparently, Captain Johnstone's connections had allowed Deng to "borrow" confidential reports authored by the CIA, FBI, and other investigative organizations whose documents were not available to the public.

He found the report readable. It was not only clearly written but crafted in idiomatic English, an extraordinary feat for one whose native languages were other than English. In Deng's case, English was his fourth language.

On the final page, Durham read Deng's three-point summary.

- *Although the CIA trains and funds the Contras, some U.S. politicians —
  both House and Senate members — give political support to their adversaries, the Sandinistas. When they support the Sandinistas, they often do so in the name of liberation theology, the official ideology of the
  Sandinistas, which is an approach to Christianity that employs political and even military tactics to address the conditions of the "poor and
  oppressed."*

- *Those politicians supporting the Sandinistas tend to be open about their
  rationale, citing liberation theology's authorities and concepts to secure
  the support of Christian/Catholic voters when campaigning for re-election in their home states or districts. These politicians, it must be noted,
  are <u>always</u> campaigning. Campaigning is what they do.*

- *There are repeated references in certain documents to an unnamed
  Nicaraguan who appears to work as a conduit for financial support for
  the Contras. Despite this individual's prominence in his role, he is never
  named, and does not appear to be among those acknowledged as the
  movement's "official" leaders.*

Deng's report concluded with recommendations that local law enforcement disengage from any politician who could be shown to involve herself or himself with either side of the Nicaraguan war. He noted that the very fact of CIA involvement comprised an excellent argument, in itself, for law enforcement to take a hands-off position vis-à-vis the Sandinistas versus Contras.

Durham made notes to himself from Deng's report. He then placed an entry in his daily calendar, reminding himself to obtain a copy of the young Sudanese's schedule at police headquarters. He intended to follow up face-to-face.

Realizing then that he had not read the first section of his newspaper — only the sports and editorial sections — he rose from his desk and walked to the kitchen table, where he had tossed the newspaper. He stood to scan the 20 pages of news reports, but paused when he encountered a small headline on page 18, announcing *"Contra Leaders in D.C. for Meetings with House Members."*

He read the article, still standing at his kitchen table, but then, having at first merely glanced at the photo accompanying the piece, pulled the newspaper closer to his face. The caption read, *"Contra emissaries meet with House mem-bers."* The names of the three men in the photo were listed, left to right.

The face on the right, though its features were not sharp in the news photo, struck him like a thunderclap. Sarah's word-portrait of the second person in her dream — the man who appeared alongside Millicent Thomas — looked back at him.

The caption identified him as Reynaldo Acosta.

Durham immediately changed from deck shoes to running shoes and moved Deng's report from his briefcase to a lightweight, zippered document case. He took off his shoulder holster and Beretta and placed them in a lockable drawer.

He unbuttoned two of his shirt-front buttons and tucked his necktie into the opening. His tie thus secured and the document case in hand, he began a 1-mile run to the precinct office, the same distance of his previous day's run to Sarah Wilson.

But this run was in the direction opposite that to Sarah's apartment. And, running at a comparatively leisurely pace, he covered the distance in eight minutes, rather than the six minutes he had managed the morning before, during his max-energy response to her phone call.

Once inside the office, he pulled his necktie from its secured position inside his shirt, re-buttoned the shirt, and walked to the research area where Deng would be working, if he were present at the office that morning. And indeed he was there, bent over his work desk, scribbling notes on a legal pad as he worked through some impenetrable document. Durham approached and spoke quietly, so as not to startle the intent Sudanese scholar. Deng looked up, recognized Durham, and stood.

"Good morning, Kazim," said Durham. "I'm Jim Durham, one of the detectives working in our precinct."

They shook hands.

Durham, at 6 feet, 3 inches, looked down at the compact, muscular, 5-foot-9-inch Deng. The thought flashed through Durham's mind that, although he had seen the researcher often before, he had never looked closely at him. And what he saw surprised him.

This was no delicate research beetle. This was a coiled spring of a man, ebony of color, physically dynamic even while standing motionless.

This is an impressive guy, thought Durham, *and I don't even know him. How has he not gotten my attention until now?*

Durham's answer to his own question was obvious to him — he had not bothered to pay attention to a "mere" part-time researcher — but now he needed to concentrate on the reason for his coming to talk to the author of the research report.

Deng spoke before Durham could begin.

"How can I help, sir?" asked Deng respectfully.

"Oh … well … I'm not 'sir,' please, Kazim," replied Durham, "but let me start by saying I apologize for interrupting your work. You're obviously deep into something important, and I'm going to ask you to do something entirely different. I think, though, you'll find it at least as important as what you're working on now."

Deng displayed his bright, white teeth with an engaging smile.

"I'm not sure that what I'm doing right now is particularly important, Mr. Durham, and I'm *certain* it is not time-sensitive. So, if you have something you need that might be time-sensitive, let me have a look."

"Okay," replied Durham, "but you've got to drop the 'sir' and the 'mister,' and just go with 'Jim.' I mean, we're probably about the same age, and what I do here is surely *not* more important than what *you* do here … I've just read your 25-page research report on the situation in Nicaragua. Very impressive work, Kazim."

"Oh," replied Deng, "so *you're* the one who's read it."

They shared a laugh, then Durham asked, "Is there some place where we could speak privately, Kazim?"

"Sure … if you don't mind sitting in the cloak room. It's where I go to be solitary, and it's got a couple of chairs … and a window!"

After walking side-by-side past a half-dozen cubicles, they each took a seat in the dimly lit, elongated coat closet, and Durham pulled Deng's report from the zippered case. He turned to the final page of the report and read aloud the three summary points, just to place the conclusions freshly in the author's mind.

"Kazim," he said, "I'm going to tell you something that will sound strange … maybe impossible … but, well, impossible or not … it's what I and some of my colleagues are dealing with right now. And it is indeed time-sensitive and hugely important."

Deng nodded. "You're going to tell me," said Deng, looking at Durham forthrightly, "that Rebekka Yahalomin is being called into action, and you want to know if it's possible that the Yahalomin are being activated in connection with the fighting in Nicaragua."

Durham's jaw sagged.

Deng smiled. "I thought I'd just get straight to the point, Jim," said the Sudanese researcher. "That way, you don't have to launch some tortured explanation about visions and dreams and … you know … that sort of thing."

Durham was still too nonplussed to speak.

"See," continued Deng, "last summer I got hooked into Yahalomin stuff, at first by accident. Or it *seemed* accidental at the time.

"Captain Johnstone asked me to pick up Marie Campbell and a couple of men at the Soviet Embassy in the taxi I sometimes drive … one thing led to another … and I found myself eventually right in the middle of everything. But, as for the *strangeness* of visions and dreams, Jim, I had a good conversation with Rebecca Clark, just as she was leaving Andrews for England last summer.

"I explained to her that I myself have been the recipient of … what I've always called 'Christian visitations' … at several points in my life. She and I agreed that we were likely at some point to meet again.

"So … there you go," he said with finality.

Durham shook his head incredulously.

"I'm stunned."

"Yes, sir," replied Deng. "I can see that."

Once Durham had recovered enough to become functional again, he removed the news section of that morning's paper from his zippered case. He showed Deng the photograph of Reynaldo Acosta. Deng bent over the photo and looked closely, first at the image itself, then at the caption. Deng shook his head.

"I don't know these men, and I've never seen these names in any of my materials. Who are they?"

"This man on the right," Durham said, "is, I'm fairly certain, the person who appeared in a recent vision alongside Congresswoman Millicent Thomas. The visioner, in this instance, was not Mrs. Clark. It was a young woman named Sarah Wilson, who is the administrative assistant for Marie Campbell and Jack McGriff, both of whom you know from your involvement last summer with the Yahalomin.

"Sarah's dream portrayed only these two — Millicent Thomas and the man in this newspaper photograph."

Deng was silent while he scanned the article. When he'd finished, he looked up at Durham and said, "There is really nothing newsworthy in this piece, Jim, but these three gentlemen are here in D.C. right now, it would appear. And they are presumably lobbying House and Senate members for further support for the Contras."

Durham nodded.

"Yes," he said, "that's my assumption."

"What do you want from me?" asked the Sudanese.

"I want to know if you can research the connection … the *dreamed* connection … between Millicent Thomas and the man in this photograph."

"And," Durham continued, "if there is one, I'd like to know what that connection is … and I'd like to know it *before* Monday's conference on liberation theology gets underway at Georgetown University."

CHAPTER SIX

Saturday noon, Georgetown University, luncheon for panelists

THE SEVEN PANELISTS SCHEDULED TO BE FEATURED DURING the three-day conference that would begin Monday were gathered in one of the university's small reception halls. Along with the seven were two dozen other speakers who would participate in the conference's lower-profile morning sessions, plus another dozen or so faculty members and administrators. The reception began at noon, giving the group a half-hour to socialize prior to the luncheon to be held in their honor.

Dr. Eleanor Chapel — the only featured panelist whose perspective on liberation theology was not well known from her earlier publications — found herself chatting with another panelist, a Cambridge University professor. A knot of listeners clustered around them, curious to hear the exchange between two of the higher profile visitors.

"Dr. Chapel," the Englishman was saying, "I've read several of your published Old Testament articles and was intrigued by your analysis of some of the writings of the Minor Prophets. If I may be candid, I did not expect to learn anything useful from a woman, having had little contact with your species in my university work."

Eleanor's tinkling laughter bubbled from her, attracting numerous glances from those in nearby conversations. Laughter was often a casualty when self-important professionals gathered to bask in their self-importance.

The Cambridge don's face reddened.

"I do not recall, *Ms.* Chapel," he said, dropping her academic title and emphasizing, instead, the generic feminine prefix, "saying anything that could be interpreted as even the slightest bit humorous."

He paused, looking closely at the diminutive, gray-clad, gray-haired Old Testament authority. He saw that she, still laughing, though more quietly now, rummaged in her purse, extracting a tissue. She dabbed at her eyes.

"I do apologize," she said, looking up from her 4-foot-10-inch height at the elongated, 6-foot-7-inch Brit. "But I seldom encounter anyone who can issue an insult so gracefully. Are you always misogynistic, or are you befuddled by jet lag?"

There were audible gasps from those listening.

The Englishman drew himself up to his full height and lifted his chin, so as to exaggerate the extent to which he looked down upon her, both literally and figuratively. He cleared his throat noisily.

"I demand an apology, madame! If you were not a woman, and not so ridiculously small, I would issue an invitation to a duel ... pistols at 20 paces!"

In this, he appeared serious.

"Apologize at once!"

She smiled up at him.

"I am so sorry," she said simply.

There was an extended pause.

During the silence, she continued to look up at the Englishman, her face relaxed, smiling, secure ... displaying the settled confidence of a woman who knows who she is ... and knows Whom she serves. He continued to look down at the American, his face tracing a series of uncertain frowns and grimaces, settling finally on one that bespoke grudging acceptance of her apology.

After all, he had demanded one. She had then proceeded to offer exactly what he had demanded. He had won.

Rarely had he experienced that sequence: demand ... then apology.

He decided to change course.

First, he cleared his throat once more, signaling the new tack.

"You've no doubt read some of my published pieces on liberation theology. I do not recall seeing anything in print, from you, on that topic. Have you written on liberation theology? Or merely on the Old Testament?"

She suppressed the laughter that tried again to escape at the man's gratuitous use of the word "merely" in his effort to diminish her scholarly accomplishments.

"I admit," she said sweetly, "that I've published nothing on the topic of this conference ... on liberation theology."

"Then why," he asked, genuinely puzzled, "were you invited?"

"Perhaps for that reason ... I've written nothing on this topic."

"But how could you possibly not?" he said, adopting his lecturing manner. "Jesus Christ Himself made plain that 'the poor' must be the focus of much that is done in His name. Take, for one example, His response to the emissaries sent by John the Baptizer, as reported in Luke's Gospel, Chapter 7."

He proceeded ostentatiously to recite Christ's words verbatim.

"'*Go and tell John what you have seen and heard: the blind receive their sight, the lame walk, the lepers are cleansed, the deaf hear, the dead are raised, the poor have good news brought to them.*'

"The *poor* are singled out, madam," he reiterated. "That is the thrust of Christ's message … we *must* reach the poor. We must utilize every means possible — political and even, in certain instances, military — to rescue them. And you know as well as I, that if Jesus were walking the earth today, He would spearhead an international political movement to overthrow economic tyranny wherever it manifests itself. And Jesus would call attention to the fact, if He were here now, that economic tyranny is strongest where it is most strongly disguised.

"And economic tyranny is most strongly disguised *in the democracies*, where it is alleged that all people have economic opportunity, but where, in fact, the downtrodden poor have no opportunity whatsoever … absolutely *none*, madam!"

He was shouting now. Conversations around the small venue had stopped. Everyone present had turned toward the Cambridge don as he pontificated wildly, still looking down at the silent, smiling, Old Testament teacher.

"I must conclude, madam, that your silence on liberation theology is nothing but *cowardice* … pure, abject *cowardice.*"

He waved his arms as he spoke the words, his face turning purple.

As he finished, the target of his diatribe stepped quickly forward and reached up, placing her hand gently on his forearm. He looked down at the hand, seemingly surprised to see it there. Then she began to speak. And her words carried through the hall like church bells. Others in the hall began unconsciously to move toward her.

Though soft, her voice was so high, and the room so silent, that every person present could hear her response to the Cambridge don.

"Sir," she said, her hand still on his arm, "our Lord was indeed concerned for the poor … and for the rich … and for all of those in between. As the opening of John's Gospel tells us, 'In the *beginning* was the Word … and the Word became flesh and lived among us.' And the Word, sir, 'became flesh' on behalf of every person living then … every person living before … every person living after. *Every* person.

"Christ rejected," she continued, "all invitations to become political … to become a revolutionary. You recall His words, in the language of the King James translation: *'Render therefore unto Caesar the things which are Caesar's; and unto God the things that are God's,'* just as you recall, as well, the passage in which the Tempter shows Jesus the kingdoms of the world, saying, *'All these things will I give thee,'* to which Jesus replies emphatically, *'GET THEE HENCE.'*"

She removed her hand from the Englishman's forearm and was quiet for a moment, seemingly deciding whether she wished to offer him more. Meanwhile, the Cambridge don stood silent, transfixed by the soft authority in her words, in her demeanor, in her easy command of scripture.

She decided she would offer just a bit more.

"I've been re-reading Thomas Merton, sir. One of his observations comes to mind. He once wrote of Jesus' *'… incomprehensible and infinite sacrifice, in which all history begins and ends, all individual lives begin and end, in which every story is told, and finished, and settled for joy or sorrow …'*"

She looked down, thinking, then up again, fixing him with her startling blue-green eyes, eyes that seemed to look through him into Something beyond. "Sir," she said, "I ask you to recall, in fear and trembling, the five-word retort Christ made to those who challenged His revelation about Himself."

She paused again. The room was utterly silent.

"Those words were these: *'… before Abraham was, I AM.'*

"How can you *possibly* speak of Him," she continued, her voice still soft, still non-accusatory, "in the context of *politics?* How can you listen to yourself speak of Him in that way, sir, without being overcome with shame?

"You have taken Our Lord's life, death, and resurrection — the resurrection which changed the conditions under which we all live, and die, and rise again, *forever* — and attempted to reduce it to something trivial in comparison.

"Trivial … transitory … and *spectacularly* wrong.

"Excuse me, sir," she said, still speaking quietly.

"Your words make me feel unclean. I need to wash my hands and face."

She turned and walked away, scurrying in her quick, erect way, her gray Adidas squeaking rhythmically on the polished hardwood floors.

The tall Englishman, suddenly thoughtful, watched her go. The studied severity of his countenance slowly relaxed.

The ghost of a smile appeared.

Sunday afternoon, Andrews Air Force Base, Chapel-Belton guest unit

The Yahalomin had crowded together that Sunday morning in Eleanor and Sid's unit to worship under the leadership of Father McGriff, and then had lunched on sandwiches while standing around the kitchen table. Following lunch, two international calls were placed from the guest unit's newly installed military-secure line.

One phone call was from Rebecca to her husband and children in England, who reported themselves happy and safe at the Lodge with Rebecca's parents, and with the dogs that served as Joanna and Samuel's daily playmates. The other call was from Luke Manguson, freshly arrived, to his wife, Kory, who reported not only on their household matters, but on plans and progress at International Security Perspectives, known worldwide as ISP, where she, Luke, and Matt Clark all worked.

One more call went from Belton to his agency partner in New York, Jaakov Adelman. Much of the agency's New York City business was on hold while Belton was in the D.C. area, and so most of the talking in that call was done by Sidney, reporting to Adelman on D.C. events.

"Sid," Adelman said at the end of the call, "are you going to need me there? I can get the next AMTRAK whenever you say."

"I think it could go either way," Belton replied. "Keep yer go-bag ready, Jaakov. This could get complicated in a hurry.

"Oh," Belton added, "we're speakin' on a secure line that th' lieutenant colonel set up our guest unit. Ya can call direct, if ya need to."

Later in the afternoon, Rebecca and Sarah entered their room together. They took turns in the small bathroom, changing out of the dresses they had donned for the morning worship service, Sarah having supplied Rebecca with one of the two dresses she had hurriedly packed for Sunday worship.

They changed into workout clothes and running shoes.

"Sarah," said Rebecca when her roommate came out of the bathroom, "I'll shop for a few clothes at the post exchange tomorrow, so you won't need to lend me your things anymore. I should have packed a few items, other than what was in my ready-satchel, but I felt that every second was important and … well … I just didn't."

"You traveled in your tennis warm-ups and you brought your throwing knives, Rebecca," replied Sarah. "You were dressed and armed for combat. And because you were, and because you came so fast … I'm here, and safe, instead of …"

Rebecca smiled and nodded.

"Yes," she said. "Things have worked out for us, haven't they? But I'll still want to buy a few things of my own tomorrow. I'll need something nice to wear to Eleanor's session tomorrow night at the university.

"Is there anything I can pick up for you?"

The discussion then moved in the direction of shampoos and other items that would make their shared bathroom — equipped as it was, in bare-bones military fashion, with exactly two tiny bars of soap — more readily usable for two young women. That discussion finished, Sarah sat on the edge of her bed and changed the subject to one she had found herself praying about during that morning's worship service.

"Rebecca," she said, "I'm still not right in my head … about the vision thing. Can you help me see how I ought to … um … how I ought to think about myself, now that this enormous thing has come into my life?

"How have you coped with the possibility … no … with the *likelihood* … that God will again, at any time, send you these kinds of … crisis messages … which will turn your life inside out … and, it would seem, often put your life in danger … and, you know … sort of … um … take your life out of your hands?"

Rebecca sat down on her bed, pushed a pillow against the headboard, and, sitting erect in her tennis togs and propped against the pillow, considered her response. She took her time, and Sarah waited patiently, having already learned that Rebecca would always respond thoughtfully, but only after turning a question over in her mind. Sometimes this took minutes.

Sarah lay down on her bed, on her side, facing Rebecca.

"Yes," Rebecca said finally. "It's not quite fair, is it, Sarah?

"One moment you have a position in a detective agency, a position that you understand and enjoy, working for two people whom you like and admire, being courted by a young man with whom you feel you may be falling in love … and suddenly, it seems, your life is no longer your own. Your innermost self — the one around which you have formed a nicely protective shell — has been breached by Something against which you have no power … and breached not just once, we can assume, but at indeterminate intervals, perhaps for as long as you will live.

"And what, you may find yourself asking, does this enormous intrusion do to all your plans? To your employment … to your church life … to your involvement with Jim Durham? You had your hand on the tiller of your boat, but now it's as if Someone else has commandeered the boat, to navigate at His discretion."

She paused.

Sarah was staring at Rebecca, her hazel eyes wide with a sudden fear. She had wanted to be comforted. Rebecca was, instead, frightening her, and frightening her more and more with every sentence she spoke.

Rebecca smiled at her new friend, her gray eyes warm with affection. "Sarah," she said, "I learned that, in fact, nothing had changed at all. God had *always* had His hand on the tiller. God could *always* intervene in my life … could *always* redirect my plans … could *always* lead me in some direction that I had not foreseen, and which, at times, could bring risks I had not imagined.

"Sometimes … in my life …" continued Rebecca, "and long before the visions began … I found, for example, that the risks of attending to God's guidance might involve the uncertainties of ending a relationship … at other times the risks of starting one. Sometimes the risks were of the sort that could become dangerously physical, as when I had to confront men who had begun to stalk me during my tennis career.

"I learned, however, that, in the long run, the changes attendant to experiencing an occasional vision were simply a change in degree. Yes, my prayer life needed to become more disciplined. Yes, my commitment to my family needed to become more whole-hearted. Yes, my devotion to my church needed to become more focused.

"But," Rebecca concluded, "in the actual doing of it all … the actual living of it all … this just meant that I *simplified* my life. It meant that I reduced my social and organizational commitments … learned to say No more often … learned to choose more carefully when to say Yes … learned to be better at prioritizing."

She paused again, then continued.

"I learned to be, above all, at peace with God and with His control and direction of my plans and purposes. I became *happier*. I've never been an unhappy person, but only when the visions started did I surrender my life more fully to God and to His direction. I became fully at peace, Sarah.

"And happier than I've ever been.

"I am just so grateful."

Sunday evening, Andrews Air Force Base, Chapel-Belton guest unit

The Yahalomin, well rested, assembled once more in the Chapel-Belton guest unit. Eleanor and Marie attended playfully to Penelope, whose food and accoutrement had been placed in the Chapel-Belton unit from the start of the Yahalomin's stay at the base, that unit being considerably more spacious than the other units. And Penelope was almost as comfortable with Eleanor as with Marie, the little calico's human parent, since Penelope had had an extended stay in New York during the previous summer while all except Eleanor had gone to England to address that crisis in person.

Durham, who had just arrived at the base after a worship-and-work day in the city, was being introduced to Luke Manguson.

"Jim," Rebecca was saying, "this is my twin brother, Luke.

"He flew up last night from Naval Air Base Oceana and will be with us as long as we need him. He brought with him, incidentally, five more of our Barringtons Swords throwing knives. My supply was depleted during Sarah's ... incident."

Durham looked at Luke in wonder.

"You *both* can throw those things?"

Rebecca laughed.

"My brother taught me everything I know about that," she said. "He knew I'd never have the upper-body strength to fight the way he can, so he felt this would be the best way for me to perform non-lethal rescues of threatened people.

"And we were sure that, sooner or later, that kind of emergency would find us. As things turned out, we didn't have to wait long."

Durham nodded. "You led boarding parties with the Royal Navy, Lieutenant?"

Sarah, just joining the conversation, hit Durham playfully on the arm. "You *must* speak that word correctly, Jim," she said. "It's 'leftenant,' as anyone knows. I'm sure Luke is insulted that you Americanized his military rank."

The four talked together easily. Rebecca noticed that at one point, Durham reached over and took Sarah's hand in his. Sarah blushed happily.

In minutes, Belton called the session to order and everyone found chairs in the small living room or brought chairs in from the kitchen table.

"Ms. Clark or Father Jack," Belton said, "would one of you pray fer us?"

Rebecca did so, starting with the familiar, *"Father, be present ... be present ..."* and concluding with *"... please help us to understand Your will for us ..."*

Eyes turned to Belton.

"I need t' report," said Belton after the Amens had been murmured, "that I let th' NYPD guys know how t' reach me on the secure line here, an' one a' my buddies called this afternoon t' say that th' effort t' investigate th' congress-woman had gone nowhere fast.

"Once th' suspects that tried t' assault Eleanor on Monday, an' then set up surveillance at our place, broke down an' gave up Millicent Thomas' name, th' NYPD investigation process started up. It broke right back down when 'er New York attorneys said they'd make mincemeat a' th' investigation … 'cause th' detectives sweated those thugs so long … an' didn't formally place 'em under arrest … an' didn't record anything … ya know … th' lawyers would just claim th' thugs gave up Ms. Thomas' name just t' get themselves outta th' interrogation room."

Belton shrugged.

"We were never gonna get somethin' useful from those people, anyway," he said resignedly. "Ms. Thomas has got layers a' lawyers in both cities, an' gettin' at 'er through legal channels was always gonna be a long shot."

"What's next, then, Mr. Belton?" asked Marie after a moment.

Durham moved forward in his chair.

"Marie … everyone …" Durham began, "I spoke with Mr. Belton earlier, and he asked me to go over my Friday and Saturday activities with the group. So … I'll start with Friday morning, when I saw a newspaper article about three emissaries from Nicaragua, here in D.C., to lobby congress on behalf of the Contras.

"The photo accompanying the article showed three men. One face in that photo jumped out: his features were exactly those described by Sarah in her dream … the face that, she explained, appeared alongside that of Millicent Thomas. The man's name was given as Reynaldo Acosta."

Murmurs of wonder infused the small room, together with soft clapping in the direction of Sarah, who smiled shyly. "Jim showed me the newspaper photo Friday evening," she said, "and I've been … um … a little 'off' since then … until I had a chance to talk with Rebecca this afternoon about the whole thing … you know … visions … and what receiving 'message dreams' does to a person's life."

She looked at Rebecca.

"Rebecca put me together again."

Luke nodded. His sister was good at that … putting people back together when they felt as if they were coming apart. He was hugely proud of his twin.

Durham resumed his account.

"I switched into my running gear," he began, "and ran to the office, where I hoped Kazim Deng, our part-time data analyst, would be at work. I think everyone here … except Sarah … will remember this Sudanese gentleman from last summer?

"He drove the taxi that picked up Marie, Father Jack, and Sid's detective agency partner, Jaakov Adelman, from the Soviet Embassy, in the midst of that crisis. But he then found himself snatched and sequestered in an underground complex of the Soviet Embassy, until a man named Ivan Ivanovich — a Soviet Christian and, along with his family, a member of Father Jack's church — extricated him.

"When I got to the office Friday," continued Durham, "Kazim was there. Since he had become familiar with Rebekka Yahalomin and the 'message dreams' last summer, I was able quickly to make clear to him everything that was happening. I asked him if he would, as highest priority, research the connection between the two faces that Sarah had dreamed: the face of Millicent Thomas and the face of Reynaldo Acosta. Kazim said he'd put everything else aside, starting then."

"Jim," said Rebecca, "I should mention that last summer Mr. Deng confided to me that he had experienced what he called 'visitations' … When I asked him for an example, he said that, just days before he had met me … or had even *heard* of me … my image was transmitted to him in a dream, along with three commands … commands that were, to use his term, 'planted' in his brain.

"When I asked what the commands were, he said they were, '*Help this woman. Defeat her enemies. Have courage.*'

"He said that he didn't know what to do with that 'visitation' until he was being interrogated at the Soviet Embassy, and *all* the questions had to do with me. He inferred that I — identified by the interrogators as Rebecca Clark — must be the woman in his visitation. And then he met me … and he knew.

"I suspect, Jim," concluded Rebecca, "that your rush to involve Mr. Deng on Friday morning may have been a decision that had more layers … more levels … more height and more depth … than seemed apparent to you at the time. I am *very* pleased that you went immediately to him."

Durham was thoughtful, weighing Rebecca's comments. "Thank you, Rebecca," he said finally. "That explains aspects of that conversation that had mystified me. Kazim seemed to know why I was there before I had told him anything at all about … about *anything*."

Rebecca nodded.

"Yes," she said simply.

After a few more moments of thoughtful silence, Durham resumed his account of his weekend activities. "Well," he said, "that was Friday morning. Kazim worked all that day and into the night and, Saturday morning, he knocked on my apartment door at 6:00 a.m. He came in and we sat down at my kitchen table, drinking orange juice, and he gave his preliminary report.

"It seems that, with considerable help from Captain Johnstone, he was given access to Millicent Thomas' FBI file.

"When I expressed surprise that she even *had* an FBI file, he said her connections with various … um … questionable individuals and groups had led the FBI to start a file. Kazim also mentioned her enormous wealth, and that the FBI sometimes looks into an individual's networks for no other reason than that.

"In any case," Durham continued, "the deeper he got into the congresswoman's file, the more complex her networks appeared to be. Among them, Kazim explained to me on Saturday, was a communications and financial trail to Reynaldo Acosta, whom I'd discovered on Friday morning to be the other image in Sarah's dream.

"The complexity of the Thomas Acosta connection, Kazim said, was evident in monies that she divided equally between the Contras, for whom Acosta ostensibly works, and the Sandinistas, whom Millicent Thomas publicly supports.

"She appears to fund Acosta, in other words, to work for both sides."

Durham paused, thinking, then added, "There is one more shocker. It appears that Ms. Thomas also has connections, according to her FBI file, to a Middle Eastern faction … specifically, to a Muslim terrorist cell now operating in the U.S."

There were audible gasps.

After a moment, Eleanor turned to her husband.

"Sidney," she said, "tell them what you said to me before we left New York Monday night … about that very thing."

Belton straightened in his chair.

"I told Eleanor that my mind went back t' somethin' my agency partner — Jaakov — said last summer. I remembered some a' the documents he talked about.

"Some a' those documents, from th' Chaos people who were terrorizin' England, showed that they were th' U.K. branch of … an' these words stuck in my brain … 'a multifaceted, full-service, criminal organization whose origins were Middle Eastern.'

"Jaakov said we might be lookin' at one branch a' somethin' that was becomin' global … an' he thought CIA an' MI6 an' Mossad would need t' start lookin' at *Muslim* threats. He said they'd need eventually t' be lookin' at terrorism that had been imported with th' idea of spreadin' panic … panic an' distrust … through th' whole U.S. society … an' maybe through th' societies in *all* th' democracies."

The room fell silent for long minutes. When several began at length to turn their faces back to Durham, he resumed.

"Kazim explained to me that the FBI file traced links from the congress-woman to a Muslim cell that entered the U.S. a year ago. The FBI found large sums of money flowing from Ms. Thomas' financial holdings into that cell. They also found that the members of that cell had scattered and multiplied, so that the FBI no longer had a fix on any particular individual or even a recognizable group of individuals.

"The cell had multiplied and then melted into the fabric of U.S. society.

"And separately," Durham continued after a moment, "Kazim reported that Millicent Thomas will be announcing her intent to run for the U.S. Senate *next week*. The incumbent in her state decided not to stand for re-election, and candidates from each party have already announced they would seek that seat.

"This all suggests, Kazim and I thought, that she is on a fast track to the Senate, presumably so she might get consideration as the current vice president's running mate in two years, when he will, no doubt, become a candidate for president."

Durham took a deep breath, consulting his notes.

"Finally," Durham concluded, "the FBI file noted that there was evidence that the Muslim leadership that Ms. Thomas has been working with — no longer identifiable as individuals — intends, first, to help her get elected to the Senate, and second, to assist her efforts to become increasingly visible nationally.

"The file also mentioned that she is expected to give vocal support to liberation theology at this week's conference to highlight her appeal to Christians … Catholics and non-Catholics … in her home state of Louisiana … and beyond."

More silence, as the group tried to absorb the avalanche of information.

"Jim," said Marie finally, *"how* would Muslim terrorists try to help Ms. Thomas get elected to the Senate, and *how* would they support her efforts to become increasingly visible nationally? How would they do that?

"I don't get it."

Luke looked at Marie, whom he had known since the previous summer's Rebekka Yahalomin activity. He shook his head at her, smiling.

"Think, Marie," he said. "How do terrorists 'help' anybody do anything?"

She looked puzzled, but then her face fell.

"Oh, no!" she said, her eyes wide.

She covered her face with her hands.

"Oh, no!"

Luke, stricken by Marie's response, rose and stepped to her side. He placed a muscled hand gently on her shoulder. She had begun to cry.

Her husband rose, too, and knelt on her other side.

"Marie," Luke said, "I'm sorry. I could have introduced that idea differently. That was thoughtless of me. I was flippant … and callous. I am so sorry."

McGriff, still kneeling beside his wife, reached into her purse, on the floor beside her, and pulled out several tissues. She smiled at him through her tears.

Then, looking up at Luke, she said, "It's alright, Luke. It was just the shock of realizing that 'helping' could mean 'murdering.' I don't usually put those two things together in my mind. They're not supposed to go together."

"No," he agreed. "They're not."

He patted her shoulder again and, seeing her husband intended to stay at her side, returned to his seat.

Durham, having waited until Marie seemed settled, and seeing that McGriff remained beside her, then said, "Mr. Belton, Kazim told me that he was going to drive his taxi over here tonight … to the base … in case we wanted him to join us at some point. He's probably here by now … at the guardhouse. Everyone?"

The group unanimously endorsed the idea of Deng joining them, and Belton quickly placed a call to the guardhouse. In minutes, Deng was knocking at the door of Sid and Eleanor's guest unit.

Rebecca flung open the door and embraced the young Sudanese.

"Kazim!" she said delightedly. "I am *so glad* to see you again. Please come in and join us. Jim has just given us a summary of your weekend's work. I'm amazed at what you've been able to unearth in such a short time. We are so grateful, Kazim … really … this is astonishing!"

Deng looked down, embarrassed, but clearly pleased that his work was being praised so effusively … and by Rebecca Clark herself.

There were no more chairs in the small guest unit, but Rebecca insisted on giving him hers. Deng accepted reluctantly, and she stood behind him.

For the next 20 minutes, the conversation retraced the details of Durham's report of Deng's work with the FBI file. Deng occasionally offered minor corrections or additions to the overview Durham had provided. No significant new details emerged, and the group eventually agreed that there were three highest-impact findings.

First, that the congresswoman would announce her Senate candidacy that week, having endorsed liberation theology and the Sandinista government. Second, that a now-scattered Muslim terrorist group intended to "assist" her in winning the Senate seat, presumably by pressuring her opponents to withdraw by means of threats to their families, or worse. The terrorists then planned, it would appear, to participate in the senator's efforts to become nationally visible.

Third, that the connection between Millicent Thomas and Reynaldo Acosta — suggested by Sarah's early Thursday morning vision — appeared to be confirmed and, to an extent, explained, by the FBI file's careful delineation of the congresswoman's directives and funding, both of which were shown to flow steadily to Acosta, apparently in clandestine support for both sides in the Nicaraguan war.

Violence for violence's sake.

After a break, the group reassembled to discuss next steps. Rather quickly, however, the discussion dried up. No obvious next steps were apparent.

Faces gradually turned to Rebecca. She smiled.

"I know," she said. "We need a 'message dream' ... and as of now, we don't have one that can push us in the right direction. We'll just need to be patient. We know that we will receive direction when God deems that appropriate and necessary. The fact that we would *like* to have His direction in hand right now ... and we do not ... simply means that we should get a good night's sleep.

"Let's stop."

Kazim Deng, still seated in the chair previously occupied by Rebecca, turned and looked up at her, as she continued to stand near his seat. "Mrs. Clark," he said, "have we talked about Congresswoman Thomas' actions as a possible ploy to draw Rebekka Yahalomin ... and you, ma'am, specifically ... into range?"

Rebecca looked to Belton, her eyebrows raised questioningly.

"Yeah," he said to Deng. "Yeah ... sometime last week, some of us were meetin' at Marie an' Jack's office ... an' Eleanor said exactly that."

He looked to his wife.

"Kazim," said Eleanor, "I recalled that, last summer, there was clearly some of that thinking behind the Soviet menace we faced then. And, in the session just last week in Marie and Jack's office we discussed that idea again ... the idea that elimination of Rebekka Yahalomin might seem to our adversaries a necessary first step in reaching their ultimate goals.

"In addition," Eleanor continued, "Sidney wanted to know how those assaults on Sarah and me could have had anything to do with big-picture efforts by the congresswoman to sow widespread disruption in society.

"I suggested that Evil at that level does not discriminate. Assaults on individuals ... or the corruption of individuals ... or detonation of explosives that wound or kill hundreds ... it's all of one piece in the mind of the greatest Evil. However, I also at that time suggested that Evil at such levels ultimately wants the moral and spiritual destruction of every *individual* human being, and corruption of whole societies is nothing more than a means of corrupting the individuals in those societies.

"Father McGriff then added that this corresponded precisely to Christ's ultimate objective: saving every *individual* human being on the planet."

Deng replied immediately.

"So," he said, "doesn't that help us in thinking about next steps? Shouldn't we be thinking, for example, of tomorrow evening's event at the university as the adversary's opportunity to destroy or otherwise incapacitate Mrs. Clark herself ... and maybe all the rest of you here in this room? Shouldn't we be laying out plans to protect Dr. Chapel and ... well ... everybody who is part of the Yahalomin?"

"Rebecca," said McGriff after a moment, "are you planning to attend the event?"

"Oh, yes," she said. "I will be there ... absolutely."

This was met by a lengthy silence.

Finally, Belton spoke.

"Yeah, Kazim," he said. "We *should* be thinkin' about that."

He turned to Durham. "Jim," Belton continued, "can ya bring us some good maps a' th' university campus, includin' some good schematics of th' auditorium an' th' buildin' it's housed in, tomorrow mornin', first thing?"

Durham nodded and turned to Deng.

"Kazim," he said, "I'll pick you up at 7:00 a.m., okay? We'll head for the office and see what we can dig up. Mr. Belton ... we'll plan to be back here by 9:00 a.m.

"Everybody good with that?"

Everybody was.

Within minutes, the meeting broke up. Deng headed for his taxi. Durham headed for his truck after spending several minutes with Sarah in a lingering goodnight. Luke Manguson called after them as they approached their vehicles.

"Jim … Kazim …" he called. "Hang on a second."

They waited.

When Luke caught up, he said, "I'm concerned about your safety, Kazim. As soon as you leave the protection of the base, you're vulnerable."

He turned to Durham.

"I think, Jim, we ought to follow Kazim home. You're going to pick him up at 7:00 in the morning, but I'm concerned about tonight."

Durham nodded.

"Can you borrow Father Jack's Cherokee, Luke? We could follow Kazim singly to his house in Anacostia. If things look okay, I'll just continue across the river to my place and you can drive the Jeep back here."

"Right," said Luke. "Wait here for a couple of minutes. I'll go back and get my rig and Father Jack's car keys."

While they waited, Durham inquired of Deng if he had seen the "rig" that Luke had just mentioned.

"No," said Deng, "but I know that it's loaded with non-lethal stuff. You know … knives of various sizes, including those throwing knives he taught his sister to use, plus ropes and ties and, maybe, saps and the like. I'm told it's something he had made specifically for his own use some years back."

Durham nodded.

"Yes," Durham replied. "And I've learned about his reputation as a Royal Navy boarding party specialist. Non-lethal weaponry was his calling card."

"Easy to imagine," replied Deng. "I mean, just *look* at him. He has the build of … I don't know … a weight-lifting champion or some such thing … That chest and those biceps are absolutely ridiculous."

Luke jogged back to them, wearing his shoulder rig and carrying the keys to Jack McGriff's Jeep Cherokee. "Alright, gentlemen," he said. "Let's go."

The three-vehicle caravan, the taxi followed by the truck, and the truck by the Jeep, snaked its way north from the air base across the state line from Maryland into the District of Columbia. Deng maneuvered his taxi skillfully through the streets of Anacostia, stopping finally at his home, just a few blocks from the

Anacostia River, the waterway separating Anacostia from the city of Washington. Without needing to discuss arrangements, Durham and Manguson parked their vehicles a half-block from Deng's apartment building, both of them having extinguished their headlights before turning onto Deng's street. They parked on opposite sides of the street within view of the front door to the building.

As Deng walked into his building, two large men, wearing hooded sweatshirts despite the warmth of the night, emerged from the tall shrubbery lining the property. Their hoods were pulled low over their faces.

Deng ignored them.

They closed rapidly on him from behind.

Deng continued to ignore them.

CHAPTER SEVEN

"KAZIM DENG!" CALLED ONE OF THE MEN. "YOU STOP THERE."

Deng continued without slowing toward the building entrance. He climbed the three steps to the small landing, stopped, and turned to face the men. They followed him up the steps and stood close, towering over the 5-foot-9-inch Sudanese.

"You show us ID," said one, the words heavily accented.

"Show me *your* ID," replied Deng, taking a long step to one side.

The men turned their heads to follow him.

"What you doing?" one asked, puzzled.

"Moving out of the way," replied the Sudanese.

A razor-sharp, 12-inch Barringtons Swords competition throwing knife thudded heavily into the wooden front door to the building, having arrowed through the narrow space between the two would-be assailants. The two men froze.

"Drop your hands to your sides. Turn to face us," ordered Durham.

The men glanced at each other, then did as ordered. They found themselves facing two men, one as tall as they, but slender, and the other shorter than they, but massively muscled. The latter held a second throwing knife in his hand, while the former held up a D.C. police badge.

Both wore shoulder holsters, though only the policeman's holster appeared to hold a firearm. The other's holster seemed to hold a bewildering array of knives, ropes, ties, and other assault-and-restraint implements.

"As the young man was saying," continued Durham, "we will need to see your identification. Remove your IDs slowly. My associate can throw that knife into whatever part of your body he chooses. So be careful, gentlemen."

Deng, thoroughly familiar with police procedure after nearly three years as a part-time analyst for the department, stepped around the men, accepted their IDs, and handed them to Durham. Deng then removed a small pad and pen from a pocket in his summer-weight jacket and recorded the contact information for each man, as Durham read the information slowly to him. Deng then returned the IDs to their owners.

"Who employs you?" asked Durham.

No response.

"Inform the congresswoman that we have your names and contact information," said Durham. "Tell her she will need to be more careful in her efforts to intimate Mr. Deng and others, like me, who work in the police department."

Durham smiled. "Go home," he said.

The two would-be assailants turned and walked back in the direction from which they had approached. Durham watched them go, then turned to Deng.

"Kazim," he said, "why don't you go in and pack for a week at my apartment? We may be working together on more than just tomorrow morning's assignment. Millicent Thomas is not going to send her thugs after a D.C. detective. The whole world would come down on her head.

"You'll be safer at my place, and the two of us can be more efficient."

In minutes, Durham had pulled away in his truck with Deng in his taxi following. Luke had retrieved his throwing knife from the thick wooden door, returned to McGriff's Jeep, and headed back toward Andrews. The evening's work was done.

Soon it would be Monday, a day that promised to be eventful.

Sunday night/Monday morning, 30 minutes past midnight,
Andrews Air Force Base

Rebecca was startled into wakefulness by the rare, yet always unmistakable, call from sleep to mental alertness, coupled with the surge of inner heat that produced whole-body perspiration almost instantly.

Although her eyes had opened in response to the paired stimuli of mental shock and physical heat, she closed them again in practiced preparation to "watch" the impending vision and to prepare to recall and recite every detail to her brother, sleeping in the guest unit next to hers. The vision rapidly materialized, with its usual bright contrasts and clear borders. Rebecca was presented with a view from the stage of a large auditorium. The auditorium was distinguished from any others she had seen both by the elaborate art on walls and ceiling and by a unique balcony design.

The envisioned balcony appeared to wrap entirely around the main floor's seating area, and to wrap so completely that the extreme wings of the balcony reached almost to the stage itself. An audience member seated at the extreme end of either wing would be almost over the edge of the stage, and only a few feet above it.

She studied the scene, concentrating not only on the dramatic art and the encompassing balcony, but also on an effort to estimate the seating capacity of the venue. She was interrupted in this last, however, by the emergence of an envisioned instrument that, at first, she could not identify. As the image became larger and clearer, now obscuring her view of the auditorium, she saw that it was a monocular … the size of one half of a pair of high-quality, military binoculars. The exterior surface of the instrument appeared to her dreaming mind as black, grainy, and somehow modified in an indeterminate fashion to give the device more than one function.

And as the vision began to fade, the dreamed monocular appeared to rotate slowly so that, rather than presenting itself in its longitudinal aspect, the objective lens — the end opposite the eyepiece — turned fully toward her, so that she was then staring into the "wrong" end of the instrument. And what she saw was not a lens.

She saw the muzzle of a gun.

The vision then left her. This vision had seemed to Rebecca to persist for longer than most of her dreams, despite the apparent simplicity of the images. And as usual, she was now drenched in perspiration. Her thick, black tresses were as wet and confused as if she had just emerged from swimming, as was her nightgown … her roommate's nightgown. And she was, also as usual, thoroughly enervated. She found it a struggle just to sit up in her bed and swing her feet to the floor.

Nonetheless, Rebecca was absolutely determined to walk to the adjacent room to awaken her brother and to narrate for him the details of the vision. She could sleep later, she told herself.

But before she could rise to her feet, she realized that her roommate was dreaming, too. Sarah was struggling in her sleep, appearing to concentrate on something that Rebecca could not see … something only the dreamer herself could perceive. She watched the young woman, fascinated.

Finally, Rebecca lay down again on her side, facing Sarah … and waited.

Two minutes later, Sarah awoke. The first thing she realized was that she was drenched in her own sweat. Her beyond shoulder-length, auburn curls were damp all through, and her nightgown and sheets were soaked. Her bare arms glistened.

She turned her head and saw that her roommate, lying on her side on her own bed, was looking straight at her. She saw Rebecca stand quickly and lean over her bed, taking Sarah's sweaty hand in her own equally sweaty hand.

"Sarah," said Rebecca, "I know you're exhausted … so am I, having just been sent my own message … but we need to deliver our reports right away. No delay.

"I'll go next door and get Luke awake. I'm thinking you probably want to report to Dr. Chapel, since she heard your first report … yes?"

Sarah thought about this.

"Can I not report to you, Rebecca?" she asked.

"No," Rebecca answered. "That would muddle my brain. I need to get to Luke right now, without hearing anything else, Sarah. You can choose anyone else here, but I'd think you'd want to talk again to Eleanor."

Both women quickly dried off, towel-dried their disordered hair, and donned their workout clothes, all without further conversation. Rebecca went next door, rapped softly on Luke's door, and found him awake, alert, and ready to listen. Luke was always a light sleeper and had heard the women's muffled voices through the thin wall separating their units. He was dressed and ready when his sister knocked.

Rebecca took five minutes to report and five more minutes to hear Luke's near-verbatim summary. She then strode back to her unit and lay down fully clothed on her bed, avoiding the damp center spot where she had lain while she dreamed.

As often before under the circumstances, she then fell into an exhausted sleep in less time than it took her to give her report to her brother.

Meanwhile, Sarah walked softly to Eleanor and Sid's unit and began knocking on their door. They were both sound sleepers. The time was not yet 1:00 a.m.

Several minutes passed before Eleanor, her unbound gray hair falling below her shoulders, opened the door for Sarah. Despite the hour, Eleanor's blue-green eyes were wide and inquisitive.

"Another dream, dear?" she said.

"Yes … I'm sorry."

"Don't be silly, Sarah … this is just what we need.

"Please come in. Sit while I start the coffee."

She scurried away while Sarah sat and composed herself.

In minutes, the two women were sipping fresh coffee. Eleanor Chapel, clad in her "ratty" bathrobe, was on high alert, a pen in one hand and a notepad on her lap.

"Go!" she said simply.

"Dr. Chapel," Sarah began, "Rebecca dreamed, too … but she is reporting to her brother. She didn't want to hear my report until that was done."

"No, dear," replied Eleanor. "That would be risky … to hear about someone else's vision prior to completing the report of one's own. We're doing this right."

Sarah nodded and took a moment to organize her thoughts.

"This vision of mine," Sarah began, "started with the image of a house … a very large, three-story house … surrounded by woods … but not completely isolated. I sensed there were other homes around, just not close by.

"The house itself had several unusual features, Dr. Chapel. The most prominent feature in my dream was a large cupola, centered along the roofline, looking sort of like an observation post on a fort … as I imagine a fort might look. In addition, there were several … I'm not sure how many … gables that faced the roadway, which was where I 'stood' in my dream. There was also a three-car garage extending to the right of the house itself, and a driveway that seemed to curve into the garage from somewhere to the right of my dreamed position on the roadway."

Sarah paused in her narration while the older woman wrote rapidly on her notepad. At length, Eleanor looked up and nodded.

"Go on, dear," she said.

"Then," continued Sarah, "I was somehow taken inside … and to the rear of the house, on the main floor … and placed in what seemed to be a personal library … or maybe a study … with a very large, rectangular wooden desk situated against the far wall, near a single window, which overlooked expansive grounds. The vision gradually narrowed its focus to a thin, dark green binder in the center of the desk.

"At first, although I could see that there were words printed on the cover of the binder, they were indistinct … blurry. But even though I was asleep, I somehow knew that it was necessary for me to read those words. So, I fought … somehow, I fought … and I fought … and I fought … to read those words.

"And, finally … my perspective was slowly brought closer and closer to the binder, and at last I was able to decipher the words. Although the binder itself was dark green and the words were printed in black … not much contrast there … my perspective was eventually so close to the binder that I could read what it said.

"There were four words: Thomas-Acosta-Hasan Pact.

"And that was all, Dr. Chapel," Sarah concluded. "The dream faded immediately, as soon as I was shown the binder and its label: Thomas-Acosta-Hasan Pact. Just those four words … and then I found myself awake.

"There was nothing else."

Eleanor took a moment to complete her notes, then looked up.

"Is there anything else I should know, Sarah? Anything before or after the dream that might provide additional context?"

Sarah thought for a moment, then shook her head.

"Nothing helpful, I think," she replied.

"When I finally did awaken," she added, "Rebecca was lying on her side, on her bed, looking right at me. She had been waiting for me to finish. She said the onset of her vision awakened her immediately, so that she was fully awake during her vision. But my entire vision was given while I slept."

Eleanor nodded, then gestured at the younger woman's workout clothing.

"You've changed your clothes," she observed.

"Yes," replied Sarah. "We were both soaking wet … *drenched.*

"We hung our nightgowns — actually, they're both mine — from the shower-curtain rod, just as if they were bathing suits. We *had* to change clothes."

Monday, 5:00 a.m., Andrews Air Force Base, Chapel-Belton guest unit

Belton convened the scheduled 9:00 a.m. meeting four hours early. The change meant that Durham and Deng had been forced to race to the precinct office in the middle of the night to complete their assignment: collecting maps and building schematics of the Georgetown University campus.

The change had also meant that the two visioners had less rest than would have been ideal following their draining experiences shortly after midnight, but they were both present and doggedly alert. Belton began by asking Father

McGriff for a prayer, which he then delivered with obvious emotion, knowing that the first crisis — perhaps of many crises to come — was upon them.

He began.

"Father, be present … be present …

"Make Thy Holy Spirit fully a part of each one of us … every single one of us … so fully a part of us that we feel Thy hand and Thy direction in every thought and in every word that we may choose to form in this session.

"Give us Thy wisdom … Thy courage … Thy strength to go face-to-face with the Enemy … and, with Thy assistance, to prevail …

"Father, be present … be present …

"Amen."

The responsive Amens echoed through the small living room. All looked then to Belton, who turned to his wife. "Eleanor, you were up in th' middle a' th' night with Miss Wilson … would ya go ahead an' lead us along?"

The Old Testament scholar nodded and shifted the lightweight burden of Penelope to the little calico's actual human parent, Marie, who happily accepted the sleepy feline. Penelope curled into Marie's lap and fell quickly asleep.

Eleanor began.

"I was asked by Sarah to hear her vision, and I did so, taking notes, a little before 1:00 a.m. today. While Sarah was reporting to me, Rebecca was reporting her concurrent vision to her brother. Although I obviously did not hear that report, Luke has told me that his sister's vision appears to apply specifically to an auditorium, presumably the one in which tonight's session at the university will be held.

"Sarah's vision, on the other hand, seems to me to depict a setting and a document that may demand our immediate attention, which is what led Sidney to decide to change our 9:00 a.m. session to this 5:00 a.m. hour. That suggests to me that we should deal with Sarah's vision before Rebecca's.

"Does anyone disagree?"

Hearing no disagreement, she turned to Sarah Wilson.

"Sarah … please?" she said.

With Eleanor following along in her notes, Sarah proceeded to relate her vision to the group, emphasizing equally the woodsy setting, the unusual characteristics of the featured house, the expansive grounds to the rear of the structure, and the specifics of the green binder and its revealing title: Thomas-Acosta-Hasan Pact. Despite the fact that Durham was sitting close beside her, meaning that she was not able to look directly at him while she spoke, she felt him tense when she described the structure … its cupola … its gables … its three-car garage and swooping driveway.

When she finished, she turned to him.

"Jim," she said, "did you recognize the house?"

He grinned widely.

"That's the congresswoman's home," he said. "That's where Millicent Thomas has lived for at least three years. That's when I started as a patrolman with the D.C. police. The Chevy Chase and Rock Creek Park areas were part of my regular patrol beat in those first years with the force. There's no other house even remotely like that in D.C. that I've ever even heard of, and I don't know where you'd find a setting like that one anywhere else in the district."

"And," added Jack McGriff, "given the Millicent Thomas-focused thrust of everything that has been researched or reported — or dreamed — thus far, it's certainly no surprise that Sarah's dream would feature the congresswoman's home."

He looked at Sarah.

"You've certainly been called, Sarah," he said, "and richly blessed. I'm so glad you agreed to come to Washington to be part of what Marie and I are doing … and, obviously … much more than what the two of us are doing.

"You've been called to fill a role in a drama that now looks as though it may encompass half the globe!"

Sarah beamed.

By unspoken consent, silence descended on the group. All understood by now that after receiving a revelation of such magnitude, time — time spent in silence — was needed for each person to process the new information, to integrate the new data with what was already known, to begin to form conclusions … and to consider next steps. At length, Marie turned to Eleanor.

"Eleanor," she said, "you mentioned that it was Sarah's vision that led your husband to move our 9 o'clock session to now. What were you two thinking?"

Eleanor looked to her husband, and he responded to the question.

"We thought," Belton began, "we'd need t' get into Ms. Thomas' house this mornin', while she's at th' university speakin' about liberation theology, so we could get a look at that binder. We figured we'd need t' get into that woman's study with my document camera t' get photos of every page that's in th' 'pact' that Sarah saw.

"Sounded t' me like there aren't many pages. Sarah said it looked thin an' I think that, while Ms. Thomas is at th' university doin' 'er talk this mornin', 'er house is gonna be clear, an' we oughta be able t' lift those document pages right into th' camera."

"But, Mr. Belton," objected Durham quickly, "what do you mean when you say that the congresswoman's house is going to be clear and that we should be able to get into her study? If you're thinking about breaking and entering, sir, I need to get out of this room and away from any conversations about that.

"I'm a detective in the District of Columbia, Mr. Belton. I not only can't be involved in any such action, I can't even *know* of any such action."

Durham was angry.

Belton, phlegmatic as usual in the face of anger, responded.

"Ya gotta understand, son," he said, "that when we get special messages sent t' us, we don't have a choice. We hafta act on th' visions, an' we hafta act without any sorta delay. We hafta move, an' we hafta move *now*."

Rebecca stood quickly and moved across the small room to Durham's chair. She knelt slowly in front of him, her gray eyes soft with understanding.

Durham was stunned by her movement … stunned that Rebecca Clark would actually kneel in front of him. And he was suddenly ashamed that he had objected to something that must, he now thought, have been an obvious course of action to everyone in the room … to everyone except himself.

His face turned red.

Rebecca reached out and touched his knee with her fingertips.

"Jim," she said softly, "you are not wrong. But neither is Mr. Belton.

"It seems we should photograph the pages in the pact, and we should do it immediately. Scripture is filled with examples of Old and New Testament people who hesitated to take action upon receiving a divine message. Obedience … and without hesitation … is the divine expectation in response to any such message.

"Such messages *supersede* humanity's rules, regulations, laws.

"But that doesn't mean," she continued, "that *you*, Jim, need to be engaged in the actions that we will undertake this morning. I suggest that you — and Kazim, too, if he feels the same professional constraints that you obviously do — get in your truck, with your pager, and let us approach the problem however we think we should. When our discussion is finished, we'll buzz your pager, and you and Kazim can come back into the room, if you think it appropriate.

"Then we can discuss my dream … my vision of the auditorium … and you and Kazim can help us with the campus maps and schematics you've pulled together overnight. Mr. Belton has your pager number, yes?"

Durham nodded, silent. He was filled with conflicting thoughts, including the one in which he inwardly called himself a coward, and in front of the woman with whom he was falling in love. At that moment, that very woman placed her hand on the same knee occupied by Rebecca's fingertips, and said, "Jim … go. You need to maintain your professional integrity. Rebecca's suggestion is the right one.

"Go, Jim."

He rose from his chair and left the room, Deng close behind him. The group heard the front door close. They refocused quickly.

Belton looked at Luke.

"This is where we need yer wife's tech talents, Lieutenant," he said. "She'd be able t' get us past th' alarm systems in that house."

Luke smiled.

"No need to deal with the alarm system in the congresswoman's home, Sid," he said. "Kory has already prepped me for this morning's work. She foresaw that we might need to do a B & E, just as she herself did last summer at the bad guys' HQ near Cambridge. I should be able to get into that room easily."

"How, Luke?" asked Sarah.

"I travel with a small toolbox, Sarah," he replied, "in addition to the ready-satchel and the shoulder holster that contains my knives and ties. Kory made sure, when I left the ISP office — the security firm that she and I and Rebecca's husband work for — that my toolbox included the ISP-issued building-entry tools, including the circular glass-cutting device, the rubber hammer, and the attached suction cup that will allow me to pull the circle of glass toward me after the cutting is done.

"I'll then drop the circle of glass to the ground, reach through the aperture, and flip the window lock. It's all low-tech, but sometimes low-tech is best.

"Sid has palm-sized document cameras; I'll take one of those. And I'll wake up the base logistics officer — the lieutenant colonel who has taken such good care of us — and ask him for his best military map of the Rock Creek Park area, one that includes the Chevy Chase neighborhood. I have already looked at one map, but it's just a visitor's map of the city. I need detail. I'll want to approach the house from the rear, where Sarah pictured the room, so I'll need to see the access points from that direction."

He looked to his sister.

"Rebecca," he said, "I'll need you to act as close support. We'll take Jack's Cherokee — if that's okay, Jack — and we'll want to get started soon. We'll be dealing with city traffic during Washington's morning rush hour.

"If we leave here at 0630," Luke continued, "we can be parked in one of that area's commuter lots by 0730 or 0745. We can be confident that Ms. Thomas will need to leave home by 0815, at the latest, to be at the university and ready to participate in her session by the scheduled 0900 start time. So, using 0900 as the preferred 'safe entry' time, we should have more than an hour, if we need it, to negotiate those wooded areas, do some reconnaissance, and move up close to the structure. The entry itself, and the photography, shouldn't take more than 15 minutes."

He turned to Belton.

"Sid," he said, "since the lieutenant colonel understands that this is *your* outfit, would you wake him up and secure that map for us?"

Belton was already struggling to his feet, the cane providing the necessary leverage. "Got it," he said.

Luke addressed the group.

"Since my sister and I are the only ones who know the details of her overnight vision of the auditorium, there is nothing any of you can do now, by way of planning for tonight. I'd suggest everyone try to get some sleep ... or at least some rest. We hope to be back here by 1030 hours this morning, but that's more than four hours away.

"Rebecca, I'll get my gear now, while you get your ready-satchel and anything else you'll need for this. Sound okay?"

"Yes," she replied as she rose from her chair.

"Wait!" said McGriff sharply. "Everyone ... just wait."

Rarely had those present heard McGriff speak peremptorily.

Rebecca stopped. Belton stopped. Faces turned to McGriff.

He stood. Rebecca sat. Belton sat.

McGriff circled his chair, stood behind it, placed his hands on the chair back, and leaned on the chair thoughtfully, his eyes down. He looked up.

"Are we *certain* that Sarah's vision implies this kind of home invasion?" he asked. "Rebecca, you talked about obedience to divine messages ... immediate acts of obedience ... and you're correct, of course. But, Rebecca, how is Sarah's vision a directive to which we must respond at all? She simply envisioned Millicent Thomas' home and a document of interest to us.

"I don't see a directive there.

"And, aside from that, I must say that this seems quite different from breaking into the Soviets' Cambridge headquarters house last summer … something you mentioned a few minutes ago, Luke. The USSR is the avowed enemy of the U.S. That struck me, at the time, as being, as we say, in the national interest."

He turned his face to Sarah.

"Sarah," he said, "you were the recipient of the vision. Do you think your vision implies this kind of forcible entry into Millicent Thomas' home?"

She looked down at her hands.

"I'm so new at this," she replied. "And Rebecca and Luke and Mr. Belton and Dr. Chapel seem so certain that this is the right thing …"

"Actually," Eleanor interrupted, "I am anything *but* certain, Sarah, that this is what your vision implies for us. I'm discomfited by the forced entry idea."

"As am I," added Marie.

The room once more fell silent.

McGriff turned to Rebecca.

"Rebecca," he said, "do you feel confident that this is what we must do, in response to Sarah's vision? Have you any doubts about this course of action?"

"Yes, and yes," she said without hesitation.

"Yes … I feel confident that this is the action implied … and yes … I have doubts about this action. You're right, Father McGriff, that this is different from other forced entries we have executed over the years.

"When I think," Rebecca continued, "of the variety in our past 'directives,' I think that highest priority … lowest levels of doubt … has always gone to outright rescues of people. For example, using my knives last week to prevent Sarah from being kidnapped, and to save her from whatever might have befallen her once she had been taken … or last summer, using my knives to keep you, Father, and Marie from being executed by that KGB agent and his colleagues. There was highest priority and lowest doubt about those kinds of interventions.

"And those also had the strongest flavor of our Rebekka Yahalomin ruling concept — *'the blueprint of the universe: my life for yours'* — especially last summer's KGB-defying intervention, since Luke and I could easily have been killed during that confrontation. That was an example of the most obvious, most compelling type of 'case for intervention' … for stopping evil exactly where we found it.

"This certainly does not have that flavor, Father," Rebecca concluded, "but I still, despite that, think that a forced entry is implied by what was sent to Sarah.

"I just don't have certainty."

McGriff turned to two of the other women.

"Eleanor? Marie?" he inquired.

"The *fact* of the vision," said Eleanor, "inclines me to endorse the action Luke has outlined. But, as Rebecca just said, this is nothing like other interventions in which she and Luke ... and Jaakov ... and Sidney ... have been compelled to action in order to prevent real injury, or torture, or death.

"This has nothing of that taste.

"And," she continued, "I think we need to acknowledge that the message ... the whole, complete message ... *could* simply be the fact of a linkage among these three people: Thomas; Acosta; Hasan. It's possible that we are not being asked, or directed, to do anything at all. The message may simply be that these people are linked, and that we need to be conscious of the fact that they are working together.

"And so, Father, I'm thoroughly ambivalent."

"As am I," added Marie. "And, aside from my uncertainty about an actual directive we are being given ... aside from that ... I fear that, even though Ms. Thomas will be elsewhere at 9:00 a.m., she may have security in place at her house ... not merely a state-of-the-art alarm system.

"Luke told us last night about two very large, armed men who had apparently planned to do something to Kazim when he arrived home after leaving here. Those two men could very well be guarding Ms. Thomas' house.

"I'm worried, Jack," concluded Marie. "I'm worried about whether we are, in fact, being directed to break into Ms. Thomas' home — completely aside from the illegality of it all — and I'm worried about what may happen to Luke and Rebecca if they do. If there were a hostage there, it would be different ...

"There isn't. There is no hostage."

Another silence ensued.

Finally, Luke spoke.

"We need to go, Rebecca," he said. "Unless Sidney, as our *de facto* commanding officer, orders cancellation ... we need to get on the road now."

All turned to Belton. He did not hesitate.

"Th' reason Rebecca an' Luke carry non-lethal weapons is so that, if they hafta fight, they'll leave th' dirtbags in one piece ... or, at least, still breathin' ... An' I think what Luke outlined is th' best guess we got, as t' what we oughta do."

He nodded at Rebecca and at Luke.

"You two ... get goin'," he said.

Monday 7:45 a.m., Chevy Chase, Washington, D.C.

Rebecca, having maneuvered McGriff's Jeep across the city through Monday morning traffic, parked the vehicle in a lot set aside for daily commuters. Luke pulled out the map Belton had secured from the base logistics officer to confirm the direction in which they would need to trek in the next 45 to 60 minutes.

Rebecca wore her dark-blue tennis warm-ups, black tennis shoes, and dark-blue, billed cap. As always when prepared for action, she had drawn her jet-black hair into a ponytail and passed it through the slit in the back of her cap.

Luke was dressed in full-body camouflage and combat boots. His custom-designed shoulder holster was in place, and his array of knives, both conventional and competition, protruded menacingly from their slots in the holster.

Rebecca carried her ready-satchel, stocked with, beyond its usual contents, Belton's palm-sized document camera, two Barringtons Swords throwing knives, a pair of ISP-issued image-stabilized binoculars, and the ISP-issued building-entry window-cutting device that Luke had transferred to her from his toolbox.

She slung the satchel's shoulder strap over her head and across her chest, making it secure for the difficult hike through the area's woods and underbrush. Their progress was as rapid as could be expected, but they found, upon emerging from the thicket of vegetation, that they were, according to the map, at least a quarter-mile east of the congresswoman's home.

They re-entered the woods, moved the necessary distance west, and emerged in good position at 8:40 a.m. Rebecca pulled the binoculars from her satchel and passed them over to her brother.

Luke lay down just inside the tree line and began to study the rear of Millicent Thomas' home and the terrain separating himself and Rebecca from what appeared to be the most likely window. Fifteen minutes later, without needing to speak, the two of them moved forward, Luke in front and Rebecca just behind.

Upon reaching the structure, again without needing to talk, Luke turned, bent his knees, and formed a stirrup with his hands. Rebecca placed one foot in the stirrup, Luke straightened his legs to lift her higher, and Rebecca, keeping her face away from the window itself, steadied herself with her hands against the wall of the house.

She looked down at Luke, who seemed to be holding her effortlessly.

"Okay, Luke?" she asked.

"I'm good," he replied.

She moved her head slightly, so she could see into the room that, they hoped, would be Millicent Thomas' study. It was not.

Rebecca dismounted and they moved to a different window, but found that it, too, provided a view into a room other than the congresswoman's study. That left but one window. A quick look inside showed what they were looking for.

The siblings then reversed their positions.

Rebecca, strong enough to hold her brother's weight for the 45 seconds required, though not longer, provided the stirrup while Luke worked the window-cutting device. Standing in her cupped hands, he applied the device to the glass.

Using the rubber mallet to tap the cutting surface hard enough to gain penetration of the glass, he pulled the circular section back to himself by means of the suction cup that was part of the device. Then he turned, dropped the whole array to the ground behind his sister, and reached through the opening to pop the window latch. Finally, he lifted the window and stepped from Rebecca's hands to the ground.

Without discussion, they immediately knelt in the soft grass, while Rebecca prayed softly, and Luke silently joined her in prayer.

Father, be present … be present …

Be present, Father, while we do our best to respond to Your message as given to Sarah, our sister in Christ …

Be present, Father, while we do our best to carry out the implications of Your directive to us …

Keep us safe, Father, and make it so that we do not injure terribly any adversaries we may encounter …

Help us and protect us, Father …

We pray in the name of Thy Son, the Lord Jesus …

Amen.

Without words or signal, they again reversed positions, Luke providing the stirrup while Rebecca stood and, with an upward boost from Luke's hands, pushed herself headfirst into the room. Luke, with his enormous upper-body strength, simply grasped the windowsill and, doing a hands-reversed pull-up, hoisted himself up and, also headfirst, entered the congresswoman's study.

Rebecca already had the document camera in her hands and was standing over the green binder: Thomas-Acosta-Hasan Pact. She snapped a photo of the cover, then proceeded to photograph each page of the slender document.

Consistent with Sarah's vision, the document contained a mere six pages. Rebecca noted, as she glanced at each page, that the document was not a plan. It simply stated the terms of an agreement among the three parties.

She did pause long enough to read the opening Purpose Statement. The statement was both brief and explicit.

Purpose Statement

The purpose of this three-person alliance is to facilitate the political rise of Millicent Thomas, congresswoman, first to the position of junior senator from Louisiana, and second to the position of vice president of the United States.

Once the vice presidency has been achieved, a new pact will be developed.

Pursuant to these objectives, Millicent Thomas will supply the other two parties to this agreement with all financial support — and, where needed, all political support — required to achieve success.

Beyond the financial support expressly required to achieve, first, election to the U.S. Senate, and second, selection as her party's presidential nominee's running mate, both Acosta and Hasan will receive from Thomas regular payments to their personal accounts equal to that of a U.S. senator's salary. Bonus payments may be made at the discretion of Thomas.

While Rebecca worked the camera, Luke moved directly to a four-drawer file cabinet that stood in one corner of the room. He systematically went through each drawer, dropping file folders randomly onto the floor and rearranging those that remained in their drawer. His objective was to create the impression of an intruder's attempt to find something specific in the congresswoman's files. He studiously avoided anything on her desk, including the green binder Rebecca had photographed.

Since the 8-inch-diameter hole in the window would be obvious, Luke wanted Millicent Thomas to conduct a search of the room, trying to determine what had been taken. She would need no more than 15 minutes to find that nothing was missing, that nothing was broken, and that her desktop computer had not been violated.

Apparently, then, merely a failed attempt at document theft.

Suddenly, as the twins moved toward the window to begin their withdrawal, the door to the study was flung open with a thunderous crash and two enormous men burst into the room, both with weapons drawn. Luke and Rebecca wheeled to face the men, their hands at their sides in practiced response to threat.

To the gunmen, the twins appeared preternaturally calm, a confusing response and one that was immediately disconcerting to them. They glanced at each other uncertainly. Then, turning back again to the twins, one said in heavily accented English, "Give me purse … now."

Rebecca smiled agreeably and pulled off the ready-satchel's strap, then stepped forward to hand the satchel to the one who had demanded it. He glanced again at his partner, holstered his Glock 9mm, and accepted the "purse" from the woman. He placed it on the floor and bent to examine the contents. After a moment, he seized the document camera and held it up.

"What this?" he said to her.

"That is a camera," she said simply, smiling and relaxed.

He looked at the camera, apparently weighing his response.

"I keep this," he said finally.

"No," she said softly. "I'll need to take that with me.

"Please," she added, stepping forward again, her hand outstretched.

He laughed and stood up.

"You crazy, woman," he said.

Still smiling, she stepped within arm's length and snatched the camera from the man's meaty paw. In another instant she had opened the back of the instrument and flipped the roll of film out, exposing its images to light and immediately rendering every photo she had taken useless. Not a single image would survive the exposure.

But the gunman, recovering, was lightning quick, surprisingly so for a man of such proportions. He outweighed the woman by 150 pounds.

His thick hand cuffed her with such force that she fell, spinning, to the floor. Blood flowed from her split lower lip. The second gunman, offended that his partner would strike a woman, stared at Rebecca as she rolled across the floor. His distracted gaze provided Luke the opening he needed to leap forward and redirect the barrel of the gun. The gunman's trigger finger contracted reflexively, and the resulting explosion drove a 9mm round into the wall above Millicent Thomas' desk, its impact dislodging a 36-by-48-inch gold-framed photo of the U.S. Capitol building. The heavy picture and frame crashed down, glass shattering, onto the green binder.

Having deflected the shot, Luke then forced the weapon down, twisting it violently out of the gunman's hand, then glancing down quickly to flip its safety switch into place. In that instant, the first gunman launched a thundering right hand to the side of Luke's face. Stunned, Luke fumbled the Glock to the floor as he staggered backward. The gun tumbled harmlessly out of the way as the gunman's next punch, a left cross, crashed into Luke's jaw, driving him back against the wall.

The two gunmen, now fully engaged, converged swiftly on their victim, their fists assailing him from two angles. Luke had no realistic chance to counter the two huge bodies as they pressed upon him, nor could he deflect or dodge the fists that pounded into his face from divergent angles. He sank to the floor, losing consciousness.

The first gunman, his firearm still holstered after his examination of Rebecca's satchel, suddenly screamed from the searing pain of a 12-inch Barringtons Swords throwing knife as it shredded skin, fat, and muscle, driving itself into his body inches below the left shoulder blade and producing hairline fractures in two of the smaller ribs as they radiated out from the vertebral column.

Confused, terrified, screaming, the gunman sank ponderously to his knees beside the semi-conscious Luke. Beginning then to moan piteously, the gunman reached hopelessly over his shoulder for the knife. Meanwhile, his partner, his gun still on the floor where Luke had dropped it when the first gunman struck, looked back in surprise and fear toward the knife thrower.

He saw that she was already positioned to hurl a second knife.

He held up his hands, backing away, palms toward her. Rebecca, blood flowing freely from her lip, the second knife still in her right hand, raced to the still-kneeling victim of her first throw and, reaching over his shoulder, pulled the man's Glock 9mm from his shoulder holster. She flipped on its safety switch with her left thumb, and, without turning her head, flung the gun through the open window.

She then picked up the Glock that Luke had ripped away from the second gunman, flipped it through the window also, and, her second throwing knife still in her right hand, pulled her semi-conscious brother to his feet with her left and pushed him toward the window. He haltingly exited the window while she stepped to her satchel, picked it up left-handed, and tossed it out the window where it landed beside the two handguns, the glass-cutting device, and her struggling brother.

Rebecca paused, took one last look at the two men, then gestured to the unwounded gunman, indicating with her hand that he should attend to his groaning partner. He nodded to her, his eyes wide.

"Dial 9-1-1 from the phone on this desk," she ordered. "Get an ambulance on its way now. Do not try to remove the knife yourself."

The man stood, staring at her dumbly.

"Move!"

He did.

Rebecca, the second knife still in her right hand, turned, extended her left leg fully through the open window, balanced herself briefly on the sill, and whipped her trail leg through in a classic hurdler's motion. She landed firmly on both feet and quickly picked up and opened her satchel.

She sheathed her knife, then picked up both handguns and the building-entry device, its extracted, 10-inch circle of windowpane still attached, and pressed everything into the satchel. She zipped the satchel, placed the long strap over her head and across her chest, and turned again to her brother.

Luke was now standing unsteadily, his face already beginning to discolor and swell from the pummeling he had received. She stepped to him, took his hand in hers, and led him at a trot toward the woods. As they entered the thicket, Rebecca turned and looked back toward the house. The unwounded gunman stood at the window, telephone in hand, watching them go. She turned away and continued, Luke trailing.

As the twins worked their way through the woods and underbrush toward the lot where they had parked the Jeep, Rebecca prayed her thanksgiving to God that He had brought them through such a horrific collision with two of Evil's more formidable foot soldiers. She prayed, as well, for her brother, that he might recover fully and swiftly from the beating he had received.

And finally, she prayed for the wounded man she had left behind, that he might recover, also fully and swiftly, from the knife wound that she had, in desperation, with her brother's life appearing to hang in the balance, inflicted upon him.

She shook her head.

This was not what she had wanted.

CHAPTER EIGHT

Monday, noon, Andrews Air Force Base, Chapel-Belton guest unit

THE YAHALOMIN, SANS DURHAM AND DENG, WHO HAD AGAIN been asked to wait in Durham's truck until paged, had been waiting since 11:00 a.m. for the twins to return, so that they could hear the report of that morning's incursion, followed by the details of Rebecca's overnight vision. After that, they would lay out their plans for that night at Georgetown University's auditorium.

However, only one of the twins entered the room and took her seat, roughly an hour later than had been planned. Rebecca was still dressed in her dark-blue tennis warm-ups, but the cap was gone and her hair was down. She held an ice pack to her lips whenever she was not actually speaking. Now she smiled her odd, swollen smile and began her report to the group.

She started by saying, "Our mission was not successful. We have returned without the photographs of the agreement among the three principals — Ms. Thomas, Mr. Acosta, and Mr. Hasan — and, beyond that, two people were hurt. My brother has a severe concussion and is now at the base infirmary. And I wounded one of the gunmen we faced. He and his partner were beating Luke … beating him, I feared, to death … and so I felt forced to use one of my throwing knives to stop the assault.

"That gunman is presumably in one of the hospitals by now."

She looked down, clearly disturbed, but then explained further.

"Two of Ms. Thomas' gunmen surprised us as we were leaving her study, and a four-person battle ensued. The fight was initiated when I tore Mr. Belton's camera from the hand of one of the gunmen, popped open the back cover, and exposed the entire roll of film to prevent Ms. Thomas from knowing why we were in her study. That enormous man promptly struck me hard enough to knock me to the floor and to lacerate my lower lip. The fight accelerated when Luke twisted the gun away from the other man, causing that gun to discharge and send a round into the wall above Ms. Thomas' desk. That, in turn, caused a very large, framed photo of the U.S. Capitol building to come crashing down on her desk.

"Both gunmen then attacked my brother at once. They were huge people, skilled with their fists, and Luke was almost completely helpless to defend himself … thus, my decision to use one of my knives."

The group took a moment to process this. Then McGriff spoke.

"Was Luke able to leave Ms. Thomas' house on his own steam, Rebecca?" asked McGriff, "or …"

"And how are *you*, Rebecca?" asked Marie.

"Luke was able," she replied, "to leave on his own, although he was … groggy … and so I led him by the hand. He regards himself, by now, as perfectly fine. The base physicians disagree, and he remains at the base infirmary, Father.

"And I'm fine, Marie," she added.

Rebecca scanned the small living room — Sid and Eleanor's, as usual — and saw the looks of concern on every face. Her gray eyes filled with gratitude. She looked down at her lap, breathed deeply, composed herself, and continued.

"My brother and I conducted our annual argument on the drive back to the base," she explained. "It seems that once a year we have an angry *contretemps* about something, and it nearly always has to do with one of us being concerned about the other's safety. In this case, I had *seen* those fists hammering Luke's face and head … I had seen and I had actually *felt* the force of one of those blows …"

Here she pressed the ice pack against her mouth briefly, as if to reinforce her point that she had indeed tasted some of what her brother experienced.

"I *knew* Luke was concussed. And so, I insisted that he receive treatment at the base infirmary, and that he not participate in any other actions of ours until he had cleared a concussion protocol with the military physicians. And that meant that I insisted he not be part of whatever we decide we must do tonight, at the auditorium."

She paused again to press the ice pack against her lips, then continued.

"Luke wouldn't hear of that, and I wouldn't hear of anything else. And so, we fought all the way back, from Chevy Chase to the base. Finally, I simply told him that I would not be able to trust his judgment tonight at the auditorium … knowing that he had sustained some sort of brain injury.

"Our work tonight, I insisted, would be compromised by his mere presence, because I could not be fully functional. He still wouldn't budge, and so I resorted to authority. I told him I would ask you, Mr. Belton, to *order* him to stand down from tonight's work. Interestingly, he and I were *both* quite certain that, once you had heard our complete report, you would, in fact, do exactly that."

Belton nodded.

"Yer right about that, ma'am," he said. "Whoever goes over there t'night has gotta be workin' at a 100 percent in their brain box.

"Know what I mean?

"Hm?"

Rebecca nodded her agreement and continued.

"So … my brother is in the base infirmary until further notice. As for the film," she continued, "I exposed the film because I had photographed the six-page document that Sarah dreamed, and I did not want the congresswoman to know that we were even remotely aware that an agreement existed between herself and the others.

"That's why we left the dreamed document exactly where we found it, and her desk undisturbed by anything *we* did … although, as I said, that enormous framed photograph crashed on top of her desk. Glass shattered over everything."

She paused again, looking down, remembering.

Rebecca raised her arresting gray eyes again, scanning the small group.

"Further to our efforts at misdirection," she continued, "and, of course, before we were so forcibly interrupted, my brother moved systematically through Ms. Thomas' four-drawer file cabinet and handled every file in every drawer, altering the order in which they had been arrayed and even dropping some of them carelessly on the floor. We wanted her to think that the files were our entire focus, and that our forced entry comprised a search for a particular document, or set of documents, of the sort that would be in her file cabinet. Since Ms. Thomas knows nothing of Sarah's dream, there is no reason for her to think otherwise.

"She will be free to assume that I tore open the camera and exposed the film because I had photographed something from her file cabinet."

"But," noted Eleanor quickly, "she *will* know who broke into her study and wounded her henchman. And, as a result, her existing animus toward you, Rebecca, and, more generally, toward Rebekka Yahalomin, will surely be amplified."

"Yes," replied Rebecca. "Her henchmen will describe us and, beyond that, I have left my calling card at the scene of two different incidents that involve Millicent Thomas: my intervention at the site of the attempted kidnapping of Sarah … and, now … this forced entry and the fight that ensued. My knives have, I'm afraid, become my signature in the eyes of the Evil we find ourselves facing.

"So, yes, Dr. Chapel," continued Rebecca, "she will know the Yahalomin were there, and she will assume we were on a treasure hunt … looking for something in her files that we apparently found … thus, my exposure of the film to get rid of the evidence regarding what we chose to photograph. Bear in mind, too, that she does not know we have access to her FBI file, and may not know such a file exists.

"As I've said, she'll have no reason to think we had any interest in that innocuous-looking binder sitting undisturbed on her desk … undisturbed excerpt for the shattered glass and gold-framed photo now resting face-down on it."

Marie stirred.

"Will Ms. Thomas want to report this breaking and entering event … and, maybe, the assault with deadly weapon incident … to the police, Mr. Belton?" she asked.

"Nah," replied Belton. "She isn't gonna want anything about 'er life t' be investigated … by anybody … fer anything. She'd be 'specially nervous about an investigation maybe turnin' up some connection between 'er an' th' Nicaraguan guy an' th' Muslim guy. And as Mrs. Clark just said, th' Thomas woman prob'ly doesn't know there's any FBI interest in 'er, an' she sure doesn't want any.

"Nah … she won't be doin' any reportin' to police about this."

"But, Sid," asked McGriff, "how about the gunman who presumably was taken to an emergency room, and will likely be kept at least overnight to get patched up? Won't there be some kind of police report about that?"

"Well, sure, Jack," answered Belton, "but that dirtbag is not gonna press charges, an' neither is Ms. Thomas. They don't want any police investigation … of anything. An' I'll give Cap'n Johnstone a call as soon as we finish here, just t' keep 'im in th' loop.

"He's not gonna be happy about a knife bein' used as a weapon … again … but he'll also understand that it was either another knife-throw by Mrs. Clark, or a likely homicide … an actual *homicide* … against Lieutenant Manguson.

"Cap'n Johnstone will be okay."

Another thoughtful silence ensued before Sarah finally spoke.

"Since," she said, "Ms. Thomas will know who broke into her home and searched her files and wounded her employee, won't she now come after

Rebecca … and the rest of us … as Dr. Chapel implied … with fresh determination? Might we … all of us here … now become her top priority?"

Belton nodded.

"Yeah … well … maybe not 'er *top* priority … but *one* of 'em. She'll be mad … that's fer sure … an' she'll put a target on Ms. Clark … and fast."

"That sounds like a segue to Rebecca's vision about tonight, Sid," said McGriff. "Maybe it's time to page Jim and Kazim, and get them back in the room?"

"But wait," said Sarah.

"Could we first talk for just a minute about what's just happened? When I think about the disagreement the seven of us had this morning … with four of us saying the forced entry idea was a mistake, and three of us saying it should go ahead … and seeing how it turned out … doesn't this mean that the minority — Rebecca and Luke and Mr. Belton — might have been wrong to go ahead with the plan?

"And doesn't that mean that my vision was … I don't know … just misinterpreted … or… I don't know … I just feel that somehow I should have been able to stop this thing that happened … because it was *my* dream … and now Luke is hurt, and one of the gunmen is wounded … and we don't have anything to show for it.

"I feel like I should have done something … something better … than I did."

"Yes, Sarah," agreed Eleanor, "you should have done something better, as should I, who heard your vision report as soon as you had experienced it. As should you, Marie, and you, Father Jack.

"All four of us," she continued, "were, in varying degrees, opposed to the forced entry, and for more than one kind of reason. We deferred to Rebecca … because she's Rebecca … and to Luke and my husband, because they are veteran strategic-action types … because they seemed more sure that they *should* enter that home than we were sure they shouldn't.

"But," Eleanor concluded, "we *could* have done more, Sarah … and we *should* have done more than we did."

"Like what?" said her husband irritably.

"Well, dear," Eleanor replied, "like maybe trying to get a search warrant for that house. I would guess that Captain Johnstone could have contacted a judge and gotten a search warrant pretty quickly, and that would have meant that Jim and his police associates could have entered that house legally and peacefully and simply confiscated the document we were actually interested in."

Another thoughtful silence enveloped the group.

"Yeah … well … maybe so," said Belton grudgingly, "but that woulda been a long shot, Eleanor. We'd still a' been askin' a judge t' take seriously a *dream* by a person — Miss Wilson here — that th' judge had never heard of."

"And to consider an FBI file we're not supposed to see," added Marie.

"We acted fast," continued Belton, "because we've seen time after time how important *speed* turned out t' be when we're workin' with a 'special message' … an' I just don't think this 20-20 hindsight is gonna be of much use.

"Know what I mean?

"Hm?"

Another silence.

"I'm sorry," said Sarah finally. "You're right, Mr. Belton. You and Rebecca and Luke did what you thought my dream implied, and things didn't turn out … but you did what your experience implied as the best course.

"I just need to get used to all this. And I need to understand the risks … the uncertainties … the possibilities for failure … that will always be part of the decisions and the actions that Rebekka Yahalomin face.

"I just need to get used to all this."

Rebecca, still holding the ice pack to her mouth, stirred, lowered the ice pack to speak, and added, "I do want you to know, Sarah … and everyone … that I'm not satisfied with what I did back there in that house.

"I've asked myself over and over if there were ways I could have handled that without leading to my brother's concussion or to my feeling forced to use the knife. My only answer is that my brother and I … and you, Mr. Belton … were just wrong. We didn't interpret Sarah's dream correctly.

"Those of you who had reservations were surely nearer the mark, especially the suggestion … yours, Dr. Chapel, I think … that the entire meaning of Sarah's dream was simply to inform us of a connection among three people … to make clear to us that not only can we expect to find that Ms. Thomas is operating with a Nicaraguan partner, but with an Islamic partner, as well.

"And that's valuable information, in itself."

She paused, thinking, then continued.

"It's time to bring Jim and Kazim back into the room. We need to talk them through what has happened. We have protected them by removing them from our discussions prior to our taking action … but now … after the fact …

"Things are different. They need to hear of the incident … and they need to comment … and we need to move on to my vision and to its implications for this evening at the university. Can someone page them now, please?"

Durham and Deng returned to the Belton-Chapel guest unit quickly, were brought up to speed on the morning's events, and asked if they had questions or observations about what they had heard. They did not.

"Kazim and I," said Durham, "have no interest in claiming 'we told you so' … because we appreciate the fact that Rebecca and Luke and Mr. Belton were weighing the meaning of a 'special message' against mere prudence … mere legalities … and, beyond all that, feeling the urgency that has always been layered into anything that comes to the Yahalomin by means of dreams or visions.

"They did the best they knew. It didn't work out. Let's move on."

Sarah's heart filled. She felt immense joy that the man with whom she was falling in love could display such generosity of spirit. She wanted to shout with happiness. But she simply closed her eyes and prayed her thanksgiving for such a person to have been brought into her life.

Monday, 1:00 p.m., Andrews Air Force Base, Chapel-Belton guest unit

Within an hour, plans had developed. Rebecca had described her vision: the ornate auditorium; the art on walls and ceiling; the unique balcony design, its wings extending almost over the stage.

And the monocular, modified to function as a weapon.

Durham and Deng had listened, entranced, as the visioner described exactly what their research had found. Rebecca was obviously, to them, describing Gaston Hall. And they offered more details. This was the university's 740-seat auditorium, the site of innumerable speeches, ceremonies, theatrical performances, and debates since its completion in 1901. Gaston Hall, they noted, was situated on the third and fourth floors of the north tower of Healy Hall on the university's main campus.

"Our research," concluded Durham, "did not, of course, reveal anything about the instrument … the weaponized monocular … but I'm thinking that, with that information from Rebecca, and with Captain Johnstone's high regard for Rebecca, we will be allowed to place uniformed officers at both entrances and simply confiscate any implement that looks like that. There will be metal detectors, but a monocular will have to be passed around the detectors, just like coins and car keys. We just need to have our officers in place as soon as the doors open tonight."

"So," said Marie, "we think someone is actually going to try to *shoot* Eleanor tonight … I mean … someone will *intend* to shoot her? Seriously?"

"That just seems so … so far-fetched, to me … that auditorium will probably be full, I should think, given the interest in liberation theology, and given the preeminence of the people who will be speaking. A *shooting?* Really?"

"Well, dear," replied McGriff, "Ms. Thomas' people have tried to snatch Dr. Chapel … and Sarah … off the streets … and that tells us that she considers the Yahalomin to be a serious threat. And Rebecca has left her calling cards at two sites, so far, and so Ms. Thomas knows Rebecca is here and active.

"When you couple all that with Rebecca's vision of last night … the weaponized monocular … the auditorium … the fact that Eleanor is one of the featured panelists … I think we *must* assume that the congresswoman's people are going to be there, and that Eleanor will be in their sights, figuratively and literally."

"So," replied his wife, "you think Jim's plan of confiscating any monocular that comes past the metal detectors will take care of the problem?"

Belton snorted. A dismissive noise. Eyes turned to him.

"That weapon's already there," he said unhesitatingly. "It's already in th' place. It's been there prob'ly fer a few days now. These people're too smart t' think they can just bring that thing through an' around th' metal detectors t' night. That weapon's there … somewhere in th' building … waitin' fer one a' their dirtbag goons t' go in there t' night an' pick it up b'fore th' session starts."

This observation stopped the conversation cold.

Belton continued.

"They've built th' gun t' fit inside th' monocular b'cause there's prob'ly no place in th' buildin' where th' thing can be locked up. They'll have it inside somethin' that looks like a thing college students would carry … maybe a little draw-string bag … like that … or maybe just sittin' by itself … with books an' other stuff … in plain sight."

Belton stopped to think, then continued.

"An' th' idea that Eleanor is th' target … th' main target … or th' only target … is wrong, too," he added, shaking his head unhappily.

"Th' congresswoman an' 'er partners … this Acosta guy an' this Hasan guy … an' any a' their henchmen … they're not gonna put a guy — maybe a suicide guy — into t' night's event just t' get a shot at Eleanor. She's small potatoes.

"Know what I mean?

"They're lookin' fer Ms. Clark, people."

The room was silent once again. Then Marie stirred.

"Did you say, 'a suicide guy,' detective?" asked Marie.

"Yeah ... maybe," he replied. "Miss Wilson dreamed a three-person pact, y'know. An' one of 'em is a Muslim guy. I figure there're prob'ly at least two bullets in that weapon. One is fer Ms. Clark. Close range. Th' other bullet is fer th' foot soldier himself, if he sees he can't get away after he murders Ms. Clark."

Belton delivered this last phrase with emotion in his voice, something so unusual that it got the attention of everyone present. Sarah, seated next to the detective, reached over to him and placed her hand on his shoulder.

Marie once again covered her face with her hands.

"And we'll be without Luke tonight," observed McGriff soberly.

At this, Belton looked up and smiled his crooked smile.

"Yeah," he said, "but I got a first-rate substitute, fer 'im, Jack. I got in touch with Jaakov ... my partner ... early t' day, when I didn't much like th' looks a' th' mission t' th' congresswoman's house. I know ... I know ... I'm th' one that sent 'em there, but I didn't like th' looks of it any more than most a' you didn't like it.

"Jaakov's on th' AMTRAK right now, Jack. I told 'im you an' Marie would pick 'im up at Union Station at 3:15 this afternoon.

"Sound okay, Jack ... Marie?"

They smiled.

"It will be so good to see Mr. Adelman again," said Marie.

"Oh ..." Belton added as an afterthought.

"I talked t' Horace, too ... Captain Johnstone ... he was a trainee a' mine when he first joined th' NYPD a thousand years ago, y' know ... an' I got 'im t' agree t' get authorization from th' administration at th' university t' have two armed people there t' night, besides Jim an' any other D.C. police he takes with 'im. So, Jack, you an' Jaakov, as licensed detectives, are gonna be allowed t' have yer sidearms.

"I'm puttin' Eleanor — my wife — in yer hands, y' know, Jack ... yers an' Jim's an' Jaakov's ... An' Rebecca, too ... y' know ... who's kinda like ... um ... who's kinda like ..."

"Kinda like ... your daughter, Sid?" asked Marie.

He looked down at his hands.

Rebecca smiled.

Monday, 2:30 p.m., Andrews Air Force Base, guest quarters

Rebecca and Sarah entered their room and immediately undressed. For Rebecca, this was a chance to catch up on sleep, her slumber having been interrupted first by her midnight vision and later by Belton's 5:00 a.m. emergency session.

Rebecca was under the bedsheets in two minutes.

"Sarah," she said as she pulled a sheet up to her chin, "I intended to shop at the post exchange for something to wear tonight, but I had no time. I'm sorry."

"It's fine, Rebecca," her roommate replied. "You can just wear the same dress of mine that you wore to our little worship service yesterday. Or you can wear the other one … the one I wore yesterday … if you like. The one I wore is black, so maybe it would be a better choice for an evening event at Georgetown? Anyway, just pick either one when it's time for you to get dressed for the event."

Sarah quietly changed into summer running clothes and was out the door in five minutes, leaving Rebecca already asleep. Durham was waiting.

"Do you want to ride around for a while, Sarah," he asked, "or shall we just walk around the base … in those areas that aren't restricted?"

"Oh, let's just walk, Jim," she said. "I've been doing too much sitting."

They chose a route that would allow them to orbit the guest area, giving them a loop of about a half mile. They settled into a brisk pace.

"How are you feeling about tonight's work, Jim?" she asked. "It strikes me as quite a bit less … fraught … than this morning's forced entry that Rebecca and Luke carried out, but maybe I'm wrong?"

"I think," he replied after a moment, "that this morning's effort *seemed* straightforward to Rebecca and Luke and Mr. Belton. Of course, it turned out to be … as you said … *fraught* … But tonight's problem is much more complex.

"We have Rebecca's vision of the location, and her image of a weaponized optical instrument. And from you, we have the dreamed link among three people, one of whom we *know* wants very badly to … eliminate … Rebekka Yahalomin … probably, as Mr. Belton said, starting with Rebecca herself.

"And, of course," continued Durham, "we have Rebecca's refusal even to consider staying away from the auditorium this evening. She feels compelled to be there, I think, to share the risks with Dr. Chapel, but also because it was *her* dream that is leading us there. I think she feels responsible for this evening's risks.

"The problem, of course, is that we don't know what we're looking for, other than that weaponized instrument. I, for one, am going to be *very* tense."

They walked in silence for another 50 yards before Sarah asked the question that had troubled her since she heard Rebecca's report of that morning's failure.

"Jim," she said, "given the misinterpretation of my dream … by Rebecca and Luke and Mr. Belton … how can we know we're thinking correctly about

Rebecca's dream? It does seem that the threat is clear … this weaponized optical instrument.

"But wouldn't it be simpler and, to say the least, *safer,* just to ask Dr. Chapel to cancel her appearance? If none of you went to the auditorium …"

Durham smiled as he took her hand, slowing their walk to focus on the question, but also to increase the feeling that this was a "date" of sorts, the only kind they could realistically manage during the crisis.

"I don't think," he replied, "there's *any* chance that these people would back away from their commitments, *merely* because their lives appear to be at risk. I know that's not exactly the normal way to look at things, but seriously, Sarah …"

She laughed.

"I know … I know," she said. "They don't back away from anything, do they? They just go ahead with what they think they ought to do, then take whatever precautions they can take without compromising their commitments.

"That's just who they are … right?"

"Yep," he agreed. "That's exactly who they are."

As they rounded the makeshift loop they had invented for their walk, holding hands happily, they saw Rebecca, dressed again in her tennis warm-ups, waiting for them. She walked to meet them as they approached.

They saw that Rebecca no longer carried the ice pack with her, and that the swelling on, and around, her mouth had mostly subsided. A faint blue bruise was developing under her lower lip, but her speech was not impeded.

"I couldn't sleep more than five minutes, Sarah," she said. "I just feel that I should find the man I wounded this morning. I want to talk to him … pray with him.

"Pray *for* him.

"Jim," she said as the couple came to a halt in front of her, "can you find out what hospital he was taken to? And, if you can find where he is, would you be willing to take me to him … and Sarah, would you come, too?"

Durham, as a member of the D.C. police, had no trouble contacting the D.C. hospitals and finding out which one had received a patient with a knife wound in his back earlier that day. Shortly before 3:30 p.m., the three entered the hospital.

Aleksy Kaminski, all 280 pounds and 6 feet and 4 inches of him, had been moved from his temporary room near the ER to a transitional room nearby. He was to have no visitors, but Durham's detective badge carried the day, and they were granted "no more than 15 minutes" in the recovering victim's room.

Kaminski lay on his right side, a hard pillow against his backside keeping him from rolling onto his back.

The wound was near the left shoulder blade and the surgeon wanted Kaminski to avoid pressure at that site for at least the next 24 hours. The hospital intended to keep him there for 72.

Rebecca strode directly to the patient's bedside, while Sarah and Durham stayed near the door to the private room. Kaminski's hard, black eyes tracked her as she crossed the room to him, his brain working to place the woman.

Suddenly he succeeded.

"You …" he said haltingly in his heavily accented bass voice.

"You try kill me."

Rebecca shook her head.

"No," she said firmly. "I tried *not* to kill you.

"And I see I succeeded. You are alive, Aleksy."

He thought this over.

"Why you hurt me?" he said, an apparently honest question.

"I was afraid you and your friend were going to kill my brother."

He thought this over, as well.

"Yes," he said matter-of-factly. "We kill him … except for your knife."

"He is my brother," replied Rebecca, "but even if he were not my brother, I would have tried to stop you. I can't let someone just beat another person to death."

"Why not?" he asked, seemingly puzzled by her assertion.

"God does not allow me to permit such a thing, if I can stop it from happening. Since you and your friend are much bigger and stronger than I am, the only way I had to keep my brother alive was to use my knife.

"But I am so sorry I hurt you, Aleksy. So very sorry."

He thought this over.

"Okay," he said finally.

"Okay?" she asked.

"Okay," he repeated.

"Aleksy," she asked, "do you pray to God?"

"No," he answered, "but I know God is … up there … somewhere."

She smiled at him and slowly knelt beside his bed. She placed her fingertips on his shoulder, giving her fingers just enough pressure for him to be conscious of the fact that she was *physically* present with him.

"Close your eyes," she said, "and listen to my prayer, Aleksy."

He closed his eyes.

"Father, be present … be present …" she began.

"Please help Aleksy to get better. Please help him to know that I meant him no harm, but that I had to stop him from … killing … my brother …

"Please help Aleksy to know that he can talk to You … that, if he does, You will hear his prayer … that You will help him if he asks You to…

"Please lead Aleksy to understand that his strength can be used in many ways … many ways that are good … many ways that help people …

"Please help him to understand how good he can be …

"In the name of Jesus Christ, Thy Son, I make my prayer.

"Amen."

She kept her fingertips pressed into his shoulder for another 10 seconds, then removed her hand and stood beside the bed.

He looked up at her.

"I would like to do good," he said.

"I know you would," she replied.

"Are you Polish, Aleksy?" she added.

"Tak," he replied, nodding.

Rebecca, without turning her face away from the wounded man, called out to Durham, who continued to stand with Sarah just inside the doorway. "Jim," she asked, "what is the best Roman Catholic church for Aleksy? One with other Polish members and with priests who would be pleased to help him?"

"St. Patrick," Durham replied without hesitation.

"Can you and Sarah visit the priests there, Jim, on Aleksy's behalf?"

The young couple looked at each other, both nodding.

"We will, Rebecca," said Sarah.

"Aleksy," added Durham, "Sarah and I will go to St. Patrick in the morning. First thing. Someone from there will come to see you tomorrow."

Durham walked to Aleksy's bedside and, after writing his home number on the back, placed his business card on the bed, next to the big man's pillow.

"Here is my home number, Aleksy," he said. "Call me anytime you want."

As they turned to leave the room, Rebecca heard Aleksy say something, and she turned to face him again. "Did you say something to me, Aleksy?" she asked.

"I sorry I hit you," he said softly.

She walked back to the bedside and leaned over the huge man, placing her fingertips on his shoulder once more.

"I know, Aleksy," she said simply.

Monday evening, Gaston Hall, Georgetown University

D. C. Police Captain Horace Johnstone, a large African-American now in his mid-40s, took a seat on the extreme right wing — "right," facing the stage — of the Gaston Hall balcony. It was his first time in the famed venue, and he looked with glad wonder at the artwork on the walls and ceiling.

But only for moments.

He was there on business. Sid Belton had been his mentor with the NYPD when he began his service. All these years later, Belton was still, as far as Johnstone was concerned, the best analyst in the country, one whose analytical powers were known and respected not just in the U.S., but on the far side of the Atlantic, as well.

When Belton had phoned him earlier that day to ask for his help with this evening's "problem," Johnstone not only cleared private detectives McGriff and Adelman to bring their service weapons into the auditorium, he made clear to the university administrator with whom he spoke that he would be there himself, in person. And he, too, would be armed, as would one of his precinct detectives, Jim Durham.

That meant that four armed "friends of Rebecca" — the captain, McGriff, Adelman, and Durham — would be present. Belton, with his severe physical limitations, would not himself be in attendance, but he had agreed with Johnstone that Jack McGriff should serve as Rebecca's personal bodyguard and would sit with her high in the balcony's center section that evening. This was not a compliment to McGriff; it was an acknowledgement that the Episcopal priest was the least experienced of the four at surveying crowds and taking emergency action, if needed.

Durham would be positioned on the extreme left — "left," facing the stage — of the balcony, almost over the stage; Johnstone would be on the right, also nearly over the stage; Adelman would be the "roving" agent, ready to move to any spot in the auditorium at a moment's notice.

All would be equipped with police-issued walkie-talkies, simple wireless communication devices that, although just one step up from toys, were effective short-range, line-of-sight instruments. All were aware that Eleanor Chapel would be positioned somewhere on the stage itself and could conceivably be a secondary target. But they were also confident that Rebecca Clark would be the top priority for Millicent Thomas' henchmen. Dr. Chapel, they felt, would be at risk only if, somehow, Rebecca were not present at the venue.

And she would definitely be present.

Detective Jaakov Adelman, a tall, lean-muscled scarecrow of a man, stood a few feet behind Johnstone, who had seated himself in the front row of the three rows that extended all the way to the extreme end of the balcony wing. And Adelman liked nothing about what he saw.

He saw a venue that would seat more than 700, now filled to roughly three-fourths capacity by his estimate. A few individuals and couples were still filing into the auditorium, but he saw there would be only a handful of empty seats on the main floor, and perhaps two dozen seats unoccupied around the balcony wings.

The Yahalomin had inferred from Rebecca's dream that a weaponized mon-ocular would be the instrument of threat. Such a weapon, Adelman knew, would be too bulky to hide effectively under summer-weight clothing, but could easily be hidden in a purse.

The audience appeared evenly divided between men and women, and many of the women carried purses of adequate size to conceal the weapon.

Adelman scanned the main floor and the balcony, focusing on couples. He reasoned that a man and woman could enter, split up long enough for each to visit the rest rooms or other spaces where the monocular might have been placed a day, or several days, earlier, and then return to sit together in a spot that would provide them a shooting platform for Rebecca Clark, once they had located her.

He checked Rebecca's location once more. She was seated high up on the fifth row, out of six rows, near the center of the balcony. McGriff sat beside her.

The seats on each side, and just behind them, were empty. But he tensed when he saw two couples ascending the twin staircases that led from the main floor to the rear of the balcony. Once they reached the balcony level, all four of them could come in behind Rebecca and McGriff.

Just at that moment, Adelman heard a small, high-pitched voice speak his name. He turned quickly, and for an instant saw no one. Then he realized that the speaker was more than a foot shorter than him.

A girl was looking up at him. To Adelman's eyes, her age was uncertain, partly because her head was covered by an Islamic scarf and partly because her unlined face could be that of a child of 8 or a teen of 16. She spoke his name again.

He bent down to hear her quiet voice.

"Mr. Adelman," she said again.

"I am Sari," she said. "I tried to kill you. In a hospital room. Five years ago."

His eyes widened and his mind reeled. In a two-second flashback, he recalled being told by Belton of the incident.

Adelman, then and now an observant Jew, had lain unconscious in a Birmingham, England, hospital bed when a Saudi child of nine, raised to hate all things Jewish, crept into his room. She lifted a knife above her head in preparation for driving it into Adelman's exposed carotid, only to see her wrist cracked violently by a heavy walking cane wielded by Belton, who had stood hidden behind the door in anticipation of this precise act of attempted murder.

The weapon had tumbled harmlessly onto Adelman's pillow.

That same child, now 14, continued to speak to the man she had once intended to murder, her excellent English a unique mixture of Middle Eastern and classical Oxford influences. Adelman shook off the flashback and focused on her words.

Her expressive, dark brown eyes, set against the light brown of her face, glanced urgently in the direction of the center balcony. "The Muslim woman sitting two rows in front of Mrs. Clark," she whispered, "wearing American clothes, carries a gun in her purse. The gun is housed within an optical instrument.

"As soon as the program begins, she will turn and kill Mrs. Clark.

"Then she will kill herself."

Adelman fought off his ingrained interrogation-based responses. *How do you know this? Why are you telling me this? And why are you telling ME this?*

Instead, he thought only two things: *The chances of this being a ruse are so close to zero as to be inconsequential.* And then: *This feels like the kind of intervention Eleanor Chapel likes to call "a God thing."*

He turned immediately and left the Saudi teen standing alone. He strode with the long legs of a 6-foot-plus athlete in the direction of the center balcony. As he walked toward the reported threat, he raised the walkie-talkie to his face.

"Adelman here. Suspect Muslim female, wearing American clothing, sitting two rows in front of Mrs. Clark and Father McGriff, center balcony. I'm on my way."

In 12 seconds, Adelman was high-stepping across a long row of seated audience members. He stopped directly in front of the woman identified by the girl. At the instant of recognition, the woman's face clouded with a consuming hatred of the Jewish features staring down at her. She reached into her purse.

As she pulled the weapon out, Adelman, a slender but immensely strong man, reached over the seatback in front of him and seized the instrument with both hands, forcing the exposed muzzle of the weapon toward the ceiling and twisting the weapon violently from the woman's hands. At no point had her finger reached the trigger.

The furious Saudi assassin, pulled up and out of her seat by Adelman's action, then felt both of her wrists seized from behind by the burly Jack McGriff, who, having heard Adelman's message on the walkie-talkie, had stepped over the empty row in front of him just as Adelman had arrived in front of the woman.

McGriff forced the Saudi's arms behind her back just as Durham and Johnstone arrived from each side. Durham snapped his handcuffs onto the woman's wrists, and he, Adelman, and the captain led her away and onto the near staircase.

Throughout this swift confluence of movements, Rebecca, elegant in her roommate's simple black dress and 2-inch heels, remained quietly in her seat. Minutes earlier, she had seen the Muslim girl speaking to Adelman and she had watched as he wheeled immediately to walk in her direction. Although the girl's hair was covered, Rebecca realized after a moment's mental search that she *knew* the girl. Knew the girl through Rebecca's sister-in-law in London. This was Sari, with whom Rebecca, Luke, and Kory had had tea earlier that spring.

That recognition triggered in Rebecca a flood of memories. The memories told Rebecca that this was the once 9-year-old child who had wounded Kory van Dijk — now Kory Manguson — seriously, albeit defensively, in an encounter in an Israeli desert. The memories also told Rebecca that this was the same child who had attempted to murder a helpless, hospitalized Jewish man, the very same man to whom the girl had just spoken in this auditorium.

As she watched Adelman's swift approach, Rebecca's only physical response was to shift in her seat in order to remove her shoes. If action were to be required of her, she could not afford to be encumbered with Sarah's 2-inch heels. Bare feet would serve infinitely better if she were called upon to fight or flee.

But neither was in order. Rebecca had simply watched as the four men converged on the woman sitting two rows in front of her.

She found that she was unsurprised at the appearance of the dreamed weaponized monocular, as it was torn from the would-be assailant's hands. And now, as the men took the woman away, Rebecca, with her phenomenal ability to change focus, shifted her attention fully back to the stage, where Eleanor now received 100 percent of Rebecca's concentration.

The diminutive scholar had just taken her seat on the extreme right — "stage right" — of the seven panelists. To Rebecca, Eleanor looked as small as a child, and yet at the same time she appeared to be the most formidable presence on the stage.

From Eleanor's own perspective, the auditorium looked so immense that for a moment she was unsure whether she would be able to locate anyone she knew. But she found Rebecca quickly, and, at nearly the same moment, she saw Jaakov, Jim, and Captain Johnstone forcefully escorting a handcuffed woman toward one of the staircases.

She nodded to herself, smiled in Rebecca's direction, and turned her face toward the moderator. Eleanor, too, could change focus swiftly and fully. She was determined to speak with the greatest possible clarity about liberation theology to this audience.

She considered it of signal importance that the audience members and, as well, her fellow panelists, hear her say without equivocation that Jesus Christ lived, died, and rose again for every person on the planet, past, present, and future. His time on earth had been determinedly and consistently non-political. His message, from first to last, had been individual-person-focused and eternal in perspective.

Yes, He attended to the poor, but no more so than to every other individual. Christ had suffered and risen for each person, regardless of her or his life status. There were 700 people in Gaston Hall that evening, and she wanted each one … individually … to hear her recitation of those facts.

Eleanor Chapel was ready.

CHAPTER NINE

Monday, 11:00 p.m., Andrews Air Force Base, Chapel-Belton guest unit

ALL 10 HAD NOW CROWDED INTO ELEANOR AND BELTON'S UNIT, the largest, but still barely adequate for the number of Yahalomin assembled. For Jaakov Adelman was now reunited with everyone from the original group, along with Sarah, Durham and Deng: Eleanor and Belton, Marie and McGriff, Luke and Rebecca, who had changed out of Sarah's dress and into her tennis warm-ups. She had then escorted her brother back to the guest unit from the infirmary, having assured Luke's attending physician that she would walk him back to the infirmary as soon as this late-night meeting ended.

First, the participants demanded Eleanor's account of the panel discussion.

She grudgingly offered a summary, but insisted on turning the conversation to the unexplained presence of the Saudi teen, whose role in that evening's developments seemed to Eleanor of much greater significance than the panelists' discussion.

"The liberation theology discussion was civil," she said, "and I was able to give my main points about the nature of Jesus Christ without interruption."

Rebecca and McGriff, the only members of the group who had been able to stay for the discussion, nodded their agreement. Rebecca added, "Eleanor was so amazing throughout the evening that several of her observations elicited applause, and, if you can imagine, applause even from some of her fellow panelists, including the … um … rather pompous gentleman from Cambridge University.

"I was very proud to know her."

"Yes, yes, yes," said Eleanor impatiently, rolling her eyes … but smiling at the compliment … "but can we just get on to this … *impossible* … intervention by the Saudi girl? I am *starving* to hear about her.

"Who is she? What happened?"

Rebecca placed a hand on her brother's knee. "Luke …" she said, "do you feel like telling us about Sari?"

"I *felt* like being there with you at the university," he said, showing playful irritation, "but you wouldn't hear of it, ma'am. You insisted on throwing me into solitary confinement in a military hospital."

Belton snorted.

"If you'd tried t' go t' this thing, Luke, I woulda whacked ya on yer noggin so hard ya woulda ended up in th' infirmary anyway. Just be glad yer sister didn't make me hafta beat ya to a pulp, b'cause y' know I woulda done it."

Eleanor's high voice cut through the verbal traffic.

"Boys!" she said. "The *girl!* Tell me about the *girl!*"

Luke nodded, smiling, and began.

"Five years ago, in Israel, when Kory and I were first … um … 'dating' … we were tasked with dislodging two sentries who were guarding the perimeter of a terrorist enclave. We had to get them out of their positions … and without alerting their *very* numerous colleagues. This was a dark night, and it took us a while to realize that one of the sentries we'd need to tackle was, in fact, a child … a girl child.

"We moved fast. Kory rushed the child; I rushed the man.

"In the child's defense… that child — who turned out to be a Saudi 9-year-old named Sari — looked up at the last second and thought she was being attacked … and, in a sense, she was. She pulled out her knife and slashed Kory in the neck … superficially, as it turned out … but when Kory seized the knife by its blade, Kory's third and fourth fingers… on her right hand… were cut so badly that, even after surgery, she still has only partial function in those fingers."

He stopped for a moment, organizing.

"Later, it seemed that Sari … the only name she knew for herself … had begun to regard Kory as … um … well …"

"As the first female human being she had known," interjected Rebecca, "and, thus, as an older sister, and someone to whom she instinctively gravitated … someone whom she could actually trust."

"Yes," agreed Luke.

"So," he continued, "when Kory and I later needed help finding a hidden entry to an underground passage occupied by the chief terrorist, it was Sari — whose English, even then, was excellent — who found the hidden panel, which, in turn, allowed me to track down the … er … the *dirtbag* … who was directing the group's actions.

"Subsequently, Sari allowed us to bring her back to England. By then, Jaakov had become involved with us, and, at our parents' retreat center near Birmingham, the place to which these mostly Middle Eastern terrorists had tracked us, he was badly wounded by automatic rifle fire. He underwent surgery and was hospitalized.

"Sari," Luke continued, "whom we had begun to trust, then sneaked into Jaakov's hospital room, where he lay unconscious, and attempted to murder him. We had not been smart enough to realize that she, as a fledgling Saudi terrorist, might be able to trust Kory right away, but not a male Jewish person like Jaakov, a classification of human being she'd been raised to hate.

"But Sid," Luke concluded, "had figured that out. And, because he did, he was behind the door in that hospital room. When Sari raised her knife to stab Jaakov, Sid whacked her wrist with that cane of his and saved Jaakov."

"You, Luke Manguson," said Eleanor Chapel impatiently, "are the slowest storyteller I have ever had to endure!

"Will you *please* tell me how Sari materialized at the university tonight … *in Washington, D.C., in the United States, if we can imagine* … to tell Jaakov Adelman … this Jewish person whom she once attempted to murder … that there was a terrorist sitting just in front of Rebecca!"

"But Dr. Chapel," Luke said mildly. "I don't know. I really don't."

"Well," said Rebecca, "we do know *something*, Luke. Explain Kory's aunt's role in Sari's life since then. After all, it's been five years. She must be 14 years old now."

"Oh … right," Luke agreed. "Back then, Kory and I had rescued Kory's aunt, Greta van Dijk, from her home in northern Holland. We rescued her from Nazi terrorists who were bent on exterminating the Righteous Among Nations. Those were the mostly Christian people who sheltered Jews during World War II, and who are now honored along the Avenue of the Righteous at Yad Vashem in Jerusalem.

"Greta," he continued, "who sheltered a young Jewish woman during the war, was simply not afraid of the child, despite Sari's violent history, just as it seems she was never afraid of the Nazis. She took Sari into her home in London and raised her as her own. So, for five years, Sari has lived with kindness … gentleness … prayerfulness … and the Dutch Reformed church, which was Greta's church back in Holland.

"However," concluded Luke thoughtfully, "Greta decided a year ago to allow Sari to attend the local mosque whenever she chose. Greta had seen Sari's growing curiosity about her Saudi upbringing … well, no, not exactly *upbringing* … more of a curiosity about her Saudi *roots*, I suppose …"

He looked to his sister for help.

"That's a good way to put it, Luke," said Rebecca. "Sari had been raised among male terrorists. She had no *religious* tradition. She had, as you said, *roots* in Muslim extremist perspectives. Sari wanted to know something about those perspectives.

"You've said it well, Luke. Sari had become curious about those perspectives, and Greta allowed her to go to her local mosque for … educational purposes."

"Well," resumed Luke, "a few weeks ago, with Greta's *very* nervous permission, Sari left home to live for a few weeks with a Muslim family. Greta spent time beforehand 'scouting' the family … especially the mother and the 14-year-old daughter who had befriended Sari. Then … once Sari had begun staying with that family, Sari sent notes home to Greta every day. The notes were reassuring, and so Greta was not worried. The arrangement was to be temporary … three weeks, max.

"Greta," continued Luke, "did not involve any of us in her decision. She did let us … Kory, her niece … and me … and Rebecca … know what was going on. She said she was determined to give Sari the three weeks that had been agreed to.

"And that's all Kory and I … and Rebecca … were allowed to know."
Prolonged silence ensued.

"Luke," said Eleanor finally, "what is Sari like? You must know a little about what she has become during these five years. Yes?"

"Well … not really," he said with some embarrassment.

"Kory and I … and Rebecca, too … have only seen Sari occasionally," he said, "because Greta and Sari immersed themselves in their Dutch Reformed church, whereas Kory switched to the Anglican church even before she and I married.

"So, since Greta and Sari move in different circles … you know … Greta's church … Sari's schools … we just don't see them much."

"But," interjected Rebecca, "Greta has told you, Luke, and Kory … and occasionally, me, too … that she feels that Sari has become … *good* … kind …

thoughtful … compassionate … a *prayerful* girl … and I must say that, the few times I have been with Sari, she has seemed exactly those things."

"A Christian?" asked Eleanor.

Rebecca and Luke looked at each other, then shook their heads.

"We don't know," said Luke. "Greta told Kory and me a few months ago that Sari would undertake confirmation classes at their church as soon as she turned 14 … or as soon as confirmation classes began once she'd had that birthday.

"I don't think she's yet started."

"But … of course …" added Rebecca, "that's not really what you're asking, Dr. Chapel. You … we … would like to know what is in Sari's heart and mind.

"You … we … want to know if Sari is a Christian *believer.*"

"Exactly," agreed Eleanor, who continued after a moment.

"You three apparently," she said, "don't know about that — about her beliefs — with any certainty, but you do know that she is *here* … and that she intervened tonight at a critical moment. *None* of us knows how she got here or where she has now gone.

"Luke …" she concluded, "you must have thoughts about this … about this 14-year old … and about what might be going on with her?"

"Well," Luke responded after a moment, "I would guess, given Jaakov's description of her, wearing a headscarf and an abaya, she must have come over from England with a Muslim contingent, and they must have thought she could be helpful to them. Otherwise, why would they want her to accompany them at all?"

Luke was quiet for another few moments, then continued.

"It may be that they brought Sari specifically to identify my sister for them. Sari and Rebecca have been together a number of times over these five years … always, I think, at Kory's and my house, when Kory's aunt would come to visit. My sister's face is still well known to British tennis fans, but that doesn't mean that a group of Saudi terrorists would recognize her without assistance.

"The fact that she — Sari van Dijk is her full name, you know, having been formally adopted by my wife's aunt four years ago — went to Jaakov purposely to alert him to the threat to Rebecca … suggests to me that she was brought here against her will and was … I'm guessing … looking for a chance to subvert her captors' plans. That's just speculation, but that's the best I can do, Eleanor."

Eleanor nodded to Luke, then turned to Adelman.

"Jaakov," she said, "I'm curious. What led you, a seasoned professional detective accustomed to looking for real evidence, to *believe* this teen, dressed as a

Muslim, when she pointed out the woman sitting in front of Rebecca as intending to commit murder? What went through your mind?"

Adelman responded immediately.

"I've been thinking about that exact thing while Luke was giving Sari's background, Eleanor," he said, "and I've been able to remember exactly what went through my mind when she approached me tonight. In the first flash of recognition, I remembered her attempted murder ... of me ... in that hospital room, even though I was not conscious, and did not actually see her ... but I have in my mind Sid's detailed description of what she tried to do, and what he did to stop her.

"In any case, that scene burst through my mind for a second or two. But I shoved that aside, knowing I had no time to think about that."

He paused, organizing, then continued.

"In the next several seconds, I thought two things. First, I thought that the chances of this being a fabrication — this young person saying she tried to kill me five years ago — were close to zero. How would this girl know anything about that ... about her attempt on my life ... unless she had, in fact, lived the story?

"And second, I asked myself the question, why would she be telling *me*, the Jew whom she once tried to murder?

"Why me, of all people?"

"And your answer was ..." asked Eleanor.

"My answer was that this felt *authentic* ... felt like the kind of thing that you, Eleanor, sometimes call 'a God thing' ... and I stopped questioning and *moved*."

"And," continued Eleanor, "looking back?"

"Looking back," replied Adelman, "I think exactly the same thing ... that her little presentation was authentic ... and that she came to me precisely *because* she wanted to kill me five years ago. 'A God thing' ... plain and simple.

"Which leads me to this.

"Sari has been converted ... converted by five years with Kory's aunt ... converted *probably* to Christianity ... converted *certainly* to the concept of the Good."

He paused, thoughtful.

"The book of Jeremiah tells us that God has written His law on our hearts. I think Sari has allowed that to happen in her own heart. I think she wanted *me* to hear her say that Rebecca was in imminent danger ... wanted *me* to take action to save Rebecca's life ... which would mean that Sari *also* saved Rebecca's life.

"I think, quite simply," concluded Adelman, "that this is who Sari has become. She has been stripped of her hatred … *cleansed* … She is a new person, Eleanor."

Marie stirred.

"And Sari," she said, "…this 'new person' … has willingly placed herself in mortal danger this evening, because God's law is written on her heart."

"That, certainly," said Rebecca, "but also by her coming to *feel* the meaning of Christ's sacrifice … which, in turn … has led Sari to *embrace* our guiding principle: *the blueprint of the universe … my life for yours.*"

In the ensuing silence, all thoughts turned to the girl … alone … somewhere.

"Yeah," agreed Belton after several moments.

"Ya gotta know there were others there t' night … others that saw what Sari did … saw that Sari showed Jaakov th' woman who had th' gun. Ms. Thomas' people — her own Muslim terrorists — have prob'ly already snatched that girl up. She's gone. No way are we gonna find 'er."

"Sid," said McGriff, immediately disagreeing, "after Jim handcuffed the assassin, and after Jim and Jaakov and Captain Johnstone escorted her from the auditorium, I sat back down, next to Rebecca, and noted that Sari left the auditorium just seconds after Jim, Jaakov, and the captain did. I think she followed Jim and the others closely … possibly all the way out of the building."

Durham quickly interrupted. "No … once we reached the ground floor of the building, I checked carefully behind us to see if anyone was trying to follow.

"No one followed us."

McGriff nodded thoughtfully. "Good," he said.

"I noted," McGriff continued, "that no one from the auditorium tried to pursue the girl. No one in the balcony moved … and those on the main floor were not in position to see what had happened. Millicent Thomas' associates were certainly present in the auditorium, but I think they were simply unprepared for what happened. They were either not in position to see the arrest of their would-be assassin, or they saw the arrest, but had no 'Plan B' in place.

"I'm guessing," McGriff concluded, "that Sari is running from the people who brought her to the U.S., in which case she is on foot … alone … and hiding."

Silence followed.

Finally, Belton nodded to McGriff.

"Yeah, Jack," he said. "Yer prob'ly right."

He turned to Durham.

"Jim," he said, "can ya get yer buddies lookin' fer th' girl?"

Durham shook his head.

"She doesn't *belong* to any of us, Mr. Belton," he replied. "We don't have the standing to request police help. She's not *ours*."

"Right," said Belton, "but y' could … y' know … informally … get in touch with a couple a' yer buddies an' ask … y' know … a *favor.* Right?

"A couple a' uniforms," Belton continued, "lookin' around Georgetown … askin' if anybody's seen a Muslim teenage girl … they might come up with somethin' …

"Know what I mean?

"Hm?"

Durham swiftly left the room to use the phone, and the group waited in silence for him to return, each one thinking about this 14-year-old and her astonishing bravery … and about the lethal danger that she now faced.

Monday night/Tuesday morning, 12:30 a.m.,
Andrews Air Force Base, guest quarters

Rebecca returned to her and Sarah's guest unit after midnight, having escorted her brother, grumbling all the way, back to the base infirmary. She found her roommate already in bed, asleep with her reading light on and a book in her hands. Rebecca crossed quietly to the bedside, carefully lifted the book from Sarah's hands, and switched off her reading light. She used the bathroom, checked her lip in the mirror and found the cut barely visible, along with a trace of swelling and bruising, loosened the laces on her tennis shoes to give them a more relaxed fit, and tiptoed to the door of the unit. She turned off the floor lamp, using the wall switch, and silently exited.

Rebecca wanted to walk in the darkness … and pray.

She had not thought carefully in advance about what it would mean that evening to wear Sarah's somewhat skimpy black dress, Sarah's 2-inch heels, and Sarah's gold barrette, which Rebecca had used to add a "dressy" touch to her luxurious hair. She so seldom gave extended thought to her attire — her own non-tennis wardrobe consisting of modest skirts, dresses, blouses, and flats — that her mind had been completely focused on Eleanor Chapel's safety, on the liberation theology content of the evening's program, and of Eleanor's anticipated performance.

The subsequent experience, as she walked from McGriff's Jeep Cherokee, first along the streets of Georgetown, then across campus to Gaston Hall, had been unsettling. Pedestrians stopped to stare openly at her as she passed. Eyes followed her every step … both men and women … both university students and Georgetown residents … and she became gradually aware that this was different from the attention she attracted in London. There, *some* people noticed her, but it was because she was 6 feet tall, carried herself with an erect, athletic stride, and, to more than a few, was still a recognizable sports figure.

And, of course, because of the long facial scar.

Here, on this evening in the capital city of the United States, she was attracting attention because she was, with Sarah's heels, 6 feet, 2 inches tall and … it dawned on her as she walked … a *spectacle*. She had spent her adolescence and adulthood honing a public presence consistent with her mother's advice when Rebecca, nearly two decades earlier, had begun to grow into her physical maturity.

"Rebecca, dear," her mother had counseled, "you are becoming a beautiful girl … soon to be a beautiful woman. The fact that you are a believer … a Christian believer … does *not* mean that you are to pretend that you are not beautiful, when, in fact, you are. Nor does it mean you should pretend you are not highly intelligent, when, in fact, you are. Nor does it mean you should pretend that you are not phenomenally talented, when, in fact, you are. No pretentious modesty whatsoever is required or implied by your Christian faith and commitment.

"Your Christian faith and commitment *does* imply, however," her mother had continued, "that you not seek to manipulate those around you by means of your beauty, your intelligence, or your talent. You should attend to your appearance, of course — your nails should be trimmed, your hair should be washed and brushed, your clothes should fit properly — but that is all, dear.

"You will be assailed," her mother had said, "by an unending stream of commercial messages seeking to turn you into a goddess … a goddess of people's fantasies … a goddess whose dress, accessories, and behaviors are designed to be titillating, flirtatious, and seductive.

"Your Christian faith means that you should focus your mind and heart elsewhere, my daughter … on the things that truly matter in this life … that is, on your own application of the Great Commission in Matthew's Gospel … no matter where you are and what you are doing. You're going to be highly visible as one of the top female tennis players in our country. People will notice how you conduct yourself, and not just on the court. They will notice how you behave, dress, and comport yourself.

"Keep in mind always St. Paul's words in his first letter to the church in Corinth: '… *your body is a temple of the Holy Spirit within you … not your own …* '"

That night on Georgetown's streets, Rebecca had been reminded in the most emphatic terms what it meant to dress — accidentally, in her case — to attract others. But she acknowledged to herself now, walking through the air base darkness in her tennis warm-ups, that the evening's experience had revealed something important.

And that was simply that, without the slightest effort on her part, she felt little other than embarrassment as the eyes turned toward her to gape and leer and lust. She had inadvertently become a spectacle, and it simply embarrassed her.

And that was good.

And so she continued to walk through and around the darkened guest compound, praying now for God's grace and mercy … for herself … for her brother … for Dr. Chapel, Mr. Belton, Mr. Adelman, and the rest of Rebekka Yahalomin.

And for her own children, husband, and parents, across an ocean.

And for Sari … somewhere in the darkness of the city.

Tuesday, 1:30 a.m., a secluded copse near the Potomac River

Sari van Dijk finally drifted toward exhausted sleep.

Dressed now in the English-American clothes she had carried in her drawstring bag, she had first removed the Muslim garment, donned her jeans and her tee shirt, and then wrapped herself, fully clothed, in the long abaya she had worn to the Gaston Hall program. The abaya now served both as covering and undersheet. She had lain now on the warm ground near the Potomac for hours, unable to sleep and unsure what she should do next. Her plan for that evening had extended no further than taking action to prevent what she knew her Muslim captors intended for Rebecca Clark. Beyond that, she had only expected to run from them and then to hide herself somewhere.

She had dimly hoped to be rescued, but she could not have said how that might happen or who might do the rescuing.

She had spent the hours since finding this secluded spot near the historic C&O Canal thinking back over the events that had culminated in her intervention in what would otherwise have been a highly public murder. Her mind had repeatedly gone back to the recent weeks in London during which, even after a stranger had gone to some lengths to introduce himself — first having asked permission from her temporary Muslim "Mum" to do so — she had not at first felt warning signs of any kind. On the contrary, the man had seemed, as with the women she met during her visits to the London mosque, genuinely pleased to learn that she was a Christian teen who simply wanted to understand her childhood better.

They were kind, thoughtful, generous … even sweet.

As time passed and other conversations with this man followed, she now remembered, he had revealed that he knew many things about Sari and her London family. He had seemed especially interested in Greta van Dijk's niece, Kory, and in the family into which Kory had married … the Manguson-Clark family. He had talked to Sari about how much he appreciated that family's history of "fighting against evil," as he put it. He hoped that she, Sari, would also wish to fight against evil.

He had said his name was Hasan.

A one-word name.

His familiarity with Greta van Dijk's extended family had eventually raised a red flag in Sari's mind, a mind made wary by her years of living with the male terrorists who had comprised her entire world for the first nine years of her life.

On one very recent visit to the mosque, Hasan had talked for more than an hour with Sari, just the two of them, an older man apparently passing along his Muslim wisdom to an eager teen-age girl. On that visit, he began to talk about "evil" in a different vein. He spoke about a certain member of the Manguson-Clark family, the family into which Sari's adoptive mother's niece had married.

This person, he had said, had for several years moved down what he called a "dangerous path" … a path that would take that person to "a different kind of Evil" … an Evil that purported to receive messages from God.

That person's name, he had said, was Rebecca Clark.

Good Muslims knew, Hasan explained, that truth was written in the Koran, and that she … Sari … would need to study the passages that would make clear what dangers awaited the family into which Kory van Dijk had married. He had said that he … Hasan … was part of a global organization which had "associates" in a number of countries. His was an organization that sought to spread truth by means of forceful opposition to the kind of Evil the Manguson-Clark family espoused.

In their very next conversation, Sari recalled now from her secluded riverbank hiding place, Hasan had said that he and others would be leaving immediately to travel to the United States, the country to which, they had just learned the night before, Rebecca Clark had recently flown.

And Sari had found herself suddenly being "helped" into a vehicle that, in turn, carried her, Hasan, and others to a private airfield north of London. She recalled that she had had no chance to contact either her temporary Islamic family or her permanent English one. Now, in the warm Georgetown darkness, Sari closed her eyes and recalled the prelude to that forcible abduction, the angst-filled hours in London that had been marked by her uncertain reactions to the hatred that she now felt had begun to radiate from Hasan's words. His hatred had generated four prayerful questions that had fought for her attention during those pre-abduction hours.

Should she make clear to this man that she wanted no part of his and his organization's views regarding the nature of Good and Evil?

Should she stop visiting the mosque altogether?

Should she break with her temporary Muslim family and return to Greta?

Or … and this was the question that stopped the other three questions from being answered … should she feign interest in Hasan's arguments, agree to whatever proposal he might offer, and make an attempt to derail his plan from the inside? Sari recalled that a certain quotation from C. S. Lewis had formed itself often in her prayers, an 11-word sentence taught her by her adoptive mother and cited often in conversations with her relatives, Kory and Luke Manguson, and Rebecca Clark:

Courage is the name of every virtue at its testing point.

In those desperate prayers, and again, now, on the Potomac riverbank, Sari reminded herself that Professor Lewis had not suggested that 14-year-olds ought to be exempt from that axiom. And so, she recalled, by the time Hasan demanded that she leave with him for the United States, she had already decided what she would say.

She would say Yes … she would go. No need to force her.

And Sari's mind now also played back the last few hours, and her decision, reached prayerfully in Jesus' name, hours before the Gaston Hall program was to begin. She had decided then that she would approach Jaakov Adelman, a Jew whom she had tried to kill when she was still that "other" person … that "other" person whom she no longer recognized when she looked back.

Her Muslim captors, she now recalled, had given her an assignment for that evening. She was to locate and catalogue those members of Rebekka Yahalomin who were present in Gaston Hall. To that end, she had been given photographs of the Yahalomin members other than the three whom she knew personally: Kory and Luke Manguson, and Rebecca Clark.

The photos of the others were recent.

Dr. Eleanor Chapel's picture, of course, appeared in freshly printed brochures announcing the evening's event. Sid Belton's and Jaakov Adelman's photos were published regularly in various New York City and Washington print media, advertising their detective agency's availability in both cities. The same was true of Marie Campbell and Jack McGriff, their D.C. agents. None of the Muslim women and men with whom Sari had come to America knew Sarah Wilson, Jim Durham, or Kazim Deng, or had photos of them, the three newer members of the Yahalomin. There was no expectation that Sari would be able to identify them, nor was there any need to do so.

Sari's assignment was to locate the Yahalomin who were central to the group's membership, and, if they were present, to report their positions to Hasan's deputy, who would be seated in the balcony, near the stage, on the left side as one faced the stage. He would then communicate Rebecca Clark's position, and the positions of others, to the assassin, who would be waiting for him in the lobby, so that she could select her seat accordingly. She would move to her seat regardless of whether the program was underway. Hasan himself would not be present inside the building. At some point he and others would take positions outside. Sari was confident she could do as asked.

But her *real* assignment was of a different order.

Her prayers, as she now recalled once again, had led her repeatedly to one particular Yahalomin member … Jaakov Adelman … and to that night's would-be assassin … a woman who had traveled with Sari, Hasan, his deputy, and the others, from England, and who would be dressed for the Gaston Hall event in unexceptional "American" evening wear.

Sari, as a child of God, had come to understand that her role was to warn Jaakov Adelman of the specific danger: this female assassin and her location in the audience. And when the moment had finally arrived, she had found that she easily recognized Adelman from her five years earlier hospital bed encounter, brief though it had been, and from his recent photos.

She now remembered how she had then approached the tall, solemn Jew and had told him what would happen in just minutes. While his facial expression had been enigmatic, she had seen that his action was decisive. He had spun immediately toward the assassin. He had moved … fast … in her direction.

And Sari had put her head down and had walked swiftly toward the center balcony, trailing in Adelman's wake, hoping that she could get out of the building before being stopped by Hasan's deputy or by the other members of the Muslim entourage that had brought her to the United States.

She had felt that it took forever to reach a staircase. Once there, she swiftly descended stairs that would lead from the auditorium level down to the second-floor corridor, where dozens of student cubbies were built into the hallway walls. When she had reached the second-floor corridor, she now recalled, she had broken into a run, racing down the empty hallway to the long rows of cubbies. She had quickly found her little drawstring bag — the bag in which the weaponized monocular had been placed, awaiting its use by the woman who had been assigned to kill Rebecca Clark — and had snatched the bag from its knee-level hiding place.

Having been relieved of the monocular earlier that evening by the designated assassin, the bag weighed little, now containing only toiletries, a Pocket New Testament, a set of loose document pages, and her American — actually British — clothing. Clutching the lightweight bag, Sari had flown back to the stairwell, descended to the ground floor, and exited the building at a run. And then, finally, she was free, running through the Georgetown campus in her cumbersome Muslim garments toward the commercial streets of Georgetown itself … running … running … running.

She now recalled how she had fled, hoping that Hasan and his associates had not yet taken up their positions around the building. She'd run across Healy Lawn and past the university library. She'd traced a circuitous path across Prospect Street and finally into the thickly wooded, rectangular copse that separated the streets of Georgetown from the C&O Canal.

Then slowing to a walk, she had cautiously entered the thick wood that flourished near the riverbank and, having picked her way carefully through the underbrush, had come to a halt deep within the darkened confines of the copse. The wood had proven navigable only because the moon was bright on this cloudless night and was augmented by accidental light from the streetlamps on Prospect. She also recalled how fear had clutched at her from all sides.

Despite the maze of confusing shadows cast by networks of overhead branches, Sari had eventually stumbled into a sort of natural room created by a rock outcropping's nearly circular formation. Without pausing, she remembered, she had removed the headscarf, allowing her long, thick, black tresses to cascade freely down her back. Then, having checked to see that her seclusion was total, she had removed her beige, ankle-length abaya and donned her English-American clothes. She had then lain down carefully, wrapped in the abaya, on the makeshift bed of pine needles. She had spent many of her childhood nights out of doors. Consequently, the natural surroundings brought familiarity to her mind.

Her fear diminished.

But, still restless and unable to sleep, Sari had replayed a dozen times the onslaught of sensations that had enveloped her during the hours since her act of defiance in Gaston Hall. She had had since then no second thoughts about going to Jaakov Adelman to alert him to the presence of the assassin sitting just in front of Rebecca Clark. She was at peace with that decision.

Her Aunt Greta and members of the Manguson-Clark family had taught her the Christian's "blueprint of the universe," and she had prepared herself long in advance to offer "my life for yours," should the crisis materialize.

And it had.

Sari did not realize that sleep had overtaken her until she was awakened in the early morning hours by the sound of rough, male voices. The men seemed to be nearby in the darkness, their harsh voices muffled by the thickness of the trees and shrubs. When she listened carefully, she could understand the words.

The men were speaking Arabic.

CHAPTER TEN

Tuesday, 3:00 a.m., Jim Durham's apartment, Washington, D.C.

Two minutes after 3:00 a.m., Durham opened the door to his apartment and was surprised to find his temporary roommate talking on the living room phone. Deng waved Durham over, saying, "It's Aleksy Kaminski ... calling from a pay phone somewhere ... needs to speak to you, Jim."

Durham had been getting drowsy during his drive home. Suddenly he was wide awake and at the same time mystified. How could Aleksy be calling from a pay phone when he was supposed to be in a hospital bed and filled with pain medication?

"Aleksy?" he said into the phone. "Where are you?"

The Pole ignored the question.

"The girl in danger. I know what they plan for her. They get rid of her. I know where they take girl. I show you."

Durham paused to let these rapid-fire statements register.

"You're talking about Sari ... and you're saying that Millicent Thomas' people will snatch her up and ... eliminate her?"

"Tak ... they bring her to U.S. to help them ... then throw her away."

"And you know where she has been taken?"

"I know hotel where they meet ... Ms. Thomas and the others ... and I know where we look for girl before hotel ... we look in forest ... we need hurry."

Durham thought for a moment, then asked a question.

"Father McGriff ... one of our people ... saw Sari leave the auditorium at the university, but that was ... let's see ... about eight hours ago, Aleksy. You think you know where she might be, even after so much time?"

"Check forest first ... Ms. Thomas had me ... um ... *rekonesans* ... that forest ... in case they try to grab Mrs. Clark and she run from them ... hide ... but the girl knew about the forest, too … I am thinking that after her work done … she go to forest …

"So … we check forest first … then go to hotel … find girl."

"So … you did *reconnaissance* in this forest you're talking about …

"Aleksy," Durham continued after another pause, "I've had some of my police colleagues looking all around Georgetown for most of the night. None of them saw her, and they said they looked everywhere in that area."

"Easy to hide in forest at night … they not find that girl."

"All right, Aleksy," said Durham finally. "I'll come get you. We'll go and look.

"Where are you now?"

Tuesday 3:30 a.m., Georgetown, copse near C&O Canal

Durham, Deng, and Aleksy Kaminiski, each carrying a precinct-issued flashlight requisitioned by Durham, spread out across the rectangular "forest" that separated Prospect Street in Georgetown from the C&O Canal. They moved slowly, systematically, through the close woods, stopping periodically to examine likely hiding places behind natural rock formations or within foliage-sheltered declivities.

They had almost reached the extreme western edge of the east-west axis of the rectangle when Deng called out, "Here! Look!"

When the others arrived, they saw a nondescript drawstring bag lying crumpled at the edge of a small rocky enclosure. Near the bag was a beige abaya. Durham opened the bag and found an assortment of toiletries, a few undergarments, some loose document pages, and a Pocket New Testament. Deng illuminated the tiny volume of scripture and Durham read the penciled inscription on the flyleaf:

Sari van Dijk

Contact Greta van Dijk

Dutch Reformed Church
City of London

Carrying the drawstring bag, the men hurried back to Durham's Dodge Ram. Kaminiski's enormous bulk made the truck's bench seat feel small, but

Deng's compact frame and Durham's slender physique made the arrangement workable.

While he gave turning directions to Durham, Kaminski explained the importance of the hotel toward which he was guiding them.

"Ms. Thomas not have her meetings at her house. Meetings at old hotel. Very bad hotel. Very dirty. Very ugly. Very bad neighborhood. I show you."

Kaminski knew the route to the hotel precisely. The building was located in the northeast corner of the city, not far from the park where Durham and McGriff had accosted the young man who had knocked Marie off her feet and stolen her ready-satchel the previous week. Kaminski took them first past Dunbar High School, north of the Capitol building, then beyond the park and on to the hotel.

Once there, he showed Durham where to leave the truck, one block from the hotel, then led the other two back to the rear of the structure. Kaminski pointed upward toward a darkened room on the third floor. The window to the room stood open, leading Durham to realize that the hotel probably had no air conditioning.

"That room," said the Pole, "… that where Ms. Thomas hold meetings.

"We use fire escape."

He positioned himself under the downward-sliding ladder that, when pulled down to ground level, would lead them up to the ancient fire escape's switchbacks of stairsteps and iron platforms. He made a cup with his meaty hands and gestured toward the small, but well-muscled, Sudanese.

Deng saw at once what Kaminski intended.

He placed one foot carefully in the stirrup formed by Kaminski's hands and, as the immensely strong Pole lifted him, Deng reached up and seized the lowest rung of the ladder with both hands. Kaminski then stood back as Deng's own weight brought the ladder down almost to the pavement.

"I no climb," said Kaminski to the others. "Back hurt."

He looked at Durham.

"You have gun. You go up … get girl … shoot everybody else."

Durham suppressed a grin.

"Well, Aleksy," he said quietly, knowing their voices would carry easily up to the open windows of the hotel, "I can't just climb up and shoot everybody, but I can go up to that window and see if Sari is there. If she is, I can use my truck's police radio to wake up Captain Johnstone. I'm sure he'll authorize an entry team to go up and retrieve the girl, even though he may not have time to obtain a search warrant.

"The captain saw the girl at the auditorium. If I see her in there, he'll send a team to get her. No question … he gets what's happening … it's life or death."

With that, Durham, supremely fit, scaled the ladder with ease, proceeded to the third-floor window, and cautiously peered into the room. The hotel room was dimly lit by its floor lamp and entryway overhead light and was obviously empty. The bed did not appear to have been slept in that night.

He leaned back and looked down toward the sidewalk. Only then did he realize that Deng had followed him silently up the fire escape and was crouched just behind him. Deng spoke to Durham in a whisper.

"No one in the room, Jim? Let me go in and see if there is evidence of Sari having been brought here."

Deng understood that Durham would be reluctant, as a precinct detective, to conduct a warrantless entry and search. But Deng, as a mere precinct researcher, and a part-time one at that, felt no such constraint. Durham nodded and moved aside.

The agile Deng, having slipped on a pair of evidence gloves, drew something from his pocket and Durham heard the unmistakable spring-loaded snap of a switchblade knife being unleashed from its handle. In just seconds, Deng had slashed the screen along its left side and across its base, creating a triangular fold-back opening through which he moved instantly. Durham watched as his partner moved swiftly around the room, searching the surfaces and opening drawers.

Durham saw him suddenly stiffen and look toward the closed door to the bathroom. Deng looked back and gestured with a hand to his ear that he had heard a noise from that room. He padded silently to the door to listen.

Durham watched Deng pause briefly and then enter the bathroom. In seconds, he returned, moving fast, to the window where Durham still crouched, waiting.

"She's there," he said quietly. "They chained her to the toilet bowl."

"Do you have chain or bolt cutters in your truck?"

Durham nodded, spun, and descended the fire escape. He hit the ground running and, in less than two minutes, was climbing the ladder again, a formidable chain-and-bolt cutter clamped to his belt. He handed the implement to Deng and waited while the Sudanese crossed the room again, disappeared into the bathroom for less than a minute, and emerged with Sari van Dijk in tow.

Tuesday, 4:45 a.m., Andrews Air Force Base, Chapel-Belton guest unit

Durham, Deng, and the girl, having dropped Kaminski at his hospital, where he was simultaneously welcomed and scolded by the night nursing staff, approached the door to Eleanor and Belton's guest unit. Durham rapped quietly on the door, but loud enough, he hoped, to awaken one of them.

Together, they opened the door immediately.

Early risers.

Seeing Sari standing beside the men, Eleanor rushed to the girl and reached to embrace her. Sari shrank back momentarily, but in Eleanor's tender embrace, quickly relaxed and smiled gratefully.

As soon as all were inside the cramped living room, Eleanor said, "Sidney and I were just starting to pull together something for breakfast.

"What can we get you three?"

"Sari must be famished," said Durham, "but I'm going to wake up Sarah, Dr. Chapel. She and I need to get to St. Patrick Church before the 5:30 a.m. Mass, if we can. We've promised Aleksy Kaminski that one of their Polish-speaking priests will visit him at the hospital this morning. We can get to the church and back here in time for our next meeting, Sid, if you'll wait 'til 7 o'clock. We'll beat the worst of the traffic."

Belton shook his head.

"We'll meet late morning, Jim," he said. "Do get here by seven, though. Crash fer three 'r four hours. We need everybody t' be rested … at least a little."

Durham nodded gratefully.

He headed out the door to retrieve Sarah, while Eleanor and Belton expanded their breakfast preparations to include Kazim and Sari. Conversation and explanations were placed on hold until the late-morning meeting. After downing toast and cereal, Deng was sent into their bedroom at the couple's insistence, removing his shoes and lying down softly on the edge of the bed. Meanwhile, Eleanor pulled spare sheets from the guest-unit linen closet and created a makeshift bed on the sofa for the teen.

Sari declined the pillow offered to her, saying she preferred to use her drawstring bag for that purpose, as she had done in the woods that night. In minutes, Sari van Dijk was sleeping the sleep of the saved.

Tuesday, 11:30 a.m., Andrews Air Force Base, Chapel-Belton guest unit

The session began a half-hour before noon with everyone present, including Luke, officially released from the base infirmary, and Sari van Dijk, who had awakened of her own accord an hour earlier. She had freshened herself and had also eaten again, ravenously. She was now perched on the same sofa on which she had slept, and additional chairs had been brought in that morning so that everyone could be seated. The little room was crowded, but no one seemed to mind.

Rather, it seemed all were happy just to be together again.

And Sari fairly bubbled with joy at being included in the "grown-up" meeting. She now wore an NYU sweatshirt, borrowed from Eleanor Chapel. The two were the same size, the six-decade age difference notwithstanding. With Rebecca's hairbrush, Sari had brushed her black tresses thoroughly, so that now the glistening cascade fell across one shoulder and down across the "new" sweatshirt.

At Belton's request, Rebecca opened the session with a prayer of thanksgiving for God's deliverance of them all, especially Sari, from the dangers "wherewith we were compassed" in the night. After the heartfelt *Amen*, Rebecca introduced the teen more formally to the group. She wanted to make sure that all of those present understood Sari's familial connections to the Clark-Manguson families. Several Yahalomin members murmured their welcoming words to the girl.

Rebecca then nodded to Belton, who turned to Durham.

"Jim," he said, "ya wanna fill us in?"

Durham, assisted occasionally by Deng, then supplied the group with the astonishing narrative of the late-night/early-morning events, starting with his arrival at his apartment at 3:00 a.m., and the phone call from Aleksy Kaminski. He traced their three-man search of the Georgetown C&O-Canal copse and the discovery of Sari's drawstring bag and abaya. Then he described the trek across the city to the decrepit hotel in which, Aleksy had explained to them, Millicent Thomas had held her meetings with the Nicaraguans and Muslims.

At this point, Durham had looked across the room to Sari.

"Sari," he asked, smiling, "do you want to say anything about how you got to that hotel … or shall I just keep going?"

All eyes turned to the teen, and her own eyes dropped into her lap. Durham was about to resume his overview when she began to speak, her voice high and clear.

"I ran to the woods after I told Mr. Adelman about the killer-person and found a good hiding place, I thought. I didn't have any idea what I might do next, so I just changed into my English-American clothes, laid my abaya on the pine needles, fluffed my drawstring into a pillow, and eventually went to sleep.

"But Hasan, the man who made me come with him and his Muslim friends to the U.S., found me and took me to that hotel. He did not stay long. He spoke Arabic to his friends and to me, and said he'd exchange me for … Mrs. Clark.

"Then he chained me to the toilet, and they all left."

At this, she looked back to Durham, and he continued.

"At Aleksy's direction, Kazim and I climbed the old-style fire escape and looked into the open window where Aleksy said the congresswoman held her sessions. We saw the room was empty, but Kazim whipped out his switchblade and cut through the screen. He checked the room, wearing his precinct-issued gloves, looking for evidence that Sari had been taken there."

"I heard a little noise," Deng interjected, "from the bathroom, entered, and there was Sari, chained, as she said, to the toilet. I reported that to Jim. He ran back to his truck and came back with bolt cutters. Then I freed Sari easily."

"We took Aleksy back," resumed Durham, "to his hospital, where I'm sure he was both welcomed and yelled at, and then we came straight here. I awakened Sarah, so that we could hurry over to St. Patrick before their 5:30 a.m. mass. We made it, talked to one of the Polish-speaking priests, and he promised he would visit Aleksy at his hospital at some point this morning. Sarah and I will check back with the priest as soon as we're finished here … with our meeting."

"So," said Belton, "whada we know … an' whada we *need* t' know?"

After a thoughtful silence, Rebecca offered to summarize.

"From Sarah's dream," she began, "and from my attempt to photograph the Thomas-Acosta-Hasan document in the congresswoman's office, we know the congresswoman has a formal agreement with those two men … a Nicaraguan and a Saudi. And, as stated in the FBI file that was reviewed by Kazim, we know that Ms. Thomas hopes to leverage herself into the now-vacant U.S. Senate seat from Louisiana. She apparently will announce this week.

"Longer-term, it seems clear that she hopes to become sufficiently prominent that the current U.S. vice-president will seriously consider her as a running mate when his party nominates him for president in the 1988 election year.

"And we know, too," Rebecca continued, "that Ms. Thomas is speaking in support of liberation theology here at the conference, presumably to emphasize her support for the Sandinistas, for whom liberation theology constitutes the core mission doctrine ... but also, we assume, to impress her Catholic and non-Catholic Louisiana voters. Thus, liberation theology comprises a borrowed *theological* rationale undergirding the congresswoman's political ambitions.

"And, again according to the FBI file, we know that she gives financial support to both sides in the Nicaraguan civil war."

Rebecca paused, thinking.

"And, on that subject of financial support, we know from Kazim's research that Ms. Thomas is extremely wealthy, both from inheritance and from offshore oil, and is in position to contract with ... um ... those who are available to commit violence on her behalf ... to further her personal-political agenda.

"And, as a preliminary to her other moves, we know that she has contracted with those who deal in violence ... to eliminate us ... and those helping us ..." — here she nodded to Sari — "by ordering assaults on Dr. Chapel, then on Sarah, and now on Sari ... and, of course, also by trying to murder me, and possibly others among us, to smooth the way for her longer-term agenda.

"We are a *major* obstacle in her eyes."

Rebecca paused again, then continued.

"We also know that this man who calls himself Hasan has orchestrated the two abductions of Sari, first from London and again last night from Georgetown. And, I should add, while we do not *know* this, we might speculate that he has, or will, get in touch with the Muslim cells delineated in Ms. Thomas' FBI file, as reported to us by Kazim. If so, then Hasan will presumably become part of those cells' efforts to insinuate themselves so thoroughly into the nation's social fabric that the cells are no longer identifiable. Furthermore ... Jaakov, having studied relevant documents last summer in England, has reminded us that these cells are probably just one component of something much larger ... something global."

Rebecca looked toward Adelman, who responded, "Yes ... 'a multi-faceted, full-service, criminal organization whose origins are Middle Eastern' ... now looking to spread a sense of distrust throughout U.S. society … and probably throughout the societies of the major democracies around the globe."

Rebecca nodded and added, "And we also know from Kazim that Ms. Thomas contributes large sums in support of these Muslim terrorist cells."

She paused again, reflected, then looked back to Belton.

"That's where we are, I think, Mr. Belton. Does anyone have more … anything I've forgotten? Does that seem to cover everything we have at the moment?"

She and Belton looked around the small room. To their surprise, it was the 14-year-old Saudi who responded, after she saw that no one else offered.

"Mrs. Clark," Sari said tentatively from her perch on the small sofa, "I've been carrying around a document in my drawstring bag since yesterday. It's just loose pages … maybe 20 or 30 pages, I think.

"Hasan and the others took me to a photocopying place yesterday morning. They made maybe a half-dozen copies of this … 'plan,' they called it … and they told me to stack the copies in a box. While they were busy talking, I dropped one of the copies into my bag. I haven't looked at it, but … like I said … they called it a plan."

With that, she reached into her ever-present drawstring and pulled out the document. The pages were loose, disordered, and crumpled. She pulled them together as best she could — a single, untidy pile of paper — and pushed the messy stack into Eleanor Chapel's hands, as the professor moved to the sofa to assist. Eleanor Chapel, almost identical in size to the Saudi teen-ager, sat down beside her and began to organize the confused pages.

The others waited, curious.

"Well …" said Eleanor after several moments, "this is written in both English and in what appears to be Arabic. Sari, is this Arabic?"

Sari looked at the page held out to her.

She nodded.

"Yes," she said simply.

"And can you translate this?" asked Eleanor.

"Yes …" Sari said, peering at the page.

"It seems," said the teenager, "that this page is talking about … um … 'several powerful explosives … to be placed in Gaston Hall' … and … um … it seems to say … 'the explosives will be placed' … let's see … 'Tuesday afternoon' … um … that would be *this* afternoon … yes … *this* afternoon … um … 'in preparation for destroying those who attend … this evening's panel discussion'."

The Yahalomin looked at each other in wonder.

"Sari, please read that whole section to us," asked Marie.

"No … wait …" said Eleanor.

"Let me help Sari get the whole document organized properly. This is probably a single document, written first, I should think, in Arabic and then translated into English at some point. Give us a few minutes to get the pages in order, and then we can begin to get a sense of what we have here."

And fewer than 10 minutes later, the two documents — the English and the Arabic versions — lay side by side. Sari peered at the two opening pages, comparing the two, and then looked up, nodding, at Eleanor.

"These first pages are the same," she said.

"Each of these documents," said Eleanor to the room, "is only 17 pages. Let me read the English aloud, while Sari follows along in the Arabic, just to make sure that one is, in fact, the translation of the other. Everyone agree?"

The room nodded.

"This has single-spacing in a small font. This is going to take some time," she noted. "Everyone ready?"

Several stirred, picking up pencils or pens and notepads.

Eleanor waited, and then began, reading slowly while Sari followed in the Arabic. After nearly a half-hour of tedious reading, Eleanor stopped. She turned to Sari.

"Same … on your pages?" she asked.

"Same," said the girl.

The group, many of them having made notes to themselves while Eleanor read the document, then sat back to consider the revelation they had just heard. The silence was long, as each Yahalomin member struggled to process the enormity of the Thomas-Acosta-Hasan Pact and Long-Range Plan.

Rebecca had recognized the first several pages as the same ones she had photographed in the congresswoman's home office. That document, a simple agreement among three individuals to align themselves in support of Millicent Thomas' political goals, had been less than a third the length of this. The longer portion of this document, which Rebecca and the others were hearing for the first time, put forth a staggering agenda, starting with the explosives to be detonated that evening.

The explosives were to be placed in Gaston Hall at the university as a means, according to the document, of killing Eleanor Chapel and any other Yahalomin who might be present. The document assumed that Rebecca would have been assassinated Monday night by the shooter that the Muslim group would put in place.

Thus, Rebecca was not mentioned.

But the projected Tuesday evening action consumed only one page of the 17. The document went on for many more pages, and extended more than *two decades* into the future, long *after* Millicent Thomas envisioned herself as having served eight years as the first woman to become president of the United States.

In the near term, the document described other explosives to be planted at the U.S. Capitol building — the framed photo of which had crashed onto the congresswoman's desk during Rebecca and Luke's incursion — and went on to describe other agreements soon to be developed among the plan's leaders in Iran, Iraq, Saudi Arabia, Syria, South America, and Central America.

These projected agreements, some of them already tentatively in place, would funnel oil, drugs, arms, and human trafficking money to Millicent Thomas and her associates before, during, and after she had achieved election as senator, as vice president, and then as president of the United States. In fact, the long-range goal was to elevate her global power to something *above and beyond* the mere U.S. presidency. She would eventually, if the plan came to fruition in the longest term, be in position to buy and sell nations, corporations, and peoples at her whim.

To most of the Yahalomin listening to Eleanor's reading of the document, the plan sounded insane, the ravings of a lunatic.

When she finished, another long, thoughtful silence ensued.

Luke broke the silence eventually, saying, "Could I just see the hands of anyone here who thinks that, aside from tonight's planned bombings, this is anything we should even discuss seriously? Does anyone in this room think that this is anything other than 17 pages of nonsensical megalomania?

"After we tackle tonight's Gaston Hall problem … does *anyone* here think we should take the rest of this seriously?"

After a moment, four hands went up. The hands belonged to:

Rebecca Clark.

Eleanor Chapel.

Sid Belton.

Jaakov Adelman.

CHAPTER ELEVEN

AS THE YAHALOMIN FINISHED READING AND DISCUSSING THE document that Sari van Dijk had secreted in her drawstring bag, a disheveled, long-haired male figure moved impatiently and irritably through the passageways of Washington National Airport. Louis Bois was unhappy. He had not wanted this assignment.

He had, in fact, not wanted to travel to the U.S. at all. He felt at home in London or in his native city of Paris, was contemptuous of American politics and politicians, and wanted simply to do his job, preferably in England. That job was that of an investigative journalist. Bois had, for several years now, been affiliated with the *New York Times'* London bureau. He was regarded as the bureau's top-ranking investigator.

His British editors had told him only two days previous that they needed him in America right away, because he was, they insisted, the only journalist in the world who had any meaningful background with the mysteries they grouped under the editorial heading of "unexplained and unexplainable data sources." And he had had to admit that indeed he, and only he, knew the players involved.

Bois *knew* Rebekka Yahalomin.

He had, in fact, been so trusted by the Yahalomin during the previous summer that he had been sought out by none other than Sid Belton, another disheveled figure, whose reputation, like that of the journalist, was not constrained by national boundaries. The two were widely known and respected on both sides of the Atlantic.

Bois had been told, as well, by the London bureau's senior editor, that Rebecca Clark, former internationally ranked tennis star and central figure in the news staff's intermittent efforts to understand and uncover "unexplained and unexplainable data sources," was reported to have intervened recently in downtown Washington, D. C., to stop a kidnapping attempted in broad daylight.

The kidnap target, Bois was told, had been a young woman who served as administrative assistant in a Washington detective agency. That agency, he was given to understand, was a branch of the New York City agency of Belton and Adelman, the very men who had engaged Bois the year before to assist in an ultimately successful rescue attempt of yet another kidnap target.

That target had been Rebecca Clark herself.

The editors had reasoned that, given Bois' relationship with the Yahalomin, and given the fact that Sid Belton and Jaakov Adelman were now reportedly immersed in efforts to derail a volatile plan involving a U.S. congresswoman, a Nicaraguan political operative, and the leader of several Muslim terrorist cells, he would be the journalist of choice to uncover the facts, including the identities of the three leaders of the plan, none of whom was known by the London desk. It promised to be a "groundbreaking story," said the editors, with Bois as the brilliant centerpiece.

One problem, however, was that Bois had no interest in being seen as the brilliant centerpiece of anything. He loved investigative journalism for its own sake. He loved the work. He loved to see the outcome in print, but not so much to see his own byline as simply to read the article. His joy was the story.

Bois had been told that Rebecca Clark had employed her skill in the use of 12-inch Barringtons Swords competition throwing knives to quash the abduction of the D.C. detective firm's assistant. He had also been informed, during his two-hour layover at New York's Kennedy Airport, that Mrs. Clark had subsequently been the target of an aborted assassination attempt at Georgetown University.

Beyond that, Bois knew only that the unknown-to-him congresswoman had been rumored to have provided payments, not only to the would-be attackers of the administrative assistant, but also to another group that had attempted to kidnap Dr. Eleanor Chapel, a longtime member of Rebecca Clark's entourage. Bois' editors had emphasized to him that the assassination attempt on Mrs. Clark and the attacks on the New York professor and the administrative assistant were probably linked. The congresswoman herself was, they suggested, the link.

The editors expected Bois to uncover the plot quickly, while the liberation theology conference in Washington was still underway. Bois had been told that he would be met at Washington National Airport by one of the mid-level editors who had been assigned to facilitate this effort to generate a high-profile, "groundbreaking story" about the developing crisis and its lead characters. Still unhappy and still irritable, Bois finally secured his luggage and proceeded to the pickup area near baggage claim.

Bois had been told to look for a beige, four-door, 1984 Toyota Corolla. The vehicle sounded so bland that Bois was not sure he would be able to distinguish the car from the airport's walls and pillars. But after fewer than 10 minutes, a vehicle matching the description stopped just in front of him. The driver motioned for him to toss his single piece of luggage onto the back seat.

He did.

"Did you have a good flight?" asked his escort when Bois was seated.

Bois looked at the man carefully. Then he looked out the front windshield, where city traffic crowded in on itself and an unwelcome investigative assignment loomed. Bois had not slept on the overnight flight from London, nor on the connecting flight to Washington, and he was in no mood to chat.

"Non!" he said simply.

"I wish to go," he added, "to the detective agency leased by Marie Campbell and Father Jack McGriff … the Washington branch of the New York firm owned by Sidney Belton and Jaakov Adelman. Do you know this agency's location?"

"I do," said the driver. "We'll be there in … about 15 minutes."

"May we not speak during that time?" asked Bois.

The driver nodded.

And so they negotiated the city's noon-hour traffic until, 25 minutes after they left the curb at Washington National, they came to a stop at the Campbell and McGriff detective agency. The mid-level editor looked at his passenger questioningly.

"Merci," said Bois simply as he rose from the front passenger seat, stepped to the rear door on that side, and removed his single piece of luggage.

Tuesday, 1:35 p.m., Campbell and McGriff offices, Washington, D.C.

"Thank you," Bois said again, and slapped the roof of the Toyota, his signal for the driver to leave him there. The car pulled away and Bois walked to the door of the agency. He stepped inside and was confronted immediately by a large man wearing a shoulder holster from which the handle of a 9mm weapon protruded.

The man indicated by a gesture that he intended to frisk the visitor. Bois dropped his luggage to the floor and extended his arms out to the side, not in the least annoyed by the unanticipated level of security. On the contrary, he fully approved.

The weapons search completed, the security guard gestured for Bois to follow him to the reception desk, where Marie and Jack's part-time assistant waited nervously. She asked Bois if she could be of assistance.

"My name is Louis Bois," he said, producing his identification. "As you can see, *madame,* I am a journalist with the London desk of the *Times.* I assisted Monsieur Belton and Monsieur Adelman last summer when they were in England, and I have been asked by my editors to contact them again. Now."

He stopped and waited, his face impassive.

She smiled uncertainly, then said, "Please follow me to Mrs. Campbell's office."

She turned and walked down the hallway, Bois and the security guard close behind. She entered the office, crossed the room, and sat at her employer's desk. She pressed the intercom button that had been set to buzz in Sid and Eleanor's guest unit at Andrews. Then she handed the receiver to Louis Bois.

Belton, in mid-sentence as he drew the Yahalomin's midday discussion to a close, heard the buzz and looked a request to his wife. Eleanor bounced to her feet and trotted to the wall-mounted phone in the small kitchen.

"Eleanor Chapel," she said brightly.

"Madame," said Bois, "I am Louis Bois. I assisted your husband and Monsieur Adelman last summer during the … ah … crisis with Madame Clark."

"I know who you are, Louis," interrupted Eleanor. "It's good to hear your voice. Are you here … in the United States?"

At this, Belton stopped again and turned his eyes to his wife, standing in the kitchen. All others in the cramped living room followed suit. In the silence, Eleanor's high-bells voice carried easily through the room.

Not everyone knew this "Louis" to whom Eleanor was speaking, but all of them realized immediately, from the instant alertness in the demeanor of those who did, that the phone call was being treated as consequential.

"Yes … I understand," Eleanor was saying. "And do you have transportation, Louis? No?

"Please wait a moment, Louis."

She looked to her husband.

Belton turned to his partner.

"Jaakov," he said, "ya wanna talk t' Bois an' see what's goin' on?"

The session's conclusion was paused while Adelman and Bois conversed. The listeners realized immediately that Jaakov was screening the call. Although his tone was congenial, his questions were businesslike. He was clearly not going to offer transportation to the journalist, a man whose contributions the previous summer placed the Yahalomin in his debt, certainly, but whose potential contributions in the current crisis, if there were to be any, were not obvious.

The presence of a journalist, in fact, seemed to Adelman a distraction.

"Louis," Adelman was saying, "give us a few minutes here. I'm sure that Ms. Campbell or Father McGriff will want to talk to their receptionist in a few minutes. Stay there with her, please, and wait for one of them to call her back."

Adelman hung up and remained standing by the wall phone. He then addressed the group, specifically the four — Sarah, Durham, Deng, and Sari — who knew nothing about the previous summer's dealings with the journalist.

"Louis Bois," he said to them, "is an investigative journalist with the London desk of the *Times*. He is, I understand, their top investigator. He says he's been sent to 'sort' our issues for his publication. He wants to interview Rebecca. His editors are somehow aware that Rebekka Yahalomin is facing something sinister here in the U.S. involving a congresswoman, a Nicaraguan national, and the leader of reputed Muslim terrorist cells. He doesn't appear to know their names, or, in fact, anything else at all.

"We do owe him an enormous debt for his help last summer. Without it, I don't know how we would have gotten Rebecca back."

He stopped and looked inquiringly at Belton.

"Whad'ya think, people?" Belton asked the group.

After a moment, McGriff responded.

"He first approached us" — he indicated Marie with his eyes and a nod — "when we were walking near the security firm in London last summer. My view is that in every instance he did exactly what he said he would do. When he learned a great deal about our issues, but saw that publishing the story would do little other than to increase the dangers, he and his editors did not go forward with the story."

"Right," said Belton, "an' when he got th' crucial info fer us, an' when th' MI6 guy asked what he wanted in return, Louis just said he wanted an 'exclusive' with MI6, once th' crisis was over. An' he did exactly what he promised."

"You trust him, then, Sidney?" asked Eleanor.

"Yep."

"Jaakov?" she asked.

"Yes."

"I'll buzz our office," said McGriff, "and suggest that Louis get a taxi to Andrews. We can let the gate sentries know he's coming."

"And I must say," added Rebecca, as McGriff walked to the phone, "I think we might benefit from this man's study of the document Sari has salvaged for us. I'd very much like a fresh pair of ... um ... 'investigative eyes' to review this plan of Millicent Thomas' ... and to help us think long-term about its implications.

"I realize, Luke, that only four of us indicated we think all this should be taken seriously. Eleanor, Mr. Belton, Jaakov, and I raised our hands to show that we think these fantastic complexities — oil money, drug money, human trafficking money, money from a half-dozen outlaw nations, all being funneled toward Ms. Thomas' agenda — could, in fact, materialize. But, Luke, we think this woman has the funding and the political leverage ... *and perhaps, in addition, the commitment to Evil* ... to make it happen. And I'd very much like an investigator of Mr. Bois' caliber to weigh in."

Tuesday, 3:30 p.m., Gaston Hall, Georgetown University

Sarah and Durham stood outside the police tape, 100 yards from the doorway to the Healy Building on the Georgetown University campus. As they watched, three K-9 Corps teams of handlers and bomb-sniffing Belgian Malinois entered the building to climb the stairs leading up to Gaston Hall.

Durham had taken one copy of the Thomas-Acosta-Hasan Pact and Long-Range Plan, secreted by Sari in her drawstring bag, directly to Captain Johnstone at police headquarters, as soon as the Yahalomin midday session had ended, and before Bois had arrived at the base by taxi. The captain had immediately contacted university officials and ordered them to vacate the Healy Building and to move that night's liberation theology panel discussion to a different space.

By the time Johnstone had arrived at the university, that had all been done. When the captain saw Durham standing outside the tape, he approached.

"Jim," he said, "the K-9 teams are gonna go up right now, and the bomb disposal squad is ready to follow as soon as the dogs find something. And everything is closed in Healy ... everybody's out ... and tonight's program has been moved."

"I think we're gonna be okay. You did good, Jim."

"Thank you, Captain Johnstone," replied Durham, turning toward his companion. "This is Sarah Wilson, sir. She was the near-victim of the assault last week … the one stopped by Mrs. Clark's knives."

Johnstone nodded to her, then looked back and forth from one to the other. He shook his head disapprovingly at Sarah.

"You're not thinking of *dating* this detective, are you, Miss Wilson?" he said. "I can tell you for sure … you're gonna find he's nothing but trouble."

She smiled.

"Oh, I've already found that, sir, but I'll straighten him out for you."

Durham reddened, then changed the subject.

"Captain," he said, "any news on the assassin we arrested last night?"

"Well," answered Johnstone, "she is a foreign national who has apparently entered the country without going through customs … has no passport … has not been willing to say anything about how she got here. We're just going to turn her over to the FBI, Jim. They'll figure it out.

"And we can't technically view her as an assassin, you know, because she did not have a chance to aim that weapon at anyone, and so her illegal activity last night in Gaston Hall was simply possession of the firearm. The FBI will put that together with her unauthorized entry into the U.S. and decide what's next.

"You and I," Johnstone concluded, "can move on and just concentrate on the document the Saudi girl got for us."

Durham nodded.

He and Sarah exchanged glances, then he turned back to the captain.

"If you don't need me here, sir," he said, "Sarah and I would like to visit the Polish man who was one of the congresswoman's henchmen, but who is now helping us. He led us to the hotel where the Saudi girl was held. He's in the hospital, recovering from a knife wound he received at the hands of Mrs. Clark.

"We'd like to keep him working with us, partly because he knows some of the ins and outs of how Ms. Thomas and her gang operate."

Tuesday, 4:15 p.m., Aleksy Kaminski's hospital room

Sarah and Durham entered Kaminski's room quietly, but found him conversing in Polish with one of St. Patrick's priests. Introductions were done quickly.

Switching easily to English, the priest said, "We're grateful to you two for taking the initiative on Aleksy's situation. I think this is going to have a beneficial outcome for all concerned. We can certainly use an increased Polish-speaking security presence at our church, especially at night, and, after some training and mentoring, Aleksy ought to be exactly what we've been looking for.

"Further," added the priest, "we have an English as Second Language course just starting next week, and his security responsibilities will not interfere."

"Men's group, too," said Kaminski from his bed.

The priest laughed good-naturedly, turning his head to the patient.

"Right, Aleksy," he said.

Turning back to the couple, he added, "We have a men's group — mostly a social thing, encouraging our Polish men to get to know each other, but also fostering discussions of how to live in accord with Christ's teachings — that also starts next week. There are some good people coming into our church.

"Thank you, Sarah and Jim, for giving us one more exceptional member."

From his bed, Kaminski beamed.

Tuesday, 5:30 p.m., Andrews Air Force Base, Chapel-Belton guest unit

Sarah and Durham entered the Chapel-Belton guest unit to find Belton talking to them as soon as he began to open the front door. He had a great deal to say and was clearly in a hurry to say it.

"Jus' got off th' phone with Cap'n Johnstone. He's sendin' a squad car t' pick up Eleanor an' Jack fer tonight's thing. He's talkin' t' 'er right now on our phone."

Belton did not pause for breath.

"He's moved tonight's thing t' a little room that'll hold maybe three dozen. Each a' th' panel people gets one guest — we're sendin' Jack with Eleanor, b'cause he can be armed — plus there'll be a few uniformed police an' a couple a' university people.

"Th' squad car'll be here in 15 minutes t' pick up Eleanor an' Jack."

As Belton talked, he and the couple moved slowly toward the kitchen where Eleanor continued to speak on the phone with Captain Johnstone. She appeared mostly to be listening.

Belton took a breath and continued.

"An' wait'll ya hear what Louis Bois has got t' say about th' document that th' girl stole fer us. An' wait'll ya hear what Cap'n Johnstone tol' me on th' phone about th' congresswoman an' her Nicaraguan sidekick ..."

"Wait!" inserted Durham in desperation.

"What?" replied Belton, irritated at the interruption.

"Why," said Durham, "am I not part of the group that will be present this evening with Dr. Chapel and Father McGriff? I'm armed all the time, Mr. Belton, and better prepared than Father McGriff to go into action if that becomes necessary.

"Why not me, Mr. Belton? I'm younger and in better shape and more current with handguns than Father McGriff. I don't understand the thinking here."

"Well," snapped Belton, "if ya would just hol' yer horses, maybe you'd see what's goin' on without makin' a nuisance a' yerself. Could ya just hol' yer horses, Mr. Washin't'n DC Super Detective a' th' Month?"

Belton, angry now, continued, again not pausing for breath.

"You're jus' showin' off fer yer girlfriend, anyway, tryin' t' get 'er t' think you're better an' more important than Jack ... when he knows more about this kind a' stuff than ya ever even heard of in yer whole rotten life ..."

Suddenly Belton, shuffling along with his cane and intent on the evisceration of his young victim, was wrapped up and brought to a halt by Rebecca Clark's forceful, yet somehow careful, embrace from behind. Reflexively Belton tried to jerk away from her, but Rebecca simply held him tighter.

"Dear Mr. Belton," she said quietly in his ear, "let's allow Sarah and Jim to catch their breaths, have a glass of juice, take a seat together on your little sofa, and consider the news we have. After all, Mr. Bois' observations alone have taken the rest of us quite a while to absorb, and this other information about Congresswoman Thomas and the Nicaraguan gentleman ... well ... none of us has had a moment to think through what any of that might mean for us...

"Let's just slow down ... please."

With that, Rebecca released the chastened detective. She took his free hand and led him, clumping along with his cane, to a chair near his wife, who was just finishing her lengthy conversation with Captain Johnstone.

Eleanor, having witnessed the brief drama with Rebecca and her husband, swiftly took a seat beside him on the other side from Rebecca. Meanwhile, Sarah and Jim did as Rebecca had suggested, moving into the kitchen to sample the excellent tomato juice that the ever thoughtful lieutenant colonel had carried into their kitchen earlier. They then carried their glasses to the sofa, squeezing in next to Sari.

When they were settled, Rebecca addressed Eleanor Chapel.

"Is there anything more we ought to talk about from your conversation with Captain Johnstone, Eleanor?" she asked.

"No, dear," she replied. "Captain Johnstone just wanted to go over the details of tonight's arrangements, so that I would have a clear picture. I told him I really didn't need the details and that I was appreciative of how solicitous he was of my welfare, but he insisted. So, I have mostly been listening to things we don't need to discuss."

Rebecca nodded to Eleanor, and glanced toward Louis Bois, who was sitting quietly on the other side of the small room. She turned back to Belton.

"Mr. Belton," she said, "shall we ask Mr. Bois to review his observations about the Thomas-Acosta-Hasan document for the benefit of Sarah and Jim?"

"Yes, ma'am," said Belton quietly, embarrassed at his display of temper.

He looked to the new arrivals.

"Sorry, Jim," he said to Durham. "I get carried away, y' know."

He then shifted his gaze to Durham's companion.

"Yer boyfriend," he said to Sarah, "is not really th' lowlife I just made 'im out t' be, ma'am. He's a very good detective … an' a very good man … an' if I was in his place, I'd be tryin' t' show off fer *my* girlfriend, so … y' know …

"Sorry, Miss Wilson."

Sarah smiled.

"Jim needs the occasional scolding, Mr. Belton," she said. "Keeps him humble, you know. We don't want him to think he's *too* important."

Durham shifted uncomfortably, wishing the spotlight would turn elsewhere.

And it did. Eyes had already turned to Louis Bois, and he began.

"I understand," he said, looking at Durham, "that you delivered a copy of this document … this pact … to the chief *gendarme*, Monsieur Durham, and that he has taken action already. Thank you for that. Your alacrity is commendable."

Durham nodded quietly, still unsettled.

"My editors in London sent me here," he explained, looking now at both Sarah and Jim, "because I worked with Monsieur Adelman and Monsieur Belton last summer in England, and because they — the editors — became aware of Rebekka Yahalomin's engagement with a plot … a plot about which the editors knew almost nothing … other than that the plot involved a U.S. congresswoman, a Nicaraguan national, and the leader or leaders of Muslim terrorist cells beginning to operate on American soil.

"Because my editors knew so little, they did not emphasize to me a fact that has leaped to the fore as I reviewed this pact upon my arrival here early this afternoon. I, as our London desk's chief investigative journalist, have been responsible for tracking Muslim terrorist cells as they have begun to take up residence in the United Kingdom. And as a result," Bois continued, "of my investigations into those cells, I have become familiar with this Hasan person whose name is on the title of the pact document that young Sari so boldly secured for us."

He smiled in Sari's direction, but the smile failed. The gesture looked to the teen more like a grimace than anything she had ever seen. Bois soldiered on.

"Although I have never personally encountered this Hasan person, I have known of his activities for more than three years now.

"I was not happy with the assignment. I do not like United States politics or politicians. I did not want to come."

He paused and shook his head in disgust. Then he sighed and continued.

"My flights, hastily booked," Bois said, "took me from London Heathrow to New York Kennedy to Washington National. I got no sleep, but I was here fast … almost as fast, it would seem, as Hasan and his people."

Adelman moved his hand to get Bois' attention.

Bois nodded to him.

"So … you've actually known of Hasan for years, Louis?" he asked. "I didn't catch that when you briefed us earlier this afternoon."

"Oui, Jaakov," answered Bois.

"Hasan is Saudi and, although he arrived in England alone almost four years ago, he has steadily collected a capable and versatile cadre of associates. He has made sure that his people are scattered throughout the U.K., so that their presence in any one locale is unlikely to become obvious to local law enforcement.

"During my two-hour layover at Kennedy Airport this morning," Bois continued, "a *Times* editor met me and explained the facts of Hasan's presence in the U.S. I was still unhappy, because I did not know Hasan had such powerful connections here. I did not become less unhappy until I read this Thomas-Acosta-Hasan pact and plan this afternoon, the original of the copy you took to Captain Johnstone, Monsieur Durham. Then I became interested. I became … happy …

"I suppose."

Durham stirred.

"Mr. Bois," he said, "how did Millicent Thomas bring Hasan into her orbit? How did she attract him to this … um … Thomas-Acosta-Hasan pact and plan? It seems to me that the pact … and the plan that goes with it … must have been pieced together within hours of Hasan's arrival here in Washington.

"I mean," Durham concluded, "this document Sari secured … the one you spent the early afternoon reviewing … seemed pretty sophisticated to us when we studied it before you arrived … and yet, Ms. Thomas has had almost no time with Hasan."

Bois smiled broadly.

"Ah, monsieur," he said. "You have provided a superb segue."

"I have?" said Durham.

"Oui," Bois responded. "I think your associates here — your Rebekka Yahalomin people — have been wrong, Monsieur Durham … *completely* wrong to think that Madame Thomas has had the leadership role in this Thomas-Acosta-Hasan triumvirate.

"My view is that Hasan almost certainly assumed control of all Muslim terror cells in the U.S. the instant he arrived here. And more importantly, the strength of his Muslim support from Europe and western Asia, not just from Saudi Arabia, *dwarfs anything* the Thomas woman or the Acosta man can muster. My reading," Bois continued, "of the situation is that Madame Thomas and Monsieur Acosta are … what is your amusing phrase? … being 'led by the nose' … by this Hasan.

"He is a man whose resources … please think carefully about this … outweigh those of Madame Thomas and of Monsieur Acosta by a factor of at least 10 … whether one is speaking of financial resources, of human resources, of resources in weaponry, of resources in the political sphere, or of any combination of those factors which can be brought to a focus for the purpose of conducting terroristic activities.

"It is Hasan who is in charge of this pact … of this plan … and yes, even of the long-range goal of winning the U.S. presidency for Ms. Thomas. In fact, if she does manage to become president in a decade, it will be under Hasan's aegis. And she, as president, will be forced by him to act in accord with his priorities.

"Mark my words, Madame Wilson and Detective Durham," Bois concluded, "what you face now … what Rebekka Yahalomin faces now … is a Muslim terrorist thrust into the heart of the United States government and its people. Thomas and Acosta are nothing more than tools in the hands of Hasan and his legions."

Bois paused, thinking, then continued.

"You have thought of Madame Thomas as … embodying great evil, have you not? Well, my friends, *multiply that evil by some large number* and you will arrive at an estimate of Hasan's potential in that regard."

Sarah and Durham looked, first, at each other, and then at Belton.

"Mr. Belton," said Sarah, "can he possibly be right?"

"Well," answered Belton after a moment's pause, "we turned th' thing over an' over this afternoon while you two were … doin' whatever ya were doin' … an' we tried *not* t' agree with Louis … but we ended up thinkin' Louis is prob'ly right, Miss Wilson …

"So … yeah," Belton concluded. "Yeah … he's right."

The telephone buzzed and Eleanor jumped to answer. She listened, said "Yes … good," into the phone, and hung up. She turned, lifted her compact briefcase from the floor, and spoke to Bois, still seated across the room.

"Louis," she said, "Father McGriff and I are leaving now in a city police vehicle for our session at the university. I'm sorry to leave you all, but I do want to thank you, Louis, for turning us around in our thinking about Millicent Thomas.

"We were certain that she was the driving force behind this allegiance with the Nicaraguan and the Saudi. The idea that she … and Reynaldo Acosta … are, in fact, Hasan's lieutenants … or even his lackeys … has gone down hard. You've made our task more formidable, I'm afraid, because opposing the Muslim terrorist world is a more fearsome prospect by far than opposing Ms. Thomas and her allies.

"But, Louis, you have turned us toward the true adversary.

"Thank you."

She and McGriff swiftly exited.

Belton paused momentarily to watch his wife and McGriff depart, then turned back to Sarah with the intent of finishing his response to her question about Bois' analysis and conclusions. Belton glanced down at a small pad on which he had scribbled a few notes to himself.

"Th' idea that it's Hasan that's runnin' this show, an' not Ms. Thomas or this Acosta guy, Miss Wilson, might help explain somethin' that Cap'n Johnstone was tellin' me a few minutes b'fore you two lovebirds came in. I haven't had a chance t' say this t' anybody yet, so this is gonna be news fer everybody here in th' room."

Belton paused for effect.

"Cap'n Johnstone tol' me that Ms. Thomas an' Mr. Acosta are missin' … haven't been heard from in 24 hours … nobody has any idea where they are."

The group took several moments to think about this.

"But," said Marie, "wasn't the congresswoman supposed to participate in small-group discussions this morning at the university?"

"Yeah, she was," answered Belton. "She didn't show."

"An' this Acosta guy was s'posed t' appear in front a' two Senate subcommittees today. He didn't show up at either one. That's why they're considered missin'."

Another pause ensued as the group turned this news over in their minds.

"What does it mean, Mr. Belton?" asked Marie finally.

"Well, ma'am," replied Belton, "it might mean that Hasan decided he didn't need those two anymore. He mighta decided t' get rid of 'em.

"Know what I mean?

"Hm?"

"Oh, surely not, Mr. Belton," said Marie, aghast. "He would surely not … 'get rid of' a U.S. congresswoman and a representative from another government … simply because he wanted more control of this ridiculous planning document?

"Would he?"

But Marie knew as she spoke the words that "getting rid of" people, regardless of the soundness of the rationale and regardless of their stature, was exactly what terrorists would do. She slumped in her chair.

Meanwhile, Rebecca, her hair freshly washed and brushed, now dressed in a modest skirt and blouse combination she had purchased at the base exchange, crossed her legs at the knee, her most comfortable sitting position, and leaned into the group. Her intensity was apparent despite the fact that her shimmering hair, falling forward around her face, obscured her eyes and covered her scar.

"It sounds to me," she began, "as though we need to pray … and pray earnestly … for Millicent Thomas and Reynaldo Acosta … whether their disappearance portends their demise or something less catastrophic."

She sat up straight again and her hair fell back away from her face. The deep gray of her eyes and the exquisite drama of the long scar were, once again, the dominant features of her face.

The room had become utterly silent … waiting.

After a full minute, Rebecca continued.

"It is just occurring to me, right now, in light of Monsieur Bois' observations, that we have also been wrong in our inferences about Ms. Thomas' history of supplying funds to both sides in the Nicaraguan war. We thought her actions were simply a function of her eagerness to prolong the conflict while seeming to her public to favor the liberation theology-themed Sandinista government.

"But consider …"

She paused again.

"Does it not seem plain, in view of this new perspective, that Ms. Thomas has been *buying influence* within the framework of Muslim terrorism's global aspirations? By investing heavily in the Muslim terror cells, does it not seem apparent that she is purchasing for herself a voice in those terror cells' plans and actions?

"Ms. Thomas," Rebecca continued, "is not, in contrast to what we have thought, in charge of anything at all. It is, rather, her wealth and her willingness to fund terrorism that buys her access to power. And that power ranges from simple violence against street targets like Eleanor and Sarah; to large-scale mayhem via the detonation of explosives in Gaston Hall or, suggests this planning document, inside the U.S. Capitol building; or even to whole-population violence via illicit operations originating in the Middle East or South America or Central America, involving oil, drugs, weapons, human trafficking ... the ingredients in a colossal, worldwide 'Muslim mafia' operation.

"Much of that enormous power, right now," Rebecca concluded, "is vested in this man who calls himself Hasan."

She paused again, then continued.

"Millicent Thomas and Reynaldo Acosta will be allowed to co-exist with Hasan and his ... legions ... only so long as they are perceived by him to be useful. I regret to say that ... perhaps ... that time has passed."

She stopped and looked at Belton, still seated next to her.

"Mr. Belton, would you permit me to give us a prayer?"

He smiled his crooked smile.

"I was hopin' you'd say that, ma'am."

Heads were bowed, eyes were closed ... and Rebecca began.

"Father, be present ... be present ...

"We pray now for our missing sister and brother, Millicent and Reynaldo ...

"Please forgive them their transgressions, and, if they have entered into the final transition, please welcome them, forgiven, into Your kingdom ...

"And Father, if they remain here with us, please comfort them if they are in distress, and, if they are not in peril and free to choose their actions, please lead them to right decisions and compassionate choices ..."

Rebecca paused, while she and her listeners concentrated, in prayer, on their "missing sister and brother, Millicent and Reynaldo." Then she continued.

"And Father, we pray also for our sister and brother, Eleanor and Father McGriff ...

"Please be present with them this evening as they work on Your behalf to speak Your truth to those who will hear them … those who are teaching alongside Eleanor … those who are listening … and those who are protecting, alongside Father McGriff …"

She paused again, concentrating on Eleanor and Father McGriff. Then she continued.

"And finally, Father, we pray for us, here assembled in Your name …

"Please guide our thoughts and embolden our actions on Your behalf …"

After one final pause, she reached her prayerful conclusion.

"And we give thanks to You, as well, Father, for Sari … for bringing her safe here to us … and for Aleksy, who helped us to find and rescue Sari …

"We ask Your special blessing, Father, on Sari, on Aleksy, on Eleanor, and on Father McGriff … those of our number who have been and who remain on the front lines in this struggle we face in Your name …

"Father, be present … be present … for we pray these things in the name of Jesus Christ, our Savior and Redeemer …

"Amen."

CHAPTER TWELVE

Tuesday, 7:30 p.m., Andrews Air Force Base, Chapel-Belton guest unit

DURHAM HUNG UP THE WALL-MOUNTED TELEPHONE IN THE kitchen of Eleanor and Sid's guest unit. He turned to the group, which had just finished another take-out dinner of sandwiches and salad. Those present included Rebecca, Luke, Belton, Adelman, Marie, Sarah, Deng, Bois, and Sari.

Eleanor and McGriff were elsewhere … at the university for her presentation.

Those present looked up expectantly.

"Captain Johnstone reported on three things," announced Durham.

"First," he said, "the bomb squad and the dogs found and disarmed three explosive devices in Gaston Hall this afternoon.

"Although the captain considers the auditorium to be cleared now, he will not permit Healy Hall to open until the squad has cleared the entire building. He thinks that will take the rest of tonight and possibly tomorrow, as well.

"Second," continued Durham, "Millicent Thomas and Reynaldo Acosta are still missing. There is no word on their whereabouts. The captain added that, given the document Sari brought us and that we shared with him early this afternoon, he would arrest them both immediately if he could find them. He does not take lightly a document that talks about detonating explosives within his jurisdiction and in places where large numbers of people will be assembled. He noted, too, that both the FBI and the CIA have been alerted.

"And third," Durham concluded, "the captain requests that I transport Sari to the downtown precinct office, so that the police artist can, with Sari's help, construct a sketch of Hasan's face: he wants a head-on, full-face drawing; and, as well, a profile sketch. He notes that Sari is the only person here in the U.S., other than the missing congresswoman and the Nicaraguan, who has seen Hasan …

and so, Sari is the only person who can help the police artist construct an accurate drawing."

Durham turned his eyes to Sari.

"Sari, if you are willing to do this, Miss Wilson and I will drive you downtown right now in my truck, and we will stay with you until your work with the police artist is done. We'll bring you back here as soon as you have finished.

"Is that okay?"

She nodded.

"Sarah will stay with me while the artist works?" she asked.

Sari and Sarah had been sitting next to each other, talking comfortably, throughout the dinner hour. Their connection had been quick and obvious.

"I will be with you every minute, Sari," replied Sarah.

Durham smiled and nodded.

"If you two want to freshen up, then," he said, "we can leave for the precinct office in the city in … say … 15 minutes?"

As the session was breaking up, Marie, who had been holding Penelope in her lap while feeding tidbits of tuna to her grateful calico, stood and approached Rebecca, carrying the little feline with her.

"Rebecca," she said, "I'm going to do my after-dinner walk now … my substitute for the 20-minute walk from our Washington office to our house … would you be willing to join me? I'm terribly anxious about what Jack and Eleanor are doing right now at the university. I'd be grateful for your company."

"Of course, Marie," replied Rebecca. "I'll just need five minutes to change into my tennis warm-ups. I'll meet you then … outside?"

Marie returned Penelope to the pet carrier, the cat-sized enclosure where she would remain until everyone had departed. At that point, Belton, alone while his wife was presenting, would release Penelope to patrol her small queendom at will.

Belton had never, until these last few days, spent any time around cats and at first was disappointed in the inquisitive animal. Eleanor, who had kept Penelope for several weeks the previous summer while Sid was in England, had finally explained to her husband that he should stop expecting Penelope to be a dog.

"She is not a dog, my dear. She will never behave dog-like. She will not wag her tail and bark to be let outside. She will not jump for joy at the sight of you when you come in the door. She's a cat, Sidney.

"This is *her* domain, not ours. Accept the idea that she is simply indulging our presence. Observe her. Be amazed at how she investigates everything … how she poises to attack imaginary mice … how she leaps effortlessly to the top of the kitchen cabinets … how she decides every night where she will sleep, sometimes between your feet, sometimes between mine … sometimes in another room.

"She's a cat, Sidney."

With his wife's lecture in mind, Belton had come to value Penelope's company. He now looked forward to releasing her from the pet carrier, so that the two of them could have their evening chat without interference or distractions.

Meanwhile, Marie and Rebecca had rendezvoused just outside Penelope's unit to begin their circuit. Rebecca immediately adjusted her pace to conform to Marie's much shorter strides and began by asking, "Marie, did Father Jack seem nervous about his assignment tonight? Or are you just nervous on his behalf?"

Marie smiled.

"Oh, it's just me, Rebecca. I still get uncomfortable each time I see him slip that shoulder holster on. He always checks the gun to make sure its safety switch is in the right position. It's automatic with him.

"But sometimes I think I'll never get accustomed to that."

Rebecca thought for a moment, then offered a suggestion.

"You might consider a familiarization experience with that firearm, Marie … you know … handling it and maybe even firing it at the police range … Jim could probably arrange that for you … in order to … um … demystify the weapon a little bit. I'm guessing you've never handled a gun?"

Marie shook her head.

"I've never wanted to."

"They're precision instruments," said Rebecca, "and, given the career on which you and Father Jack have embarked, you probably should consider gaining a certain comfort level with that gun, and with your husband's use of it.

"But don't misunderstand me, Marie," Rebecca quickly added. "I'm not suggesting that you carry a firearm routinely. I don't. I do, however, usually carry three of my Barringtons Swords throwing knives in my ready-satchel. Whenever I have that satchel with me, I am … armed … so to speak. Just not with a firearm.

"The thing is," Rebecca continued, "we do whatever we can, as Christian people, not to take the life of an adversary, if we are called upon to intervene at a critical moment. But Marie, it is very difficult to shoot a human being *carefully*.

"And it is often *impossible* to shoot a human being … *carefully* … in the midst of what may be violence-filled bedlam. Mr. Belton and Mr. Adelman and Jim and Father McGriff have all trained, either in the military or in police settings or both, to use their pistols with great care and precision. And they train continually."

She thought for a moment, then continued, as they completed the first of what would become three circuits around the guest units.

"I have found it necessary," Rebecca said, "to use my throwing knives several times over the last few years, and I think that Aleksy Kaminski's wounds are the most serious I have inflicted. And yet, Aleksy was able to leave his hospital room to help Jim and Kazim find Sari less than 24 hours after my knife stopped him from beating my brother … possibly to death. Had I been forced to use a gun … even from that short range … I don't know if I could have damaged him so … moderately.

"Bullets tend to keep going, Marie, once they've penetrated human skin, and some are manufactured so that they expand on impact, much like shrapnel from artillery shells. And that's why Luke and I use other means.

"So I don't suggest you *carry* a gun, Marie … just that you get more comfortable with your husband's carrying and handling one."

They walked for another minute in silence, each mulling the idea of a familiarization experience for Marie with McGriff's pistol. Then Rebecca continued, returning to her own experience by way of illustration.

"I doubt," said Rebecca, "if knife-throwing would work for you, Marie. Your physical gifts are modest, compared to those God has given me.

"You don't have my length or athleticism … nor do any of us have my brother's strength and experience of fighting without any weapons at all. My recommendation for you is that you simply avoid situations in which you find yourself alone when a potential physical conflict might materialize nearby.

"As St. Paul teaches us," she said, "we all have different gifts. Yours may be to help the rest of us think through our best approaches to the crises that we face, and occasionally to place yourself at risk … purposefully … when you are the best one to do so. None of us is ever likely, as members of the Yahalomin, to live in full safely. We will each, from time to time, find ourselves confronting danger.

"You will sometimes be the one to commit to a dangerous act on our behalf."

Marie, beginning now to breathe more deeply from the sustained pace of their walk, took a moment to consider. Finally, she laughed.

"I know you're right about that first thing, Rebecca. If I'm to be a partner in our detective firm ... a partner to Jack in every sense ... I need to get comfortable with the fact of his carrying a weapon. I need to get rid of my knee-jerk response to seeing him put on that shoulder holster. I'll speak to him tonight, when he gets back.

"As for the other thing, I don't see that I have the courage to do *anything* that involves placing myself purposefully in danger. I don't have that in me."

Rebecca made a noise that sounded like, "Hmph."

Marie looked at her questioningly.

"You," said Rebecca, "have all the courage you will ever need, Marie."

"I do?"

Rebecca smiled.

"Who was that," she said, "at enormous risk to herself, who infiltrated the Soviet Embassy in Washington last summer?

"Who was that who opened a wall safe, extracted a document, and photographed each page of that document, exposing herself to discovery and capture at any moment? And who was it who then went into that foreboding place a *second* time to retrieve a list and memorize it, standing fully exposed *again* to discovery and capture?

"Who was that, Marie?"

Marie laughed.

"You know, Rebecca," she replied, "when I think back about those ... incursions into enemy territory ... it seems as if it was someone else doing those things.

"And yet," she concluded, "it was me. I know.

"It really was me."

The two women completed their walk, much of it in comfortable silence, thinking about their lives and their roles in Rebekka Yahalomin. They had made three circuits of the guest-room compound in just under 30 minutes. As they finished, Marie invited Rebecca to stop briefly in her and Jack's room for a glass of juice.

In their compact guest quarters, Rebecca took her juice glass to the one chair in the room — a straight-backed wooden affair — while Marie sat on the edge of her and her husband's bed. Neither found the arrangement particularly comfortable.

"Well, Rebecca," said Marie, "I wish I could offer you more generous seating, but this will have to do, I suppose."

"It's nice to sit, Marie," Rebecca responded, "but you're right … we were actually more physically comfortable during our walk."

They laughed together, two women who had become relaxed in each other's presence during two summers of relying on the other's judgment and faithfulness through a series of often-violent threats to themselves and to others.

"I just wanted to hear you talk, Rebecca," Marie began, "about this … messy … situation we're facing. I really don't have a handle on *anything* that's happening now. Especially now that the … impetus for things … no longer appears to be one person's mania for power … you know … for grasping at power in any way, legal or not … in any possible way that might occur. But now … well … Ms. Thomas is missing, and this Hasan person and his terrorist allies seem to be leading the charge to … to what?

"I mean, when it was focused on Ms. Thomas and politics, I thought I understood where such evil might originate, and how it might play out, but now …"

"Yes," said Rebecca immediately, "the political thing seemed obvious, didn't it, Marie? Eleanor showed me recently a C. S. Lewis quote about that. It seems he conducted a years-long correspondence — in *Latin*, mind you — with an Italian priest and scholar named Don Giovanni Calabria.

"The passage Eleanor showed me, from a 1950s letter from Mr. Lewis to the Italian, was so striking that it lodged itself in my brain without my making the slightest effort to memorize it. The English translation goes like this:

"'I think almost all the crimes which Christians have perpetrated against each other arise from this, that religion is confused with politics. For, above all other spheres of human life, the Devil claims politics for his own, as almost the citadel of his power.'

"Note," Rebecca added, "not *this* politics or *that* politics … just … politics."

"My goodness!" said Marie. "The citadel of the Devil's power?"

"Yes," responded Rebecca, "and the more I have thought about that passage, the more accurate it seemed to me … but … as you've just said … the issue has shifted under our hands with Mr. Bois' analysis of the problem, and with Ms. Thomas and Mr. Acosta now appearing to have been … um … removed from the equation."

"Yes," agreed Marie. "The political thing seemed to provide a … channel, of sorts … for Hasan's terrorism. His goal was her goal: the U.S. Senate, then the vice presidency, then, no doubt, the presidency. But, absent that structure, Hasan's terrorism becomes, in my mind, completely unpredictable."

"Right," said Rebecca. "The goal now may be exactly that: to create unpredictability in the minds of Americans ... and then, later, citizens of other democracies ... to generate that very unpredictability ... that very uncertainty ... that very doubt ... that things always work in a certain way and will always continue to work in a certain way. Thus, we see Hasan's focus on explosives ... on blowing things up ... on widespread and unpredictable destruction and devastation.

"He and his compatriots may simply want to focus on increasingly visible acts of public violence. They may want to ... I don't know ... blow up the National Cathedral, here in Washington ... or collapse America's most famous bridges, such as your Golden Gate in San Francisco ... or ... maybe ... even commandeer airplanes and fly them into buildings, such as your Empire State building ..."

Marie gasped. "You really think ..."

"I do," said Rebecca, "but here is something that Evil at Hasan's level may be blind to, Marie, because that level of Evil has so little understanding of the Good. His level of Evil may not understand that, in the face of unfathomable horror, Good people unite. I think, for example, of the British people during the nightly bombing of our cities in World War II ... or of the American people in response to the Japanese attack on the U.S. Naval base at Pearl Harbor ...

"It seems to me that neither the Nazi leaders nor the Japanese leaders foresaw that those attacks would bring their chosen adversaries to a unified determination to confront and eventually to defeat the aggressors.

"I wonder whether this Hasan person understands that."

Tuesday, 10:00 p.m., Andrews Air Force Base, Chapel Belton guest unit

As Eleanor and Sidney were just thinking of getting ready for bed, the wall-mounted kitchen telephone rang. Eleanor popped up from the sofa where she and her husband had sat, reading and holding hands.

"I'll get it, dear," she said cheerily, trotting to the kitchen.

"What?" she said into the phone. "Oh, no!"

Belton struggled to his feet and clumped toward his wife, who stood, distraught, the phone down at her side. He reached her and she handed him the phone.

"Belton!" he rumbled in his customary telephone salutation.

Durham was on the line.

"Sir," he said, his voice tremulous, "About 30 minutes ago, Sari finished working with the sketch artist and said she needed to go to the Ladies Room. Sarah went with her. The restroom on this floor was closed off for cleaning, so they went downstairs to the ground floor. When, after 15 minutes, they weren't back, I went down the stairs and stood at the door of the Ladies Room and called out to them.

"When there was no response, I went in. The window to the street was wide open and they were gone, Mr. Belton.

"I ran to the dispatch desk and we got an APB out immediately, which got a half-dozen patrol cars searching the area. But, of course, unless Sari and Sarah were taken on foot, which is hard to imagine, the patrol cars don't know what to look for and we were too late to set up checkpoints around the area. We have no information whatsoever about the vehicle in which they've presumably been taken."

Belton was silent for 10 seconds, thinking, then asked, "How'd th' dirtbags know Sari an' Sarah would even be there at th' p'lice building, t'night? An' how'd they get into th' building t' get that window open? An' how'd they know th' upstairs Ladies Room was gonna be closed fer cleaning?

"Hm?

"How'd they know any a' that?"

"We've been talking about that here, sir," replied Durham.

"We've speculated," he continued, "that they knew Captain Johnstone would be coming here to the HQ building sooner or later, that they knew what he looked like from the Gaston Hall event or from newspaper photos, and that they set up a stake-out, thinking they would try to kidnap him and use him as a hostage … or as leverage. Since 'they' would be Hasan and others who brought Sari to the U.S., they obviously know Sari on sight. We think that, once they saw her enter the building with Sarah, they posed as a cleaning crew, got the upper-floor Ladies Room closed for cleaning, and then just waited for Sari in the ground-floor Ladies Room.

"We really don't know, sir, how they did any of this. We're just guessing.

"But it does seem to us," Durham concluded, "that they had Captain Johnstone in mind, then adjusted on the fly when they spotted Sari, and then took her and Sara … no doubt delighted to have them rather than the captain.

"Snatching a police captain would have brought the whole law enforcement world down on their heads. Taking a foreign teen and a young local woman probably struck them as less risky, although I don't know if Hasan cares about degree-of-risk."

Belton nodded to himself.

"Sounds about right," he said after a moment.

Another pause.

"How're ya doin' with this, Jim?" Belton asked.

Durham swallowed hard, then tried to answer.

"I've fought off the panic, sir, just trying to focus on what action we could take. Once we had the patrol cars out on search, though, I couldn't think of anything else I could do, other than phone you to let you know."

Belton nodded to himself again, then had a new thought.

"Ya think yer Polish friend at th' hospital might be any help?" he asked.

"'Aleksy? Well, I suppose he might. And nothing else is coming to me right now, sir. That's a good thought.

"I'll head over to the hospital and see if Aleksy can think of anything we might do. I'm convinced that he's committed to the right side now. I'll go by the hospital and then drive on out to the base, Mr. Belton. Unless Aleksy sends me off in a different direction, I'll be with you in less than an hour.

"Thanks for the idea, sir. I didn't have any."

"Yeah, okay," said Belton.

"An' listen," he added. "Ya won't do those two girls any good t' go off by yerself, lookin' all over creation. Come on out here. We'll put somethin' t'gether. It might take us all night an' mornin', but we'll have th' best brains in th' country workin' on it.

"Know what I mean, Jim?

"Hm?"

"Yes, sir. I do."

Tuesday/Wednesday, midnight,
Andrews Air Force Base, Chapel-Belton guest unit

"So," summarized McGriff after more than an hour of mostly fruitless speculation and suggestion, "first, we agree that Hasan and his minions realized they had no chance to get at Eleanor or Rebecca or other Yahalomin targets tonight at the university, and so shifted their focus to Captain Johnstone in hopes the captain could be taken from police HQ and used as a bargaining chip, but Sari and Sarah appeared and they snatched them, probably by posing as a cleaning crew.

"Second, we agree that Jim's effort to elicit information from Aleksy Kaminski at the hospital came up empty, though Aleksy was willing, and that Jim's check of the hotel room where Sari had been taken earlier was, as expected, not productive.

"Third, we agree that the congresswoman and the Nicaraguan, now missing for at least 36 hours, have been kidnapped … and are possibly dead … and, either way, were taken by Hasan and his 'dirtbag' associates.

"And finally, we agree, that unless we are contacted by Hasan in an attempt to exchange Sari and Sarah for Rebecca — who is always, we think, the number one target — we have no realistic idea as to how we might search for them.

"Agreed, all?"

Heads nodded somberly.

"Rebecca?" McGriff asked, requesting from her the obvious.

Rebecca stood to pray, standing straight and motionless in her dark blue tennis warm-ups, her hands clasped in front of her chest, her hair unbound and falling as usual to frame her face as she bowed her head.

The room was silent, as she began.

"Father, be present … be present with us …"

She paused for long seconds, the room utterly still.

"Father … we need Your help …

"Please guide us … guide us to our missing sisters …

"Comfort the girl, who is new in Your service, yet incredibly brave …

"Protect the young woman, whom You have already chosen to receive, like me, Your special messages …

"Father, give them to know that we will, with Your help, come for them …"

Rebecca paused again, reflecting, then concluded.

"Father, be present … be present with us … we need Your help …

"Urgently … desperately …

"We pray in the name of Your Son, the Savior, Jesus Christ.

"Amen."

CHAPTER THIRTEEN

Wednesday, 6:00 a.m., shipboard, interior of a 40-by-8-by-8-foot metal container

HE TURNED HIS HEAD AND LOOKED BESIDE HIM AT THE WOMAN, and he saw in her eyes the contempt with which she held him. He knew what he looked like. He knew his face was soft, almost pudgy, and that it showed every day of his 70-something years. He knew that he was nearly bald, and he knew his habit of combing a few wispy strands of hair across the crown of his head only made his baldness more obvious and, to this woman, made him an even more contemptible figure. He knew that his lips were irregular and were seemingly cast in a permanent snarl under his broad nose.

But he knew more than that about himself. He knew that his intelligence was at least equal to that of this woman. And he knew also that the woman's contempt for him was based on more than his singularly unattractive appearance.

He knew that her contempt for him was grounded, above all, in her certainty that he understood Goodness as thoroughly as she understood Evil … and that his alliance with her was one of convenience, at best … and that his view of her egomaniacal lust for power repulsed him. Above all, he knew she hated him because he was a believer, heart and soul, in Jesus Christ as the only begotten Son of God, whereas her publicly held "belief" was no more than a marketing pose.

He knew in his heart that his support of the Contras was driven by his early realization that the Sandinista government's embrace of liberation theology was also a pose, a politics-driven embrace of a flawed theology that nonetheless gave them leverage with much of the poorly educated Nicaraguan populace. And he knew that the Sandinistas' day-to-day methods of operation were as murderous as any examples that world history could provide.

He knew that his commitment to the Contras was real; he knew that the woman's commitment to the Sandinistas was as false as the Sandinistas' embrace of an allegedly Christian political platform.

His beliefs, he knew, were real; hers, he knew, were nothing.

He turned his head away from her and closed his eyes in the sweltering gloom of their 40-by-8-by-8-foot metal container — already placed onboard its container ship — a container that admitted light and air only through 1-by-1-foot openings at each end, each opening 7 feet off the floor, each housing a battery-driven fan that, at one end, pulled air into the container and at the other, pushed air out onto the decks of the massive, fully loaded container ship.

His hands, like the woman's, were bound behind his back and secured to one of the metal eyelets placed regularly around the base of the container, eyelets designed to be used to tie down the container's contents against the pitch and roll of the ship. He and the woman were seated on the hard metal flooring of the container, their ankles bound tightly and the distance between the two of them fixed by the spacing between the container's adjacent eyelets, in this case 6 feet.

He opened his eyes again and turned his face fully away from the woman and toward the far end of the container, peering through the dimness toward the girl and the young woman who had just been thrown, literally, into the container, both of them unbound, but both injured. The girl sat with her back against the container wall, pressing her hands to her rib cage, apparently in an effort to manage the pain from whatever blows had been earlier directed against her small body. From time to time, she would stroke the face and hair of the woman whose head lay in her lap.

The woman was unconscious.

The woman appeared to him, at this distance, to be in her early 20s. He could see the traces of dried blood on the woman's forehead and cheek. Injuries other than those to her face were not visible from where he sat.

Perhaps five minutes had passed since the two had been tossed unceremoniously into the container and the metal door slammed behind them. The girl had immediately positioned herself so that she could cradle the woman's head in her lap. The girl breathed with difficulty, struggling to maintain composure.

He sensed, however, that this girl was not a newcomer to pain. He spoke to her softly through the silence of the tomb-like container.

"Young lady, my name is Reynaldo. Are you hurt badly?"

She looked at him warily and said, "I'm sorry?"

Her confusion reminded him that his English was heavily Spanish-accented, and he repeated his question, speaking more carefully.

"No," she said, now understanding the question and grateful to be asked. "My side is hurt … my ribs … but not terribly … I think."

"And your friend?" he asked.

Sari looked down at Sarah, looked up at Reynaldo Acosta, and said softly, "I don't know. They hit her … *he* hit her … with a club of some kind, because she was fighting him, trying to give me a chance to run away. She has been unconscious for a long time now, and I don't know what I can do to help her."

"When you say that 'he' hit the young woman, are you making reference to the man who calls himself 'Hasan'?"

Sari nodded.

"Shut up, you fool," hissed Millicent Thomas, seated near Acosta. "They're monitoring everything we do or say in here. Just shut up!"

Acosta did not turn his head to look at the congresswoman. He continued to address the girl at the far end of the container.

"What is your name, child?" he asked kindly, now beginning to enunciate as precisely as he could when speaking to her.

"Sari."

Just then the container shuddered as the ship's engines were engaged by its massive reduction gears, beginning now to turn the twin 65-foot shafts, which would drive the screws through the water. At that moment, the door opened and Hasan entered. He slammed the door closed behind himself and strode past the newcomers, stopping 10 feet from Acosta and Thomas and looking down at them coldly.

"Sunrise was about half-hour ago, my friends, so we're backing out of our berth here in New Jersey. We'll take a southerly course down the Hudson and into New York Harbor. We have brought with us from England a skilled ship's pilot who is dedicated to our cause. He has known from the start that this would be, for him, his last voyage … a 12-mile, 90-minute suicide voyage of destruction.

"Since we do not want this dedicated man to … um … reconsider his commitment after we leave the ship … we have chained his wrists to the ship's wheel, but with enough play in the chains that he will be able to reach the engine controls and, when the time comes, also able to reach the trigger which will blow up this ship, everyone left on board — the pilot himself and you four — and the Verrazzano Bridge."

Hasan smiled, waiting for this information to do its work on his listeners. He saw fear in the eyes of the woman, and, in equal or greater measure, hatred. But he saw none — neither fear nor hatred — in the eyes of the Nicaraguan.

Hasan continued.

"The containers beside and above this one," he said, "are filled with enough explosive to destroy not only the ship and everyone on board …" here he glanced at Sari … "but also everything nearby. Our pilot will set a course across the harbor and toward the east tower of the Verrazzano, which, as you are probably aware, spans the entrance into, and the exit out of, New York Harbor.

"The explosives' trigger mechanism," Hasan continued, "is a simple off-on switch. As the bow of the ship smashes into the east tower of the Verrazzano, our pilot will pull the trigger and detonate the explosives. The explosion will not only obliterate this ship, it will collapse the east tower like a twig.

"The blast," Hasan further explained, "will bring the eastern half of the Verrazzano down into the water, taking all transiting vehicles, private and commercial, with it. Possibly, the collapse of the eastern half of the bridge will cause the west tower to collapse, immediately or gradually, as well. That is uncertain.

"But, if so, the entire Verrazzano will be in the water and the harbor will be completely blocked. Loss of life will be immense, including the lives of any unfortunate individuals driving their vehicles near the Brooklyn approaches to the bridge.

"This is," Hasan concluded, "as you know, but one of the … ah … *special events* … that I have planned for the next few months. The Capitol building in Washington will be next … then will come the major airports … eventually we will send large commercial aircraft flying into some of this country's greatest buildings and … eventually … we will wreak sufficient destruction to cause the complete collapse of this country … known to us in the Muslim world as 'the Great Satan.'

"We will achieve its total disintegration."

Hasan turned his face toward Sari and the unconscious Sarah Wilson.

"You, child," he said, "chose to betray me in the university's auditorium when you informed the Israeli. You pointed out our assassin to him. You prevented our assassin's completion of her mission … to end the life of the Clark woman.

"You betrayed me …and our cause. Now you will die."

Sari stonily returned his gaze, her face impassive.

Hasan turned back and faced Millicent Thomas.

"Your childlike naivete," continued the Saudi terrorist, "in thinking that I would make myself subservient to your own personal agenda goes beyond any that I have ever encountered. You, Millicent Thomas, do not understand the meaning of selflessness … of commitment to a cause … of living in accordance with the dictates of a Higher Power. You are a pathetic excuse for a human being.

"Your miserable life will end in …" Hasan glanced at his watch … "less than 90 minutes. It will be no loss. No one will mourn your departure from this earth. In a week's time, no one will so much as remember your name."

He turned and strode out of the container and onto the ship's deck, slamming the container door behind him. The container fell silent.

After several moments, Acosta smiled toward the girl.

"Sari," he said carefully, "I think we should leave the ship before it sails all the way to that bridge tower. Do you not agree?"

She nodded gravely.

"Yes, sir," she said, "but how can we do that?"

"I keep a switchblade knife in my shoe," Acosta answered. "Come over here and use the knife to cut through my wrist bindings. Once you have freed my hands, I'll take care of the rest. And if your friend remains unconscious, I'll carry her out.

"I'm old, but I'm still strong as a bull, Sari."

And he laughed aloud at his own exaggerated self-assessment.

"Let's get started, *senorita*."

Sari carefully lowered Sarah's head to the floor, stood, and moved through the container's semi-darkness to Acosta's feet. She looked at him questioningly.

He wiggled his left foot.

"There," he said. "Just pull my trousers' cuff up and pull my sock down. The knife is right there. Its blade is encased inside its handle. You can't cut yourself."

Sari followed Acosta's directions and in seconds freed the knife.

"Press that little button, Sari, and the blade will spring out. Hold it away from you. The blade is very, very sharp."

Sari did as Acosta said, and an impressive 5-inch blade sprang out.

"Come around behind me, Sari, and cut through these bindings."

Acosta leaned forward as much as he could and in seconds his hands were free. He took the knife back from the teen, thanking her courteously, then sliced through the bindings at his ankles. He then rose to his feet and stepped over to the congresswoman. Kneeling, he swiftly freed her hands, then her ankles.

He stood, reached down, took her hands, and pulled her to her feet. She faced him, rubbing the circulation back into her wrists and hands.

"What do you propose to do now?" she asked.

As she said this, they felt the engines shudder, shifting from "reverse" to "stop" to "forward." The shudders told them that the ship had backed into the Hudson and would be turning south toward the harbor. Twelve miles and 90 minutes from their current position, the lumbering ship would reach the Verrazzano. The subsequent explosion would dwarf anything that had ever been experienced in or around New York City.

Acosta considered the congresswoman's question.

"I imagine," he replied, "that Hasan has either disembarked already or is prepared to disembark with his henchmen as soon as we pass from the river into the harbor. When they brought us on board yesterday, I saw that the port side of the ship has a collapsible ladder — a metal staircase — that hugs the side of the ship and offers an easy descent from the deck to the waterline.

"I also saw that, fixed to the lowest rung of the ladder, there is an … I'd say … an 18- or 20-foot rubber dinghy, powered by an outboard motor. That little craft, tied to the ladder, will move alongside the ship as it sails toward the harbor.

"I assume," continued Acosta, "that Hasan and his people will use that port-side ladder at some point in our passage through the harbor. They've chained their suicide pilot to the wheel; they'll kill or incapacitate the harbor-licensed pilot; they'll descend to the dinghy, and they'll proceed to a Lower Manhattan pier, possibly near the Battery, well before the suicide pilot works the ship to the eastern end of the Verrazzano. Hasan and his associates are certainly not part of the suicide scheme, Millicent. You heard him recite some of his plans.

"They won't be around for the explosion.

"Only the suicide pilot … and you and I and these two … victims … and presumably the harbor-licensed pilot … are part of Hasan's suicide-and-murder plan. We're very small bits in his grand strategy, Ms. Thomas.

"We're fully expendable."

Millicent Thomas frowned.

"You told this girl you plan to leave the ship before it reaches the bridge. I'm curious … how do you plan to do that?"

"Simple," he said.

"I plan to wait until Hasan and his people have used the ladder and the motorboat to flee, if they've not already done that.

"Then we'll pop out of this container, find one of the ship's own life rafts, lower it to the water, and use the life raft's oars to row to the nearest shore.

"Easy."

"And the destruction of the bridge?" she asked.

He shook his head.

"You *want* that bridge destroyed, don't you," said Acosta, "but you've lost control of your plan, Millicent. Now you just want to save your own neck. Well, if we get to shore in time, I'll contact the harbormaster and ask him to close the bridge to traffic, and to get all vehicles off the span."

"And why would he pay attention to you?" she asked skeptically.

"He wouldn't," Acosta admitted.

He was thoughtful for a moment, then continued.

"And I acknowledge," Acosta said, "that I don't see how we can do anything at all to keep the bridge from being blown up."

"Why not?" the congresswoman replied. "Just go up to the wheelhouse and kill the suicide pilot with that knife of yours. Then disable the trigger mechanism."

"I'm not going to kill anybody," he said. "That's something *you* do, Millicent. *You* don't mind killing. Here … take the knife."

The congresswoman snorted.

"We *might* save ourselves," she said, "but I don't understand why you seem so confident about *that*. What is it that makes you think that the door to this … this tomb … is not locked from the outside?"

Acosta turned his face to the metal door at the other end of the container, but he did not move toward it.

"I haven't wanted to think about that," he said.

The congresswoman, however, turned immediately, strode to the far end of the container, placed a hand on the interior handle, and tried to move it.

Nothing.

She turned back to Acosta.

"We're locked in here, genius," she said sarcastically.

"We *might* have 90 minutes to live."

Wednesday, 4:00 a.m., Andrews Air Force Base, guest unit

In the early morning hours of a soon-to-be-eventful Wednesday, while it was yet dark, Rebecca Clark dreamed. The dream was brief and uncomplex.

Needing to report the dream immediately, as always, she rapped on the thin wall to alert her brother, then threw on her tennis warm-ups and exited her unit. He opened his door before she had taken a step in his direction.

"I heard your knock through the wall, Rebecca. A dream?" he asked.

She nodded and he stood aside to let her pass into his small living room. They both remained standing while she delivered the substance of her vision. It was one of the simplest of her visions. She had, she said to her brother, dreamed of an aging, rusting cargo ship of some kind — she did not know commercial ship types — and the featured component of the dreamed image was the ship's flag.

Flying from a staff rising from the stern, the flag exhibited a dark green background that contrasted dramatically with bright, white Arabic-language lettering, along with a white sword superimposed over the lettering. The dream had contained nothing else and had been completely static, but there was the sense, transmitted inexplicably to her sleeping brain, that Sari and Sarah were aboard.

Luke nodded and repeated her description.

"Yes," she said. "Correct."

He nodded again.

"Rebecca, that's a Saudi-flagged cargo vessel."

He thought for a moment.

"No hint of its location?"

She shook her head.

"Do you think it was at sea, or was it at anchor … or tied up to a pier?"

She looked away, thinking.

"Oh … excellent question, Luke," she said. "It was tied up. Definitely not at sea or at anchor … but there was no hint as to the location of the pier."

With those barebones yet nonetheless critical bits of "unexplained and unexplainable data," the two had walked to Belton's unit. As before, despite the 4:15 hour, he was dressed and breakfasting, his eyes bright and alert.

Taking in the dream's import in a flash, Belton said, "If that ship is tied up t' a pier, chances 'r good it's New York. Not much chance of a Saudi ship bein' somewhere else — some other U.S. port with a deep enough harbor an' quick access t' th' ocean — an' a place that Hasan could get to, from here, in a hurry, with captives in hand.

"It's gonna be New York."

Belton, going through a long-distance operator, quickly telephoned his former NYPD precinct office and asked the overnight duty sergeant, a man whom Belton had helped to train when the sergeant had been a mere police academy recruit, to contact the precinct captain at his home in Morningside Heights, on the Upper West Side, to request an immediate return call to Belton at his Andrews guest unit.

Within five minutes Belton was talking to the NYPD precinct captain, another former mentee, asking him to find out immediately from the local harbormaster whether there was a Saudi-flagged ship at one of the piers, and, if so, which pier. Fewer than 15 minutes after that, the hour not yet 4:45 a.m., a Saudi-flagged cargo vessel was identified by the harbormaster, and its New Jersey pier pinpointed.

The precinct captain then informed Belton of those facts and added that the Saudi vessel, a container ship, had booked a licensed pilot and two tugboats for a 6:00 a.m. departure that morning, slightly more than an hour from that moment.

Belton then telephoned the "convener" of the CIA's five-person Rebekka Yahalomin Unit, the small group charged with addressing "unexplained and unexplainable data and their sources." That CIA officer, at his home in northern Virginia, picked up on the second ring. Clearly, 4:45 a.m. was not early for the CIA officer, any more than it was for Belton.

"Belton here. Sorry about th' hour."

"Not a problem for me, Sid. What's up?"

"We just got one of our 'special messages' an' we need yer help … fast."

"You'll have it, Sid. What do you need from us?"

Belton explained that a container ship berthed in the Hudson River on the New Jersey side, in the city of Hoboken, needed to be targeted immediately, that the threat was generated by Muslim terrorists — thus, falling within the purview of the CIA — and that a successful intervention would require boarding-party skills and experience.

"Well," replied the CIA officer, "we can certainly get you there, but we don't have people with boarding-party experience … not available on short notice."

Belton responded immediately. "We've got th' Royal Navy's Luke Manguson, right here with us … at Andrews … best boarding party guy on the planet.

"He's ready to go right now."

"We can get him up there fast, Sid, and we can provide our New Jersey helicopter, too, once he's on the ground."

In just minutes, the time now 5:00 a.m. exactly, the same CIA pilots who had brought Sid and Eleanor from New Jersey to Andrews were scrambled to fly the same route as previously, but in the reverse direction. This time, however, there was to be more to their assignment than simply getting the boarding party team to New Jersey.

The two pilots were qualified not only to fly the 10-passenger Learjet 55C, but also the Sikorsky S-76B helicopter, a five-passenger, state-of-the-art aircraft leased by the CIA and maintained at Teterboro Airport, just north of the

Hoboken pier identified by the New York and New Jersey harbormaster as the registered docking site of a Saudi-flagged container ship.

By 5:30 a.m., having been notified nearly a half-hour earlier by the CIA Rebecca Unit at Langley, the New Jersey maintenance crew at Teterboro was fueling the Sikorsky chopper and giving it the required pre-flight checks prior to the pilots' anticipated arrival in the Learjet, expected to be 6:15-6:30 a.m.

At Andrews, the same process had been undertaken with the Learjet, and, by 5:45, the plane was ready, the pre-flight checks finished, and the "payload" — Luke, Rebecca, and Jaakov — seated and going through their own checks: examining their ready-satchels for the expected-to-be-needed tools of their interventionist trade. Those tools included, for Rebecca, three of her competition throwing knives; for Luke, his array of knives, tools, ties, and short-handled bolt cutters, in case Sari and Sarah were being restrained with chains; and for Adelman, his Glock 17 service weapon.

In addition, the Sikorsky had been supplied with a tactical shotgun, retrieved by the CIA maintenance staff coordinator from the CIA's top-secret weapons cache, located a few miles from the George Washington Bridge across the Hudson.

Wednesday, 5:50 a.m., Washington to New York

Lifting off at 5:50 a.m. and cruising at over 400 mph, the agile Learjet covered the 200-mile distance in 35 minutes, from takeoff to touchdown, descending into Teterboro at 6:25 a.m. This was 25 minutes *after* the container ship had reversed out of its pier and, aided by tugboats and guided by a harbor-certified pilot, headed downriver. The boarding party members knew only that Rebecca's dream had identified a Saudi-flagged ship as one likely to conceal Sari van Dijk and Sarah Wilson.

The boarding party members did *not* know the ship's mission or destination. They did *not* know that three of the ship's containers were filled with enough explosive power to obliterate the ship itself, and, if detonation was in proximity to one of the Verrazzano Bridge's two suspension-support towers, with enough explosive power also to bring at least one-half of the bridge down into the water, along with hundreds of vehicles.

They *did* know, however, that the history of Rebecca's divine messages dictated the critical importance of moving with the greatest possible speed to intervene. Rarely had an emergency been encountered and rectified by Rebekka Yahalomin with more than a few minutes to spare, if that.

When the co-pilot announced to the three-member boarding party that the Lear would begin its descent in five minutes, Rebecca unbuckled her seat belt, knelt next to the two men, and took their hands while she prayed. Her prayer asked for God's presence … "Father, be present, be present …" and for His steadying hand in the upcoming struggle … and, above all, she asked that God would spare the lives of all concerned — both friend and foe — in this attempt to bring Sari and Sarah safely out of captivity and home to those who loved them.

At the sound of their murmured Amens, Rebecca moved back to her seat, buckled the seatbelt, and closed her eyes again, adding a silent prayer of her own to the spoken prayer she had led with the men. Then she looked up, thought of her children and her husband, waiting for her in England, and nodded to herself.

She was ready.

As the Learjet descended toward the airstrip at Teterboro, Luke and Jaakov studied the ships docked on the Jersey side through their military-issue binoculars. They saw no Saudi-flagged vessels, for, in fact, the ponderous container ship in which Sari and Sarah were held had already made its way out of the river itself and into the harbor, moving slowly toward the Verrazzano.

The Learjet pilots brought the aircraft to a full stop just feet away from the idling Sikorsky. They cut the engines and then all five — two pilots and three passengers — leaped from the jet and raced to the chopper. The pilots executed a perfunctory instrument check, engaged the rotor, and lifted off.

They swiftly brought the helicopter and its boarding party to 500 feet and proceeded south, moving with caution given the amount of helicopter traffic around and above them, most of the swarming choppers reporting on morning traffic for local TV, but some carrying business executives to and from Teterboro.

As the Sikorsky tracked downriver and then over the harbor, moving at deliberate pace toward the far-distant bridge, Luke and Jaakov studied the southbound ship traffic ahead, searching for a Saudi flag. As the two men strained to find the target ship somewhere in front of them, Rebecca, without binoculars, looked elsewhere.

Off to the port side and falling behind the copter, she saw a dark speck now gradually nearing the Lower Manhattan park known as the Battery.

"Luke," she said after a moment, "look off to our left, just a few yards south of the Battery and moving toward shore. What is that tiny craft … is that a rubberized dinghy with an outboard motor mounted on the stern?"

Luke turned his binoculars to the northeast.

After several moments, he said, "Rebecca, that boat has three men … and … is it possible?… I think that might be Hasan and a couple of his people!"

"What?" said Adelman, swinging his own binocs in that direction.

He looked, adjusted his binoculars, looked again.

"I see where they're going, but where are they coming from?" he asked.

"They must have dropped that dinghy," answered Rebecca, "from the ship we're looking for … and if that's Hasan … he and his two associates must have just evacuated that vessel … not more than … 15 minutes ago … maybe 10?"

The men turned their binoculars forward again.

"Sirs," said Luke to the pilots, "we need forward speed … now."

The responsive Sikorsky accelerated and, within 30 seconds, the Saudi-flagged container ship could be seen in the distance, plowing methodically toward open water. Luke passed his binoculars to his sister.

She adjusted the focus and looked intently forward.

"Yes!" she said. "That's the flag I dreamed … dark green … with Arabic-language lettering in white … and with a white sword superimposed across the lettering. That's it, Luke … that has to be the ship I was given in the dream."

"Odd," said Adelman after a moment's consideration of the ship. "That thing is a rust bucket. The Saudis normally buy top-shelf vessels. I wonder …"

"But wait," Rebecca interrupted. "The ship is changing course. Why is it turning to port? The ship is heading for … for what?"

The Sikorsky pilots, hearing the question, descended quickly and maneuvered to a position directly astern the ship, lining up with its heading. Now with a clear view of the ship's new course, the boarding party realized its destination.

"Luke," said Rebecca, "it's headed for the east tower. Is it possible it will try to ram the tower? Would that collapse the whole structure?"

"Well," he answered after a moment, "it might, especially if the ship is packed with explosives, Rebecca. Maybe that's why it's a rust bucket, Jaakov. Maybe its mission is simply to sacrifice itself a few minutes from now.

"And maybe Sari and Sarah are intended merely to be collateral damage. Maybe your dream, Rebecca, was just telling you where they've been taken … and maybe they've been taken inside a container on a ship that's going to destroy itself … and them … and the Verrazzano … and everybody in those vehicles …"

His voice trailed off.

"And that," said Rebecca, "would explain why Hasan — if that's Hasan — is in a dinghy going the other way… he's getting as far away as he can from the ship."

"And," added Luke, "he has left maybe one man on board to pilot the ship … and maybe to blow himself up, along with Sari and Sarah, when the ship reaches the east tower. If the ship is packed with explosives, the detonation would kill everybody in proximity and … surely … bring down at least the eastern half of the Verrazzano."

The three Yahalomin looked at each other, incredulous.

But they knew with a certainty borne of experience. This was exactly what terrorists would do.

"Luke," asked Rebecca, "how long do we have before that ship reaches the tower? Do we have time to rappel to the deck?"

Luke looked at his watch and calculated quickly.

"Maybe five minutes … maybe less."

Hearing that exchange, the senior of the two pilots, a former U.S. Army helicopter combat pilot, did not need instructions from the boarding party. He took the controls from the co-pilot and pushed the Sikorsky forward and down, while the co-pilot stood quickly to assist Luke and Rebecca with the rappelling hookup.

In fewer than 60 seconds, the helicopter was hovering 30 feet above the wheelhouse, just 15 feet above the rotating surface-search radar antenna. Without hesitation, Luke and Rebecca stepped out of the aircraft and rappelled down, just beyond the antenna's rotation radius, landing softly on the wheel-house roof.

Adelman, meanwhile, covered Rebecca and Luke from the Sikorsky's open side panel during their descent, using the CIA-issued tactical shotgun. The Yahalomin knew that at least one man had to be on board, conning the ship. And they knew that a three-man crew, apparently including Hasan, must have abandoned the ship in a rubberized dinghy, now fleeing toward the southernmost tip of Manhattan.

That did not mean that there were no other members of the ship's crew still on board, possibly armed, and perhaps bent on their own suicide.

But Rebecca and Luke also knew they had no time. The colossal mass of the Verrazzano loomed overhead, the noise of its traffic deafening, while the immensity of the east tower stood directly in the ship's path, 500 yards and closing.

"There's no time, Rebecca," said Luke. "We've got to go in without recon."

Rebecca nodded.

Luke leading, careful to avoid the rotating antenna, they moved 10 feet aft and dropped down the conning tower's after-ladder. First Luke and then Rebecca swung their agile bodies through the open hatch, each landing solidly on both feet on the wheelhouse deck. They found themselves directly behind the unwitting man at the ship's wheel. Lying between themselves and the suicide pilot was the struggling body of the harbor pilot, bound at wrists and ankles.

The overwhelming noise from the rotor and the vehicles above drowned out every incidental noise they necessarily made during their headlong incursion.

Hasan's man at the wheel — small, wiry, perhaps 30 years old — was unaware that he had been joined in the wheelhouse by a former Royal Navy boarding-party legend and his knife-throwing sister. The man's left wrist was chained to the ship's wheel; his right, to the engine-room control levers.

And inches from his right hand was the trigger mechanism for the explosives. The man shouted a prayer and moved his right hand to the trigger. Luke, having spent five Royal Navy years engaged in work of this exact sort, recognized the trigger for what it was. He leaped over the prone form of the harbor pilot, reached the suicide pilot in two more strides, and reached over the man's right shoulder and seized his trigger hand in a crushing grip. He ripped the hand away as far as the chain would allow.

"Rebecca," he shouted over the din, "this trigger sends an electronic signal to an explosives detonator that's somewhere else on the ship, close to the explosives themselves. Nothing will happen if you sever that wire.

"Quick!"

Rebecca, one of her knives already in hand, glided over the prone harbor pilot, around her brother, and without hesitation sliced through the wire connecting the electronic signal device to the actual explosives detonator. She then sheathed the knife, spun, and lifted the short-handled bolt cutters from her brother's holster. She swiftly cut through the chain that secured the terrorist's right hand to the ship's engine-control levers, dropped the implement clattering to the deck, seized the levers, and pulled them from the "all ahead one-third" position through "all stop" to "all reverse full." She felt the ship shudder violently as it strained to comply with the new setting.

Then Rebecca stooped, picked up the bolt cutters, moved to Luke's other side, and swiftly cut through the second chain.

Luke, his own right hand still gripping the terrorist's, spun the man around and slammed him face-first against the bulkhead. He then pinned the man's wrists behind his back, extracted a set of plastic handcuff-ties from his holster, and snapped the handcuffs onto each of the terrorist's wrists. He then swept the terrorist's feet from under him with a right-leg takedown, controlled the man's fall to the deck, and snapped a second pair of handcuff-ties around the man's ankles.

Luke then turned and knelt next to the fully conscious harbor pilot and cut through his bindings. Rebecca knelt beside them and checked the pilot for any obvious wounds. There appeared to be none.

Brother and sister stood. They extended their hands to the pilot.

With their assistance, the pilot stood.

Luke addressed the man, who appeared shaken but alert.

"We're in full reverse, sir," he noted. "There is no point in making an effort to change the heading, correct?"

The pilot quickly judged distance and speed and shook his head.

"Correct," he said.

There was nothing more to be done. Trying to change the ship's heading with only 150 yards of open water before impact would be fruitless. Only the engines, now backing at full power, had the slightest chance of stopping the ship in the ever-diminishing space between its prow and the east tower of the Verrazzano.

Rebecca and Luke, paired from birth, instinctively joined hands and watched the bow of the vessel as it approached impact with the east tower:

100 yards …

75 yards …

50 …

25 …

CHAPTER FOURTEEN

REYNALDO ACOSTA, DEEP IN PRAYER, FELT THE SHIP'S VIGOROUS shudder as a brief mechanical protest, sensed the subsequent deceleration, and knew that someone had thrown the engines into reverse. He opened his eyes and looked through the oppressive gloom of the 40-by-8-by-8-foot container. He saw Millicent Thomas standing defiantly at the metal door, shouting incoherently, pounding fruitlessly on the unyielding metal, unwilling to acknowledge the likelihood that soon her life was to be demanded of her.

Acosta saw, too, that the unknown-to-him young woman had regained consciousness and now sat with her back against the far wall of the container, holding hands with the girl who had tended to her so faithfully during the woman's cognitive absence. The two of them appeared to be praying and seemed to Acosta, even from a distance, to be filled with a supernatural serenity, especially in contrast to the woman who stood near them, raging in the face of her imminent demise.

He stood up stiffly, stretched, and walked slowly to the young woman and the girl. He stood over them for a moment, then carefully knelt in front of them.

He touched the girl's foot and she opened her eyes.

"Sari," he said quietly, "I think something has happened. Do you feel … and hear … the changes in the ship's movement?"

She nodded.

Sarah, hearing the exchange, opened her eyes.

Acosta introduced himself to her and saw the instant wariness in her face. He decided to try to explain. He began by glancing toward the congresswoman.

"Ms. Thomas and I," he said, enunciating carefully to make his spoken English more readily intelligible, "have been uneasy allies in a project we undertook with a Muslim terrorist named Hasan … who is now doing what terrorists do.

"My real allegiance, however, has never been to the terrorists … nor to Congresswoman Thomas, who has her own priorities…" — here he glanced toward the woman who stood nearby, still pounding on the metal door — "but to our Lord Jesus Christ, and to His work here on the earth… thus, my opposition to the Sandinistas and their false theology — liberation theology — in my home country of Nicaragua."

The woman continued to stare at him, apparently unmoved.

"Would it be permissible for me to sit beside you?" he asked.

Sarah shook her head.

"No."

"I understand," he said.

He rose and, moving to a position near, but not too near, Sari, he sat down, his back to the cold metal wall. Sitting, he had placed himself more than 10 feet from Sarah Wilson, with Sari halfway between them.

He understood the woman's reaction. He had experienced women's revulsion to his appearance all his adult life. He knew that that would never change in his lifetime. And if he had been told that Sarah's reaction to him had nothing to do with his appearance, he would not have believed that to be true. That would have been inconsistent with his life experience. Women had always found him ugly.

He leaned back against the unforgiving metal and closed his eyes.

Adelman, still positioned at the open side panel of the Sikorsky and still holding the tactical shotgun in readiness to fire, saw the water suddenly begin to boil around the ship's stern, indicating full-power reversal of its twin screws.

"Luke and Rebecca have got control!" he shouted to the pilots over the din of vehicular traffic and helicopter rotor noise. "The engines have reversed!"

Then he watched, his heart in his throat, as the 35,000-ton ship grudgingly responded to the braking action of the propellers' reversal.

Adelman had no idea whether a fully loaded container ship of this size and weight could bring itself to a complete halt in the ever-diminishing distance between its massive prow and the east tower of the Verrazzano Bridge.

He could only hope.

As for the issue of the ship's being packed with explosives, he and the pilots were aware that they had no way to know whether that assumption had a basis in fact, but the pilots prudently began to move the copter back and away from the ship, putting distance between themselves and a possible explosion. Their assumption was that, if explosives were set to detonate, and if Rebecca and Luke had disabled some sort of trigger mechanism inside the wheelhouse, explosives could nonetheless be set off by the ship's collision with a stationary object, such as a bridge-support tower.

They also knew that, even if no explosion of any sort occurred, this fully loaded container ship, plowing into one of the two suspension towers supporting the Verrazzano Bridge, would cause colossal damage and, in and of itself, could conceivably bring down the eastern half of the structure.

In any case, the chopper was now far enough removed from the ship and the east tower that, regardless of any explosion, the pilots and Adelman — and the Sikorsky itself — would survive to continue pursuit of Hasan and his operatives. There was nothing further they could do as the critical moment approached.

They could only watch as the bow drew ever closer to the tower.

By now the ship's forward movement had become negligible, yet was still perceptible, and they watched with mounting tension as the gap between bow and tower slowly … ever so slowly… shrank to less than 10 yards.

Then … less than 5 yards.

Then … they steeled themselves as the prow appeared to touch the tower itself.

They waited, muscles tensed, abdomens hardened.

Seconds passed.

But the men gradually … ever so gradually … began to understand that this ship-to-bridge contact had been more of a caress, and less … much less … than a blow.

A metallic courtesy.

As they watched spellbound, they saw a tiny gap … perhaps 4 inches … begin to appear between prow and tower, a gap that slowly … slowly … became 2 feet … then 2 yards … then 10 … then 20. Seeing this, the pilots reacted by bringing the helicopter close once more, thereby keeping Adelman in position to fire the tactical shotgun if circumstances should suddenly demand.

"Gentlemen," Adelman called to the pilots over the noise of traffic and rotor, "please contact the harbormaster. We need to get NYPD patrol boats over here as fast as possible. No matter who turns out to be on board this ship, Rebecca and Luke are going to need help. Someone's going to have to get this ship back to New Jersey. We're going to need a couple of tugboats, too."

In minutes, the CIA pilots had radioed the harbormaster, who patched them through to the NYPD precinct captain specified by Adelman. This was the same captain who had, earlier that morning, when it was yet dark, worked with the harbormaster and Belton to locate the Saudi-flagged container ship. The captain now ordered two NYPD patrol-boat crews to embark for the Brooklyn side of the Verrazzano.

The captain wanted a SWAT onboard one patrol boat in case there was fighting to be done, and he wanted two of his K-9 bomb squads on the other, to deal with the suspected explosives-laden containers stacked on the ship.

And as the NYPD patrol-boat crews scrambled, Adelman and the chopper pilots continued to follow the ship as it reversed away from the east tower, backing clockwise, and finally began to approach the Brooklyn shoreline, stern-first.

When the ship was within 100 yards of the Brooklyn seawall, Adelman saw the boiling water at the stern suddenly melt into the surface. Concluding that the engines had been reset once again, and now were set to "all ahead," Adelman knew that the resultant braking force would bring the ship gradually to a halt.

Within 30 seconds, the ship stopped.

Then, to his complete surprise, he saw both anchors plunge into the water. The container ship was now at anchor a mere football-field's distance from shore.

"Look at that, gentlemen!" called Adelman to the pilots. "The harbor pilot must be alive and well and in control of the ship. There's no way Luke and Rebecca would know how to find whatever control mechanism would release those anchors."

Seconds later Adelman saw the twins emerging from the ship's conning tower onto the main deck, moving warily, knives in hand.

"Gentlemen," called Adelman to the pilots, "put me closer ... now closer still ... and closer still ... okay ... good ... let's hold right here."

The Sikorsky now hovered, fully stationary, 25 yards from the starboard side of the anchored vessel and almost at deck level.

The shotgun remained poised and ready.

Reynaldo Acosta sensed that the strain of the reversing engines had come to a sudden halt. He felt the now-familiar shudder of the ship as the engines passed through "all stop" and then to "all ahead full."

Then, in just 30 seconds, he felt another change. The engines, he realized, had once again been brought to "all stop," and immediately he heard the sound of two 1-ton anchors being released to crash into the water, their chains rattling violently.

The steady noise from the Verrazzano's vehicular traffic continued unchanged, penetrating the container's skin undiminished, but now a faint additional sound began to force its way through the container walls and make its glad presence known to Acosta's ears. He smiled broadly. A helicopter was in a stationary hover.

And very, very near the ship.

He leaned over far enough to touch Sari's shoulder. She turned her face toward him. She raised her eyebrows questioningly.

"Do you hear, Sari?" he asked.

She listened.

"That's a helicopter," he said. "Your friends are coming."

Acosta rose and moved to the door, where Millicent Thomas still stood, though she was now standing quietly, leaning against the side of the container, apparently having reached a state of complete exhaustion. He pulled his switchblade from the pocket where he had placed it after using it to free her from her bindings.

Blade in, he began to tap loudly on the door with the heavy metal handle of the switchblade. It made a satisfyingly sharp noise, one that echoed around and through the metallic canyons of container walls and ship bulkheads.

He continued with this for minutes, convinced that the ship's position at anchor and the proximity of a helicopter signaled imminent rescue. His three companions watched silently, their minds dulled by fatigue and anxiety.

Suddenly the container's door handle moved and the door was pulled vigorously open. Luke Manguson entered, a 12-inch Ka-Bar knife with a 7-inch blade held at the vertical in front of his face. Two seconds after, Rebecca Clark followed her brother into the container. Like him, she held a 12-inch knife, though hers was shaped for throwing and thus was held high, ready for her trademark windmill delivery, accurate at any distance up to, and even beyond, the 40-foot length of the container.

Luke and Rebecca took in the situation at a glance, realizing that, to their surprise, two strangers were present along with the two whom they sought. They immediately guessed that the strangers were the "missing" members of the Thomas-Acosta-Hasan Pact and Long-Range Plan. Without discussion, Rebecca and Luke together handled Millicent Thomas and Reynaldo Acosta exactly as they would have handled any other enemy: they forced them to face the wall of the container and swiftly handcuffed their wrists behind them.

Luke then ordered them to turn so that their backs were to the container wall. He and his sister then snapped handcuff-ties onto their adversaries' ankles and told them to sit down. They sat down.

Sheathing their knives, the twins turned to Sari and Sarah, pulled them to their feet, and embraced them. Rebecca held Sarah, by now a cherished friend; Luke held the teen to his chest, feeling the girl's tense muscles begin to relax.

But Rebecca quickly realized that Sarah was unsteady. She leaned back, placed both hands on Sarah's battered face and examined her closely.

"You have head wounds, Sarah," she said. "You're concussed."

Sarah nodded weakly.

"Luke," Rebecca said, "Sarah needs your help."

Luke knew immediately what his sister meant.

He released Sari to Rebecca, stepped to Sarah, and scooped her up in his arms as if she weighed nothing. Rebecca placed an arm around Sari's shoulders, and the four of them moved through the open container door.

Rebecca leaned over to put her face at Sari's level and said, "Sari, we think Hasan and his people left the ship some time ago. Do you think we have other enemies on the ship? Or do you think it's just those two in the container?"

Sari, her dark eyes wide, shook her head.

"We haven't seen anybody other than Hasan and two other men who brought us on board the ship ... plus Mr. Acosta and Ms. Thomas.

"But Mrs. Clark," she added quickly, "I don't think Mr. Acosta is our enemy. He may be mixed up with the wrong people, but I think ... no, I'm sure ... that he is our friend. I think he is very different from that woman."

"Really?" said Rebecca. "Interesting. I'll want you to say more about that, but ... later, Sari. Right now, we need to get medical assistance for Sarah."

Rebecca stood and looked at her brother, who had now placed Sarah's feet on the deck, but continued to hold her upright, his arm around her waist. Then, as happened so frequently, brother and sister communicated without words.

Rebecca nodded, turned, and made eye contact with Adelman, who knelt in the Sikorsky's open side panel, a mere 25 yards from where she stood, his shot-gun now held at the vertical, pointing to the sky.

Rebecca gestured to Sarah and Luke and pantomimed to Adelman the need for the rappelling chair to get the two of them into the Sikorsky. Adelman, having seen that Luke was carrying Sarah and that he was still holding her upright, had no difficulty interpreting Rebecca's gestures.

Nor did the helicopter pilots.

They immediately increased the chopper's altitude to a position some 30 feet above the topmost container, which placed them 50 feet above the main deck where their colleagues waited. Adelman swiftly attached the "chair" — a specially constructed seat that fit snugly into the rappelling harness — and lowered the device to the deck while the copter hovered directly overhead.

Rebecca attached the harness to Sarah, who sat on the small metal seat, while Luke stood in the stirrup-step mounted three feet lower than the seat, an arrangement that allowed him stand upright in the stirrup, holding Sarah from behind with one arm, while the rappelling-assist motor did the lifting mechanically.

In seconds they were both aboard the chopper.

As soon as Sarah was secure in one of the Sikorsky's passenger seats, Luke confirmed with Adelman that NYPD patrol boats were on their way.

"We've got SWAT and K-9 boats coming, Luke," Adelman said.

Adelman then looked at Sarah, whose glassy eyes spoke volumes.

"Should we request a medical team, too?" he asked.

"I don't think she needs emergency care," Luke replied, "and I'd rather we take her to Teterboro, get on board the Learjet, and fly her to the Andrews Air Force Base infirmary. Our CIA pilots can radio ahead for a concussion specialist to be ready and waiting for her. We can have her there an hour from now, which is, I'd guess, at least as fast as anything we could achieve here in New York City."

Adelman nodded his agreement, adding, "Let's get Rebecca and Sari up here."

He sent the rappelling chair down while Luke spoke with the pilots about radioing Andrews to prepare a concussion specialist team. Luke turned back to Adelman.

"Before we left the conning tower," Luke said, "we prepared the harbor pilot for the likelihood that NYPD patrol boats would be coming to make sure the vessel was clear of hostile units and to disable the detonator to any explosives on board.

"The harbor pilot," Luke continued, "is not hurt nearly as badly as Sarah appears to be. He, in fact, conned the vessel throughout that backing maneuver.

He handled the engines and the ship's wheel all the way to the full stop near the Brooklyn shoreline, and the subsequent anchoring, as well.

"And a good thing, that," Luke added.

Adelman looked puzzled.

Luke clarified.

"We had no idea how those anchors worked."

As Rebecca prepared to help Sari onto the rappelling seat, she heard Reynaldo Acosta call her name from his position, seated and handcuffed, just inside the container. As Rebecca turned to find out why he'd called, Sari gripped her wrist.

"Mrs. Clark," she whispered urgently. "He's one of *us*."

Rebecca looked closely at the teen's face, saw the earnestness, and believed her. She nodded and, after a moment's thought, said simply, "I understand."

Rebecca looked up at her brother and Adelman, 50 feet above, and signaled that she needed another minute. Then she stepped back inside the container.

"What is it, sir?" she asked.

He looked up and smiled.

"That child is a treasure, Mrs. Clark," he said. "Take care of her."

"Of course," Rebecca replied. "But what …"

"I want to give you something," Acosta said.

"My wrists are handcuffed behind me, ma'am," he continued, "but if you'll reach just inside my jacket you'll find a packet that will prove invaluable to you and your friends, going forward. It is a directory of every terrorist cell and every individual terrorist associated with those cells. You'll find contact information for every man operating with Hasan here in the United States."

Rebecca hesitated.

"It's a seven-page document," said Acosta, "folded several times and several ways to shrink it to a little block of paper. It is full and complete and up-to-the-minute, Mrs. Clark. I took this from Hasan's materials while Ms. Thomas and I were being transported to New York. I think that, with this directory, the CIA and FBI will be able to round up every member of every cell now operating here."

Millicent Thomas, handcuffed and seated 3 feet away, stared at Acosta, hostility radiating from her every pore. "You idiot!" she hissed. "You've just signed your death warrant … and mine, as well. You … and I … will be hunted for the rest of our lives by every Muslim terrorist on the planet. How could you be this stupid!"

Acosta turned his face to her.

"I have chosen a side, Millicent," he said evenly. "And so have you. I think that, perhaps, you have enough money to buy your way out of this. Whatever the case, I have done what Mrs. Clark's now well-known 'blueprint of the universe' requires of me: *my life for yours.* And 'yours,' in this case, means Mrs. Clark, Sari, Miss Wilson, and the rest of Mrs. Clark's group … plus every person on earth who views the universe in the same way that they do. I have done what is required of me.

"May God's will be done with us both."

Acosta turned his eyes back to Rebecca.

She considered his statement, thought again about Sari's judgment of this man, and reached down, moving her hand inside his jacket.

She stood again, now holding a multi-page document that had been folded repeatedly and compressed into a 4-by-4-by-2-inch block of paper. She deposited the packet in her ready-satchel and turned to go.

"Thank you," she said simply. "May God protect you, Mr. Acosta."

She strode out of the container, helped Sari onto the rappelling seat, placed a foot on the stirrup, and the two of them were ratcheted up and into the Sikorsky.

As the rescuers and the rescued helicoptered toward Teterboro to reboard the CIA Learjet, Rebecca laboriously unfolded the packet given her by Reynaldo Acosta and began to examine it. The pages appeared to contain exactly what Acosta had said they would: detailed contact information for every Muslim terrorist cell, and every individual Muslim terrorist, operating in the U.S. at that moment.

She showed the document to her companions and explained how it was obtained. She also asked Sari to say more about Acosta, and why she had come to regard him as "one of us," as she had put it while still on the ship. By the time they had landed at Teterboro, reboarded the Learjet, and achieved cruising altitude and speed toward Andrews, they had achieved consensus among themselves.

Luke approached the two CIA pilots.

"Can you contact the chair of the Rebecca Unit at CIA HQ right now?" he asked. "We need for him to meet us the moment we arrive at Andrews."

Luke then explained exactly what that meant.

Wednesday, 8:45 a.m., Andrews Air Force Base, infirmary

"Okay," said Luke to Rebecca, Adelman, and Sari, "Sarah's in good hands ... no, the *best* hands. They'll keep her under close observation for ... maybe ... 24 hours. She'll be back with us, ready to go, this time tomorrow morning."

"Do you think," Rebecca asked teasingly, "that Jim's presence with her will help or hinder Sarah's recovery, Luke?" She was smiling at the thought of Jim's rigid insistence that he stay at Sarah's side until her release.

"Well," said Luke after a moment, "I don't know that it will either help or hinder, but I know for sure that his insistence on staying with her will cement that relationship ... if it needs any cementing. All of us understand what it will mean to her to realize that Jim would accept no arrangement that did not include his presence at her bedside."

"Good answer, Luke," said his sister, delighted at the thought.

The foursome — Rebecca, Luke, Adelman, and Sari — walked together to Eleanor and Sid's guest unit. There they were welcomed by their friends, who reported they had just received a call from New York confirming the fact that more than a ton of high explosives had been packed into three of the containers on board the ship.

The phone call also described the successful decoupling by the K-9 bomb units of all detonators running to the explosives themselves. That having been reported, the welcoming Yahalomin members demanded a detailed report of everything that had happened in the five hours since Rebecca's early morning dream.

It seemed impossible to Rebecca that everything had happened in that time frame, but it was true. The dream had been received at about 4:00 a.m., and she and Luke, plus Jaakov, had, in those few hours, jetted to New York, helicoptered to the Verrazzano Bridge, rappelled onto an explosives-packed container ship, disabled and secured a suicide-bent terrorist in the ship's wheelhouse, secured two other adversaries inside one of the containers, rescued two of their own Yahalomin members, and returned home bearing a directory revealing the names and contact information of every terrorist cell and individual terrorist member operating in the U.S.

However, before she, Luke, Adelman, or Sari could begin to recount the morning's events, a knock came at the door of the unit. McGriff answered the door and was surprised to find two men dressed in dark suits. One, the younger of the two, identified himself as chair, or convener, of the Rebecca Unit at CIA Headquarters. The other, who looked vaguely familiar to McGriff, said nothing at all.

Belton, unable to see the visitors from his chair, but recognizing the voice of the younger man, called out to McGriff, "Have 'im c'mon in. He's th' one that got our people t' New York in time t' get everything fixed this morning."

The Rebecca Unit chair leaned into the room sufficiently to see Belton, but said, "Sid, I have the director of the Central Intelligence Agency with me. After receiving notification from our pilots — they radioed me from the Learjet — I went straight to the director's office. He and I have secured an appointment with the commanding general of Andrews Air Force Base. I'd like to take your three-person team with me, so that they can present the document to the director, in the general's presence."

This declaration — it could not realistically be regarded as a request — was greeted by a thoughtful silence from the room.

After several moments, Rebecca, still clad in her dark blue tennis warm-ups, rose from her seat and approached the doorway. She spoke directly to the two men, but loudly enough for her colleagues in the room to hear what she said.

"I am Rebecca Clark, gentlemen," she said in her Oxford-accented contralto. "The document appears to us — the three whom your people were kind enough to fly to New York this morning — to be just as authentic as its bearer claimed, but it is incomplete without another document which we also have in our possession. It is titled the Thomas-Acosta-Hasan Pact and Long-Range Plan.

"The two of you … and the commanding general …" she continued, "will benefit most from our presentation if we bring both documents, so that we can talk about both … and make copies of them for you to retain. I request that you allow the three of us to come with the documents, but I also want to ask that you permit the chief investigative journalist from the *New York Times'* London desk, Monsieur Louis Bois, to be part of this conversation. His experience with the Muslim terrorist units that have settled in the U.K., and now in the U.S., coupled with his insight into the true import of these documents, you'll find invaluable, as have we.

"And," Rebecca concluded, "I have no doubt that Louis will agree to treat our conversation with you as entirely off the record, unless you, at some point, declare otherwise. Louis," she said, looking over her shoulder at the journalist, "am I correct about this last ... that you'll agree to participate off the record?"

"Oui, madame," he said. "Exactly as you said."

Wednesday, 11:15 a.m.,
Andrews Air Force Base, commanding general's conference room

The three Yahalomin met with the CIA director, the chair of the CIA Rebecca Unit, and the Andrews Air Force Base commanding general — and Louis Bois — for two hours. At the conclusion of their session, the general's recording secretary printed and photocopied a list of the core items in the agreement:

- Based upon details expressed in the 17-page document titled the Thomas-Acosta-Hasan Pact and Long-Range Plan, the CIA director recommends that all three parties to the pact — Millicent Thomas, Reynaldo Acosta, and the individual known as "Hasan" — be arrested and jailed, with the FBI coordinating with local police in making the actual arrests, and with local police precinct captains supervising handling of the prisoners prior to their trial(s) and subsequent transfer to their respective place(s) of incarceration, in accordance with instructions from the judge(s) presiding.

- Based upon data found in the seven-page "Directory of Muslim terrorist cells and individual Muslim terrorists now operating in the United States," the CIA director recommends that the FBI proceed immediately to locate and apprehend every individual named in the document, turning individuals over to local law enforcement officials on a case-by-case basis. Depending upon FBI findings case-by-case, the CIA director recommends immediate deportation of every individual whose background in other countries and/or activities since arriving in the U.S. form justification for such deportation. [Note: the seven-page directory listing includes the individual known as "Hasan," whose name is in the title of the "Thomas-Acosta-Hasan Pact and

Long-Range Plan," plus both of the individuals who operated with Hasan earlier this day in commandeering a Saudi-flagged container ship that had been docked in Hoboken, NJ; the directory includes, as well, the name of the individual who was chained to the wheel and engine controls of said container ship; the latter individual was apprehended this morning in New York, along with Thomas and Acosta.]

- The CIA director will request an emergency meeting with the president of the United States and his cabinet to examine the 17-page "Pact and Plan" in its implications for future U.S. relations with the array of nations cited in the document as helping to finance the agendas delineated in the document, especially the document's emphasis on mass murder-by-explosives via the wholesale destruction of buildings and property throughout the United States. The CIA director expects, at that point, action to be carried forward by the U.S. State Department and Department of Defense, with CIA participation, as needed and as directed.

- The CIA director hereby instructs the journalist present at this meeting — Mr. Louis Bois of the London desk of the *New York Times* — to await clearance both from the CIA director and from the FBI director before publishing any of the recommendations set forth in this summary.

- The CIA director does, however, grant Mr. Louis Bois the right to publish immediately an article(s) on the subject of the events that have transpired earlier this day, including CIA transport by Learjet from Andrews Air Force Base (MD) to Teterboro (NJ) and back, as well as transport by CIA Sikorsky helicopter to and from a commandeered Saudi-flagged container ship, of Mrs. Rebecca Clark, of London, England; of Royal Navy Lt. Luke Manguson, also of London, England; and of New York City private detective Jaakov Adelman, former Israeli (Mossad) intelligence officer.

Wednesday, noon, Andrews Air Force Base, Chapel-Belton guest unit

An off-base, take-out lunch having been ordered and retrieved by Marie and McGriff, the Yahalomin sat, relaxed, in Sid and Eleanor's cramped guest unit. They had listened wide-eyed as Sari, Rebecca, Luke, and Adelman provided details of the adventure experienced by the four of them and the hospitalized Sarah between Tuesday night's abduction and Wednesday morning's rescue.

At the story's end, there were questions.

"Sari," said Durham, whom Sarah had sent to the session, insisting that he hear everything and then return to the infirmary to fill her in, "what led you to decide that Reynaldo Acosta was 'one of us,' as you said?"

"I saw," answered the teen, "from the moment Sarah and I were thrown into that container, that he and the congresswoman were as powerless as we were, but it also seemed clear that the two of them didn't like each other. And once he started talking to me … um … I just found him to be … um … *genuine* … you know … the sort of person who has more interest in others than in himself … more concerned about Sarah and me than about himself … a caring sort of person.

"I just liked him."

Durham nodded.

"Got it. Thank you, Sari."

"Sari," said Deng after a moment, "when I was … abducted … from my taxi … last summer … I found the worst moments for me were the first moments … those moments of feeling physically helpless … but that, as time went on, I found that I was able to … ah … 'find myself,' if you know what I mean … I was able to … well … *think* again … and, once I could think, I could pray … and I seemed gradually to become more the person that I'm meant to be.

"Did that sort of thing happen with you?"

Sari smiled delightedly.

"Yes!" she said. "Exactly!

"Even before," she continued, "we were thrown into that container … and while we were still being transported in some sort of truck to New York, I found that I was able to … ah … to retrieve my proper … perspective … on life, and on what my life means, and on how God's hand in my life has changed me over the years … since the time Luke and Kory pulled me out of my first life and brought me to London … to Greta.

"I was almost happy," she concluded, "to be me again."

Here she looked from Deng back to Durham.

"And when Mr. Acosta," Sari said, "began to speak to me, I felt I saw something *real* in him … something I … recognized …

"I felt I *knew* him."

After several more questions about the adventure, McGriff turned the discussion toward the just-finished meeting with the CIA director.

"Rebecca, are you three … or four …" McGriff said, remembering that Louis Bois was also present at that meeting, "allowed to tell us what transpired with the CIA people? Or is that something you are required to hold close?"

"Not only," answered Rebecca, "can we talk freely about the meeting, we have one-page copies of a summary. As you'll see, the summary has five points."

Reaching into her ready-satchel, she extracted her copies and circulated them to the group. She then waited while everyone read through the five points.

"The summary," she said, "may be clear enough so as to require no explanation, but … are there questions, anyone?"

After several moments, Eleanor turned to Bois, sitting near her, and asked, "Louis, do you expect problems with your senior editors on the penultimate point here … the prohibition against publishing anything about the CIA director's recommendations without permission from both directors … CIA and FBI?"

"Maybe," said Bois, "but I'm inclined to think they will be mollified by the permission to write about the early morning drama. We're going to be the only news source in the world that will carry the story, and it's going to read like a piece of hair-raising fiction … with a great outcome that will satisfy readers.

"I think the editors will be … willing … to grant the point, Dr. Chapel."

"Anyone else have a question?" asked Rebecca.

"Yeah … I do," said Belton. "Didja get a sense a' how quick th' director thinks th' FBI can move on th' 'directory of scumbags'?"

General laughter filled the room at Belton's creative reference to the lists of terrorist cells and terrorist individuals operating in the U.S.

Rebecca replied, "Yes … I think … the director expects the FBI to launch … what he called … 'a round-up' of these people within hours, Mr. Belton."

She turned to her brother, sitting nearby, and said, "Luke?"

He nodded. "I agree. The people on that list can expect visitors tonight."

Luke looked at Adelman, then Bois. They nodded their agreement.

The room was silent, thoughtful.

Finally, Marie spoke, petting Penelope as she did and sounding a little embarrassed. "Does that mean we could actually go home … tomorrow?"

Belton looked at her, a faux scowl on his face.

"Ya mean ya don't wanna live here any longer than ya hafta?" he said.

Marie smiled shyly.

"It's not that I don't *love* being in the company of every one of you, Mr. Belton … but I admit … I miss my house. I even miss our office."

"She's miserable here," said her husband.

"Jack!" she responded.

Then she looked at Belton and said in a stage whisper, "I'm miserable here."

Durham had just finished talking Sarah through the five bullet-point list circulated at the Yahalomin's midday session, explaining to her that, if things proceeded as quickly as Rebecca and the others seemed to expect, everyone would be going home tomorrow at some point.

She was thrilled.

"Really, Jim?" she said.

"We'll need to hear something tonight from our CIA man," he said, "but Rebecca and the others seemed confident that the FBI would move fast to apprehend every person on Reynaldo Acosta's list. I think the CIA director's view is that this will be an immediate number-one priority for the FBI director.

"Pretty exciting, huh?"

"Oh, my goodness, yes!" she said.

He stood up, leaned over the bed, and kissed her on her forehead. She reached up and drew him to her, planting an enthusiastic kiss on his lips. They were interrupted at that moment by the colonel who had taken charge of her upon her arrival. He entered the room and smiled broadly.

"She's in good shape, detective. I'd prefer no violence for Sarah for a couple of days, if you can arrange that," he said, chuckling, "but she's exactly where I want her to be, insofar as the concussion is concerned. She has no memory loss whatever, even for the minutes and seconds just before she was struck. I've asked her to check in with her civilian physician when she gets home … maybe go through a week-long concussion protocol … but I won't need to see her anymore."

"Hey," said Sarah teasingly, "I'm right here, you know!"

The colonel laughed. "Sorry, Miss Wilson … I knew the detective wanted to hear that report, so I ignored the patient. An unfortunate habit some of us develop."

She reached for the colonel's hand and took it in hers.

"I'm so grateful for your attentiveness, Colonel," she said seriously. "You and the staff have been wonderful. I've felt like a queen, and I'm not even in the military."

"Maybe not, Miss Wilson," he replied, "but that trauma you experienced was exactly the kind of thing we see often in our combat people.

"Take care of yourself and check in tomorrow with your doctor."

Durham circled the bed and shook hands with the colonel.

"I'm very grateful, sir," he said. "And Sarah's right. The staff has been great, from the first minute to the last."

When they were alone again, he sat down and held her hand. They were relaxed and cozy with each other, delighted with the prospect of getting back to normalcy. They were quiet for several minutes, happy, before she continued the conversation.

"So," she said, "everybody expects to go home tomorrow, Jim, including the England people … including Sari?"

"Looks like it. The Brits will need to await an RAF transport flight, but those happen almost nightly, and the New York people will need to arrange for the CIA Learjet to take them back to Teterboro, but that can probably be set up easily.

"So, yes … the 'scumbag directory'," as Mr. Belton calls it, "should trigger a roundup of every one of those people … and fast."

"Including that Hasan person?" she asked.

"He's on the list," replied Durham, "and, you know, the sketch artist finished the likeness Sari helped him develop. That's been distributed electronically to every FBI office in the country. I don't think he'll be able to hide for long."

Her face fell. She shook her head.

"What is it, sweetheart?" he asked.

She smiled at the endearment, something to which neither was yet accustomed, but which both of them enjoyed.

"Oh … you know, Jim … I failed," she said. "I was charged with protecting Sari and … well … I just failed. If it hadn't been for Rebecca's dream and for all that incredibly fast work by Mr. Belton … and Rebecca, Luke, and Jaakov …"

"Well," he said, "if it can be said that you failed, Sarah, then so did I … and so did all of us who thought we could go to police HQ and be safe. I admit, it never crossed my mind that there was danger waiting for us at the precinct.

"We just got outsmarted on that. All of us."

He looked closely at her face.

"You're not convinced, I see."

She smiled ruefully.

"Well," she said, "I'm convinced of the logic of what you said, Jim … but I don't think I feel any less … guilty … of failure … failure to do my job.

"Do you know what I mean?"

He nodded.

"Yes," he said. "I do. I think I'd feel just the same."

He was thoughtful for a moment, then asked, "Would it be good if Rebecca came over to talk about this to you? Might her perspective be helpful?"

She considered the question, then said simply, "Yes … yes, please."

Wednesday, 5:00 p.m., Andrews Air Force Base, infirmary

Rebecca occupied the chair, next to Sarah's bed, vacated 15 minutes earlier by Durham. Rebecca and Durham had agreed that a weighty conversation between the two women might benefit from his absence.

"I do know what you mean, Sarah," Rebecca was saying, "about the sense of guilt that goes with failing to protect someone who'd been placed in your charge. And not only failing, but becoming a victim yourself, as well. It's horrible in real time, and even worse afterward, because the feeling of ineptitude doesn't go away.

"The feeling wants to stay."

Sarah nodded.

"I've never, until now," Sarah said, "had any trouble putting failure behind me, Rebecca. I know how to fail and yet move on, having learned from the failure. I think that, in this instance, my failure seems to grow in me because … well … because of you … because you are just so … spectacularly successful, Rebecca. You've done astonishing things, over and over, that others couldn't do at all.

"I've loved," Sarah continued, "beginning to feel like your younger sister while we've been here as roommates. Feeling somehow worthy of that high honor. *I'm Rebecca Clark's chosen sister!* I've actually said that to myself."

She smiled shyly. She had not planned to say any of that.

Rebecca reached for the younger woman's hand.

"I'm going to describe a particular experience from my past … of the numerous experiences I could choose," said Rebecca. "This will take a few minutes, Sarah."

Rebecca paused to reflect.

"Some years ago," she began, "a young reporter for a Christian news-and-opinion weekly here in the U.S. had helped us secure a document — somewhat as Sari has managed to do for us, here — and the reporter and I were trying to escape from some exceptionally violent people in a small boat on the Chesapeake Bay.

"Suddenly," recounted Rebecca, "an enormously fast racing boat came out of nowhere and, with no warning, literally drove through and over our tiny craft, its huge, whirling propeller chewing up everything it passed through.

"I was at the tiller, facing forward; the reporter was in the bow, facing aft.

"She saw the racing boat coming from behind us. I never saw it at all."

Rebecca paused again, remembering.

"Perhaps three seconds before it made contact, the reporter — her name was April — hurled herself into me, Sarah, and knocked me backward, all the way out of the boat and into the water. She threw herself down on top of me, sinking me far enough down so that the propeller did not contact me at all.

"April was cut to pieces. Killed instantly."

Rebecca became silent, remembering.

Sarah felt the tension in Rebecca's hand and saw her eyes fall. Saw the sadness overtake her and so gained a small sense of the tragedy.

"Horrible, Rebecca," whispered Sarah.

Rebecca looked up.

"I was her protector, Sarah," she said, "and yet she saved *my* life. *My life for yours* is supposed to be *our* mission, and yet … the roles were reversed.

"I could barely stand it then," Rebecca continued. "I can barely stand it now … but I know that April was welcomed into Christ's arms as the heroine that she became, and that He and she forever cherish her sacrifice.

"And, as C. S. Lewis reminds us, we are to pray for her … for April … *just as she is no doubt praying for us … just as April is no doubt praying for me.*"

Rebecca smiled her glad smile, the one that compressed the scar along the side of her face. The one that seemed always to make her gray eyes glisten.

"So, Sarah," she continued, "I don't want to *forget* my failure that day. I want to *remember* my failure, because it is connected with April's heroism and sacrifice and triumph ... and it is *that* that makes my failure part of something glorious."

Sarah stared at her friend and exemplar, astonished at the emotion she saw in Rebecca's face and that she felt in the pressure of her hand.

"Sarah," Rebecca continued after a moment, "your failure to prevent Sari's abduction will be forever part of the unhesitating heroism to which that led: Mr. Belton's quickness in gaining the harbor information; our CIA committee chair's quickness in scrambling his pilots; our little boarding party's quickness in taking control of the ship; our jet and helicopter pilots' speed and boldness; the harbor pilot's skill in conning that unwieldy ship, in reverse, to anchor safely near the shore.

"And, don't forget, Sarah, the sacrifice of Reynaldo Acosta, a Christian man who stood up for you and Sari, knowing that, if he managed to survive, Muslim terrorists would pursue him for the rest of his life.

"Connect the dots in your mind, Sarah," said Rebecca. "Your 'failure' will forever be part of a magnificent story of sacrifice and heroism. Try never to think of the one without thinking of the other.

"And thank God for both."

Sarah smiled, but then shook her head slowly.

"Rebecca," she said sadly, "I don't think I am *worth* all that sacrifice and heroism. I just don't feel that ... that ... *important.*"

Rebecca suddenly stood and leaned over the bed, looking down into the hazel eyes that stared up at her. She took her friend's other hand and pressed them both into both of her own.

"You are *not* 'that important,' Sarah, nor are you *worthy* of the sacrifices and heroism that so many displayed. None of us is 'that important.' None of us is *worthy* of this kind of sacrifice and heroism.

"Christ did not die for those of us who are sufficiently important or sufficiently worthy. Christ sacrificed Himself because each of us is God's own creature. *That's* your importance. *That's* your worth. *That* is why the 'blueprint of the universe' stipulates *my life for yours* ... not *my-life-for-yours-if-you-are-important-or-worthy-enough.*

"You are immensely important ... worthy of anything that anyone could ever do for you, Sarah Wilson. And so am I. And so is Sari."

She paused, then finished her thought.

"And … so is Hasan."

Sarah's eyes widened.

"If we can save him, you know," said Rebecca, "we will."

Sarah nodded slowly, beginning to comprehend.

"And if we cannot," added Rebecca, "then he will be saved, in the end … if he is saved at all … by Jesus Christ."

Sarah thought for a moment, searching for something.

"John 3:17?" she asked.

"Exactly," said Rebecca.

CHAPTER FIFTEEN

"SIDNEY! SIDNEY! IT'S THE CIA DIRECTOR, DEAR," CALLED Eleanor.

The assembled members of the Yahalomin, which included all except Sarah, who was spending the night in the AFB infirmary, and Sari, who had gone to bed, exhausted, in Rebecca and Sarah's room, watched as Belton clumped to the wall-mounted phone.

He accepted the receiver from his wife.

"Belton here, sir!" he rumbled.

Then he listened, inserting the occasional "Yes, sir," and "Right, sir," and "Sounds very good, sir," into the conversation. After perhaps two minutes, Belton said, "Thank you, sir. We're all grateful t' ya."

He replaced the receiver in its cradle and turned to his audience.

"Th' director says," Belton began, "that they've already nabbed every single one a' those hoodlums except th' three that kidnapped our two ladies an' then tried t' blow up th' bridge. Those three guys were in New York, rather than where th' directory said they'd be, an' so none of 'em has been arrested yet."

"So … no sign of Hasan?" said Jaakov.

"Right," said Belton, "but they've got Sari's sketch of th' dirtbag, an' it's already posted everywhere it needs t' be … an' so …"

A thoughtful silence followed this sobering statement.

Finally, Marie said, "Jack … can we still go home tomorrow?"

Laughter all around, as her husband replied, "I think we can pack our things in the morning, Marie, and load the Jeep. We'll say our good-byes to England and New York …" — here he glanced at those who would be flying to Brize Norton or Teterboro — "and we'll collect Sarah from the infirmary …"

Marie clapped her hands, exclaiming to Penelope, curled up in her lap, "Did you hear, little one? We're going home tomorrow!"

From that point, conversations separated themselves by home base: Rebecca, Luke, Sari, and Bois discussing RAF transport schedules; Eleanor, Belton, and Adelman doing the same regarding CIA Learjet arrangements. Durham and Deng looking at each other in unspoken acknowledgement that there would be no need for Deng to extend any further his temporary lodging in Durham's apartment.

Rebecca and Luke had spoken previously, albeit briefly, about Sari's situation in England. Neither of them was comfortable with the idea that she would continue to live openly in a London neighborhood with Greta van Dijk, given the fact that the teenager had, in the eyes of Hasan, "betrayed" him to Adelman at Gaston Hall and then had been "stolen" from him twice: first, from the D.C. hotel where Hasan had chained her to a toilet; and second, from the container ship where Hasan had deposited her, obviously with every expectation that she would die in the planned explosion.

Rebecca and Luke had agreed that, even if Hasan were imprisoned in the U.S. or deported to Saudi Arabia where his roots appeared to be, he might already have communicated with terrorist cells in England, Europe, or elsewhere regarding what he viewed as the girl's treachery. Rebecca and Luke feared for her safety and had already spoken with her about the idea of her and her "London Mum" Greta van Dijk moving permanently to the Lodge, near Birmingham, or to the U.S., in Washington. They had described for Sari how various arrangements might work, with Greta and Sari continuing to live as parent and child, but with a much higher level of security.

Sari, ever adaptable and adventurous, had listened intently, had tried to imagine the various arrangements, and had told Rebecca and Luke that she would give the "opportunities" — her word choice — serious thought and prayer. But she insisted that she should return to England with them so that she and Greta could talk face-to-face about the best arrangements for them both.

That response was more than Rebecca and Luke had dared hope.

Thursday mid-morning, Campbell and McGriff offices, Washington, D.C.

Having parked his truck in the alleyway behind the offices of Campbell and McGriff, Durham helped Sarah alight as she stepped down from the cab.

"I'm not made of glass, Jim," she protested playfully.

"Yeah," he said, "but … ya know … I like hovering."

They laughed as they unlocked the alleyway door to the office, happy to be back. Having also tossed Marie and McGriff's things into the truck bed, along with Sarah's, they carried everything inside, where the part-time receptionist welcomed them. With the unloading completed, Durham kissed Sarah good-bye.

"I'll be at the precinct office until noon," he said, "then I'll be starting to work this afternoon on a new case in the northeast corner of the District. I'll check in by phone as I leave, just before noon, to see if you want to go to lunch. You don't like to 'waste time' by going out, but today might be an exception?"

"Hmm," she said. "It might be."

Durham departed in the Ram just before Marie and McGriff arrived in the Cherokee to join Sarah at the office. Once the three of them had settled in, they thanked the receptionist and told her that she could resume her normal schedule. They then met in Marie's office to get themselves organized after the days away at Andrews.

Once they had looked carefully through all of the accumulated notes and messages, they agreed that they would need to work late that evening, Marie and McGriff until 7:00 p.m., Sarah later than that.

A half-block away and on the opposite side of the street from Campbell and McGriff sat a diplomatic vehicle, black in color, its windows heavily tinted. While it flew no diplomatic flags from its front fenders, the license plates on the rear of the massive Lincoln indicated the vehicle was owned by the Kingdom of Saudi Arabia.

The terrorist called Hasan sat on the back seat; the two men who had accompanied him to New York sat in front, one driving, the other studying the entrance to Campbell and McGriff. They noted the departure of the receptionist.

"Will we be able to continue the work?" asked one.

"No," Hasan answered. "The theft of the directory by the traitor Acosta is fatal to the current operational plans. Our colleagues throughout the country have already been arrested and taken to jails.

"And the Saudi Embassy," he continued, "will not cooperate with us. The Kingdom must maintain a working relationship with the U.S., for financial reasons. We can gain the occasional favor from my friends at the Embassy, such as the short-term loan of this vehicle, but nothing beyond that. We are forced to abandon our plans for now, a bitter drink to swallow, but we will be back … always … we will be back.

"And we will be able," Hasan declared, "to deliver one more strike … tonight… before we return home to Saudi Arabia."

Thursday midday, Campbell and McGriff offices, Washington, D.C.

Durham pulled his Dodge Ram up to the front door of the Campbell and McGriff office, and Sarah, watching from the doorway, hurried out and climbed up onto the passenger seat. She leaned over and accepted a kiss.

"How was the morning?" he asked.

"It was so nice to be back in our lovely work spaces, Jim, but the work has really piled up. Our receptionist couldn't take action, of course, on anything much … she could only write down messages and call-back numbers. So, we're scrambling to catch up, and I had second thoughts about going out to lunch.

"But we agreed in our morning meeting that we'll all work late tonight … and probably Saturday, too. Marie and Father Jack are planning to work until 7:00 this evening, and I'm going to stay … probably … until midnight."

Durham thought about that for two seconds.

"Well … can I pick you up at midnight and drive you home?" he asked.

"Exactly what I was going to ask!" she said.

Over lunch salads, Sarah inquired about the travel plans for the others.

"Sounds to me," said Durham, "as though the England group, including Sari and Louis Bois, will board an RAF transport plane just before midnight, but I think the New York group will be staying until tomorrow. The CIA plane is tied up today.

"The three of them could take AMTRAK to New York today, but they just don't want to. As Mr. Belton said, 'We're spoiled rotten, people. Learjet or nothin'.'"

Sarah laughed, then was quiet, thinking.

"Something weighing on you, Sarah?" asked Durham.

"Yes … do you think Sari is going to be safe, Jim?"

"I don't think she will go back to her previous arrangements," he said. "I think her 'mum,' Greta van Dijk … and Luke's wife Kory, who, of course, is Greta's niece … and Rebecca and Luke … are going to work on alternative set-ups.

"For example," Durham continued, "I think they'll have the option of moving — Sari and Greta — to the Birmingham Lodge, where Rebecca and Luke grew up. I understand that it's got a perimeter wall that is monitored electronically, plus an actual guard house with security people staffing it 24/ 7, 365."

She pictured this for a moment, then asked, "Would that resemble a good life for a teenage girl, Jim? It sounds almost like a prison."

"I've never seen it, of course," he replied, "but my impression is that Rebecca and Luke think of it as idyllic. It sounds like a well-appointed hotel and retreat center, which it is, with plenty of outdoor space, indoor and outdoor activities, families coming in and going out on short and long vacations … and dogs!

"I also understand," Durham continued, "that they would bring tutors out five days a week to work with Sari on what you and I would call her high-school education. You know … an English lit teacher on Monday; a math teacher on Tuesday; French or German on Wednesday … that kind of thing. Apparently, Rebecca and Luke's parents are good at setting things up for young people. So … it might be a good thing."

"Are they also considering suggesting that Sari and Greta move to the U.S.?"

He nodded.

"Yes, I think so. At some point, Marie and Father Jack were part of those conversations, but I don't know how seriously that option was considered. I think they really do want Sari herself, and Greta, too, to weigh the pros and cons of everything."

Thursday night, 2315 hours, RAF transport aircraft, Andrews Air Force Base

Rebecca knelt in front of her brother and Sari. They were seated along one side of the RAF transport aircraft's cavernous cargo space. Rebecca looked steadily into Luke's eyes and said, her voice carrying over the sound of the jet engines warming up, "I'm not going to go with you tonight, Luke. Something is telling me that Sarah Wilson is in danger … now … and that I need to go to her.

"It's not a dream … not a vision … it's just a sense that something is threatening her. I can't stay on this airplane with this feeling gnawing at me, Luke."

He nodded.

"Got it. Go quick."

Rebecca turned her face to Sari. "I'll follow soon, Sari. Give Greta a hug for me and tell her that I will come see you both as soon as I can."

Rebecca picked up the small travel bag she'd purchased at the post exchange to secure the few things she had bought during her time in the U.S., made sure her ready-satchel strap was secure, and welcomed a crewman's assistance with the ladder.

On the tarmac, she accepted a ground crew member's offer to drive her in his utility vehicle anywhere on the base she needed to go.

"Where can I take you, ma'am?" he inquired.

"To the base logistics office, please," she replied.

With the RAF flight scheduled to depart at 2330 hours, she was confident that now, at 2320 hours, the lieutenant colonel who had been so gracious to the Yahalomin would still be in his office. She was correct.

He seemed pleased to see her but concerned that she was not on the flight.

"Is something wrong, Mrs. Clark?" he asked.

"There may be, sir," she replied. "May I impose on you to have a taxi sent out here to the base … one that can take me into the city?"

"Absolutely not," he replied with a grin. "The commanding general was quite impressed with you, your brother, and the former Mossad agent. The general would not hear of your being sent into Washington in a city cab at midnight, when his personal driver — a Military Police sergeant — is on call 24 hours.

"I'll buzz the sergeant right now."

Rebecca's protests were unavailing, and at 2330, as the RAF flight was starting its roll to the active runway, she tossed her small travel bag onto the rear seat of the general's command car, a massive 1985 Humvee in camouflage. She gave the sergeant Sarah's home address, watched him check his detailed map of the city, and sat back to experience a ride in the monstrous, unique vehicle.

The sergeant drove fast. The route to Sarah's apartment would take the Humvee directly past the front of the Campbell and McGriff offices.

In those same moments during which Rebecca knelt in the RAF transport, explaining to Luke and Sari that she felt impelled to go to Sarah immediately, Deng, now back in his Anacostia apartment, felt the same impulse, and, he would say, from the same Source. He felt, in fact, a particular kinship with Sarah — and with Rebecca, as well — precisely because he, too, had in his past experienced what were clearly "divine messages," though the "style" of communication had often varied considerably among the three of them.

In this case, much like Rebecca, he had had no vision, no dream, no visual or auditory signal. But he was unmistakenly impelled.

And the impulse came from without.

He was reading in bed when the impulse came upon him. He looked at the clock. It read 11:15 p.m. Deng put his book down, closed his eyes, and prayed.

But only for seconds. The impulse became so strong that he knew he had to get up and move. He threw on jeans and a sweatshirt, slipped into his workout shoes, grabbed his address book, billfold, and keys to his taxi, and ran to the vehicle. He started the car, turned on the map light, and found Sarah's home address. As a veteran taxi driver in the D.C. area, he did not need to consult a map.

He drove through the night fast, though not recklessly.

At some point he realized that he would be passing within a block of St. Patrick Catholic Church where Aleksy Kaminski was newly employed on the night security force. Having checked in with Kaminski earlier that day by phone, he recalled that Kaminski had been assigned a split shift: 7:30 p.m. to 11:30 p.m. and 3:30 a.m. to 6:30 a.m. on weeknights. The time, as Deng neared the hospital, was 11:30 p.m.

He brought his taxi to a halt in front of a side door just as Kaminski exited. Deng opened his car door, stood, and called to Kaminski.

"Aleksy!" he shouted. "We need you. Now!"

Kaminski broke into a run and, seeing the front passenger seat dominated by the taximeter and various maps, he jumped into the rear seat. Once seated, he asked only one question of Deng.

"Who is in the big trouble, Kazim?"

"Sarah Wilson," Deng replied.

And without further words, they sped toward her apartment, a route that would take them directly past the front of the Campbell and McGriff offices.

Durham checked his watch. It read 11:30 p.m. He would need fewer than five minutes to drive the Ram from the precinct office to the Campbell and McGriff offices, and he had promised Sarah he would be there by midnight.

He still had about 15 minutes before he'd need to leave.

But he found he was uncomfortable waiting much longer. He did not know why, but when his watch read 11:40 p.m. the pressure was no longer bearable. He picked up his keys, his zippered document case, his shoulder holster and service weapon, and ran out the door. He was in the Ram and rolling toward the Campbell and McGriff offices at 11:45 p.m. Sarah would expect him at the rear door to the office at midnight.

Running a little early, Durham headed for the alleyway that would bring him to that door. The anxiety that he felt was puzzling to him.

At 11:45 pm Deng, driving to Sarah's apartment along the most direct route from St. Patrick Church, turned a corner and headed along the street that would take him past the front of the Campbell and McGriff offices.

The streets in this section of the city were deserted, but in the medium distance he saw some kind of activity in front of Campbell and McGriff.

"Aleksy," he called over his shoulder, "what's going on down there in front of Marie and Father Jack's office? Are you seeing what I'm seeing?"

Kaminski sat forward and looked in the direction indicated.

"I see something," he said simply.

"It's almost midnight," said Deng. "Nobody's there in the office. It's been closed for hours. Why should there be activity out front?"

As the taxi neared Campbell and McGriff, Deng and Kaminski tensed. They saw two hooded figures standing in front of the plate-glass window that marked the offices' window to the city. As they drew closer still, they saw what appeared to be a black diplomatic vehicle nearby, and, as Deng slowed the taxi to look carefully, they realized that the two figures were in the process of lighting what was unmistakably a firebomb, a large jug filled with accelerant, its wick extending from the mouth of the jug.

"No!" shouted Deng to no one in particular.

He braked the cab to a lurching halt and he and Kaminski simultaneously burst out of the vehicle from its front and rear doors. Deng, a muscular 5-foot-9-inch athlete, and Kaminski, a 6-foot-4-inch, 280-pound mountain, headed for the figure nearest to each. In Deng's case, that was the hooded figure who was applying an igniting device to the wick. In Kaminski's case, that was the hooded figure who was holding the jug and preparing to hurl it through the plate glass.

They were both too late.

Kaminski's target figure released the jug a fraction of a second before he was smashed on the side of his head by the avalanche that descended upon him. The jug, its wick burning toward the accelerant, crashed through the glass. As the jug hit the floor of the reception area, it exploded into flames in a whirlwind of fire that leaped to the walls and ceiling with a terrifying whoosh.

Kaminski's blow flattened the firebomber. The instantly unconscious terrorist slammed to the sidewalk face first. Kaminski stooped, snatched the hood from the man's head, rolled him over, and beheld the man who called himself Hasan.

Meanwhile, Deng reached the igniter figure and delivered a vicious punch to the midsection, doubling the figure over, the igniting device tumbling to the sidewalk. As the hooded figure struggled to recover, Deng launched a left cross to the side of his face, followed by a right uppercut that toppled the figure backward, causing the man to fall uncontrolled onto the sidewalk. The man's head struck the concrete with a sickening crack. And he, too, lay unconscious.

Behind them, Kaminski and Deng heard a voice speaking to them from the open door of the diplomatic vehicle in which the three men apparently had arrived.

"Stand back or I kill you both," said the voice, heavily accented.

Kaminski and Deng turned to face a gunman. Both seemed to appraise him coolly, their hands at their sides, apparently relaxed. Deng spoke.

"You'd better kill us both, and quick," he said. "This fire you've started will bring police vehicles from all directions in less than 60 seconds from right now, followed by every fire truck in the city. Your chances are zero."

The gunman hesitated and, as he did, heard the sounds of a siren, then a second one, then a half-dozen, the sounds coming from all directions. He turned, tossed his Glock onto the seat of the vehicle, and ran, hard, the run of a man who knows he cannot escape but can only think of running.

Deng, now acutely conscious of the heat radiating from the flames that had already consumed everything visible in the reception area, turned to Kaminski and said, "Aleksy, there's nobody inside the office … nothing to be done here.

"Let's drag these people across the street, away from the fire."

The Military Police sergeant driving the general's Humvee, following the most direct route to Sarah Wilson's apartment, turned onto a street that would take him and his passenger directly past the Campbell and McGriff offices. He immediately saw flames billowing from an office building and beginning to push through the roof.

"Ma'am," he called over his shoulder, "we've got a fire in that building up ahead. I'll need to stop and render assistance, to see if there is anything I can do."

"Of course," agreed Rebecca, now sitting up from the rear seat and looking toward the flames. As she did, an alarm clutched at her abdomen.

"Sergeant," she said after studying the surroundings, "I think … that may be the building where Sarah Wilson works."

The sergeant glanced at her over his shoulder.

"But," he said, "Miss Wilson will be home now … nearly midnight … right?"

Rebecca paused.

The pause grew long.

"She *should* be home, sergeant, but …"

"Ma'am?"

"Turn left here!" she shouted, as the Humvee approached a narrow street that appeared to lead to alleyways that ran across the rear of the buildings in the small-business neighborhood. The sergeant braked hard and whipped the vehicle to the left. The Humvee cornered sharply, tires protesting, and barreled into the narrow corridor between the buildings, the vehicle's 8-foot width, including its side mirrors, clearing the buildings on each side by inches.

"And now right!" Rebecca shouted.

The Humvee wheeled right into the alleyway that would take them to the rear door of the Campbell and McGriff offices. As the vehicle sped down the alleyway, Rebecca's fear turned into certainty. Sarah was in there.

Flames now engulfed the roof of the building.

As the Humvee raced down the alley, Rebecca grabbed her oversized water bottle and poured its entire contents over her head and shoulders, saturating both her hair and her tennis warm-up top.

Rebecca leaned over the driver's shoulder and pointed to the Campbell and McGriff sign on a doorway they were approaching.

She shouted, "Crash that door, sergeant!"

The Humvee was equipped with a massive, hardened-steel grille-guard that framed the entire front end of the vehicle. The sergeant cut the wheel sharply to the right and drove the right-hand corner of the grille-guard into the center of the Campbell and McGriff door. The door exploded into fragments.

As the Humvee stopped, its nose wedged in the doorway, Rebecca leaped from the vehicle and squeezed herself through the narrow opening between grill-guard and door frame. Then, running in a crouch to get below the swirling smoke, she raced down the hallway, ignoring Marie's office on her left, but stopping at the guest office on her right, where she guessed Sarah might have been working.

Unable to see clearly through the smoke, Rebecca placed her hand on a desk chair and then on a small sofa to confirm that Sarah was not there. She returned to the hallway and, acutely aware of the impending collapse of the roof, followed her memory through three right-angle left and right turns until she found the conference room.

And there on the floor lay Sarah Wilson.

Sarah was face down on the floor, unconscious, her head and shoulders in the hallway, her lower body still in the conference room. Rebecca knelt, turned her friend's limp body over, and, forcing her hands and arms under Sarah's knees and back, lifted her from the floor, pulling her tight into her own chest.

Straining, Rebecca struggled to her feet, turned and, her eyes stinging and her skin feeling as though it were being seared, ran, staggering, back through the hallways toward the door to the alleyway.

She was met 30 feet from the doorway by the sergeant, who threw a rain tarp over both women and, running beside Rebecca, steered her to the doorway. He had backed the Humvee away from the door so that their exit would not be impeded, and the three of them emerged, fighting for air, into the eerie, firelit darkness.

As they did, Durham's Dodge Ram braked to a halt 15 feet away from them. Durham leaped from the cab, ran to Rebecca, took Sarah in his arms, and turned toward the truck. The sergeant stopped him.

"You got no room in that thing," he said. "Put her in the Humvee."

In seconds, all four of them had piled into the military vehicle, both women in the back, Durham in the front passenger seat shouting directions to the nearest ER. As they pulled away from the building, they heard the roof collapse with a roar.

At the front of the building, a half dozen police vehicles and three fire trucks had assembled, along with one of the fire department's ambulances. Captain Johnstone had arrived to take charge of the three prisoners, the driver having been quickly intercepted, arrested, and brought back to the scene.

Most of the police on the site knew Kazim Deng from his work as a part-time data analyst at the precinct and there was consequently no confusion regarding whom to take into custody. Deng had been quick to explain Kaminski's presence and to make clear that it had been he who had put the firebomber out of action.

Johnstone then joined the two still unconscious terrorists in the rear of the fire department ambulance, where they had both been placed, each handcuffed to a wheeled stretcher. Deng and Kaminski followed in the taxi. The diplomatic vehicle's armed driver, handcuffed, rode in a police cruiser, which followed close behind the ambulance and the taxi.

Back at the scene of the fire, the firefighters concentrated on preventing the fire from spreading, which meant that within minutes two hand-held foam guns had been transported to the alleyway behind the buildings. When the assistant fire chief arrived there, he was initially confused to see the Ram parked near the rear door of the targeted office, and the rear door itself in splinters.

"I was told no one was inside," he said to no one in particular.

"We were told there had been one employee inside and that there was an attempted rescue," replied one of his men. "I don't know whether it was successful. They left for the ER in a Humvee."

Thursday night/Friday morning, 30 minutes past midnight

An ER physician was speaking quietly in a hospital hallway with Rebecca, Durham, Deng, and Kaminski.

"She's okay … even now," the physician said of Sarah, "but I want to keep her for another couple of hours. She breathed in a lot of smoke and toxins from burning upholstery. That's why she lost consciousness, but she had come around by the time she got here. I just want her on oxygen for a while longer."

She looked closely at Rebecca, then said, "Your eyebrows appear to be singed. Do you have burns you want me to look at?"

"I don't think I'm burned, doctor," she replied, "but I breathed several minutes' worth of smoke and ... as you say ... toxins from the burning upholstery. Is there anything I should be concerned about?"

"Let's go back to a treatment room," she said, "and let me listen to your breathing, just to make sure you're not obviously damaged in that way."

The two women turned and walked toward a treatment room, while the three men watched them go. Then they heard a deep male voice from the other direction.

"Durham! Deng!" called Captain Johnstone. "How is she?"

They introduced Kaminski, then filled the captain in on Sarah's condition.

"So," he said to Deng, his star research analyst, "you had no idea the Wilson woman was in the offices?"

Deng shook his head.

"Aleksy and I," he said, "were on our way to her apartment and assumed she would be there ... at home. We stopped at the offices because we saw those two guys getting ready to firebomb the building. Didn't occur to us that Sarah was inside."

"And why," asked the captain, "were you going to her apartment at midnight?"

There was an awkward pause while Durham and Deng struggled to decide how to answer the question. Finally, Durham said, "Captain ... it seems that Rebecca Clark is not the only person who gets these 'special messages' from time to time. Kazim has been a recipient, off and on, for years ... and so has Sarah herself ... twice, now."

Johnstone looked closely at Kazim, then slowly nodded.

"So, Kazim," he said, "I suppose you'll be wanting a pay raise? ... You know ... data analyst *and* 'special messages' recipient?"

Deng looked at the captain, unsure how to respond, but then Johnstone burst into laughter, punching Deng softly on the shoulder and saying, "Just kidding, Kazim ... I'm not giving you a pay raise for being ... ya know ... *weird.*"

The men relaxed. Johnstone continued.

"Seriously, Deng and Kaminski," he said, "I'm impressed by your work in mashing those two terrorists and facing down their gunman driver.

"I'm not all that easily impressed," he continued. "But your work tonight is going to get you both a commendation from the department. You don't work for us, Aleksy, but we give commendations from time to time to civilians for extraordinary bravery.

"You deserve the honor just as much as Kazim ... so you're gonna get it."

At that moment three men entered the hallway, each dressed in a dark suit and arrowing straight to the captain. "FBI," he muttered to Durham under his breath.

For the next 15 minutes, the six men stood in the hallway talking about the apprehension of Hasan and his two associates. At that point one of the FBI agents thrust a clipboard in front of Johnstone. The captain proceeded to sign papers acknowledging his taking custody of the three terrorists under the aegis of the Federal Bureau of Investigation and pledging to keep them in police custody pending determination of their route through the U.S. judicial system.

Formalities complete, the FBI agents turned to leave just as Rebecca rejoined the men in the hallway. "The doctor is satisfied that I'm ... undamaged," she said, "and that there is no need for me to be here ... medically speaking."

She pulled her still-wet hair around to her face and wrinkled her nose. Then she pulled one sleeve of her soaked warm-up top to her face and shook her head.

"My goodness," she said, "I may be medically okay, but until I can take a shower I'm going to smell like the inside of a fireplace.

"Ugh."

She noted the FBI agents retreating down the hallway and asked, "What will be happening with the terrorists, Captain?"

"Their goose is cooked, Mrs. Clark," he replied. "The FBI has been apprehending the individuals listed in that directory you retrieved from Reynaldo Acosta, and now, with the seizure of Hasan and the two terrorists with him, the FBI has collected every single one of them. And in Hasan's case, his name on the title of that pact and plan document means that he'll be treated differently than all the others. I doubt he will ever see the light of day in this country ... although, if he is eventually sent back to Saudi Arabia ... I don't know what will happen to him there.

"He might be celebrated. He might be executed. No way to know."

He nodded and turned to go, giving the little group one of his rare smiles.

"Nice work tonight, everybody."

They watched him go, then Durham turned to Rebecca.

"Rebecca," he said, "do you want to head back to Andrews now, to wait for the next flight to Brize Norton, or ..."

She was shaking her head.

"No, Jim," she replied. "I want to spend some time talking to Sarah when she is able. I'm desperately anxious to get home to Matt and the twins, but I need to be sure Sarah is going to be alright … alright in every way … before I leave."

Just then the Military Police sergeant strode up the hallway, meeting and passing the FBI agents as he did. "Mrs. Clark," he called out as he approached the group, "do you want me to run you back to Andrews, or will you be staying in the city tonight?"

"I'll stay here tonight, Sergeant, but let me thank you again for what you did with that Humvee. I don't know if any other kind of vehicle could have punched through that door so … thoroughly … or if any other driver could have pulled off that maneuver. The precision of your handling of that enormous vehicle was astounding to me.

"We are so very grateful."

"Well," answered the sergeant, "I have to tell you … being the general's command-car driver has been far and away the most boring assignment I've ever had in the U.S. military. That little bit of action tonight was the greatest thing I've experienced in … oh … I don't know how many years. So, thank *you*, Mrs. Clark, for injecting some excitement into my Andrews Air Force Base life."

"Did the Humvee get damaged, Sergeant?" asked Durham.

"No… I hit the door clean," said the sergeant, "with a corner of the vehicle's grille-guard. That thing is made of steel and it smashed that door like it was made of plywood. There might be a scratch or two on the grille-guard, but the general will like that. Makes it seem like his command car was in a firefight.

"And," added the sergeant thoughtfully, "I guess it sorta was."

Rebecca and Durham stood comfortably in the hallway near Sarah's room while Deng drove Kaminski back to St. Patrick for the second portion of his split shift.

In 15 minutes, Deng returned just as the physician approached to say that she was satisfied with Sarah's respiration and general condition, and that they could take her home. Entering her room, they found Sarah looking pale and weak.

Durham went to her, leaned over the bed, and kissed her on the forehead. She smiled feebly and said, "I'm so sorry, everyone."

Durham took a seat on the edge of the bed, while Rebecca held one of her hands and Deng, on the other side, held the other. Rebecca looked across the bed at her Sudanese friend and said, "Kazim, go ahead. She'll want to hear."

"Sarah," he said, "I felt a message earlier tonight. It was simple. It was about you ... about you being in trouble. I jumped in the taxi and headed for your apartment. I picked up Aleksy at St. Patrick. Our route took us past the office, and that's when he and I saw the terrorists preparing to firebomb the office.

"We ... um ... disabled them ... but not before the firebomb had done its work.

"It did not occur to us that you were there."

"Of course not, Kazim," replied Sarah, smiling at him. "What sort of crazy person would be at the office at midnight? I'm just grateful that Rebecca got the same message, apparently at the same time, and had a Military Policeman at hand ... and a military vehicle ... ready to bring her to me.

"And, of course," she continued, "none of us thinks for one moment that this confluence of events was coincidental ... you know ... Kazim's taxi coming by the front of the office just as the firebomb got thrown ... Rebecca's Humvee coming to the front of the office seconds later, the timing just right to witness flames and redirect the vehicle to the alleyway ... no coincidences involved in *any* of that ... right?"

Soft laughs of agreement.

Then Sarah turned her hazel eyes to Durham.

"You know, Jim," she said teasingly, "you're the only person in this room who has never received a special message. I think there must be something wrong with you. You're somehow not ... suitable ... to be in company with us special people."

Durham nodded. "I've never thought for a second that I was," he said, agreeing amiably. "Kazim's rooming with me for a week showed me what full-commitment Christian prayer discipline can look like. I'm a novice compared to him."

Smiles all around.

"Sarah," said Rebecca after several moments, "you don't seem to me to be ... um ... afflicted with the kind of self-recrimination you experienced after your and Sari's abduction, despite your having to be rescued from tonight's emergency, just as you had to be rescued from the other one.

"I'm delighted, but how is this different, in your mind?"

Sarah thought for a moment, then replied, "I think the difference had to do with the fact that, before, I was charged with protecting Sari ... and failed. Tonight, I was just working alone, not guarding anyone ... not protecting anyone

… and … well … these same horrible people came to destroy our place of work. They weren't even trying to do something to *me* … just to the building."

She laughed again.

"I don't know, Rebecca … it seems to me that Hasan and his people lacked imagination. Firebombing a presumably empty building seems so childish. It makes me shake my head and think, 'Can't they do any better than that?'"

More laughter from the four, all relaxed and comfortable with each other.

Rebecca leaned over her friend and, as Durham had done, kissed her on the forehead, saying, "You know, Sarah, seeing you like this … happy … grateful … aware of how God took such good care of us tonight …

"I don't think you need me any longer to provide counsel and comfort. Jim can do that … and better than I. So," she added, "Kazim, I think I have changed my mind regarding your offer to drive me out to Andrews. Eleanor and Sid … and Jaakov … are still there … in their guest units … and I've still got the key to mine and Sarah's.

"If you're still willing, Kazim, I'll accept a ride back to Andrews, and that will put me in position to fly with the New York people back to Teterboro and then perhaps arrange RAF transport from McGuire Air Force Base, south of New York, back to England. I flew into McGuire just 10 days ago, and that base works for me just as well as Andrews works for my brother. In any case, I think I am *not* needed here."

She smiled her good-bye to her roommate.

"Sarah," she said, "you're ready for whatever comes next … now and in the future. I'm sure of that."

Rebecca paused, thinking, then added, "You've been *called*, Sarah. And you are aware that, although Our Lord gave Himself for us not because we're somehow worthy of His sacrifice, it's also clear that you… just as much as Kazim and I… are worthy of the calling. *You*, Sarah Wilson … are … worthy … of … the … calling."

Rebecca suddenly beamed.

"And I'm ready to see my husband and children!"

CHAPTER SIXTEEN

Saturday evening, New York City

ELEANOR AND BELTON SAT ONCE MORE ON THEIR OWN SOFA IN their own home, holding hands and chatting happily, as husbands and wives do, when marriage is at its best. And this late-in-life marriage of long-time widow to lifelong bachelor, filled as it was with both sweetness and laughter, had always been marriage at its best.

"So," he was saying, "ya think Rebecca is on 'er way by now?"

"I think," she replied, "that she is known almost as well by the senior people at McGuire as is her brother at Andrews. They expected an RAF transport to depart for Brize Norton sometime tonight … maybe not yet … but sometime tonight.

"They'll make sure she's on board."

They were silent for several moments, thinking about the sudden whirlwind that had swept them up, starting with Eleanor's near-abduction as she had approached the New York City Library on foot.

"So, Eleanor," Belton said, "whadya make of Kazim and Sarah bein' sent th' same kind a' 'special messages' that only Rebecca … I thought … only ever got? I mean … whadya make of that?

"Hm?"

She laughed her tinkling laugh.

"Why, Sidney," she said, "I don't need to 'make anything' of that. The Almighty can send His messages to anyone at all … at any time. And Rebecca would certainly not claim exclusive rights to the privilege.

"And, besides," she added, "you heard Rebecca say, when Jim was talking to us about Kazim, that Kazim had spoken to Rebecca last summer about a vision he'd been sent … about her … about Rebecca … remember?"

"Oh, right," Belton replied. "Kazim had even got some commands … somethin' about Rebecca herself …"

"Yes!" she recalled. "He'd been sent an image of Rebecca, whom he had never even heard of at the time, along with … let's see … several commands: *'Help this woman. Defeat her enemies. Have courage.'*

"Remember, Sidney?"

"Well, I do now… an' so," he said, "guess it's no surprise …"

"No surprise at all," she agreed, "that he would have been … um … 'nudged' to drive his taxi to help Sarah on Thursday night."

Belton nodded.

"Yeah," he said. "An' how 'bout Sarah bein' sent th' dream about th' people that turned out t' be Ms. Thomas and Mr. Acosta? An' then, later, th' dream about Ms. Thomas' house an' her library. How 'bout that?"

Eleanor gave her husband one of her *looks.*

"Well," she said, "how about *what,* Sidney?"

He laughed his cackling laugh.

"Yeah, Eleanor," he agreed. "How 'bout *what?*"

Their pizza had finally been delivered and consumed, and the couple was back on their sofa, happy, relaxed, holding hands again. And thinking.

"So, Eleanor," Belton began, "tell me … how'd this liberation theology thing turn out? Is it gonna be th' next big thing? Or is it just another thing nobody'll remember a few years fr'm now? Or just what?"

"It's going to go away, dear," she said, "just like all the other 'Christianity *and'* ideas and movements that have popped up and blown away over the last 2,000 years. And it won't be because of anything I say or do.

"It will go away because it does not capture the center."

"Th' center?"

"Yes," she said, "the center of the faith.

"You know, Sidney … the words in John 3:16 and John 3:17. The *reason* for 'the Word made flesh' was … and is … to alter the eternal living and dying … and living … conditions for you and me and the pizza delivery person and the pilots that flew us here from Andrews and the taxi driver that brought us home from the Teterboro airport and the gentleman who held the door open for us downstairs ..."

Belton grinned his crooked grin.

"Yeah, Eleanor," he said. "I get it."

Still smiling, he rose from the sofa and was reaching for his cane, when another thought clambered for admission to his always active mind. She saw the question coming and asked, getting up from the sofa herself, "What is it, dear?"

"I'm thinkin' about that Hasan guy, Eleanor," he said. "There was somethin' about that guy that seemed different ... somehow less ... um ... less Evil, I guess ... than some a' the dirtbags we've faced off against in other years.

"Know what I mean?

"Hm?"

She clasped his hand on the frozen-elbow side while he picked up his cane with the other hand, and together they began to make their way toward the bedroom. As they moved along, the cane thumping against the floor, she answered.

"Some of our adversaries in the past ... Anton Fedorov, last summer, for one ... appeared to have invited supernatural Evil into themselves so purposefully and so successfully that they had saturated themselves with powers that were beyond anything we think of as just ... normally ... evil. They could, for example, weaken their enemies, at times and in places, just by proximity to them."

They had reached their bedroom and Belton nodded, now carefully leaning his cane against his bedside table.

"Yeah, right ... like a super dirtbag ..." he said.

She rolled her eyes.

"Yes," she said, "if you must, Sidney ... like a super dirtbag."

She smiled despite herself and continued.

"I really do think," she said, "that Millicent Thomas had much of that *kind* of Evil within her, Sidney. Had the Muslim chieftain not decided to take over ... and to push Ms. Thomas aside ... and beyond that, of course, to murder her by throwing her onto the explosives ship ... we would have faced a similar level of Evil this time. Millicent Thomas' Evil was more sophisticated ... more complex ... less obvious ... than Hasan's.

"I've no doubt we would have triumphed in the end, Sidney, but the fight would have been, I think, more subtle. Not so crude.

"Not just brute force."

She paused, then continued.

"This Hasan man," she continued, "was not Evil at the congresswoman's level, dear. He was more of a ... well ... straightforward terrorist thug. Just a thug, Sidney, who wanted to intimidate and kidnap and torture and murder ... preferably mass murder ... but with a rationale that connected to his twisted view of his religion. He saw his thuggery as being *in service to others,* if you see what I mean.

"He was ... he is ... certainly an evil, evil, evil man. Nonetheless, as you've just noted, at a level that's a little lower ... or higher ... than some of the others."

She crossed to her closet to select her nightgown and found that she wanted to add one more thought to what she'd just suggested.

"And Sidney," she said, "it occurs to me now that that probably explains why it was not necessary for Rebecca to defeat Hasan *personally,* in the way she had to defeat Anton Fedorov last summer, with her knives. This Hasan man was defeated, as I understand what happened, by our friend Aleksy Kaminski who simply smashed him in the head and drove him down into the sidewalk.

"You know ... it was more of a thug-to-thug sort of thing.

"Our lovable thug beat up their hateful thug."

Belton collapsed on the side of the bed, laughing helplessly.

Later, as each of them closed their night-reading books and turned off the reading lamps on each side of the bed, Belton found he wanted more. He reached for his wife's hand under the summer-weight sheet and asked, "Didja ever get t' ask Rebecca about 'er housing problem, Eleanor? Where's she an' Matt an' th' kids an' their dog gonna live, once school gets started this fall?"

"I don't think that's settled, dear," she said. "Rebecca told me that their arrangements last year were just for that one school year, while a King's College London faculty member was on sabbatical in France with his family. They had hoped that their firebombed home might be rebuilt over the still-intact basement of the house, but she seemed less confident that that was going to work out."

"That'd be great, wouldn't it," he said, "since that basement was set up just th' way they wanted it fer their workouts an' fer Rebecca's knife-throwin' practice ... but if they can't find a place in London that'll work, I guess they'll just stay at th' Lodge fer th' whole school year ... an' Matt will hafta do 'is weekly commute t' his ISP office ... an' stay with Luke an' Kory in London Monday through Thursday nights, huh?"

"Yes," she agreed, "and Sari and Greta may eventually reach the same decision … that the Lodge makes the best sense for them, at least in the short run.

"I guess we'll just wait and see."

There was a pause, and so she said softly, "Good night, dear."

There was no response from Belton, which told her that he had fallen deeply asleep in the 10 seconds since his observation about Matt Clark's weekly commute to the ISP offices, or that his mind was still buzzing.

It was the latter.

"Eleanor," he said, "d'ya think Louis Bois' article is gonna be published in tomorrow's newspapers? Or is that too quick?"

"Oh, I expected it to appear today, Sidney," she replied, "and I suppose it might have, in the U.K., just not yet in the U.S., but they will want that article in print immediately. As Louis said to us, he is the only journalist in the world who has the story of Sari and Sarah's abduction and subsequent rescue.

"That's going to make for exciting reading.

"Don't you agree, dear?" she asked.

"Sidney?"

This time there was no reply. Sid was finally asleep.

Sunday midday, Washington, D.C.

Sarah and Durham walked hand in hand from Foundry Methodist Church on 16th Street to Durham's truck, which was parked on Church Street, near DuPont Circle. Durham walked on the outside, nearest the street.

"I can't walk beside a woman and be on the inside, you know," he said, "because … just because. My body doesn't know how to do that."

She laughed and squeezed his hand.

"Jim Durham," she said, "you're 27 years old but you are, as they say, 'old school,' aren't you? … And I wouldn't have it any other way."

Her 3-inch "church heels" made walking tricky on the old, uneven sidewalk, and Durham placed one hand on her upper arm to provide added support. He found that he was impressed by the musculature in her bicep.

"Hmmm …" he mused. "Do you … did you … lift weights, Sarah?"

"High school basketball and volleyball," she said. "Our coaches put us on a light weight-lifting regimen from ninth grade on. I never could see any difference in how my arms looked, but I could tell I was stronger."

He assisted her up and into the Ram's cab, then circled the truck and climbed in behind the wheel. He had left the truck's windows down in the 90-degree heat and had managed to park in the shade. He turned on the engine and then the air-conditioning, waited several moments until cold air was pushing itself into the cab, and then rolled up his window. She did the same with hers.

Their hands joined again.

"I was so impressed," he said, "to learn that you and Marie and Father Jack have been systematically photocopying almost everything in the office and setting up a duplicate office in their home. You're not going to miss a beat, are you?"

"No, we're really not," she said. "It's going to double the length of my walk to and from work, but the only problem with that will be the afternoon heat when I start home. That's going to be a long 40 minutes in the summer."

"Maybe somebody with a truck will give you a ride, most days."

She nodded and they sat silent, comfortable, and happy.

"You know," he said after several moments, "my apartment is a lot closer to Marie and Father Jack's house than your place is. If you lived with me in my place, your walk to work would be much shorter than it has been up 'til now."

She looked at him and shook her head, smiling.

"We are nowhere *near* doing that, detective. What's wrong with you?"

"Oh, I don't mean right away," he said. "I mean if we were … you know …"

She looked at him, no longer smiling.

"If we were what?" she asked.

"Well … if we were married," he replied.

There was a pause.

"Are you asking me to marry you, Jim Durham?"

He was unprepared for this direct question, having not planned for the conversation to go in the direction of marriage.

"Well," he said hesitantly, "I … um … I don't actually have an engagement ring for you … or anything, Sarah, but … well … I must confess that my mouth just went in a direction I didn't expect it to."

"So," she said, "you're *not* asking me to marry you."

He turned his face away from her and looked out his window, trying to think of a way out of the swamp he'd managed to blunder into.

She laughed.

"Oh, Jim," she said, "I'm being mean on purpose. You were just innocently pointing out how … um … *convenient* it would be if I only had to walk from your place to Marie and Father Jack's house for work every day.

"Just *innocently* pointing out …"

He looked into the hazel eyes and felt himself melting into them … again.

"Sarah," he said seriously, "I don't want to spend another day of my life without you in it. And I don't want to pretend that I don't think of a life with you as my wife … every single day …because I do.

"And," he continued, "I do know this is premature, but I'm not sorry I stumbled into the topic. We're going to learn each other, more and more, and love each other, more and more, and talk about how things would be …"

"And for now," she interrupted, "that's enough, isn't it?

"We're not teenagers anymore," she continued. "We know the kind of connection we have now … already. And we're doing the right things…

"Let's just keep doing the right things."

She paused, then continued.

"And that includes being sure that this topic — this marriage topic — is part of our every-morning prayers, yours and mine. And it means talking and praying about children, and about how we'd go about raising them …

"There is so much to talk about, Jim Durham."

She beamed at him.

"And … you know, detective … I find I can't wait."

The End

ACKNOWLEDGEMENTS

When the sixth novel in the Rebecca Series was released, the Men's Group at our church held a book event, featuring the new story, but also making Rebecca Series books 1-5 available. Many of the event's attendees chose to start at the beginning and, as the months passed, several of them asked me questions that altered the trajectory of the seventh.

Lin Wuest found herself intrigued by "the Sudanese guy," Kazim Deng, who was a member of the supporting cast in the fifth novel. Lin asked me if I planned to bring him back. I said, "Yes, but probably not in the story I'm working on now." Later, I thought about Kazim, and I began to see how he could play a pivotal role in the new story. And now he does. Thank you, Lin!

Mignon and Charlie White were interested in "the little Saudi girl," who, as a nine-year-old, played a fearsome role in the fourth novel. They asked if I planned to bring her back. I said, "Yes, but probably not in the story I'm working on now." Later, I thought about that child who, in my fictional world, would be a 14-year-old if she were to appear in the new novel. The more I considered her as a teenager, the greater the role I saw for her. And so, like "the Sudanese guy," she now plays a critical role in the new book. Thank you, Mignon and Charlie!

My wife, Dr. Linda Mason Hall, has read all seven of these manuscripts in 60-70- page manuscript chunks. Her feedback has been essential to the development of every story and every character. When I gave her the final 70 pages for this new novel, she asked if I was excited to finish. I said, "No… not until you sign off on the ending." I've learned not to get too excited about these stories until Linda is completely satisfied. Thank you, Linda!

Robin Surface, editor at Fideli, and Frances Archer, copy editor at Content Keeper, have handled the fifth, sixth and seventh books with insight and meticulous attention to detail. For example, Frances informed me, while she worked on the fifth book, that I could not write that Marie Campbell had taken the "Scrunchie" off of her ponytail when she finished her treadmill workout. "Why not?" said I. "The Scrunchie," she said, "was not invented until two years after the time-placement for this book."

Amazing!

And to the countless readers who have written their appreciation over the years I give all of you my thanks, as well. Without appreciative readers, there would never have been a second Rebecca novel, to say nothing of five more after that one.

Will there be an eighth?

Well… Rebecca is only 34 years old. I'd say she still has much to give us.

Walker Buckalew

Upon graduation from Duke University, Walker Buckalew was commissioned an officer in the U.S. Navy. He served on the 7th Fleet aircraft carrier USS Constellation, with home ports in San Diego, Pearl Harbor, and Yokosuka, Japan. After completion of his military service, Walker coached and taught high school English in Wyoming public schools. Later, having earned a Ph.D. degree from the University of Wyoming, he joined the faculty of St. Lawrence University (NY).

Dr. Buckalew then taught in the Psychology Department and served as Coordinator of the Kellogg Foundation Health Promotion Program at the University of North Carolina Asheville. After his four years at UNCA, he became President and COO of Cumberland University (TN).

He next joined the private-school consulting firm Independent School Management, Wilmington, DE, working with Boards of Trustees in the U.S. and Canada in the development of long-term sustainability plans for their institutions.

Walker now resides in Greer, SC, with his wife, Dr. Linda Mason Hall.

Other books in the Rebecca Series include:

- *The Face of the Enemy*
- *By Many or By Few*
- *Such Thy Mercies*
- *Choose You This Day*
- *A Fearful Thing*
- *A Whip of Cords*

www.ingramcontent.com/pod-product-compliance
Lightning Source LLC
Chambersburg PA
CBHW020751310726
48969CB00002B/482